Sign up for our newsletter to hear
about new and upcoming releases.

www.ylva-publishing.com

Other books by Andrea Bramhall

Norfolk Coast Investigation Story:

Collide-O-Scope

Under Parr

Stand Alone:

Just My Luck

Under Parr

Andrea Bramhall

Acknowledgements

To Astrid and Daniela—it's been a hell of a year, but here we are. Stronger, wiser, and a little more exhausted, but still writing nonetheless. Thank you.

To my wonderful beta readers, Louise and Dawn, your help with this story was invaluable.

I'd like to offer a special thank you to Simon Gorton, my newfound friend and retired Norfolk Police officer. Your advice on investigative details really helped to make this story as true to life as it could be. Should a body ever be discovered in the bunker, we know exactly what to do now!

To Ian Symington, your knowledge and time showing me around the clubhouse and the course at the Royal West Norfolk Golf Club immeasurably helped with this story. The inspiration, the setting, and the quiet stayed with me long after I left.

The North Norfolk Coast was my home for many years and it helped to shape my life and my future in ways I am still adjusting to. This series of books is just one of those. Without it, I would never have been inspired to discover Kate and Gina.

Dedication

Old age is a cruel punishment for a lifetime of living and loving. I can't decide which is worse—forgetting or being forgotten. In which do we truly cease to exist?

I will remember you.

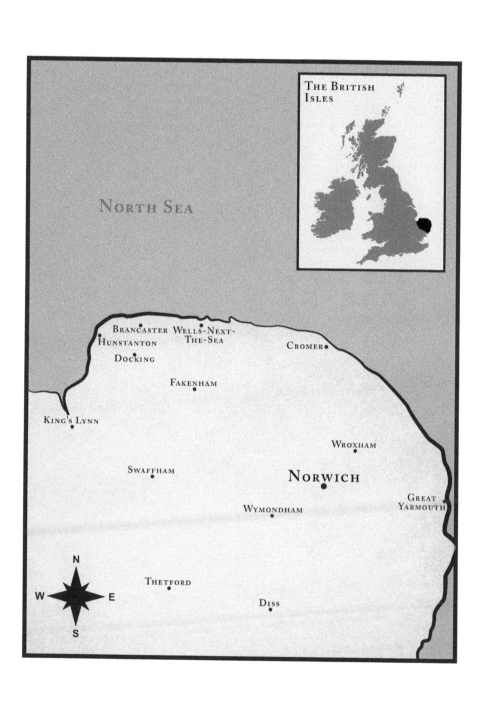

Prologue

Alan shuffled down the hallway as quickly as his feet could take him. The odour of stale piss, antiseptic, and old age assaulted his nostrils. Just like it did every minute of every day. It was no different in the dark of night as the snores of his fellow inhabitants indicated they dreamed the murky dreams of senility and medication-induced relief.

The cries of pain were something he'd become accustomed to. A fact that wore heavily on his soul. When he remembered, of course. Dementia was a cruel and unforgiving mistress. And the young people supposed to care for him—for them—were just as bad.

His dentures made his gums ache. The palette didn't sit right in his mouth, and the clothes he wore chafed. As though they were too small for him. He hobbled in shoes that didn't fit correctly and rubbed his heels while he tried to pull his dressing gown closed. It wouldn't reach. *Since when did my dressing gown have flowers on it?*

A shriek drew his attention from the ill-fitting garment and spurred him towards Annie's room as fast as he could. It wasn't the normal shriek of pain that he was used to hearing from that direction. This one was filled with fear, and then it had been muffled out.

He pushed open the door to her room and gasped.

A tall, thickly-muscled young man pushed a pillow tight against Annie's face.

"Get off her. You're hurting her!"

Her feet kicked limply at the bed covers.

"No, I'm helping her, Alan," he said softly, tucking the covers around Annie's body with his free hand. "See? You're just confused again."

Annie's feet stopped moving.

"No, no, no. You're hurting her." Alan rushed forward and grabbed his arm. "Don't hurt her. She hurts too much already."

"I know she does, I know. That's why I'm helping her. I'm making her more comfortable, Alan." He shook his arm and Alan lost his grip. "Go on. Go back to bed. I'll bring you a cup of cocoa in a few minutes."

Alan frowned. *Was he helping Annie? How was he helping Annie? Annie wasn't crying in pain as she usually did. Wait, no, the pillow. She can't breathe. Have to breathe.*

"No, you're hurting her. Let her go." He balled his fist and struck the man's back. He grabbed at his white tunic and pulled as hard as he could.

"Enough!" The big man lashed out with one powerful swipe of his arm.

Alan stumbled backwards, and his head hit the doorjamb. He lifted his hand to the back of his head and whimpered when it came away bloodied.

"I told you, I'm helping her."

"What are you doing to her?"

"I told you to go back to bed. I told you I'm helping her." His voice was quiet but roughened with frustration.

"But you're not..."

"Yes, I am."

Alan noticed the dim light of the room reflecting off the man's bald head as he reached across the small space and grabbed Alan's ill-fitting dressing gown. He pulled Alan close before slamming him against the wooden door frame again. Alan's brain rattled in his skull as his teeth smashed together through his tongue. Pain, sharp and tinged with blood, filled his mouth as his head pounded. It throbbed against the onslaught of blood that flowed around his body in preparation for him to do...something. Anything. To do what?

There was a tiny moan from under the pillow, and the man let go of Alan's clothes and turned his attention back to Annie. "Stay there."

Alan shook his head, trying to clear the pain and confusion. *He isn't helping Annie. I have to do it. I have to get help.* He stumbled out of the room, barely noticing that his hand left a bloody smear on the wall.

His legs shook as he steadied himself against the corridor. He approached the nurses station, hoping to find someone, anyone, to help him stop the man hurting Annie. But it was empty. The small room had a desk, overflowing with papers, a humming computer, and a box of paracetamol with the blister pack of pills spilling on to pages of patients' notes.

"Must get help," he whispered.

He ignored everything in the small room and stumbled along the wall to the door. He tugged on the handle, but the door wouldn't budge. He tried again. And again. And again. He cried in frustration.

"Must get help." He turned and walked down towards the back of the building. "Must get help."

"Alan, where've you gone, pal?"

Alan's heart pounded in his chest and his hands shook as he moved as quickly as he could. He ignored the pinching at his heels and the chafing between his legs. He rattled each door as he passed, looking for anything that wasn't locked. Finally, one opened and he toppled into a kitchen. The room was lit only by the fluorescent light in the tall, glass-fronted fridge. The steel worktops glinted in its light, then fell starkly into shadow.

He could make out a door at the far end of the room, but as he rushed towards it he fell. His head throbbed. Blood ran down his cheek and dripped off his nose as he tried to push himself up. He balanced on his knees and put his hand to the back of his head again. It hurt so much. He slumped against the wall and closed his eyes.

When he opened them again, he couldn't remember why he was sitting on the cold floor in a room he didn't recognise. His head pounded and his vision blurred. He put his hand to his stomach in a vain attempt to quell the awful queasy feeling that burned in his gut.

"Alan? Come on, mate, let me help you."

Help. The word reverberated in his mind and focused him on what he needed to do. "Must get help." He crawled to the door and used the handle to pull himself to his feet. He staggered, and swayed as he rattled the handle, and chuckled to himself when he saw the key in the lock. He turned it and almost fell outside.

Wind and rain pelted his face. Gravel crunched beneath his shoes, and his dressing gown was soaked, clinging to his skin.

"Must get help," he called into the wind.

He had no idea where he would find help. He didn't know where he was. Not really. There was something familiar about it, but that was all. Like a vague recollection of a dream from childhood. Dim and distant, and cold. So cold. He blew on his fingers to chase away the chill, then wrapped his arms about himself.

In the distance he saw a light. A warm, orange light shining in the vast, black nothingness, and it called to him. Beckoned him towards it like a siren's song drawing a sailor to the rocks. He didn't care. He didn't know. He just walked towards it.

The salt tang of the sea clung to the road as he walked. The roar of the wind stopped him hearing the splash beneath his feet until the cold water seeped over the tops of his shoes and bit at his toes. But still the light beckoned to him, and offered promises that it would be everything he needed it to be.

"Must get help."

He waded through water that reached above his knees now, and crawled forward when he fell. He shivered and his teeth chattered as he ploughed through the water, till the tarmac felt solid beneath his feet again. But still the light called to him.

Alan's vision blurred, and he fell as the ground shifted beneath his feet. He spat sand from his mouth and scrunched his fingers into the wet grains. Rain mixed with blood and ran down his face, and then dripped on to the sand, but he couldn't see it. He couldn't see anything. It was too dark. Even the light that had drawn him there had forsaken him now. Disappeared from the sky like a star behind clouds.

He groped through the sand, always moving. Slowly moving. *Must keep moving.* Even the sand kept moving. Shifting, drifting down and away. Into the wind and away.

He felt the coarse marram grass tucked amongst the dunes and held on to them. They offered something solid in a world where everything continued to shift and move. Including himself.

Wave after wave of dizziness and nausea washed over him as the waves continued to crash against the shore. Higher and higher they came towards him, kissing his feet no matter how high up the dune he tried to climb.

"Must get…" He tried to remember the last word. "Must get…"

A ferocious gust of wind blew him flat on to the sand and his hand brushed against a rough slab of concrete half-buried in the dunes.

"Must get…warm." He shivered and pulled himself towards the lump of concrete. Beneath it was a tunnel. A tunnel he remembered from…a long time ago. A happier time. He smiled and crawled on his belly down the shaft, tumbling to the floor at the bottom.

It stank. Empty bottles and cans strewn across the concrete floor rolled away from him as he groped about and crawled around the pitch-black space. But he knew where this was. He knew what it was. He'd played here so many times as a child. He and his friends had played soldiers in the old bunker. They'd hollowed out the openings for the guns and pretended they were on the frontline as their fathers and uncles all had been. They'd sat for hours, playing cards and smoking their first illicit cigarettes. Drank their first stolen ale and talked about the girls with the biggest bosoms in their class.

He leaned against a wall. Rough breeze blocks leeched what little warmth was left from his body as he closed his eyes and remembered better days. Days where his head didn't hurt and he didn't want to throw up. Days where he could remember why he was wearing a dressing gown that didn't fit him and shoes that rubbed his heels raw. Days where his teeth didn't feel wrong in his mouth. He remembered days where he could…remember.

CHAPTER 1

Detective Sergeant Kate Brannon tapped her fingernails on the steering wheel in time to the music. Emilie Sande sang about being a clown while Kate waited for Detective Constable Jimmy Powers to lock his front door. He had a slice of toast stuck between his teeth, his coat drawn up one arm while his other hand fumbled with the keys.

The small, square house tucked away in the council estate of Burnham Market where Jimmy lived was probably half the size of her own house in Docking. And probably worth twice as much. Even if it did lack "character" and was in the less desirable part of town, it was still in the town. What was it the man said? It's all about location, location, location. And Burnham Market was *the* location to be in if you were on the north Norfolk coast. Every inch of space was developed or being developed, car parking was a nightmare, and the prices for everything were extortionate. But that's what you got when you added a celebrity hotspot to a coastal location. *Damn you, Stephen Fry, Kiera Knightly, Natalie Portman, et al.*

She wound the window down and stuck her head out. "We haven't got all day you know, Jimmy. The DI's waiting for us."

Jimmy held up his hand and shouted, "One sec. Fuck." He cursed as he dropped his toast on to the wet ground.

Kate chuckled and wound the window back up.

Jimmy tucked his keys in his pocket, finished putting his coat on, pulled the wooden gate with chipped green paint closed behind himself, and then climbed into Kate's brand new car.

She'd gone back to her beloved Mini after losing the last one to an unfortunate incident involving a car park that flooded at high tide, and a distinct lack of local knowledge at that point. She had diverted from the lovely sky blue colour she'd picked out last time, though, and gone instead for the silver metallic grey in the hope that it would hide the road grime a little better.

She slid the stick into gear, checked her rear mirror, and pulled out on to the road.

"Can we—"

"No." She cut him off. "We haven't got time to stop at the cafe and pick you up some breakfast. Like I said, the DI's waiting for us. Stella's already called me—twice—to let me know that he's not happy."

"You've only been here ten minutes."

"Twenty. And I was about to call the DI just because I was bored. What were you doing in there? Bathing in adder's milk or something?"

"Very funny. It takes work to look this good, Kate."

Kate gave him a cursory once-over and sniggered. "You keep telling yourself that."

"Hey! That's sexual harassment or something," Jimmy said with a lopsided grin. He ran his fingers through his dark, floppy hair, then scratched at his goatee beard. At twenty-eight he was still fairly new to his detective's position, but he was learning fast.

"You're wishing, pal." She turned left at the junction and headed north towards the sea.

"So where are we going anyway? Stella just told me to get ready because you'd be picking me up."

"Brancaster beach."

"Shit. I've been dreading this starting."

Kate frowned. "What are you talking about?"

"It's just been a matter of time really, hasn't it? Before the people smugglers started trying to get the refugees ashore. I mean we've got miles and miles and miles of coastline, no way can the coastguard protect it all. No way. It was only a matter of time before they started to bring boats straight over here instead of the rest of Europe."

"And you think people smugglers have chosen Brancaster beach as their new landing site?"

"Why not? It's as good a place as any."

"Jimmy, you've got an overactive imagination."

Jimmy laughed. "Right, after the Connie Wells case, I don't know how you can even say that."

Kate had to concede the point. The Connie Wells murder case had surprised them all. What they thought was a simple—for want of a better word—murder had evolved into a case she had never expected to come across in a sleepy fishing village with only forty year-round residents. They'd uncovered a huge drug-smuggling operation. One that Connie had tried to warn the local police about only to have them laugh in her face. So, instead, she'd tried to do their job for them, and paid for it with her life.

The quantities of drugs that had been smuggled into the country through the tiny fishing harbour made her feel sick. Thousands of kilos of heroin. Millions and millions of pounds worth of drugs. And far too many of the locals involved. Kate was convinced that there were still members of the smuggling ring out there, hiding in plain sight, just hoping that neither Ally nor Adam Robbins was going to name them in the hope of getting a little time shaved off their own sentences.

"Fair point, Jimmy. But I don't think the people smugglers have discovered the north Norfolk coast today."

Jimmy seemed a little deflated as she turned up the beach road and slowed down to check for water. Jimmy snickered. "You should've got a Range Rover with a snorkel, then you wouldn't have to worry about a little bit of water, sarge."

"Salt water is the tool of the devil, Jimmy. You'd do well to remember that." She'd been told that locally this road was referred to as "Car Killer Lane" because of the way it flooded at high tide. The height of the water was deceptive, and more than a few cars every year were written off as a result. She refused to be another statistic. Again.

"You do know that only part of the road floods, don't you?"

"Part or all," she said with a shrug, "it's all the same to me." The road was clear, fortunately, and she put her foot down to make the last half mile to the beach car park.

Police tape cordoned off the entrance of the beach. It stretched across the ten-metre-wide expanse of sand from the gates of the golf course on the right to the concrete slabs on the left. The latter created a barrier, to protect the clubhouse from the tide. There were huge boulders at the base, half-hidden by sand. Tufts of marram grass poked out along the cracks. A short police community support officer—PCSO—stood in front of the tape, bobbing from one foot to the other, hands jammed into his pockets, head hunkered deep down into his collar against the wind.

Kate quickly found a parking space in the almost-empty car park and grabbed her coat from the back seat. "Right, let's go see what we've got then."

She clicked the lock as she stuffed her keys in her pocket and fastened the zip of her down jacket, immensely glad she'd allowed Gina to talk her into investing in something that offered a little more protection from the elements than her old leather jacket did. The jacket and the thermal leggings Kate wore under her jeans were her biggest concession to a bout of hypothermia that had resulted from her attempting to collect evidence in the Connie Wells case just six weeks ago.

"'Bout time you two got here." The stout, balding figure of Detective Inspector Timmons called to them. "Getting your hair done, were you, lad?" His ruddy face was even redder than normal.

She hoped that was just the wind and not a case of his blood pressure rising because they were late.

"Sorry, sir," Jimmy mumbled.

Timmons continued to scowl, but Kate thought she saw a twinkle of merriment behind those wily eyes. His usually smart suit was decidedly dishevelled today, and there were wet, sandy patches on his knees that aroused her curiosity even more.

"What do we have, sir?" Kate addressed DI Timmons with a glance over his left shoulder, trying to get a glimpse of the body they were there to see.

"It's not on the beach. Thankfully. The crime scene techs said we're fine to go in, so follow me." He turned away from the clubhouse and led them about a hundred yards down from the beach entrance and up into the dunes.

Kate saw a thick slab of concrete, sand piled on top of it and on either side, and a small hole underneath it that looked to disappear into the sand. "A tunnel?" she asked.

"Yup. Leads to a bunker that was built during the Second World War. It was the front line of the home defence. If they tried to invade from the North Sea." Timmons pointed to the concrete. "Well, our lads were going to try and blow 'em out of the water from here." He waved his hand up the line of the dunes. "There's a whole network of them up and down the coast. Most of 'em are buried now, and the ones that aren't bloody well should be."

"Why? That's our history. Our heritage, sir," Jimmy said.

"That it may be, lad, but the ones that are still visible are used for nothing more than kids' hangouts. They're full of beer cans, used condoms, and used needles. The walls are covered with graffiti, and they stink of piss and vomit." He knelt down beside the hole. "Not my idea of a heritage to be preserved. Come on." He slunk down onto his belly and disappeared head first into the hole.

"You've got to be fucking kidding me." Kate sighed. She hated small spaces. She wouldn't go so far as to say she was claustrophobic, but that was more to do with the fact that she hated to admit a weakness than anything else.

"Want me to go first, sarge?" Jimmy offered.

"No, I bloody don't." Kate's sense of competition was stronger than her claustrophobia. Just. She flipped her hair over her shoulder and tied it into a hairband she kept around her wrist. Kneeling at the entrance, she stared into the black hole. "How far is it, sir?"

"Not far. Maybe six feet before you can stand up again." His voice drifted closer. "We've got lights down here, but there's a corner to go round. You'll see it when you start to make your way."

"Right." Kate swallowed and got down on to her belly. She used her elbows and knees to push herself down the incline. It almost felt like she was falling as she shuffled her way down the sand. At one point she lifted herself too high in her haste to make progress and banged her head on the rough concrete ceiling above her. "Bollocks," she hissed, and rubbed the tender spot on the back of her head. No lump. Yet.

"Nearly there, Sergeant," Timmons said, his voice too loud in the darkness.

Everything seemed too loud. Her own breathing, her heartbeat, the scuff and scrape of cloth on sand.

"I've got you." He wrapped a hand around her bicep and helped her to her knees, then her feet, before offering the same help to Jimmy, and leading them from what had obviously been a corridor into a small anteroom.

Huge banks of lights had been brought down in pieces and assembled to illuminate the room. The rough breeze blocks were covered in graffiti, and the debris was exactly as Timmons had described. Except everything was covered in a layer of silt, and the scent of putrefaction and decay was as pervasive as the darkness that the lights were attempting to keep at bay.

"What a place to die," Dr Anderson said as she examined the body. Well, what was left of it anyway.

"Good to see you again, Ruth," Kate said as she squatted beside the coroner.

"You too, Kate. You okay? You're looking a little pale."

"Not as pale as our friend here."

Ruth Anderson took the hint and moved on. "Well, he's got an excuse."

"Male then?" Kate looked at the remains—no, the bones. In the harsh fluorescent light, they appeared white, and covered in scraps of dirty, half-rotted cloth and mud. The small bones of the feet and hands didn't appear to be in place, but they could have easily been covered by the silt that squelched beneath her feet.

"Based on the hips, yes, definitely."

"And it's definitely human remains, not one of those skeletons you see in biology class?"

"Oh no. This was very definitely a real person." Ruth's voice had a distant quality to it. Like she was trying to figure something out that didn't belong. Other than the skeleton in a bunker.

"What is it? What's got you all frowny and distant?"

"There are a few inconsistencies."

"Such as?"

"Well, take a look at the shoes."

Kate glanced at the feet of the skeleton. Two shoes. One a man's black loafer, the other what looked to be a fur-lined slipper boot, the same as she'd seen her gran wear when she was in hospital. Both were clearly different sizes, and both for the left foot. Kate looked more closely at the scraps of cloth covering the bones, but they were too dirty to make out any more details.

"I'll be able to tell you more about the clothes once I get them back to the lab and examine them under better light and with the use of a little clean water, but we also have these." Ruth held up a set of false teeth. Just the upper plate, but there was a name inside the bridge.

"What the—"

"The dentist puts a label inside the resin before it sets, so that's in there permanently but it doesn't affect the wearer in any way," Ruth supplied. "It's a practice that's used a lot in hospitals and care homes."

"That makes sense."

"True."

"So why is our gentleman wearing Annie Balding's dentures?"

"You're the detective, Kate. Not me." Ruth smiled at her with a wink.

"Helpful, thanks," Kate muttered and continued to stare at the dentures.

"Now, now, don't get sulky, Kate. At least we'll be able to reconstruct the face of this victim for you."

"Uh-huh. Good job, since I don't see you getting me any prints."

"True. And DNA isn't going to be possible either."

"It won't?"

"No. Submersion in salt water would cause the DNA to denature after forty-eight to seventy-two hours."

"But you get DNA from bodies pulled out of the sea all the time."

"There's the difference. Bodies, not skeletons. If we still had flesh, I could get you DNA. Skeletal DNA is useless after seventy-two hours. I couldn't get you a profile from this lot if I had a million years to try."

"Okay. This is getting better and better. How long has he been here? I'm guessing you can give us a rough guideline to start with."

"This place was sealed off by a storm on the fifth of December 2013. No one's been able to get in since then."

"How do we know he wasn't in here before then?"

"The rate of decomposition is consistent with a three-year estimate, but until I do some testing, I couldn't be more exact."

"Fair enough." Kate looked up at Timmons. "So why are we down here now? Why's it open again?"

"The National Trust boffins have decided to open it and do it up so that they can bring kids in here as part of a history trip," Timmons said. "They were planning to dig it all out fully, put doors back on, and keep it safe and clean for the youngsters."

"And they're doing this in the middle of December because...?"

"Low season and it gives them plenty of time to get it ready for the kiddiewinks at Easter."

"Right. So this was found when they started excavating?"

"Yes. They've been working on digging out the tunnel all day yesterday, and found Skeleton Stan just about an hour ago when they broke through and came in to take their first look around."

"Lovely surprise for them."

"Indeed."

Kate turned back to Ruth. "Any idea how he died?"

She shook her head. "I'll be able to give you more when I get back to the morgue, but without flesh to examine, I may not be able to give you a definitive cause of death. It depends what the bones tell me."

"Accidental? Suspicious?"

"Possibly."

"Which one?"

"Either."

Kate sighed. "Fine."

"Nice try, Brannon," Timmons said. "Until we know differently, we proceed as though this is a murder enquiry. I won't lose vital evidence by sitting around and waiting for the autopsy results if it turns out this is suspicious. If it's not, then maybe we'll at least have identified who the poor sod is in the meantime. I've got another case over in Lynn that needs my attention. You and Stella and the boys can handle this one. Just keep me informed as you go."

"Understood, sir." She turned back to Ruth. "How long before you can get us the facial reconstruction?"

"I'll process the skull as soon as I get back and get it in the scanner. As soon as I send the file to Grimshaw over in tech, he should be able to run it through the computer, and I'd imagine he'd be able to get you an image pretty quickly. Later this afternoon maybe."

Kate smiled. "Thanks." She stood up and turned to Jimmy. "Come on, we'll go and start pulling missing persons from that period and see if we can find stuff to compare that image to once we get it."

Jimmy nodded.

"Good plan, Brannon," Timmons said. "Goodwin, Brothers, and Collier are heading over to Hunstanton again to set up. I've already spoken to Inspector Savage, and they're all expecting you over there. I think someone mentioned something about you bringing coffees. I said you'd stop on your way over."

"Thanks, boss. I appreciate that," she said sarcastically. "Before we go play errand boy, though, I'd like to talk to the people who were digging the tunnel out and found the skeleton."

"Of course. I have them waiting in the snug over at the golf house." He led them out of the room and back to the tunnel. "Bit more civilized than keeping them waiting in this bloody wind. Especially as I didn't know how long Powers' haircut was going to take."

Kate chuckled and followed Timmons up the sand-covered tunnel, pushing and pulling herself up while keeping her head as low as she could. Even though it was physically harder to pull herself out, mentally it was a million times easier.

"Better?" Timmons asked quietly as he gave her a hand to her feet. She nodded and offered him a small smile of gratitude.

"Good. Well done."

He'd known, and let her do what she needed to maintain her focus while she was down there without making a fuss. She'd asked questions that should really have been his to ask, but he'd let her get on with it and not interjected as she dealt with the situation. Her respect for her boss rose a little more. He might look like a throwback to the eighties with his trench coat and leather driving gloves, but he certainly didn't act like it. "Thanks."

"Oh, bloody hell." Jimmy crawled out of the tunnel rubbing his head. "Fuck me. That hurts."

"Oh yeah, Jimmy, watch your head on that ceiling, lad," Timmons offered, then pointed them both back up the beach.

CHAPTER 2

Gina pushed her fingers through her hair and winced when she got her ring tangled in a knot. She had to pull it from her finger before she could untangle the mess and reclaim her ring.

"You okay?" Sarah asked.

Gina looked up to the door of her office. "Yeah, I'm good. Just got my ring stuck in my hair." She rolled her eyes and then looked back down at the papers strewn across her desk. "Good" was probably not the right word. Overwhelmed. Swamped. Scared. Those were much more appropriate options; good...not so much.

"Look, I'm sorry to have to push, but I kind of need to know where I stand."

Gina knew what Sarah meant, but she was in no mood to play the subtle guessing games that Sarah had been playing for the past six weeks. Gina was doing her best in extremely difficult circumstances, and quite frankly, Sarah wasn't doing much to help the situation.

Since Gina's best friend, Connie, had died without leaving a will, Gina had been doing her best to keep the business afloat so that they had jobs and wages coming in, while still trying to figure out what was going to happen to them all in the long term. Neither of which was easy to do. A tourism business in the dead of winter was always a money drain, and Her Majesty's Revenue and Customs information was, well, difficult to get to grips with.

It also meant that Gina's patience was at an end, and if she were truly honest, if Sarah decided to quit, it would make her life much easier. So she decided to make the young woman spell out her issues. "What are you talking about?"

"I know you're doing your best to keep the campsite and hostel running, and after everything that's happened, I think you're doing an amazing job of it. But I really need to know what's going on."

Gina could feel the crease on her forehead deepening as she watched Sarah simper. "I've told you everything I know, Sarah. Connie didn't leave a will. She had no relatives that any one knows of, and she wasn't married. Her entire estate is now the property of the state."

"Yes, I know, you've told us that. But what does it all actually mean? To us. In practical terms. I mean, will I still have a job and somewhere to live next month? Or are they going to close us down and kick us all out?"

Gina was just as worried as they were. More probably. She had responsibilities they didn't. She had Sammy to take care of, after all. And trying to get to the bottom of what was going to happen was like trying to find the end of the rainbow. Complex didn't even begin to cover it.

She half wished it had all gone to Leah, Connie's junkie ex-girlfriend. At least then they'd know exactly what pile of shit they had to deal with, rather than the uncertainty they were left with right now. She'd even gone so far as to speak to one of her old friends from school who'd gone on to become a solicitor. She was looking into it for her—as a friend—as it wasn't the kind of law she usually dealt with. Gina hoped "as a friend" meant "no fee required", because money was becoming thin on the ground.

"I don't know what to tell you, Sarah. I don't have those answers right now."

"And how long will it be before you do?" Sarah folded her arms across her chest.

"In all honesty, I don't know."

"Well, that's not good enough, Gina. We need to know."

"We?" Gina queried.

"Yeah, me, Emma, and Rick. We need to know what's going to happen here so we can make plans if we need to."

More than half her staff were mutinying. *Ungrateful bastards.* "And Will?"

Sarah shrugged. "He said he'd wait. Something about him owing that much to Connie. He's a bloody fool if you ask me."

He's a bloody angel if you ask me. "Well, I'm sorry, Sarah, but I can't tell you any more without making shit up. Which I'll happily do if you want? I've already told you as much as I know of this process. The estate is registered on the Bona Vacantia. People have two years to come forward and try to make a legitimate claim if they think they are entitled to the estate in the absence of a will."

"How do you know all this shit?"

"It truly is amazing what you can find out on the internet when you go looking. Plus, I have a friend who's a solicitor. She gave me a few tips."

"Right. So what happens after two years?"

"Well, if no one has come forward, then the state can do as they wish with it all. In this case, I would presume that would mean selling the business and her house."

"And in the meantime?"

"I assume I keep running the business as it is."

"And am I to assume you can do that?" Her response emphasised all the assumptions Gina was having to operate under, and underscoring the fact that she was basically pissing in the wind and hoping to stay dry.

Gina shrugged. It was a question she'd been asking herself for the past month. She'd spent two weeks recovering from her ordeal with Ally Robins—well, the physical side of it anyway—before she'd thrown herself back into work and tried to keep together the business that her best friend had built up. A business that was now ownerless and rudderless in the wake of Connie's murder and the subsequent vacuum. "I will for as long as I'm able to."

Sarah nodded and pursed her lips. "I'm sorry, Gina, but that's just not enough for us." She held out a small stack of white envelopes. "We need more security than that. We're not just talking about our jobs after all. We live here as well as work here."

Gina couldn't argue with her. She couldn't blame her...them, apparently. Gina took the envelopes and leafed through them. Sarah, Emma, and Rick. "Notice?" Gina asked, knowing she held their resignations in her hand.

"A week."

Gina lifted her eyebrows. "Do you all have jobs lined up?"

Sarah nodded. "We wanted to give you a chance to match the offers we have on the table, though." She shrugged. "You can't."

Bitch. "Well, I wish you all the best of luck then."

Sarah scowled. "What? That's it? You're not going to beg us to stay or anything?"

Gina dropped the envelopes into the in tray. "You already told me I couldn't match the offers you all have on the table, so no. You've clearly made up your minds and it's time for you to move on, so, thank you for all your hard work, and if your new employer needs a reference from me, please give them my e-mail address."

Sarah's scowl deepened as she turned on her heels and slammed the door closed behind her.

"B-bye then." Gina muttered under her breath and opened the booking system on her computer. The hostel was fully booked for the weekend, but fortunately, there were no rooms booked for Sunday night or the rest of the week. Making a quick decision, she blocked the weekdays throughout the winter. With only herself and William left to run the hostel and campsite until she could find some new staff—and money to pay them—that was about as much as they'd be able to manage. It also meant she could turn off the heating during the week to preserve fuel and running costs. Her wages bill was down by three quarters, and suddenly she felt a little bit more optimistic about running the place for the winter. Or at least until the money started to come back in.

She picked up her phone and opened the messaging app. She clicked on the last message Kate had sent her—a simple "What did I do?"—and wondered what it was that was stopping her from responding. No, that wasn't true. She knew what was stopping her, she just didn't know when she was going to get past it and get back to being Gina again. She closed the app and used the phone to set an alarm instead—2.45 p.m. should give her plenty of time to get to the school to pick up Sammy. Now she had paperwork to deal with.

CHAPTER 3

The clubhouse stood at the entrance to Brancaster beach like a sentry towering over the sands. The two-storey structure looked like a large house with a sprawling collection of buildings behind it, and huge picture windows in an upstairs balcony. Almost like it was upside down.

Kate and Jimmy were greeted at oversized double doors by a tall gentleman with a shock of dark hair, a firm handshake, and a warm smile.

"Edgar Spink, club secretary. Terrible business all this. Terrible."

"It is. Detective Sergeant Kate Brannon and Detective Constable Jimmy Powers. Pleased to meet you," Kate said and followed him into a hallway covered in dark wood panelling, polished until she could see her face in it. "Detective Inspector Timmons said there were some folks here from the National Trust."

"Yes, yes, of course. This way, please." He led them into a large social room—again covered in dark wood, highly polished—where the scent of coffee and brandy hung in the air.

It was exactly how she'd always pictured a "gentleman's smoking room". Testosterone and machismo had carved every bold line, painted egos upon plaques, and etched names into glass for prosperity. She couldn't imagine how out of place she must look. She glanced over and saw another woman sitting with two younger men. *Ah. That out of place.*

Kate introduced herself and Jimmy as the woman stood and shook Kate's hand.

"Jo Herd, I'm the manager of the National Trust Brandale Centre." She flicked curly blond hair over a painfully thin shoulder and smiled insipidly.

"So you're the supervisor on this project?" Kate asked.

"Yes. Danny and Steve are two volunteers from our inner city outreach programme. They were doing the actual digging and found... *the remains.*" She whispered the last two words.

"Have you been into the bunker today, Ms Herd?"

She shook her head. "Heavens, no. It must be just awful down there."

Kate nodded. "I'm sure, but I'm afraid it's Danny and Steve that we need to talk to right now."

"Of course, of course. I'm here to support them."

Kate caught the stockier of the two rolling his eyes behind Jo Herd's back and smothered a chuckle. "I'm sure they appreciate that as much as I do, but we have to get official statements from them. Are either of them under the age of eighteen?"

"No, no, of course—"

"Are either of them impaired in any way and need a guardian to protect them in a situation like this?"

"Well, no, of course not."

"Okay, then I'm afraid I must ask you to let me speak to them alone. I can do that here or at the station, but I do need to get their official statements."

Ms Herd's lips tightened and the top one disappeared between her teeth. Her eyes pulled into slits as she stared hard at Kate.

Kate didn't flinch.

"Of course. Anything I can do to help."

"Thank you." Kate moved past her to the table with the two young men and introduced herself again.

"Steve Nicholls, he's Danny Batty," the stocky eye-roller said.

"Nice to meet you both. Are you okay? Must have been quite a shock for you."

"Well, yeah. But it was just bones, like. It's not like it was totally gross or anything."

With his cocky grin, his hand tucked down the waistband of his tracksuit bottoms, and his baseball cap turned so that the peak was stuck over one ear, she could practically see him swaggering down the street with his arse hanging out the back of his pants. Danny didn't seem quite as unfazed as his friend. He sat with his arms folded across his chest like a shield, and his chin tucked into the neck of his hoodie like he was trying to hide.

"What about you, Danny? Are you okay? We can get you someone to talk to if you think it'll help you."

Danny shrugged and slunk lower in his chair, his head almost disappearing inside his hoodie. "I'm good."

Yeah, right. "Okay, so why don't you tell me what happened."

Steve sat up straight in his chair and started gesticulating wildly with his hands. "We were diggin' out the sand like we was supposed to. Just diggin' and diggin'. We put the sand on this, like, tray to pull it out of the tunnel. I was pulling 'cos I've got these guns. And Danny boy, well, he's skinny as, so he was doing the diggin'."

"I get the picture. So what happened next?"

"Well, Danny finally managed to unblock the tunnel and then he just went, like, silent as the grave." He started laughing at his own joke. "Get it?"

"Yes," Kate answered without so much as a smile, and turned to Danny. "What did you see?"

He tucked his hands into his pockets. "You've seen it. You know what I saw."

"I did, but, you saw it first, Danny. I need to see what you saw."

"I saw a dead man."

She leaned forward, rested her elbows on the table, and spoke quietly. "How did you see him?"

"I had a head torch on. So I could see and keep my hands clear. At first I thought there was someone down there with me. Wearing a mask or something. Trying to scare me. I could only see a bit at first. Like out of the corner of my eye. Fucking freaky."

Kate smiled reassuringly. "I'm sure it was. When you saw it, did you touch it?"

Danny shook his head but cast a quick glance at Steve. "Nah, I didn't."

She looked at Steve. "Did you?"

Steve shrugged. "I might have accidentally knocked into something when I was down there."

She blew out through her nose. "You're not in any trouble. I just need to know what you saw and did in there. Did you move anything, accidentally or not, I don't care. I just need to know."

Steve stared at her.

"Did you?"

"He did." Danny said quietly. "He picked up one of the arm bones, but he put it back exactly where it came from and we didn't touch nothing else. We crawled out of there and called you. Well, the police. You know."

"Thank you, Danny. After you crawled out, did either of you go back in, or did anyone else go in before the police arrived?"

Steve stared into space and Danny fidgeted his legs. Opening and closing his knees like he was dancing to a beat in his head. "The man from the golf course tried to, but the plastic policeman arrived and stopped him."

"Which one?"

"I don't know which copper it was. Little and dumpy. He's stood at the tape now."

"No, I meant which man from the golf course?"

"Oh, erm, the tall one with the limp."

Kate looked quickly at Jimmy and caught the tiny shrug. "Thanks, that's a big help." She pushed her card across the table. If you think of anything else or you just want to talk, call me."

Danny picked up the card.

"Okay?"

He nodded and stuffed the card into his pocket. "Thanks."

She stood up and followed Jimmy away from the table.

"Mr Spink didn't mention anyone else out there today. Nor did Timmons," Jimmy said.

"Nope. But more to the point, why didn't the plastic policeman tell us when we got here either? Danny said he was talking to him."

"You shouldn't call the PCSO's that. The police community support officers are a vital part of our team, sarge," Jimmy said.

She shrugged, wondering how he managed to keep a straight face when he came out with bull like that. "Then they should do their jobs properly and I wouldn't have cause to." She spotted a door at the end of the hall with "Club Secretary" stencilled on the dark wood in gold lettering. "I'll speak to Dumpy later. Right now, let's see what he's got to say about it."

She knocked on the door and opened it when the voice called, "Come in."

"Mr Spink, do you have a staff member on shift today with a limp?"

He frowned slightly. "Well, yes. That would be Malcolm, the head groundskeeper here."

"Would it be possible for us to have a quick word with him?"

"Of course. I'm not sure where he'll be at the moment, but I'll just give him a call." He indicated the pair of chairs opposite his desk.

"Thanks," Kate said as she and Jimmy sat down, and waited for Mr Spink to make his call.

The room was bright and airy, not at all like the rest of the building they'd seen so far. The computer perched on the desk looked several years old but still perfectly serviceable. Files were neat and orderly, and the old wooden filing cabinet with tiny drawers for stacks of index cards was again so highly polished that she could see the shed and parked cars outside the window in it.

"Malcolm? There are detectives here and they would like to talk to you," Mr Spink said down the phone. "I don't know. Where are you?"

Kate could imagine the other side of the conversation easily enough.

"No, no. It'll be faster for me to bring them over to you." He hung up and smiled. "He's over at the tractor shed. If you wouldn't mind a quick ride, I'll take you over there."

"I'd appreciate it very much. Thank you." Kate smiled, and they followed him out of the room.

The ride turned out to be a golf cart that Mr Spink drove them across the golf course in. There wasn't a single person about, and the only sound was the small engine of the buggy.

Kate glanced out towards the sea and wondered what it would be like on any given day. Would you be able to hear hoards of tourists just the other side of the dunes during the season? Or was it only ever the roar of the tide that detracted from the silence? Or perhaps the call of the birds? "Is it always this quiet?"

He shook his head. "Yes and no. Even when there are people on the course it's the thing I love most about this place. The quiet." He glanced at her. "I've worked at a number of different golf courses over my career, Detective. But this is the only one where I can stand on the course and hear nothing but the wind and the sea."

"What do you normally hear on a golf course?"

He smiled sadly. "Traffic, mostly."

"Ah." She looked across the well-tended lawns and swathes of rough sod to bunkers, which had been cut into the grass and held back by sawn and weathered railway sleepers. Flags of red and yellow fluttered in the breeze as they zipped by, and birds cried overhead.

When he pulled off the fairway and turned behind what looked to be another mound on the course, Kate was surprised to see a large plant works. The tractor shed was a huge building of corrugated steel, painted a deep green so that it was more difficult to see against the grass. A man in his late fifties stood outside with a cigarette rolled between thin lips. A dark woollen cap covered his head and shaded his eyes as he walked towards them with a pronounced limp.

"Malcolm Slater." He held out his hand, and Kate quickly introduced them. She waited until Mr Spink moved away.

"Did you hurt yourself?" Kate asked, indicating his leg.

"In a manner of speaking, miss." He cocked his leg to the side as he bent forward and knocked on it. It sounded hollow. "I can take it off if you like."

Kate waved her hand. "No, not at all. I take it isn't a recent injury?"

"Nah. Been like this for thirty years now. More, in fact. Army."

"Ah," Kate said.

"Iraq?" Jimmy asked.

Kate and Malcolm both stared at him.

"Iraq?" Malcolm asked.

Jimmy shrugged a little sheepishly.

"History's not your strong suit, is it, lad?"

"Sorry." Jimmy had the good grace to look ashamed.

"Northern Ireland, son."

"Oh, right."

"Yeah, stood on something I shouldn't of, and got myself discharged right quick for me troubles. I've worked here ever since. But that's not what you want to hear about today, is it?"

"No, it isn't," Kate agreed. "Why were you trying to get down into the bunker this morning?"

"I needed to know if it was true or if those young lads were playing a dirty, rotten trick on us."

"Why would you think that?"

"Because I thought I was the last person alive in that bunker before it got shut off from the world."

Kate cleared her throat. "Can you explain that please?"

He nodded his head solemnly. "December fifth, 2013."

"The night of the flood," Jimmy said.

"Aye. Hell of a night." He paused, seemingly waiting for an acknowledgment.

"That it was," Kate said, trying to urge him to continue.

"You were here?"

She shook her head. "No, I was working in Norwich then. They sent me over to Cromer that night. I've never seen anything like it. Houses were just crumbling into the sea."

Malcolm nodded. "Well, we didn't lose any houses that way, but by God did we get some flooding. We were prepared, of course. The weather idiots were all over it, warning us of the perfect storm that was heading our way."

"The perfect storm?" Jimmy asked.

"Are you not local, lad?"

Kate knew it rankled when strangers, and perpetrators, saw Jimmy's boyish looks as a way to poke and prod. But he often used it to get witnesses to open up to him. It made him far more approachable than many of her colleagues, and sometimes people open up when they think you're on their side. No matter what they've done.

"I was away at the time of the flood. Working in London."

"Ah. Well, you don't know then. The perfect storm was a high spring tide, highest in a decade, and a wind storm out at sea. They all combined to make the tide so high that it breached all the flood defences up and down the coast."

"But no one was hurt. No one died in the floods."

"True. We were well warned and we evacuated. Went around checking everything to make sure there was no one left that could be hurt." He pointed out towards the dunes. "You know all those boulders out there?"

Jimmy nodded.

"They're all new. The water picked up the old ones and took 'em away. Same size as those—bigger, some of 'em. And the water just took 'em away like Lego bricks. The dunes were washed away. Every house on this side of the main road suffered flood damage to some extent or another. Every one."

"I'm sorry," Jimmy offered.

Malcolm waved his hand. "Not your fault, lad. Mother Nature can be a bitch when she's in the mood." He offered a weak smile. "So, anyway, we knew what time the road was going to flood, we knew that the chances were this building was going to flood, and that the golf course was going to spend a considerable amount of time under water. So we checked everything. Work sheds, the outhouses, the wheelie bins, and yes, I even checked in that bloody bunker. I didn't want the death of a kid on my conscience just because it was a ball ache for me to get myself down that half-buried tunnel."

"And what did you find down there?" Kate asked. The wind kicked up, tossing her hair over her shoulder and into her eyes. She brushed it back and tucked it into the collar of her coat.

"A load of half-rusted cans and some used johnnies."

Kate nodded. "A local hangout for the kids?"

"Something like that. Anyway, there was no one down there, except maybe the odd rat or two. There was no one, living or dead, in that bunker when I left it."

"And what time was that? Do you have any idea?"

"We had to be clear of the road by five, and it was the last place I checked."

"And there was no one on the road when you drove away?"

"No. The roads were empty."

"Anyone on foot?"

"No one I could see. The water was literally coming up the road behind me."

Jimmy smiled. "You make it sound like one of those films where there's a tsunami chasing you down or something."

Malcolm laughed. "Nothing so dramatic as that here in Norfolk, lad. But I can tell you that no one would have made it down the road within ten minutes of me coming up it. Not in a car anyway, and there was no one passing me as I left. So, at five o'clock, it was empty. By the time we came back in the morning to assess the damage, the bunker was sealed and has been until this morning."

"Why was it never opened before now?" she asked. A seagull squawked as it hunted the shoreline. Kate was glad she had nothing in her hands. The thieving birds were known to steal anything they could get their beaks around. Even from the hands of the unsuspecting.

Malcolm shrugged. "The beach is managed by the National Trust, not us. So it was up to them what happened to it. You'll have to ask them why they left it till now."

"If it was theirs to manage, why did you check it that night?"

"Like I said, I had to. I knew that local kids went in there, drinking, shag—excuse me—fooling around, and whatnot. While the adults were all preoccupied with the flood preparations, I wouldn't have put it past some of the little blighters to go sneaking in there for a bit of fun, not realising it was dangerous." He sighed. "I couldn't have lived with it if I'd had the thought, not bothered checking just because it was someone else's job to do, and then a kid turned up missing or dead."

Kate smiled. "I understand."

"Happened anyway, though didn't it?" He plucked a strand of tobacco from the tip of his tongue and spat out in an attempt to rid his mouth of the foul taste and debris.

Kate didn't think it was really the tobacco that was offensive to him. The taste of failure was always so much worse.

"You did your best, Malcolm. It was clear when you had to leave to keep yourself safe. That's all you could do. It's all anyone can do."

"Wasn't enough for that poor bugger, though." He shoved his hand under his hat and scratched at his scalp.

Kate noticed the red tinge to his fingernails before he crossed his arms over his chest.

"What did you do for the rest of the night?"

"Night of the flood?" Malcolm clarified.

"Yes."

"I spent most of it with some of the village locals. It was the weekend of the Christmas Market over by the campsite. The marquees were already out and we were hoping and praying that the water wouldn't come up so far as to ruin everything for the weekend."

"Why did they not cancel if the weather was so bad?" Jimmy asked.

"Bloody Sands. Thinks he can hold back the bloody tide with a flick of his wrist."

"Edward?" Kate asked.

"No, the son. Rupert. The Christmas Market's his baby. Big money-spinner for all the shops in the area, so it increases his revenue."

"I'm sorry, I don't understand," Kate said.

"The Sands own the buildings that the shops operate out of and that the market stalls sit on. They pay a base rent of, say, fifteen grand a year, more in some cases, depends on the size of the property, but they also have to pay a premium on top of that. Fifteen per cent of turnover on top of the base rent. So the more each shop and stall makes every year, the more he lines his pockets."

Jimmy whistled. "That's a pretty nice earner."

"Isn't it, lad. Extortion at half the price."

"How do you know about this deal?" Kate asked.

There was a harsh clanging from inside the shed and the doors slid open. A small earth mover trundled out with a figure wrapped up so much that Kate couldn't tell if it was a man or a woman at the wheel.

Malcolm lifted his hand to acknowledge the driver as they passed and waited for the noise to dissipate before he spoke.

"My wife used to run the bike hire out of the old forge on the farm. Robbing bastards drove her to bankruptcy. We nearly lost the bloody house. She had a breakdown. Spent three years popping pills because of those robbing gits."

"I see. I'm sorry to hear about that, Malcolm." Kate stuck her hands in her pocket. "Who's your wife?"

"Pam Slater. She works behind the bar at the Jolly now. Helen and her go way back. Schoolkids together, you know how it is. Anyway, Helen said she couldn't see us struggling, and took her on in the summer. She works in the kitchen."

"Was she with you that night?"

"She came down to the front line—that's what we called it at the campsite—after she finished work. She finished her shift at nine, but there were lots of other people there. All the staff from the campsite, Connie, even Leah was there that night. We were all stood on the white line in the middle of the road, arms linked like we were a bloody barrier ourselves. Just willing the water to stop rising."

"Did it?" Jimmy asked.

"At me toes, lad." Malcolm smiled. "At me toes." He put his hands in his pocket and pulled out a packet of tobacco.

The wind carried the damp, pungent smell to Kate's nose. It was one that still reminded her of her father. It was almost thirty years since he'd died, but she could still see him sat at her gran's kitchen table, rolling a ciggie, and doing everything he could not to look at her. For some reason it was the scent of the fresh tobacco that reminded her of him rather than the acrid odour of smoke. Probably because her gran made him light up outside. She shook her head and focused on Malcolm again. "Do you have any idea who it could've been? Was there anyone in particular you knew went in there?"

He shook his head. "Like I said, only the kids messing about, and none of them ever turned up missing or anything like that, so..." He stuck the roll-up between his lips and held a lighter to the tip before dragging a deep breath through the poisonous little stick. "Anything else you need from me?"

Kate shook her head and handed him her card. "No, thanks for all your help, Malcolm. If you think of anything else, please give me a call."

"Will do." He flicked ash from the tip of the cigarette and limped away.

"So we've got nothing useful," Jimmy said.

"Au contraire, *mon ami.* We know when our victim died—the fifth of December 2013 after 5 p.m.—and we know he's a bloke, who had no teeth of his own."

Jimmy chuckled. "My mistake, sarge. Open-and-shut this one, then."

"No need for that level of sarcasm, Jimmy," Kate said as they climbed back into the golf cart and allowed Mr Spink to drive them back to the clubhouse.

CHAPTER 4

Gina parked her beat-up old Astra on the main road and walked the short distance down the gravel path to the schoolhouse. Most other mums had done the same. Trying to find a spot in the tiny school car park was the butt of many a joke. And you couldn't even think about being able to turn around. There was a reason the teachers—both of them—came to work on bikes.

She nodded to a few people, but most of the women ignored her. After giving her dirty looks. Gina sighed. She couldn't even blame them. Not really. No matter how much it fucking hurt. They blamed her for the troubles the village was now facing.

The entire fishing fleet—all three boats—were impounded, and the fishermen and captains were either in prison or out of work. Every one of them had a wife or a girlfriend in the village. Many of them had kids that went to school with Sammy. And while Gina had had nothing to do with the drug-smuggling ring that had been discovered, she was the closest they had to someone to blame. The key witness against the criminals was Matt Green, another member of the smuggling ring and also the father of Gina's daughter, Sammy. As far as the village was concerned, that was strike one.

Add to that the fact that she was the manager at the campsite. The campsite that was the second biggest employer in the village, and *the* biggest source of tourist pounds that flooded in every season. And the well-known fact that the future of the campsite was up in the air was very definitely strike two.

It was now also known that she was seeing Detective Sergeant Kate Brannon. The detective they all credited with bringing down the drug-smuggling ring and inviting misfortune to their doors. Strike three.

Gina was a visible and convenient target for their disapproval and venom.

At least it's just dirty looks today. She plastered a false smile onto her face as Sammy trundled out of the door beside her teacher. *Shit. What now?* She glanced at Sammy, but the little girl wouldn't look up from her shoes. Gina couldn't see any obvious signs of problems, though. Her dungarees were grime-smeared as they always were at the end of the day, but they were intact. Not a rip or hole to be seen. There was no blood on her face, her hair was still in the twin braids Gina had put it in that morning—just—and she couldn't see any bruises either. Nothing to indicate that Sammy had been in a fight. She tried to think if they'd missed any of Sammy's homework assignments, but couldn't think of anything.

"Miss Temple," the older woman started. Her brow was furrowed in a tight frown, and her lips had thinned.

Mrs Eastern was a woman who dressed the part of schoolteacher. Hair tied in a bun at the back of her head, her fringe cut over her eyebrows, and spectacles hung from a chain about her neck. A thick turtleneck sweater, royal blue today, and a black skirt made up the rest of her teacher's uniform. It made her look older than she was, and almost unrecognisable when she was "off duty" and wandering about the streets in her everyday clothes. Gina guessed that was the exact reason why she did it.

"Mrs Eastern." Gina nodded. "Is something wrong?"

"Perhaps we could go inside and discuss this." Her voice was stern, her demeanour sour.

Gina felt a knot in the pit of her stomach.

Mrs Eastern's hand was clamped tightly around Sammy's shoulder as she turned and led them both back into the schoolhouse. She continued ahead in stony silence through the main entrance, past another two of the mums who volunteered at the afterschool clubs for kids whose parents worked, and into the head teacher's office.

The head, Mrs Partridge, wore an even deeper frown. She stood up as they all entered the room and pointed to the chairs on the opposite side of her desk. "Please sit down."

It wasn't a request.

Sammy moved away from Mrs Eastern and hitched herself into the chair. Mrs Eastern closed the door behind them with a resounding thunk.

Sammy looked up for the first time and grinned at Mrs Eastern.

"Was that stern enough for you, Sammy?" she said. The gentle smile that played across her face made her look younger and much more like the teacher Gina was used to dealing with, despite the many times she'd had to deal with Sammy's "issues" at school.

"Yep, fanks."

"Thanks. It starts with a T-H not an F." She ruffled Sammy's hair.

"I'm sorry," Gina said, "but what's going on?"

"Miss Temple," Mrs Partridge said, "I'm afraid Sammy's been having a bit of a rough time of late."

Gina swallowed and fought the instinct to drop her head. "I know. The past few weeks have been really hard on her."

Mrs Partridge nodded. "Yes, they have, but I'm not sure you do know. Sammy's been keeping secrets from you."

Gina turned to her daughter. "You have? Why?"

Sammy shrugged and looked down at her lap. "S'nuffink, Mum."

"Sammy, if your teachers are calling me in to see them about it, it most certainly is not nothing. Especially when they're acting so weird." Gina glanced at them both. "I'm sorry, but you are. Out there you were all stern and acting like Sammy's done something wrong, now you're acting like she hasn't. What's going on?"

Mrs Eastern knelt next to Sammy and spoke softly. "Sammy's been getting a really hard time at school from the other kids. They're hearing a lot of rubbish from their mums and dads at home, and they're acting out on it here at school. It isn't really the kids' fault, but they're worried and not sure what's really happening. They just know that bad stuff is happening."

"The harbour," Gina said.

Mrs Eastern nodded. "There are twenty-nine children in this school, Miss Temple, and only Sammy and two other children didn't have a parent who worked at the harbour, either on the boats, processing the catch, or in what passed for the offices of the fleet, doing the paperwork."

"I've been getting a lot of dirty looks and nasty comments from the other mums when I come to pick Sammy up." She turned to look at Sammy. "Is that what's going on?"

Sammy shook her head. "Well, yeah, but not just."

"Sammy?"

Mrs Eastern ran her hand over Sammy's head. "At afternoon break I found Sammy at the back of the bins. She had a bloody nose, and was hiding. She didn't want to come back into class. She also refused to tell me what had happened. She said she fell and hurt herself. I brought her in to Mrs Partridge to deal with the bloody nose and clean her up, but neither of us believed that she'd fallen. I went and asked the class what had happened to Sammy, and every one of them told me that she'd picked a fight with one of the boys, and got hurt when she fell over. But none of them would admit which boy or where the fight happened."

Mrs Partridge took over the story. "When we told Sammy this, she was understandably upset, and told us the truth. That a group of eight of them had circled her, calling her names, and taking turns pushing and hitting her until she fell on her face, then they ran off laughing."

Gina was torn. She was so upset for Sammy that she wanted to pull her into her arms and cry with her. But equally she wanted to march up to the little shits that had done this and give them the slapped arse their own parents clearly needed to, but wouldn't. *Violence is not the answer, Gina.* She repeated it in her head. Trying to convince herself of its truth. She took a deep breath and exhaled slowly. "Sammy, is this true?"

Sammy nodded.

Gina inched her chair closer to Sammy's and pulled her into a tight hug. The need to comfort her daughter won convincingly in the end. After all, others were much better placed to deal with bullying children than she was.

"So, what are you going to do to these other kids?" Gina asked. She stroked her hand down Sammy's hair soothingly. She wasn't sure if it was soothing Sammy or her, but it was keeping her in her seat instead of going to look for the little bastards and showing them what bullying really was. Mrs Partridge was a good headmistress; she'd have an appropriate punishment in mind. She just knew it.

Mrs Partridge cleared her throat. "Nothing."

"Nothing! Are you kidding? They're bullying Sammy, en masse, and you plan to do nothing?" Only Sammy's weight was keeping her in her chair. She tried to lift Sammy away from her but Sammy clung tight, not willing to be moved.

"It's what Sammy wants," Mrs Eastern said quietly.

"With all due respect, Mrs Partridge, she's nine. You're the adult here. The teacher. What do you plan to do to stop this from happening again?"

"Miss Temple, if you'd let me explain," Mrs Partridge started.

"Please do. I can't wait to hear this."

"As I was saying, the entire school is affected by the events that unfolded six weeks ago. Those children who bullied Sammy today—"

"Attacked. They attacked her."

Mrs Partridge nodded. "Very well. The children who attacked Sammy today are the children whose fathers are facing jail time for their part in the operation."

"So is Sammy's dad."

Mrs Partridge nodded. "I know, but they blame Mr Green rather than consider him one of them. I'm not saying this is right. On the contrary, it is very, very wrong. But Sammy is coping far better than any of us would have predicted and far better than the other children in her class. In my opinion, that is due to how you have dealt with the situation, and how Sammy hasn't been lied to or kept in the dark about what's happened."

"Well, I'm sorry, but there are lots of things Sammy doesn't know about what happened, and to be completely honest with you, I wish she didn't know half of what she does."

"I'm sure. Believe me, I understand the sentiment, but the fact remains that in knowing the truth behind the situation, Sammy is able to deal with the consequences of it all much better than her classmates. Taking action against these children will undoubtedly cause a great deal of anguish to children who are already suffering through things they don't understand. Because of everything Sammy saw, she understands what's happening in a way the others don't."

"So she's suffered the most and because of that she must continue to suffer. That's what you're telling me?"

Mrs Partridge shook her head. "No, not at all. It's our job to make the children understand the right and wrong of what's going on and what they're doing to Sammy. What I'm asking is that you give us time to teach them the things that Sammy already knows. And it will take time, because we are going to have to teach them something that is contrary to what their parents are teaching them at the moment."

Gina clenched her teeth together. No. She ground her teeth together. Her jaw worked as she tried to contain the anger—no, the rage—that was growing inside her. Sammy had done nothing wrong. She'd witnessed a murder. The gruesome, horrible murder of someone she had loved. Her little girl had seen it in all its wretched detail, and for three awful days she'd believed she'd caused it. For three brutal days, she'd believed she'd killed someone she'd loved. By accident. She needed empathy, some understanding. She needed a little fucking slack, and instead she was being treated like the town whipping boy. It was one thing for the adults to give her dirty looks and snub her. But not her daughter. No. That was going too far. "So let me get this straight. Treating Sammy like she'd done something wrong in the playground was for their benefit?"

Mrs Eastern nodded. "And Sammy's. If they think she's being badly treated by us too, they may ease off a bit."

Gina raised her eyes to look at Mrs Eastern. She focused on her breathing, and keeping her voice controlled. "Or they may see it as them having permission from you as well as their parents to treat my daughter like a punching bag." The ice in her voice surprised Gina.

Probably as much as it surprised them, judging by the look on their faces.

Mrs Eastern rounded the desk and knelt beside Gina and Sammy. She clasped her hands in front of her chest like she was intending to pray. "Miss Temple, you have my word, they won't touch Sammy again," Mrs Eastern said. "I'll see to it personally."

"How, exactly, do you plan to do that?" Gina demanded. A sneer curled her lips, and she fought back the urge to snap her teeth. Anger would let you get away with so much, but it wouldn't let you get away with complete crazy. No matter how good it might have felt.

"I need a new assistant to help me organise the Christmas party. I usually do this during break times and lunchtimes, so I think my assistant will have to stay with me to help me do that. Don't you, Sammy?"

"Do I get to pick the music?"

Mrs Eastern smiled. "I think we can come to a compromise."

"So you're going to punish Sammy, keeping her inside all the time."

"I know it's not ideal. I know it may sound like a punishment, but in all honesty, during winter, the kids don't always get out at break or lunchtimes anyway. So it really won't be that big an issue, but it will give Sammy something interesting to help me with while we work on educating the rest of the school."

"And how do you plan to do that?" She pointed her finger at Mrs Partridge. "Those things don't just happen like that." She snapped her fingers. "You can't just wish that the kids will suddenly have better manners and do what you bloody well want them to do."

"I know." She held her hands up as though she were surrendering. "Believe me, we do know that. And we also know that this won't be easy. But we do have a plan. We're taking a little side step into criminology." Mrs Partridge smiled. "With the older kids anyway. There are books about the law, and what's right and wrong, out there that we can start to look at with them. I'm trying to get them to think about what's right and wrong in a society, then we can scale it back down to a more local level and see if they can apply it to the things that are going on around them."

"We're also going to start reading a lot of books about bullying with the kids. There are books to suit all levels of reading, and for the very youngest we'll read them at reading time," Mrs Eastern added.

"It won't be a fast process." Mrs Partridge drummed her fingers on the desk. "And I expect that there will be setbacks, especially when the trials begin. But I do believe this is a better way forward than by approaching the parents of these children at this time. After all, the kids are getting this from their parent or parents, and I can't see that approaching them would actually improve things for Sammy at this stage."

It made sense. They were trying to deal with a school crisis, not just one little girl being unpopular, and Gina had to admit, it certainly sounded like a well-thought-out strategy that they had come up with. She turned to Sammy. "Are you happy with that solution?"

Sammy shrugged. "S'pose so."

"Sammy, if you're not, then we find another one."

"Like what?"

"I don't know. Maybe we find you a different school. One where they don't know about what happened."

"I like my school. I've got friends here."

"Where were your friends earlier when you were getting pushed? What was Emily doing then?"

Sammy stared at her lap again.

"I believe Emily was the one who pushed her down and told her she was a liar just like her dad," Mrs Eastern said.

Gina shook her head and held Sammy close as she started to cry.

"I believe Emily's dad was the captain of one of the other boats in the fleet."

Gina nodded. He was, and he was looking at a long stretch. From what Kate had said, he could be looking at fifteen years in prison. Gina eased Sammy away from her and wiped her cheeks with her thumbs. "Are you sure, Sammy? Are you sure you want to stay here?"

Sammy nodded. "I just want them to be my friends again. If I go away they'll hate me forever."

Simple child logic. She couldn't argue with it as Sammy was probably right. After all, running away from her own problems had never solved them for Gina, why would it work for Sammy? She stared into Sammy's eyes. The eyes of a nine-year-old who had seen far too much. Eyes that had seen Gina's best friend after she'd died, with her face blown off. Eyes that had looked upon that scene believing she was the cause. Eyes that had seen the scars that covered her mother's body as a result of Ally Robbins trying to find out where Sammy's father was hiding. And eyes that she knew still saw nightmares when they closed at night. Why did she have to go through more?

Sammy sniffed and wiped her face with the back of her sleeve. "I'm sure, Mum." She smiled a small smile. "I want to pick the music for the Christmas party." She turned to Mrs Eastern. "Can we put 'I'm Sexy and I Know It' on the list?"

Mrs Eastern closed her eyes and bit her lip. "I'm not sure that would be appropriate for a school Christmas party."

Sammy frowned. "What happened to negotiation? I open with 'Sexy and I Know It', and you're supposed to counter with somefink stupid like 'Raindrops on Roses' or 'The Birdy Song', and then we settle on 'Bat out of Hell'." She shook her head and looked at Gina. "She needs to watch *The Apprentice* a bit more, Mum. I could run this school."

Gina chuckled and looked down at Mrs Eastern. "Are you sure you want to do this?"

Mrs Eastern smiled back. "Someone has to keep me on my toes, Miss Temple." She looked at Sammy. "'Bat out of Hell' is on the list."

"Awesome." Sammy pumped her fist, licked her finger, and scored a number one in the air.

"Sammy?" Mrs Partridge drew their attention. "I'll only agree to this plan on one condition."

Sammy frowned. "What?"

"You have to promise me that you'll talk to us."

"I am talking to you."

"I mean about what's happening with the other kids, and about how you're feeling."

"But I don't want to be a snitch. That's why they hate my dad."

Mrs Partridge smiled sadly. "They hate your dad because he did things wrong, just like they did, but telling means he'll get in less trouble than they will. I'm not asking you to tell us things to get yourself out of trouble. I'm asking you tell us things to keep you safe. To keep you well and to help you feel better. Do you understand the difference, Sammy?"

Sammy looked at her thoughtfully and bit her lip. "I fink—sorry, I think so."

"I need you to tell one of us if someone hurts you or tries to hurt you. I need you to tell us if the things we're doing help make things better for you with the other kids or if they are getting worse. You have to promise not to keep things to yourself anymore."

"I understand," Sammy said, even though she didn't seem to like what she understood.

"You've also got to promise that you'll talk to us about the other things that are bothering you."

Sammy narrowed her eyes suspiciously. "Like what?"

Mrs Partridge leaned forward and rested her elbows on the big desk. "I know you have bad dreams, Sammy."

Sammy's eyes widened and her face paled.

Mrs Partridge nodded. "I want you to come and talk to me about them. About the things you saw, and about your dad. I want you to come and talk to me about how you feel about it all."

"I don't wanna."

Gina swallowed, both her saliva and her anxiety. She'd tried taking Sammy to a counsellor that the Victim Support unit had put her in touch with. They'd got nowhere. Sammy had simply refused to say anything, and eventually they'd given up. They couldn't help if Sammy wouldn't even talk about her experiences. No one could. She wished she could take the images that plagued her from her head, but she couldn't. She wished she could make her forget it all. Who wouldn't? Instead, she was left with waiting. Waiting for Sammy to be ready to put voice to her demons...or for them to swallow her.

"I'm sorry, Sammy. It's a non-negotiable part of the deal."

"I don't like counselling."

"I'm not a counsellor."

"But you want me to talk, just like she did."

Mrs Partridge nodded. "Yes, I do. Do you know why?"

"'Cos you're a nosey old biddy who wants to know all my business!" Sammy bounced out of the chair and knocked the squatting Mrs Eastern over as she tried to get to the door.

The woman sat on her bottom, stunned.

"Sammy!" Gina called horrified.

Mrs Partridge was faster than Sammy. She simply stood with her back to the door, crossed her arms over her chest, and blocked Sammy's only means of escape. "It's okay, Sammy," she said quietly as Sammy tried to pull her away from the door. "It's okay."

Gina pulled herself from her shocked stupor and went to get Sammy away from the teacher.

Mrs Partridge shook her head. "Leave her. We're okay. Aren't we, Sammy?" she asked as Sammy continued to scream and cry and pull at her sleeves.

"Get out of my way, you old bitch."

"It's okay, Sammy," she cooed. "No one here will hurt you."

"Move. Move. Move!" Sammy balled her hands into fists, but still Mrs Partridge didn't move. "Get out of my way!"

"No, Sammy. I'm not going anywhere."

Sammy raised her hands as if to attack and charged at her.

Mrs Partridge still didn't move.

Before touching her Sammy threw herself on the floor and beat her fists into the carpet tiles that covered the concrete. She kicked and pounded on the hard floor, her tears falling, and her body wracked by each heart-breaking sob that was torn from her.

Mrs Partridge slid down the door and sat on the floor beside Sammy. She laid one hand on her back and began to form slow, soothing circles across the back of her jumper.

"That's it. Let it out."

Sammy slowly curled herself into a ball, and whispered something too quiet for Gina to hear.

"It's okay, Sammy. I know you didn't mean it. Thank you for saying sorry." Mrs Partridge nodded at Gina and smiled.

Gina trembled as she knelt beside Sammy and pulled her into her arms, holding her close. Tears wet her own cheeks. She felt like a failure. For six weeks she'd tried and failed to get Sammy to open up to her. To cry like she knew she needed to. To release the emotion, the fear, the anger that had to have been hiding inside her little girl. And the more time that had passed, the more she had feared that Sammy would bottle it up forever. That it would affect her for the rest of her life in ways they couldn't even begin to fathom yet.

"Thank you," she whispered over to Mrs Partridge.

"No need," she said, clambering to her feet. "This place wouldn't be the same without the Sammy we all know and love." She put a hand on Gina's shoulder. "We'll be outside just clearing away. Take your time."

"Thank you."

Mrs Partridge nodded. "And Sammy?"

"Yeah?" Sammy looked up.

"Lunchtime tomorrow. My office."

Sammy was glued against Gina's shoulder, but she nodded.

"Good girl." The two teachers left the room.

Gina stroked Sammy's hair until she was quiet and her face had dried. "Why didn't you tell me?"

Sammy shrugged.

"Please don't do that, Sammy. I'm your mum, I want to make sure you're okay, but I can't do that if you don't talk to me."

"But you were hurt worse than me, and they're all being mean to you too." Sammy wiped her nose on her sleeve. "I caused too much trouble before. I didn't want to cause any more."

Gina's stomach clenched and she fought the desire to curl into a ball. She couldn't afford to do that. Sammy needed her mother. She needed a strong mum to look after her. Not one she felt she had to protect. How weak must she seem to have a nine-year-old think she couldn't handle anything else? How pathetic was she that her own child needed to shield her from her problems? How wrapped up in her own shit must she have been not to even notice what Sammy was going through? Well, no more. Sammy was her priority. She might have forgotten that for a little while, but it didn't make it any less true. Nor did it change what she needed to do now. "Oh, Sammy. You didn't cause the problems before, and you haven't caused the problems now. You're just stuck in the middle of it all, and I'm so sorry for that, baby. I wish I could change it. I really do."

"It's not your fault, Mum. You didn't do anything wrong either."

"I did. Or you would have told me what was going on."

"No, you didn't. I just didn't want to upset you."

"Sammy, sweetie, that upsets me more. I'm the mum here. I protect you. Not the other way around, okay?"

Sammy nodded and rested her head on Gina's shoulder. "I'm sorry."

"No more secrets, okay?" Gina cuddled her tight again. "I want you to tell me everything from now on."

"Everything?"

"Yes, everything."

"Okay." Sammy smiled wickedly. "You put your jumper on inside out this morning and haven't changed it."

Gina glanced down, mortified to see that Sammy was right. *Bloody kid.*

CHAPTER 5

Kate pushed open the door and smiled at Stella hunched over her desk and Tom shaking a whiteboard marker trying to get it to work. Some things never changed.

"Looks like the gang's all here then," she said.

Stella looked up and smiled. "Glad to see you're here in one piece. Did your new car make it without the snorkel?" She pushed her short, wavy, blond hair behind her ear. Her smile made the lines around her brown eyes crinkle, and she had a habit of hunching her shoulders towards her ears when she was taking the piss. Just like they were doing now. Her grey blazer wrinkled and parted across her ample chest. Stocky was probably the best way to describe Detective Sergeant Stella Goodwin. Broad shoulders, wide hips, and powerful thighs were hard to hide under an off-the-peg pant suit. Not that Stella really tried.

"Funny." Kate dropped herself heavily into a chair, slumped back, and lifted her feet on to the corner of the desk, noting the sand filing the tread of her knee high boots. She frowned. She hated sand. Loved the beach—but hated sand. *It just gets everywhere.* She tapped the sole against the edge of the desk and watched with satisfaction as the damp clumps dropped into the bin.

"So, what do we have?" Stella asked. "Tom's put a tenner on it being a load of refugees washed up and the beginnings of a people trafficking operation."

Kate laughed. "Jimmy reckoned the same thing. Do you two share a brain?"

Collier guffawed from across the room and was rewarded with a swift slap across the back of his head by Tom. "Watch it, pretty boy, you have to earn piss-taking privileges."

"Really?" Collier sneered. "And how do you do that? Spend twenty years going nowhere?"

"Ooo," Tom cooed. "Listen to her sharpening her nails," he said affecting a high-pitched voice and curling his fingers into claw-like talons.

"Now, now, boys," Kate said, "play nice or I'll have to take your toys away." She crossed her feet at the ankles and leaned her chair back on its legs. "What we have is diddly-bloody-squat. A skeleton that we know has been buried in a bunker for just over three years."

"Male," Jimmy added.

"With a set of ladies' dentures in."

"Are we sure he's male?" Stella asked.

"Doc Anderson said the pelvis was definitely male. Why? What're you thinking?"

"A cross-dresser maybe. Or maybe even transgender."

"Hadn't thought of that," Kate admitted. "I'll ask the doc when I go to the autopsy, but maybe we should run the name of those dentures in the meantime."

"I'm on it." Jimmy tapped away at his keyboard as he spoke.

"You said almost three years. I know Dr Anderson wouldn't be so exact without her tests first, so how do you know that?" Stella asked.

Kate quickly gave them a run through of the conversations she and Jimmy had had with Danny, Steve, and Malcolm. "So I think we also need to start running missing persons from that time."

"Agreed," Stella said. "I'll start a week before and run for two weeks after. See where that leads us to begin with. What's Timmons' thinking on this? Accidental?"

Kate shook her head. "He said until we know more, we treat it as suspicious and proceed accordingly."

"Right. Good job I started a new bible then," she said, referring to the murder book that was compiled for each investigation they undertook. "Collier, you can start plugging the info we have into the computer and see if it spits anything out."

The young DC sighed. "Fine, but from what I heard, we don't exactly have a lot to plug into HOLMES 2," he complained as he clicked buttons on his mouse and tapped away at his keyboard.

Kate knew he was opening up the massive program they referred to as HOLMES 2—the Home Offices Large Major Enquiry System, the second generation. It was a huge, unwieldy national program designed to organise and sort the data from every crime entered. Investigators could then sort through the masses of information from crime scenes, witness statements, and anything else the subsequent investigation uncovered.

It helped ensure that no scrap of evidence was overlooked, and helped them direct the course of the investigation. But it was so much more than just a database. The embedded dynamic reasoning engine in the software allowed the program to combine the skills and experiences of the investigating officers with the acquired knowledge of the system and identify new lines of enquiries as a result. It was a stroke of programming genius. At times it seemed to think for itself. Well, sort of. Kate had no idea how it worked. She just knew it was bloody brilliant. When used properly.

Collier scowled at his computer as he pecked away at the keys.

Kate was not entirely convinced that his use fell into that category.

She studied him as he worked. He had dark hair slicked back with a razor-sharp side parting and a pronounced widow's peak. His face was clean shaven, his strong jaw, wide mouth, and straight nose were topped off with piercing blue eyes. He was a good looking guy. Very good looking. And he knew it. Always well-turned-out in a sharp suit, polished shoes, and well-groomed, he looked more like a model than a police detective, but Kate had seen him use that to his advantage. Witnesses and perps had been known to fall for his obvious charms— well, the ladies, anyway. But there was something about him she didn't like. Perhaps he was just a little bit too...perfect.

She shook her head and jolted herself out of her reverie. "Anything on that name, Jimmy?"

"Yes. Annie Balding was pronounced dead on the morning of the sixth of December 2013. Doctor declared her after being called in by nursing home staff. They found her dead in her bed in the morning."

"Cause of death?"

"It says natural causes." His eyes flicked back to the screen. "I've got her medical records here. She was diagnosed with lung cancer over a year before. She also had Parkinson's disease, so they weren't treating the cancer. The last time the doctor visited he'd prescribed oral morphine to keep her comfortable, and written that it was just a matter of time. No autopsy was performed, and her death wasn't a surprise."

Kate sighed. "Poor thing. How old was she?"

"Sixty-eight."

"No age," she said quietly to herself. "Missing persons?" she asked Stella.

"I've discounted women and anyone under the age of fifty—"

"Why fifty?" Collier asked.

"The dentures. Probability of the victim wearing dentures and being under fifty are slim."

"But not impossible."

"No, not impossible, but highly unlikely," Stella said in a tone that was clearly warning him to back off.

He seemed to get the hint and remained quiet.

"Anyway, I've still got quite a few. Too many, really. As soon as you get some more info from the doc, we'll be able to see if any of these are our victim."

"I'll take that as my cue to scarper, then. Jimmy, you coming?" Kate asked.

"Yup." Jimmy stood up and grabbed his coat in one fluid motion. "Lead the way, boss."

"Oh, so now you're being nice to me. No. You cannot drive my new car."

Jimmy shook his head. "Like I'd have the guts to even ask."

Kate smiled. "I'm so glad we understand each other, Jimmy."

The artificial smell of formaldehyde and decay hit Kate as she pushed open the door to the morgue. She hated the place. The cold atmosphere had little to do with the air conditioning, and everything to do with the emptiness that lingered inside. Despite the few living people who littered the tables and benches with the mementos of life, it was death that permeated the air. Death that whispered in the ear of the over-imaginative, and death that lingered in the shadows.

Dr Ruth Anderson stood at the head of the steel table in her medical gown and gloves. The skeleton was laid out anatomically already, and she was holding one of the long leg bones.

"Glad you could make it," Ruth said with a small smile.

Her dark hair was held back with a rubber band and there was a pencil stuck into the bunch. She had on a pair of safety glasses that Kate wasn't sure were strictly necessary, but Ruth was always one to follow procedure in her lab. Not a bad thing. It made her witness testimony harder to dismiss, and her work was impeccable. Kate was glad to be working with her again—they'd become friends of sorts over the past couple of months.

"Oh, you know me, doc. I wouldn't miss something like this," Kate joked back. She motioned her hand up the length of the table. "He looks like a tall chap."

Ruth held out the thigh bone. "Skeletons always look bigger when they're spread out. The length of the femur indicates he was of average height for a man. 5'9"."

"And he's definitely a man?"

"Definitely."

"Is there any way, given what you've got here, that you could determine if he was transgender or a cross-dresser or something like that?"

Ruth frowned then smiled. "You mean because of the teeth and the flowery dressing gown?"

"It was a dressing gown?"

"Looks like it from the scraps I was able to get together. But no, from what I have of the remains, there would be no way to tell you that. If he was transgender, pre- or post-op, I'd need flesh to ascertain that information. As to lifestyle choices, I can't give you any details on those. He may have been, or he may have grabbed something as quickly as he could for some reason. More for you to figure out, I'm afraid."

"Just one more thing, right? What about his age? Can you give me something on that then?"

"Very difficult with a mature skeleton. It's actually much easier to get a close approximate age in young people."

"Why?"

"The developmental patterns of maturation are very specific. The older we get, though, the fewer clues we have to use as determining markers." She waved the long bone again. "For example, in the femur of a person under the age of twenty-five the growth plates would still be open, so I could use the measurements to determine the age of the skeleton at death. But over twenty-five, the growth plates are closed and of no help in determining age."

"Well, if you're going to tell me the best you can do is over twenty-five, then I don't think we're ever likely to figure out who our victim is."

"Ye of little faith, Kate." Ruth smiled as she put the leg bone back in its place. "I'm much better than that." She winked at Kate, and Jimmy chortled. "In the absence of clues in the skull or the long bones, I have to look at the pelvic symphysis, the ribs, and the bone density to get you a clearer age bracket to work with."

Kate frowned.

"The pelvis symphysis is that thin band of cartilage just there." She pointed to the juncture of the pelvis and the spine. "That straightens over time and becomes perfectly straight by the time a person reaches the age of fifty." She looked at Kate. "What do you see?"

"It looks pretty straight to me."

"Exactly. So next I look at the ribs. The sternal area, where the ribs meet the breastbone, has predictable changes over time too. The ends of those bones start off all smooth and rounded, and then become pitted and sharp over time. Can you see how pointed those rib ends look?" She lifted one from the table and showed them both the point on the end of the curved bone. "This puts our victim closer to the age of seventy, but evidence shows that the older the rib the greater the room for error, so I'd have to say between sixty and eighty, looking at the ribs."

Jimmy whistled. "Still a pretty big gap, doc."

"That's why I'm waiting for the results of the bone density analysis to come back. I'll be able to get you a five- to ten-year range then." She put the rib bone back.

"Okay, thanks. How long will the results take?" Kate asked.

Ruth shrugged. "Before the end of the day, but not by much."

"Got it. What about the skull and the facial reconstruction?"

"I've had the skull through the scanner and sent the data file to Grimshaw. He said he'd have the results for you in a couple of hours."

"Thanks, that's great." She looked down at the remains. "Any clues as to how he died yet?"

"Actually, yes." Ruth picked up the skull and turned it to show them the back. "See that?" She pointed to a series of cracks along the clean bone.

"Looks like a fractured skull," Kate said.

"Yes. A stellate fracture of the cranium, to be exact." She turned the skull upside down and pointed inside. "See that inside?"

"Looks like a dirty mark."

"Intracranial bleeding has stained the inside of the cranium."

Kate had heard that phrase before. "So a massive cranial bleed inside the skull."

"Very good, Detective. You've been doing your homework."

"Nah. I've been watching that TV show that you hate again," Kate said referring to the popular American series about a forensic anthropologist and her crack team of nerds helping the FBI solve case after case.

Ruth scowled. "I'm not sure we can be friends any more."

Kate laughed out loud. "Yeah, yeah, yeah. So you keep saying."

"Does that mean he was killed by a blow to the head?" Jimmy asked.

"An injury to the head like this, if left untreated, would have undoubtedly killed him. But not immediately."

"An injury?" Kate asked. "Not a blow to the head?"

Ruth frowned. "It's not impossible that it was from a blow, but it would have to be with something quite flat and heavy."

"Like the bottom of a frying pan?" Jimmy asked.

Ruth smiled. "More like a breeze block. Whilst a frying pan is not impossible, the shape of this fracture is more consistent with hitting your head on the floor after falling downstairs or something like that."

"A fall?"

"That's one possibility."

"And the others are?" Kate asked.

"You're the detective, not me."

"I know, but I'm asking for your medical opinion on what could have possibly caused this kind of injury."

Ruth sighed. "Fine, but I will not swear to any of this."

"Understood." Kate nodded solemnly.

"A fall downstairs is highly likely, but the other possibility is banging it into a wall. With significant force."

"So not just stumbling and banging it against the wall?"

"No. I mean more like someone slamming the victim against the wall. But as I said, the fall downstairs is more likely."

"Yes, you did say that, doc. Why?"

"Do you see how these lines don't cross over those ones?" Ruth traced her nitrile-covered finger across the faint lines on the skull.

"Yes. What am I looking at?"

"They're from a secondary fracture. The first one caused the stellate fracture and the cracks that radiate out from it, but the secondary fracture lines can't cross what is already broken matter."

"So you're saying if it was from someone slamming him against a wall, it had to have been done more than once."

"Correct. Hence why the stair falling is more likely. The victim could have easily hit his head multiple times on the way down the stairs."

"I understand what you're saying, but in my experience, one shove against a wall very often leads to another."

"You said it wouldn't kill him right away," Jimmy said. "How long would he have lasted?"

"Good question, Detective Constable Powers, and I'm afraid that's difficult to tell. I'd say more than an hour, but less than four from the time of the injury."

"Are any of the other bones broken?" Kate asked.

"No, none. There are signs of arthritis and historic skeletal damage. Some old cracked ribs, a broken arm, and it looks like a fractured collarbone at some point too, but nothing else at time of death."

"That sounds to me like a tick in the box against a fall down the stairs." Kate ran her fingers through her hair. "Wouldn't you expect there to be other bone fractures and breaks if he'd done that much damage to his head?"

"Not necessarily. If he was falling, leading with the head, then it's possible that the rest of his body may have suffered only bruises and scratches. Given his age, a fall is much more likely than a fight, Detectives."

"Fair point, doc, but are both possible explanations for his injuries?"

"Yes, definitely."

"Okay, good. So cause of death is the head injury, cause unknown at this time."

Ruth shook her head. "I can't say that."

"Excuse me?"

"I said this kind of injury would have killed him, but without the flesh I couldn't rule out that something else killed him before this had the time to."

"I don't follow, doc," Jimmy said.

"Given where he was found, and what we know happened on that night, I couldn't rule out that he drowned or died of hypothermia. So while the head injury would have killed him, I can't say that it was the cause of his death at this point."

"That sounds like an exercise in semantics to me, doc." Jimmy crossed his arms over his chest and frowned.

"I don't mean to be pedantic, Detective, and I'm not trying to make your job more difficult. But I wouldn't be doing mine if I were to let you chase down something for which I have no definitive supporting evidence."

"But you said the head injury could have killed him."

Ruth nodded again. "Yes, but think about this scenario for a moment. Our victim here falls down the stairs and causes himself a serious injury. One that would not have left him thinking clearly. Perhaps he was at home alone when the accident occurred, and he went outside to look for help. In the bad weather and his growing confusion, somehow he ends up wandering to the beach and into the bunker where he gets sealed in and dies of hypothermia or drowns when the bunker filled up with water."

"There was no water in the bunker," Kate interjected.

"No, it seeped away over time, through the cracks in the brick, the sand, and the concrete. But it was filled with water shortly after our victim went in there."

"How do you know?"

"The silt that was covering the floor and the body had microorganisms in it that came from the ocean."

"This bunker was on the beach, couldn't that account for the microorganisms?"

"No, these little buggers are only found in the water. Not just from being close to it. Also, it was the water in there that stopped the sand from filling the rest of the bunker and not just the entrance tunnel. If the water hadn't acted as a counter then the sand would have just filled the entire space."

"I'd been wondering about that," Kate said. "Why we weren't digging the remains out of sand, rather than them just sitting in there." She looked at Ruth again. "So you're thinking accidental death?"

Ruth shook her head. "No. It'll be an open verdict. There isn't enough evidence to support accidental or suspicious death in this case."

Kate stared down at the yellowed bones. What a piteous end. She couldn't imagine anything worse. To die alone, anonymously. To remain that way. She shuddered.

"You okay?" Jimmy asked.

"Yeah, just feel sorry for the poor old bugger." She looked over at the doctor again. "Anything else you can add to help us find out who he is and let his family know what happened to him?"

Ruth shook her head. "I'm afraid not. I sent all the scraps of cloth and the dentures over to your crime scene guys. Len Wild is taking a look at them."

"Right." She turned to Jimmy. "Let's go see what Len's got to tell us then. Thanks, doc," she said and led Jimmy out of the door.

Male. 5'9". Bashed-in head. Not much for a gravestone.

CHAPTER 6

The crime "lab" was housed in the basement at King's Lynn Police Station. It had a total of three windows. All three were too high for anyone to reach, and looked out on to the ankles of the good people of King's Lynn.

Kate had walked past those windows so many times and paid the four-inch square blocks of thick glass no attention whatsoever. Today there was a tiny shaft of light filtering through them as the sun went about its business of setting in the middle of the December afternoon.

Jimmy tapped her shoulder and pointed back at the door behind them. "Is that for real?"

Kate chuckled. Someone had crossed out the carefully-stencilled "SOCO" that decorated the door for as long as the crime lab had been down in the dungeon, and taken a Sharpie to the glass. The newly-christened CSIs were hard at work, ignoring their curiosity at the new appellation.

"Some creative nit has decided that we're dinosaurs and in need of a little 'Hollywood' flair," Len Wild said, curling his fingers in quotation marks.

"I don't know, Len. I can see you on a red carpet."

"Yeah, collecting particulates maybe." He grinned at her. "How're you doing, hoppy?" he asked, referring to the leg injury she'd sustained jumping from the smouldering wreckage of a houseboat in the last case they had worked together.

"Better than you will be if you carry on like that," she said with a grin as she reached over and gave him a quick hug. "I never did get to properly thank you for taking care of me that day." Len had driven her from the hospital to pick up her written-off car before spending a few hours with her going over case details, and finally driving her home.

At six-foot-four he was a good head taller than Kate. His greying hair gave him the distinguished look she knew many women would attribute to a silver fox. She smiled to herself as she suspected how Len would react to such a descriptor.

"No need to thank me. What's that Mona Lisa smile for?"

"Can't a girl just be pleased to see you?"

"Some girls, maybe. You? Not so much." He winked and leaned in a little closer. "How is the lovely Gina these days?"

Kate felt her cheeks warm, pushed her hair over her shoulder, and wondered exactly how to answer the question. Things had been going well with Gina. Romantic dates, lots of talking, lots of hand-holding, some kissing, but nothing more. She could hardly blame Gina for taking it slowly. After all, it had been Kate who'd said that she wanted more than just a long weekend after Gina had told her that was all her previous relationships had ever been. But Kate thought that in the six weeks since they'd met, there should have been a little more forward traction than they'd had. She was beginning to wonder if Gina was as interested as she'd said she was, or if it was more a case of Gina knowing very few lesbians and Kate being "handy".

"She's very well, thanks, you nosey old codger."

Len laughed. "You'll have to bring her over to dinner with me and Val. She's sick of me only bringing blokes home from work."

Kate squinted at him. "You do realise how that sounded, don't you?"

"I meant work colleagues, you dirty-minded wench." He laughed again.

Kate and Jimmy chuckled along with him.

"Anyway, enough of the fun. What can I do for you today?"

"The victim from the bunker," Kate said, still smiling. "Dr Anderson said you were processing the evidence."

"Ah, yes. Our Mr Bones. Well, I've got quite a collection for you to look at. Has she made any determination on the bones yet? Are we looking at a murder?"

Kate shook her head. "She seems to think accidental death, but there isn't enough evidence either way."

"Ah, so she's going with an open verdict."

"Probably."

"And what're your thoughts?"

Kate frowned. "You've got something, haven't you?"

Len shook his head. "I've got a puzzle, is what I've got." He waved them over to a work bench. "Look at this." He held up plastic bags covered in official seals and labels. "I've got two different shoes. Different sizes, both for the left foot. One a man's, the other most likely a woman's, though I have seen men in them in a hospital. And before you ask, no, it can't be his. It's probably three sizes too small."

"How'd he get his feet in them and walk?" Jimmy questioned.

"With difficulty, I suspect. They must have blistered him to hell and back."

"Maybe he grabbed his wife's shoe," Kate theorised.

"Yeah," Jimmy said, picking up the train of thought, "if he'd hit his head and was confused, he might have grabbed odd shoes before going out."

Len sniffed. "Maybe. But that doesn't explain the rest of this get-up."

"Show me," Kate said.

"I've got scraps of fabric from a flowery dressing gown. The gown would fit a small woman, definitely not our bloke."

"Stella was wondering if he might be a cross-dresser."

"If he was, he wasn't doing a very good job with this rig-out." Len shook his head. "No, this collection doesn't suggest to me a cross-dresser, or a person who actually chose any of the clothes they were wearing."

Kate frowned. "Explain."

Len grinned. "I thought you'd never ask." He lifted a bag up. "Underpants with the name Edward Bale on a sewn-in label." He lifted another bag. "A vest with the name Dorothy Kinder, and the teeth, as you know, with the name Annie Balding on them. And there are two other names on the shoes: Rose Harvey and John Wood. All these labels are just like the ones that the wife used to sew into the kids' uniform when they were nippers. So that got me thinking—"

"Where are grown-ups treated like children and have labels put into their clothes because the people doing the laundry don't always know whose clothes belong to whom?" Kate finished off his question.

"Exactly," Len said. "Now I see why they pay you the big bucks and give you the fancy title."

"A care facility of some sort."

"Precisely, my dear Watson." Len grinned.

"Len, you do know it's a bit odd to be grinning every time we get a dead body in, don't you?"

He chuckled. "I don't grin when we get a dead body in, Kate." He winked at her. "Only when you come to see me."

She elbowed him in the ribs. "Careful, or I'll tell your wife. Jimmy, have you got the details of that nursing home where Annie Balding died?"

"Yup."

"Okay, I think we need to pay them a visit." She headed for the door. "Len, it was good to see you again."

"Don't be a stranger."

"I won't. You've still got Grimshaw with my facial reconstruction to sort out for me." As the door swung shut behind her she pulled her mobile from her pocket and punched in the number for Stella back at the Hunstanton office.

"Bonjour," Stella said down the line.

"Those French classes are really paying off, then."

Stella chuckled. "Go ahead, mock me. Then tell me what you want me to do for you."

"Aw, am I that predictable?"

"Yes."

"Fine, can you check out a few more names for me?"

"Hit me."

"Okay, Edward Bale, Dorothy Kinder, Rose Harvey, and John Wood."

"Anything more? Some of those names are pretty common."

"See if you can find anything in common with Annie Balding."

"And why am I looking up these folks?"

"Because our body was found wearing clothing with their names written all over them."

"Right. And?"

"Well, I'm thinking that there are a limited number of ways a person could get dressed up like this. Either they're a vagrant and stole them, or they were dressed in them by someone who really doesn't care. Now, I'm not saying that every nursing home or care worker doesn't care about the people staying there, but some don't. I..." she paused, not wanting to go into the details of why she knew such things. "Anyway, residents' clothes always go to a central laundry. From there it is really easy for clothes to get mixed up, and if the resident can't recognise the mistake, or can't argue against it, for whatever reason, then you end up with a situation where everyone can be wearing anyone else's clothes at any given time. Other times, guests who die, well, their families don't want the clothes they leave behind and donate them to others there. It's really the only way I can make sense of the things he was wearing."

"Understood. I'll get those searches under way. I'll have some results by the time you get back."

"Okay. Be there soon." She hung up and slid the phone back into her pocket.

"Aren't we going straight to the nursing home?" Jimmy asked.

"Where is it?"

"Brancaster."

Kate shook her head. "No, we have to go through Hunstanton to get there, so we might as well head back to the station first and fill the others in on what we have. Stella also said she'll have the initial searches back on our label names, so maybe we'll have better questions to ask at the nursing home by the time we get there."

"Makes sense."

Kate smiled and clicked open the car. "I do try, Jimmy."

Jimmy snorted and shook his head as he climbed in.

"Any news on your new car?"

"Yup."

"And?"

"It'll have to wait."

"How come?"

Jimmy shrugged. "Money's tight."

Kate frowned as she turned on the engine and pulled out of the car park. Jimmy lived alone, and to her knowledge had no girlfriend or kids to worry about. *So why was money too tight for a full-time-employed police officer to get himself a new car? Burnham Market's expensive, but...* "Everything okay, Jimmy?"

Jimmy didn't say anything, he just stared out the window as she entered the roundabout and took the second exit towards the Hardwick industrial estate. Traffic was heavy and the rain had started while they'd been inside. Bright lights refracted through the raindrops on the windscreen before falling beneath the merciless blade of the wiper.

"It's my mum."

Kate glanced at Jimmy. "What about her?"

"She's not well, so I've been helping her out. You know how it is."

"What's wrong with her?"

Jimmy fell quiet again.

"Sorry, Jimmy. I didn't mean to pry. You don't need to tell me."

"It's okay. It's just hard."

Kate nodded and waited for him to continue when he was ready. She indicated left and took the cut through beside Sainsbury's to avoid the huge busy roundabout on to the flyover. She knew she'd still have to queue in the traffic, but it would be a hell of a lot shorter queue.

"She's bipolar."

Whoa. She glanced at Jimmy. *Poor sod.* "Recently diagnosed?"

Jimmy shook his head. "No. She was in and out of hospital when I was a kid. I was eight when she was diagnosed. It's always been a part of our lives."

"How's your dad coping?"

"Dad left twenty years ago when she was first diagnosed."

"Shit, sorry, I remember you saying they weren't together. Sorry."

Jimmy shrugged. "Doesn't matter. We were better off without him around, really."

Eight years old and struggling with a mentally ill parent, somehow I doubt you were, Jimmy. "Is she in hospital now?"

"Yes. But she wants me to keep her flat going for her. So she knows where she's going when she comes out." He crossed his arms over his chest like a shield. "The familiarity of it is comforting to her. Helps her recover quicker."

"But it means you have to fund two homes on your wage."

He nodded.

"Brothers or sisters?"

"I've a sister, but she's at uni, training to become a vet. She doesn't have any money to help with mum's costs, so the car will just have to wait a bit longer."

"Anything I can do—"

"No," he said quickly. "Thanks and all, sarge, but no thanks. I can manage."

Her respect for the young DC rose even further. He'd proven himself to be a dedicated, hardworking officer with a bright future in the police force ahead of him. He'd also proven himself to be a strong and determined young man, who took family loyalty and pride to a level she rarely saw any more. She felt a lump in her throat and swallowed with difficulty. "Fair enough, but if you change your mind, you know where I am."

He didn't say anything, just nodded once.

"And if you need to talk..."

He smiled gently. "Thanks, but I've been down this road before, sarge. I know the journey."

"I know. But you don't have to do it all on your own, you know. It doesn't hurt to have a little company along the way."

"I'll bear that in mind."

The rest of the twenty-minute journey passed by in silence. Kate couldn't help but wonder at what his and his sister's childhoods must have been like. Her own hadn't exactly been ideal, but she'd never had to deal with looking after a parent in a situation like that. Her gran's cancer had been difficult enough to deal with when she was sixteen, but physical illness somehow seemed easier. The symptoms were easy to see, and the results of the cancer eating away at her body had been increasingly evident every single day.

Mental illnesses were not nearly so accommodating. They didn't provide a measured, quantifiable progression of degeneration. The steps towards recovery were not nearly so tangible as they were in a cancer patient where you could see the removal of a tumour, the shrinking of a growth, the regrowing hair. Quite frankly, mental illnesses fucking sucked.

Kate pulled up outside Hunstanton Police Station and reached for the handle of the door.

Jimmy put his hand on her left arm. "Sarge, I'd appreciate it if you'd keep what I told you just between us." He flicked his gaze towards the upstairs windows. "I don't really want the lads to know." He shrugged. "You know how they are. It just...well, you know how they are."

Kate did, but she thought they may well have surprised Jimmy had they known. Not that she'd had any intention of mentioning what he'd told her to anyone anyway, but if reassurance was what he needed, so be it. "Jimmy, I would never have dreamed of telling anyone what you told me about your mum. It's none of their business. I'm glad you told me, so that I can help if you need or want me to. That's it. As long as you do your job and this doesn't interfere, you'll never hear me mention it."

"Thanks, sarge."

Kate nodded and smiled. "Come on then, let's go and see what Stella's managed to find for us."

CHAPTER 7

Kate opened the door to the office and held it for Jimmy as he carried a cup holder and carryout bag from a well-known coffee shop.

"Beware! Greeks bearing gifts!" Tom hollered across the room.

"That had better be a gingerbread latte you've got for me." Stella crossed the room, sniffing the air as she came, hands outstretched.

"Would we dare to bring you anything else?" Kate plucked the correct beverage from the tray. "Madam's gingerbread latte, skimmed milk, no cream, extra sprinkles, and there's a chocolate croissant in the bag for you too."

"I don't know why you bother with the skimmed milk, then go and undo the good work with a chocolate croissant," Collier said with a grin. "Shouldn't you donate your croissant and reap the rewards?"

Stella frowned at him, clearly trying to work out if he was teasing or serious. To be fair, the serious young detective rarely seemed to tease, so it was a legitimate cause for wonder. "Are you trying to say I'm fat?"

"No." He poked into the bag and pulled out the jam donut Kate had got for him. "That I'm hungry." His smile widened.

Well, well, well. Looks like the kid's got a sense of humour after all.

"Don't even think about touching mine, pretty boy," Tom shouted as he finished making some notes on the board before coming over to grab his own snacks.

"Play nicely, boys." Kate took a sip of her own cappuccino and a bite of her "death by chocolate" muffin. She moaned and closed her eyes to savour the deep, slightly bitter taste of the chocolate. Heaven.

"So, what do you know, girls and boys?" Stella asked as they all sat around eating and drinking.

"Male, aged sixty to eighty. Had a head injury, but the doc wouldn't say it was the cause of death, only that it would have killed him eventually," Jimmy said around a mouthful of Danish pastry.

"We've got the victim wearing scraps of clothes from a whole lot of people. One of whom he may be," Kate added.

"Or not," Jimmy continued.

"The doctor also said that she couldn't rule on accidental or suspicious death on the strength of what she had, so she would end up recording an open verdict." Kate took another sip of her drink.

"Damn," Tom said. "So it's identify and notify, then on to the next case."

Kate shrugged. "Maybe. I guess that depends a little bit on who he is, where he came from, and I still want to know how he got into that bunker."

"You may never get those answers, Kate," Stella said.

"I know. But I feel we at least need to try and get them." She glanced at Tom.

"Fair enough." Stella reached across her desk and handed her a stack of pages. "Missing persons reports from the twenty-eighth of November 2013 to the end of December."

"How many?"

"Twelve hundred."

Kate dropped the pile onto her knee and looked up at Stella.

"No way," Collier said. "There'd be no one left in Norfolk!"

"That's got to be the national results, right?" Kate said.

Stella nodded. "I can't find a local report of a missing person that meets the description, as vague as it is, of our bony friend. So we've got to look at national results and see what crops up."

"Bloody hell," Kate said. "Right. You start looking into those then, and see which ones are still alive and accounted for and which are actually still missing." She dropped the pile on to Collier's desk.

"What? Why me?"

"Because I asked you to, and it's your job to do what your superior officer asks you to do."

He scowled but picked up the sheaf of pages. "Yes, boss."

Kate offered him her sweetest smile. "Thank you. Stella, what about those names? Any connection to the nursing home where Annie Balding died?"

"I'm sure this won't come as a shock to you now, but yes. Every one of them lived there."

"Excellent."

"And died there."

"Bummer."

"Indeed."

"How long ago?"

"Did they die?" Stella asked and Kate nodded. "Edward Bale passed away in November of 2013, and all the others were well after. May 2014 onwards."

"All died in the nursing home?"

"Yes. And before you start getting a bee in your bonnet about that, old people die in nursing homes. It's kind of what they're there for."

"I was just going to ask if any of them died of the same thing. That was all." Kate sniffed.

Stella glanced at her notes. "All look like they were suffering from different illnesses. Cancer, Parkinson's disease, Alzheimer's, one with motor neurone disease, one with a stroke. They were all signed off by a doctor as natural complications of the illnesses they had."

"Just like Annie Balding," Kate said.

"Just like a lot of old people," Stella replied.

"True," Kate conceded. "But if they're missing a dead old person, why don't we have a missing person's report about it?"

"Maybe they aren't."

Kate looked at her sceptically. "Our victim was wearing clothes, shoes, and the dentures of people in their nursing home. How else did he come by them if he wasn't a resident there too?"

"Maybe a vagrant who stole things off the washing line?" Tom suggested.

"A washing line? Are you having a laugh?" Kate said.

"What?" he asked.

Jimmy cleared his throat. "A commercial-sized laundry like those places have wouldn't have a washing line. They'd use tumble driers. That's why relatives are asked to bring clothes along that can be tumble dried when the residents move in."

"And you know this how?" Tom asked.

"My gran was in a nursing home for the last few years of her life."

Tom grunted but accepted the facts.

"Any other believable suggestions for our body ending up in those clothes, other than him being a resident at this nursing home?" Kate asked.

Everyone shook their heads.

"Right. So why does Collier have to go through a stack of national reports to try and find our victim? Why didn't they report him missing?"

"Don't know, kiddo," Stella said. "But good luck finding out."

CHAPTER 8

Gina parked the car outside the hostel's storage barn and turned off the engine. Will opened the door of the barn and nodded to her.

"You got a minute, Gina?" he asked.

Gina sighed. "I have, but please don't tell me you're going to hand in your notice too."

Sammy climbed out of the car and opened the gate to the small compound where Gina's office was located.

Will smiled. "No, but I was wondering what was going to happen with that lot doing the dirty on us."

"Thank God for that." She pulled her office key out of her pocket and held the fob to the electronic pad on the handle. "Come on in, then. You can get your homework done, madam."

Sammy nodded and slumped into the comfy armchair in the office before pulling her books out of her bag.

Gina pointed to the other office chair.

"Them leaving, does it mean we have to close?" Will asked. He didn't sit down. He rarely did through the day. Whenever she saw him he was wandering from one job to the next with a cigarette stuck between his lips, or rolling one between his fingers. His beanie hat was pulled low over his brow, covering his blond hair and eyebrows. His blue eyes sparkled with a mixture of curiosity and concern. The jogging bottoms he wore had huge rips across the knees, and his uniform coat was far too big for him, but gave him plenty of space to wear the layers he always did. Usually three, but four wasn't unheard of through the winter.

While all the staff except Gina lived on site, she knew it was Will who had the most to worry about if Brandale Campsite did close. He had nowhere to go. Sarah, Emma, and Ricky may not have liked their options, but they weren't looking at the streets as their next address.

Gina shook her head. "No. I've got a plan." She quickly opened the computer program and talked him through her decision to close the hostel during the week to give the two of them the chance to get everything changed over and ready for the busy weekends.

"Whew, I've got to admit I was worried," Will said.

"Think I was going to pack you off into the night?"

He grinned. "Something like that." He rubbed his hand over his face. "What can I do to help?"

"Just keep doing what you're doing, Will. When we get to the painting and maintenance, we may have to do it in sections, and I'll close those down for a couple of weekends too, to give us the time we need, but we'll worry about that in the new year. I figure I'll wait till after Christmas to start looking for new staff too. It's only three weeks away and the big shops will be laying off the seasonal staff then. Lean January might be a good time for us to find some good new staff members."

"Can we screen 'em for loyalty this time?"

Gina snorted. "I'll see what I can do, Will, but I don't think I can make any promises on that one."

"Fair enough."

Gina squeezed the bridge of her nose with her finger and thumb.

"Everything okay?" Will asked.

Gina cast a quick look to Sammy, who was focused on her reading book, and shook her head. "It will be eventually, I suppose."

He nodded his understanding and changed the topic. "Haven't seen your copper around for a while."

"Hm," Gina mumbled noncommittally.

"Trouble in paradise?"

"Very funny," Gina responded, but couldn't help thinking about Kate and how little they'd seen of each other lately, and made up her mind to call her later. "She's just busy at work. As am I."

Will chuckled. "Hint taken. Want me to take the shrimp in the barn with me? I've got a whole load of stuff she can do in there."

"Like what? Juggle axes and hedge trimmers?"

"Nah, I did that myself before. There was a log delivery earlier that needs crating. Delivery driver just dumped it in the middle of the floor again."

"What do you say, kiddo? Want to help Will pick up a bunch of logs?"

Sammy was already stuffing her reading book back into her bag. "'Course."

"We'll do your reading later, then."

Sammy sighed as she pulled open the door. "'Course," she said again, with a great deal less enthusiasm.

Will and Gina both smiled. "Thanks, Will."

"No problem. Come on, shrimp. First one to fill a crate gets to pick the tunes for the rest of the afternoon."

"You're on!" Sammy raced him to the barn.

Gina heard the huge doors slam close behind them.

She pulled her phone out of her pocket and flipped open the cover of the pink case with white stars on it that Sammy had got her for Mother's Day. She quickly flicked through to her text messages and pulled up the conversation between herself and Kate.

It had been two days since she'd last had a message from Kate and she couldn't blame Kate for that. She was the one who hadn't responded to the message Kate had sent after the last time they'd actually seen each other.

Kate had been working late and turned up after Sammy was in bed with a bottle of wine, a box of chocolates, and that beautiful smile of hers. They'd talked and laughed, and got more than a little merry sharing the wine. They'd kissed. A lot. They'd both got turned on. A lot. They'd both wanted nothing more than to go to bed and finally take their relationship to the next level.

But Kate had made one error. One tiny moment, in an otherwise perfect evening, had ruined it all—Kate's fingers had brushed over the top of Gina's breast.

The touch had been electric. But for all the wrong reasons. It was like ice water being poured over Gina, shocking her back to her senses, back to reality, and the fact that there was now a series of scars all over her body. The beginnings of a game board on her back. A cross on her stomach. And a line along the top of each breast. Marring her skin. Defiling her.

Kate had told her that they didn't matter to her. That she still found Gina attractive—beautiful even—not in spite of the scars, but, in part, because of them. They represented the strength with which Gina had survived the ordeal she'd gone through. The ordeal that Kate had saved her from. And she believed Kate. She really did.

It was her own reaction to the scars that was the problem.

She couldn't find herself attractive with them. When she couldn't see them, she didn't think about them. She could forget that they were there and carry on her life. The old Gina. But the moment Kate touched her breast the whole thing came rushing back. Just like it did every time Kate touched her.

Gina looked at her own body and found it hideous. Untouchable. Unlovable. How could she relax when she was waiting for Kate to look at her with pity in her eyes? How could she respond when she was waiting for Kate to flinch at the sight of those ugly, jagged, lines? How could she enjoy Kate's touch when she felt she didn't deserve it?

She knew she should tell Kate it wasn't going to work and let her get on with her life. She was a beautiful woman, a wonderful woman, who deserved to be happy. She deserved to have someone in her life who could make her happy. But selfishly, Gina didn't want to let her go. She knew she couldn't make it work, but she didn't want Kate to want anyone else. Just the thought of Kate kissing another woman burned.

"But what right do I have to keep hold of you?" she whispered to no one.

CHAPTER 9

Brancombe House Nursing Home was the very last property on Beach Road. Beyond it was nothing but salt marsh for half a mile, until you got to the golf course, and then finally the sea.

It was huge. A Victorian schoolhouse that had been converted many years ago into a facility where families shelved their "loved" ones. The north side had gorgeous views out across the sea, while the southern and eastern perspectives were surrounded by mature oak, sycamore, and ash trees. The long, gravel drive way up the western approach crunched under Kate's tyres. The car park was empty as she pulled in. *Wonder where the staff park?*

"Nice place to live," Jimmy said.

"Yeah." Kate turned off the engine. "I bet that's what the residents families said when they parked them here too." She opened her door. "Right before they forgot about them."

"You don't know that, sarge. They probably come and visit all the time."

Kate looked around. "You see any cars around here?"

"It's the middle of the day."

"And?"

"They're probably working."

Kate offered him a wry smile. "Right," she said slowly. "You keep telling yourself that, Jimmy." She pointed to the door. "Do you want to do the honours?"

Jimmy rang the bell.

Kate glanced up the building and spotted the keystone in the archway above the large double doors with the year 1898 stamped into it. She also spotted the twitching curtains in one of the upper bedroom windows and wondered if it was a member of staff or a resident who was enjoying a little excitement.

A creaking hinge drew her attention back to the door as it swung open. They were greeted by a short, painfully thin woman wearing a white nurse's tunic and black trousers. She was smiling and frowning at them.

"Good afternoon, I'm Detective Constable Powers and this is Detective Sergeant Brannon. We need to speak to the manager or owner please."

"I'm afraid owner is not here. I am Eva."

Kate put her accent as Eastern European. Maybe Czech?

"I will get Sister for you. Please." She waved them inside and closed the door behind them, turning the big latch, and then a second one.

"Do you always lock the residents in?" Kate asked.

She smiled and nodded. "Our residents have memory issues. It is safer for them if they stay inside, but they do not remember this. Some want always to be going outside. Always, always. Even when too cold or too wet. It is safer for them to stay inside."

"Of course," Kate agreed, knowing that logically it made sense. Staff were undoubtedly limited, and there was no way they could give one-to-one care to a large number of inmates—patients, Kate corrected herself. "How many residents do you have here?"

"Forty-two."

"Is that the maximum capacity?"

"We have one space at the moment. One of our gentlemen passed last night."

"I'm very sorry to hear that," Kate said sincerely.

The woman shrugged. "I think—I think he is better off now." She sounded more upset than she looked.

Kate frowned. "How do you mean?"

"He was very ill. On much medication all time. Now he has peace. He has God."

"Ah." Kate nodded. "I'm still sorry for your loss. It must be difficult."

"It is life." She led them down a corridor. "Now we can help someone else. They will be arriving soon."

"Wow. That's fast," Jimmy said.

"There is much waiting list. Many, many people needing our help, our care."

"Boom time," Jimmy said. "An ageing population has to be a bonus for someone, I suppose."

Kate snorted but the woman didn't look impressed with Jimmy's poor humour.

"Sorry," he muttered under his breath.

"Eva, how long have you worked here?" Kate asked.

"I work here few years now."

"Were you here during the flood in 2013?"

Eva nodded. "Oh, yes. Was huge drama. I only just started that week, on the Monday, and I finished my shift at three that afternoon. I was very scared that I would not be able to get home. That they would stop the bus, and I would be here all the time."

"Where do you live?"

"Now, I live in Heacham. Then, I had to go always to King's Lynn by the bus."

"That's a long way."

"Yes."

"I wonder if you remember anyone who might have disappeared around that time? A man."

"A man?"

"Yes. One of the residents. He may have been here that day, and then just disappeared."

Eva frowned, clearly deep in thought, before she shook her head. "No. I don't remember anything like that. I remember coming back after the weekend was over and Annie had passed one night. It was on the Friday, I think. She was sweet lady. Very sick. Much medication too. I remember her because she was first lady I care for here." She sighed. "Was very sad."

"But you don't remember a man around that time? One who would have been here on the Friday when you were and then gone when you came back to work?"

Eva wrung her hands as she led them through Brancombe House. A frown marred her smooth forehead. She looked concerned that she couldn't remember the details they were asking of her. "I sorry. I don't remember anything like that. I was still very new. Still learning all the peoples here."

"Okay. Thanks."

Eva tapped on a door. When a voice called, "Enter", she ushered them inside.

"Sister, these are police." Eva said, and backed out of the door.

"Thanks for your help, Eva," Kate said, and held out her card. "If you do remember anything else about that night, please give me a call."

Eva took the card, nodded, and closed the door behind her as she scurried away.

The room was small and stuffed to capacity with an old, scarred desk, three tall filing cabinets, a key locker on one wall, a drugs cabinet on another, and shelves filling every other available wall space. There were two visitors' chairs in front of the desk. The desk itself held a computer and a stack of lever arch files a foot high. There were no windows in the room, and the air was stale. The smell of day-old coffee, day-old uniform, and well-worn trainers hung in the air.

Kate held her hand out to the heavyset woman behind the desk. Her navy blue tunic strained against her heaving bosom as she shifted forward to accept Kate's hand. "I'm Detective Sergeant Kate Brannon, Sister, and this is my colleague, Detective Constable James Powers."

"Diana Lodge," she said with a wheeze in her voice. "Not often we get detectives through our doors here. Please take a seat." She waved to the chairs in front of her desk. "How can I help you today?" she asked as they sat down.

"Well, we're investigating a mysterious death."

"Mysterious, you say? And how's that? Dead's dead, isn't it?" She chuckled.

Kate and Jimmy glanced at each other. "Mysterious as in, we believe he was a resident of this establishment, but we can't find a record that he was reported missing, from here or anywhere else."

Sister Lodge frowned and leaned forward, hands braced on the desk top, and bowing at the elbow to make space for her chest. "I can assure you, Detective, all my residents are present and accounted for. I can take you around and introduce you personally, if need be."

"That's okay. This is a resident who would have gone missing in 2013. December 2013."

The woman visibly relaxed. Her shoulders dropped and she slumped back in her chair.

Kate was certain she could hear the woman thank God under her breath before she addressed them again. "That's before I took over here. I'm afraid I've only been here for six months, since the previous head nurse passed away after a sudden illness. Well, it was unfortunate, but it did make things easier for the owner. They were going to have to find reason to sack her otherwise." She snorted a derisive laugh. "Not that they'd have had much of a problem with that. So far, I've spent most of my time trying to sort out a number of...issues, shall we call them, that had been prevalent during my predecessor's tenure here at Brancombe House."

"Such as?" Kate asked.

"Shoddy paperwork. Lax standards of patient care. Misappropriated medications. Residents missing cash from their personal belongings. Petty cash receipts missing. Tardy staff. Massive amounts of sick leave being taken. Huge agency staff bills." She shrugged. "I could go on, but I think you get the picture."

Kate did. "Any issues with violence towards the residents?"

Sister Lodge shook her head. "If there was, nothing was reported, and I've seen nothing to support that option while I've been here."

"Why were the owners bringing you in? You said they were looking for a reason to get rid of her. Was something reported to them that gave them cause to worry?"

Sister Lodge shook her head. "Nothing concrete at that time." She clasped her hands on the desk and leant forward again, resting her weight on her elbows. "The concrete stuff didn't come until after I started and uncovered them all. They were concerned because the mortality rate was higher than expected."

"According to what?"

"National statistics. From what I understand, the owner liked to get a brief overview of the home each year and compared it to the national averages to see where we lay in comparison. If things needed to be addressed, then, in a broad sense, he'd inform us of his directives, and we, or rather my predecessor, were supposed to put them in place."

"Other than mortality rate, what kinds of things was he looking at?"

"Costs per head, wage bills, agency staff usage, sick days, holidays, all the usual stuff a business owner needs to know."

"Okay, and at that point the owners suspected, what? That the deaths were the result of poor care or something?"

"Possibly. The mortality rate was higher than the national average for a care facility like this, but when I looked into them all, every one was explained." She shrugged. "Just a lot of poorly people, unfortunately. It happens sometimes. That's why it's an average. No doubt next year or the year after it will fall for us and climb somewhere else, and vice versa. As the Lion King likes to say, 'it's the circle of life'." She giggled at her own joke. "What's this all about, anyway?"

"The remains of an elderly gentleman have been found not far from here. He was between the ages of sixty and eighty, and we suspect he would have been a resident here until the fifth of December 2013. Could you have a look through the records, please?"

"I can certainly take a look." She cracked her knuckles and pulled the computer keyboard closer. "I take it you don't have a name?"

"Oh, if only life were that simple, Sister," Kate said with a chuckle.

"Okay. Let's start with anyone leaving on or shortly after that date then." She clacked away at the keys and frowned at her screen. "A man, you said."

"Yes."

"No, I've got a woman who died on the fifth, but no man. No man checking out all the next week either." She wiggled her fingers over the keys as she seemed to think. "Let me try earlier that week. Just in case." She crunched the keys some more. "No. The last man we've got leaving is Edward Bale in November. Could it be him?"

Kate shook her head. "No, he was buried by his family. Not missing."

"Can I ask why you think he was a resident here?"

"I'm afraid I can't give out the details of an ongoing case."

"But perhaps there is a simple explanation for whatever you think makes him a resident here when he never was."

Kate leaned back in her chair. "Well, if you can come up with a different explanation, I'm all for it. How would you explain our man being found wearing the dentures of Annie Balding, whom you mentioned died on the fifth, and the underwear of Edward Bale? Whom you also mentioned."

Sister Lodge raised an eyebrow, but her face remained impassive. "Mysterious, indeed, Detective."

"How many members of staff do you have here, Sister?"

"Let me think. We have six full-time nurses, twelve care workers, three catering staff, three cleaners, and a laundry woman. Then we have some bank staff, and of course the ever-present agency staff that we all are pretty much reliant on these days."

"How many of your permanent staff were here in December 2013?"

"I'd have to check the records, but I can work you up a list."

"I'd appreciate that. I don't suppose you can get me a list of agency staff who worked here regularly at that time too?"

"Define regularly?"

"Regular enough to have a chance of recognising a picture."

"I'll probably have to go back through old payroll and time sheets to get those details for you. It'll take me some time."

"I'd really appreciate it." Kate handed her a card. "My e-mail address is on there."

Sister Lodge squinted at it and sighed. "I'll send it over as soon as I've got it together. You'll have to give me a few days, though."

Kate held up her hands. "Of course, Thank you."

"Do you know how he died?"

Kate shook her head. "I'm afraid not. There is evidence of trauma, though."

"Trauma? Like an accident?"

"Possibly."

Sister Lodge scratched her head. "But you don't think so, do you, Detective?"

"I'm afraid I can't comment on that, Sister. I can only comment on what I can prove."

"Fair enough." Sister Lodge tapped at her keyboard again, then clicked the mouse. The printer churned to life and quickly spat out a small sheaf of pages. "The names and addresses of all the staff who were working here in 2013. Including those who no longer work here and who left shortly before December."

Kate held out her hand. "Thank you."

"Find out who he is, Detective."

Kate cocked her head to the side as she looked at her. "I'll do everything I can."

"No one deserves to die and just be forgotten." She crossed her arms over her chest. "I can't think of anything worse."

"My gran told me once that immortality lay not in the afterlife but in how we're remembered in this life after we are gone. That as long as one person remembers us, we're not dead."

"And do you believe that, Detective?"

Kate shrugged. *Do I?* She thought about all those she'd loved and lost. The mother she never knew. The father who blamed her for her mother's death. The gran who had battled for every last breath. All dead. All gone. *Who's left to remember me when it's my turn to kick the bucket?* "It's a nicer thought than being buried and becoming worm food."

Sister Lodge laughed. "True. A damn shame, but true."

Jimmy was quiet as Kate drove them away from the care home. Seemingly lost in thought.

"Penny for them?" Kate asked.

"Sorry?"

"You were miles away. Anything interesting?" She indicated right on to the A149 heading for Hunstanton on the coast road.

"Was it just me or did it seem like she was hiding something?"

"It wasn't just you. There was definitely more to why she'd been brought in to that place."

"What do you think's going on there?"

Kate shrugged. "Don't know yet, Jimmy." She checked her rear-view mirror and pulled out to avoid a car parked on the road. "But tomorrow I intend to find out."

CHAPTER 10

"Can you leave the light on in the hall?" Sammy's voice was quiet as she pulled the duvet over her shoulder and shifted her head on her pillow. Her blue eyes looked even bigger than normal, scared, as she watched Gina approach the door.

Gina turned and crossed the room. She perched on the edge of Sammy's bed and ran her fingers through her recently brushed but already unruly blond hair. "If that's what you want, kiddo."

Sammy nodded, her gaze fixed on the doorway.

"Why?"

"S'nuffink."

"You promised no more secrets. Remember?"

Sammy looked up at her and Gina wanted to weep for the sadness, fear, and pain she saw etched on her little girl's face. "I remember."

"So why do you want me to leave the light on?"

"It's so I can see when I wake up and it helps me not be scared so much."

"Doesn't the light keep you awake?"

Sammy shook her head. "No."

The dark circles under her eyes were more than enough evidence that something was keeping her awake. And as much as Gina suspected what that was, she knew that Sammy needed to admit it, to both of them, before she could begin to move forward and heal.

"Then what does, Sammy?"

"Connie," Sammy whispered and seemed to shrink in her bed.

"What about Connie?"

Sammy seemed to struggle to find the words.

Gina wasn't sure if it was because she didn't know them or just didn't want to voice them. "Tell me, sweetheart."

Sammy sniffed. "I see her face."

"Okay."

"After she got shot."

Gina continued to stroke her fingers through Sammy's hair, sensing that she needed a little space to get the words out, and hugging her would only stop her saying what she needed to.

She hated that Sammy had seen Connie's body after she'd been shot. Gina had only seen a picture, and it had been enough to make her throw up. Connie's face had literally been gone. There were no distinctive features. No nose, no eyes, no mouth. Just a mangled mass of bloody tissue, bone fragments, and brain matter. And her nine-year-old daughter had seen it with her own eyes.

I still wish I could string her father up by his testicles for this. Knowing that Matt Green was going to prison for the foreseeable future and would never again see his daughter on his own didn't feel like nearly enough punishment to her. After all, Sammy was going to be dealing with the consequences of his thoughtlessness and disregard for the rest of her life.

Connie had been someone Sammy had looked up to and respected. And for three days she'd believed she'd killed her. All because her irresponsible father had sent her out on the salt marsh—alone—to shoot him a rabbit for his tea.

"Is it a dream?"

Sammy nodded.

"Do you have the dream every night, Sammy?"

Sammy nodded again, and a tear snaked its way down her cheek.

"And what do you do when you have the dream?"

"I try to...not be scared and go back to sleep."

"Okay, and how do you do that? What helps you not be scared?"

"I dunno, Mum. Nuffink works. Even Sir Galahad doesn't help." She grabbed the one-eyed bear and held him out. His red coat was torn and falling off one shoulder, and his ear was holding on by a thread. Again. Gina had lost count of the number of times she'd sewn that ear back on over the years.

Sir Galahad was Sammy's favourite stuffed toy. She'd slept with him on or in her bed since she was five. She remembered when Sammy had picked the name for him, after Gina had told her some of the tales of King Arthur and the Knights of the Round Table. Sammy had decided that her bear, just like Sir Galahad, was the best and bravest in all of England and deserved to be knighted just as Sir Galahad had been. She'd even conducted the ceremony herself.

"I fink I'm always gonna be scared now."

Gina's heart broke, and she finally pulled Sammy on to her lap and held her close. "Next time you have the dream, I want you to come and wake me up. You don't need to do this on your own, kiddo." She soothed her hand over Sammy's head and back. "Do you understand? I'm your mum, I'm here to help with stuff like this. Okay?" She felt Sammy's head move against her shoulder.

"But Ally hurt you. Aren't you scared too?"

Terrified. "I'm a grown-up, sweetheart. You have to pass tests and all sorts of stuff to get your grown-up card. And one of those tests is a bravery test." She pretended to buff her nails on her shirt. "I passed that one with flying colours, I'll have you know."

Sammy grunted a small laugh. "Fibber."

Gina smiled. "Made you laugh, though."

"That wasn't a laugh. It was a hiccup."

Gina chuckled. "You keep telling yourself that, kiddo." She ruffled Sammy's hair and helped her lie back down. "I'm going to leave the light on, but if you wake up, I want you to come and wake me up."

"And you can make me not feel scared?"

"I hope so, kiddo." She kissed Sammy's head. "It might take a while, but we'll get there." She smoothed the duvet over her chest. "I promise. Me and Sir Galahad won't let anything happen to you."

Sammy shifted on to her shoulder, wrapped her arm around Sir Galahad, and held out her little finger. "Pinky swears?"

Gina wrapped her own little finger around her daughter's. "Pinky swears," she whispered solemnly. "Now go to sleep."

Sammy closed her eyes, and Gina slowly left the room. She left the door open a crack and the light on in the hallway.

The stairs creaked beneath her feet and she hurried through the downstairs corridor. She hated being in there and wished to God she could afford to move them to another house. But right now, that wasn't an option.

Instead, every time she walked through her hallway, she couldn't help but see herself bound, her arms tied over her head with the rope looped over the upstairs banister as Ally Robbins had sliced her flesh open with a fish knife. She ran a hand over her stomach and tugged at the high collar on the turtleneck jumper she'd begun to favour.

Sammy wasn't the only one fighting demons. But she was determined to get Sammy past her nightmares. Her own...well, just like the scars on her breasts, they weren't going anywhere anytime soon.

The doorbell rang as she put the kettle on to boil. Her heart pounded in her ears and she could feel a trickle of sweat run down her neck. She glanced at the clock on the wall. Eight o'clock. She moved closer to the block of knives on the kitchen counter.

"Who is it?" she called.

"It's Kate."

Gina smiled and tried to ignore the tightening in her belly as she crossed the hallway again. She pulled open the door and quickly ushered Kate into the kitchen, taking the time to admire her as they went. It was certainly a pleasant distraction from the memories. Kate's jeans clung tight to her backside and her knee-high leather boots creaked softly as she walked. Her red hair tumbled down her back like a sheet of burnished copper, swaying along with her hips. Gina licked her lips. *Lovely distraction, indeed.* "I was just making a brew. Would you like one?"

"Lovely, thanks," Kate said with a gentle smile. "How are you?"

Gina blew out a huge breath, and Kate chuckled. "That good, hey?"

"Something like that." She put coffee and milk in Kate's cup before pouring the water and joining her at the table.

"Tell me," Kate said, accepting the coffee with a bob of her head.

Gina had wondered if Kate would immediately want an answer to the text message she still hadn't responded to. That she still hadn't figured out how she was going to respond to. To have Kate walk in and not mention it felt like Gina was off the hook. For the moment, at least. She knew Kate would need an answer eventually. She needed to give her one. After all, Kate hadn't done anything wrong. She'd been doing everything right.

Gina took a seat next to Kate, wrapped her cold fingers around the hot mug, and smelled the steam rising off the liquid. "Sammy's teacher called me in for a chat today."

"What happened? Is she okay?"

Gina loved the way Kate cared about Sammy. She had from the first time she'd met the child. While Gina had gone overboard with a bottle of Rioja trying to drown her sorrows, Kate had offered Sammy comfort the night Connie had been killed.

"She's being bullied."

"The little bastards." Kate put her cup down and pushed away from the table. "Give me their names, I'll go and put the fear of God—"

Gina put a hand on her arm to still her. "That won't help."

"I'll make sure it will."

Gina shook her head and slipped her hand into Kate's, twining their fingers together, and caressed her hand with her thumb. It wasn't enough. She lifted Kate's hand to her lips and kissed it. "Thank you," she whispered against her skin. "And as much as I share the sentiment, the teachers at school have a plan. One that Sammy agrees with and will work better in the long run. We think."

"It'd better."

"If it doesn't, then I'll put her in a different school."

"And I'll incarcerate the little sods."

"That's kind of the problem."

Kate frowned. The confusion clear in her green and gold eyes. "I don't understand."

"The kids that are picking on her. You've locked up their dads."

Understanding dawned on Kate and she frowned. "Oh, Gina, I'm so sorry. I can't not do my job, but what can I do..."

"You didn't do anything wrong. Nothing at all. It isn't really you that's the problem. If anything, it's her dad."

"Because he ratted them out."

"Exactly."

"And they're tarring her with the same brush? They're nine, for God's sake. Nine-year-olds don't think like that."

"They do if that's what their parents tell them. Or more if that's what they overhear their parents saying."

Kate sipped her coffee. "So what's the plan?"

Gina quickly filled her in on what Mrs Partridge and Mrs Eastern planned to do.

Kate whistled. "It's a good plan, but it's going to take a while, and there are no guarantees it will work."

"No, but it may be better in the long run. Even if I take Sammy out of school at Brancaster and move her to Wells or Docking primary school, she's still going to end up running into some, if not all, of these kids again in a couple of years when she goes to secondary school. Short of leaving the area completely, I can't think of a way of getting her away from this forever." Gina twisted her cup in her hands, trying to draw warmth from the hot liquid inside. "And I'm not sure that's the kind of message I want to give Sammy."

"What?"

"Running away from your problems isn't solving them. If I teach her that running when things get hard is okay, then what's to say she won't run from everything?"

"Don't you think that's a bit, I don't know, overdramatic?"

"She's having nightmares."

"Still?"

Gina nodded. "Every night."

"Shit."

"This afternoon, she blew up in the meeting with her teachers when one of them told her she'd have to talk to her about everything that happened. I thought she was actually going to attack the woman."

Kate paled. "She didn't?"

"No. She stopped just short. Called her a lot of nasty names—which she apologised for—and kicked and beat the floor."

"But the counsellor at Victim Support signed her off."

"Because Sammy refused to talk. She couldn't make any progress with her. She didn't sign her off because Sammy was fixed, Kate."

"Damn it."

"Still think I'm being overly dramatic?"

"I'm sorry. I didn't mean to—"

"Doesn't matter."

"Yes, it does. I'm used to dealing with horrible stuff at work every day. I see the worst that humans can throw at each other, and I forget that this isn't every day stuff for you and Sammy. This is change-your-life stuff." She knelt beside Gina's chair. "Forgive me?"

"Nothing to forgive."

Kate reached over and kissed Gina's cheek. "I'm still sorry for being thoughtless." She paused and stroked her fingers down Gina's jawline. "I was thinking about stuff today and I think, well...I think there may be other things I've been thoughtless about. Haven't there?"

"I don't know what you mean."

Kate smiled gently. "I think you do." She cast a glance down towards Gina's chest.

Gina couldn't help but flinch under her gaze.

Kate took hold of Gina's hand and slowly threaded their fingers together. "Maybe Sammy isn't the only one who needs to talk to a counsellor."

Gina snatched her hand away. "I'm fine."

Kate raised an eyebrow. "Really?"

"Yes. Really."

"Then why have you changed the type of clothes you wear? Why all the turtlenecks, and roll-neck collars? Hoodies zipped up to your chin all the time."

"It's winter and it's cold."

"Not in here, it isn't."

"I haven't been in long."

"Is Sammy wearing one to bed?"

"Don't be ridiculous." She crossed her arms over her chest.

"I'm not the one being ridiculous, Gina. It's completely understandable that what happened will affect you. That's normal. Just like it's normal that it's affecting Sammy. You don't want to teach her that running away from her problems is the way to deal with them?" Kate took hold of her hand again. "Then teach her that you won't do that either. Show her that you can deal with what Ally did, and she'll do the same."

"You don't know what you're talking about, Kate Brannon."

"Don't I?" She leaned in closer and covered Gina's lips with her own. The kiss was long and slow, but every caress of her tongue was filled with passion, and Gina responded. She couldn't stop herself.

God, she wanted this woman. Gina slipped her hands to Kate's shoulders and tugged her closer. Kate's fingers cupped her cheeks, holding her still, then they disappeared. Gina felt them through the thick wool of her jumper, slipping down her chest and over her breasts.

She froze. The feel of Kate's fingers closing in on the pink and puckered scar tissue along the edges of her breasts was too much. She pulled back as far as her chair would allow her to.

"I'm sorry. I'm so sorry, sweetheart. But why? Why didn't you tell me?" Kate whispered. "Why didn't you say something?"

"I...I...can't." She turned her face away and squeezed her eyes closed. So this was how it was going to end. This was how she would lose Kate. Bloody Ally Robbins. *Is there nothing in this village you haven't destroyed?*

"If I bring you the number of a counsellor tomorrow, will you talk to her?"

Gina opened her eyes quickly and stared at Kate. "Excuse me?"

"I think you need to talk to someone, Gina. Someone professional who can help you come to terms with what happened and how it's changed you. I'll do whatever I can, but I don't know what you need. What's going to help you." She stroked her fingers down the length of Gina's jaw. "I've already told you that they don't matter to me. That you're just as beautiful as before. More, even."

Gina closed her eyes, and looked down at her chest. "They matter to me."

Kate nodded. "I realise that now." She held Gina's hand again. "I'm sorry I'm so slow on the uptake."

"You aren't leaving me?" Gina glanced up and held Kate's gaze. Those expressive green eyes were filled with so much emotion. Concern, guilt, anger, confusion, and the lingering remnants of lust.

Kate bent her head forward, shaking it as the curtain of her red hair slipped over her shoulders and framed her face. "Leaving you?" She looked up from under her hair. Her jaw was clenched tight. "Is that what you thought I'd do?"

Gina looked down again at their joined hands. "It's what I'm scared you'll do."

Kate leaned back. "I thought we'd been through this, Gina. I'm not going anywhere unless you tell me you don't want me here. That you don't want to be with me. I'll grant you, you've been giving off mixed messages for the past month or so. A lot of mixed messages. Hot one second, and then ice-cold the next." She held her hands up to forestall any argument. "But I understand that now. I can work with that now." She took a deep breath and held Gina's hands. "If you want to?"

"Yes." Gina smiled and felt a weight tumble from her shoulders. She hadn't realised how worried she'd been about potentially losing Kate. "Definitely, yes."

"Okay then. So will you call her?"

Gina pulled in a deep breath. "Do I have a choice?"

"You always have a choice, Gina. It might not be one you like, but you always have one."

"So what's the choice?"

"Talk to her and get better, or don't."

"And if I don't?"

"Then it's going to make it really hard for us to really enjoy each other." Kate's voice dropped as she moved forward and kissed her again. Nipping and tugging Gina's bottom lip between her teeth before caressing the tiny hurt with her tongue, then pulling away. "But it's your choice."

"I say again," she whispered and wrapped her arms around Kate's shoulders, pulling her in for another kiss. "What choice do I have?"

CHAPTER 11

Kate stared at her computer screen then glanced back at the page resting on top of a two-inch stack. The records of each employee working at Brancombe House Nursing Home during 2013. Some were clean. Nothing more impressive than a parking fine or three points on their licence for speeding. One or two others were a little more circumspect. A drunk driver here, a drunk-and-disorderly there, and one chap with a long record of police being called to domestic disturbances, but no record of a single arrest or charge brought against him.

She looked at the picture Sister Lodge had provided with his employee record. Bald, missing front teeth, and a tattoo visible on his neck. He looked like the poster boy of football hooliganism rather than a care worker with an exemplary work record. "Angel at work, devil at home, hey, Mr Warburton?"

She glanced at her watch and sighed. Ten o'clock in the morning and still no sign of the facial reconstruction. She knew time was running out. Without an ID and a recorded open verdict, Timmons was going to have to cut back resources on the case. Without something to justify the cost of the investigation, this case was very soon to become another John Doe case gathering dust on the cold case files.

She picked up the phone and punched the buttons for Len Wild. "Where's my picture?" she said, smiling, when he picked up the phone.

He chuckled. "Good morning to you too, Detective. Lovely day, isn't it?"

"Yeah, yeah, enough with the chit-chat. Where's that picture, Len? It was supposed to be here yesterday afternoon."

"And you've not got it?"

"Wouldn't be bugging you if I had. Honestly, Len, we're going absolutely nowhere without it."

"Okay. Let me see what's holding up our young Mr Grimshaw and get back to you."

"Thanks." Kate hung up and shifted to the next employee on the list. She'd decided to concentrate on those still working there and those who'd left close to the time of their victim's death. Those still there after all this time must care, and those who'd left, well maybe they'd remember something significant from that time. Or maybe they'd left because there was something wrong at Brancombe House that they didn't want to be a part of.

The phone rang. She reached for it, knocking her coffee cup over as she did. "Bollocks," she shouted and reached for the box of tissues she kept in her drawer.

"Well, that's uncalled for," Len said down the line.

"Sorry. Sorry." Kate mopped up hot, dark liquid. "Spilt my coffee."

"You want to be more careful."

"I'll try and remember that, mother."

"Ooh, someone's tetchy this morning."

"Len, I'm warning you, if the next words out of your mouth have anything remotely to do with PMS, I'm going to come back to King's Lynn and introduce your tonsils to your testicles."

He sucked in a sharp breath. "See what I mean?" he said with a chuckle. "Get another coffee and it'll all get better."

"Uh-huh."

"I'm e-mailing you the file with the facial reconstruction now."

"Thanks. What was the hold up?"

Len chuckled. "Grimshaw got PMS."

"Huh?"

"Or rather his computer did. He did tell me the technical information about a cascade failure and some sort of blue screen of death, and how he spent all night rebuilding his architecture and bolting on additional hardware and software support before he could run the reconstruction software again for you. But I'm not sure you'd want to hear it all." He paused. "You still awake, Kate?"

"Just about." Her e-mail program pinged. "Got it," she said as she clicked open the file.

He was just a man. Just a normal, elderly man. His nose was straight, not too big, not too small. His cheekbones were a little wide and his forehead fairly high, but there was nothing about him that stood out. Nothing to make you notice him. The true downside to facial reconstruction was the guesswork that had to come into play. Yes, the depth markers and muscle placement was a science and it was accurate. The basic shape of this face was correct. But they had no way of knowing what colour his eyes were. How he wore his hair. Did he have a beard or was he clean-shaven? Was he fat or thin? How wrinkled was his skin? Did he have jowls? Glasses? A scar? Was he missing his eyebrows? Did he have freckles, or moles, or liver spots?

There were so many unknowns. So many guesses. But at least they had something to start showing around. See if anyone recognised him.

"Thanks, Len."

"No bother. Sorry for the delay."

"It's fine. Thank Grimshaw for me. Sounds like he had a hell of a night trying to get this done."

"Will do."

She hung up and sent the file to the printer. The machine clunked and hummed its way to life before spitting out half a dozen copies. She placed one on each of their desks and stuck the other up on the whiteboard next to the clear, crisp lettering spelling out John Doe. "Right then, mister, let's see if we can find you a name."

The door to the office swung open and Collier stormed in. His face was red, his shoulders hunched up tight to his ears. He grabbed the back of his chair and spun it around violently before dropping into it heavily and folding his arms across his chest.

Tom scowled as he entered the room behind him. "Knock it off, pretty boy. You've got a lot to learn about this job, and if you can't take a bit of advice, a bit of constructive criticism, then perhaps you should think about what it is you're doing here," he said. "You can't talk to people like that and expect to get anywhere with them."

"I didn't ask anything wrong. It was a legitimate question."

Tom nodded. "It wasn't what you said that got his back up so much. It was how you said it. You can't ask delicate questions with a sneer on your face. If people think you're looking down on them or judging them, they won't talk to you. Full stop. And if people won't talk to you, you're poison in this job."

Collier didn't say anything. He just got up and walked towards the door.

"Running off doesn't help matters," Tom shouted behind him. "Real mature, prick."

"I'm not. Is it all right if I go for a piss, grandad, or do I have to run that by you too?" He stormed away, not waiting for a response.

Stella whistled. "Trouble in paradise?"

Tom leaned against the wall and crossed one ankle over the other, folded his arms over his chest, and dropped his head. "I'm sorry, sarge," he said to Stella. "I can't teach him." He ran his hands over his shaved head, then leaned back against the wall, looking up to the ceiling.

"Why not?"

"He won't listen to a word I say. He's hostile. All the time. He clearly has no respect for me, and nothing I've tried so far has made a blind bit of difference."

"Is it him or just a personality clash?"

"In all honesty, sarge, at this point I couldn't tell you."

"It's that bad?"

"Yeah."

Tom was a seasoned detective with hundreds of hours of mentoring junior officers under his belt. For him to admit that he couldn't get through to Collier was not a good sign. Kate knew they had limited options now, but most the likely one was going to be pairing her or Stella with Collier, and Jimmy with Tom for a while. If it was a personality clash, then the switch in personnel would soon sort it out. If not, then they'd have a better idea of what was going wrong with Detective Constable Collier.

"Okay," Stella said, "when he gets back, we'll have a word." She indicated her head in Kate's direction.

Kate nodded in return. "In the meantime, we have a face."

"About bloody time," Tom said, looking over at the board. "Have we run it through the databases yet?"

"Not yet. It's literally just come in," Kate said.

"I'll get that started." Jimmy spun his chair to face his computer and clacked away on the keys. "You want the usual, sarge?"

"Yeah. Police records and missing persons too. Just because we didn't get a hit off our search parameters doesn't mean he might not be in there. Then hit the DVLA records, government employees, armed forces. Anything that stores picture IDs," Kate said.

"Yup. The usual. It'll take a while, as always, but that's started."

"Thanks, Jimmy," Kate said. "It's worth a try."

"Want to fill us in on the nursing home last night?" Stella asked.

"Hm. That's an interesting one, actually. There's definitely something not quite right there."

"Meaning?" Stella prodded.

"Too soon to tell really. And to be honest, it could be all sorts." Kate sat down again, leaned her chair back, and propped her feet on her desk. "The sister, Sister Lodge, was hired about six months ago to deal with 'issues' in the place." She curled her fingers in the air as she said issues. "She started just after her predecessor left due to illness and then died."

"What kind of issues? And died of what?" Stella asked.

"She was vague about them. She mentioned shoddy paperwork, poor standards of patient care, issues with medications, theft from residents, as well as a high mortality rate. And she just said illness. I was going to check that today and see what happened there."

"So basically anything that could be wrong in a place like that?" Stella said.

"Pretty much."

"And?"

"It felt like too much of a coverall."

Stella frowned at her. "Explain."

"It felt like she was saying that she knew there were things wrong in there. But I'm not sure she knows exactly what it is. Otherwise why mention everything? Why not just mention the one thing you're dealing with? The one thing she was brought in to sort out?"

Stella tapped a pencil to her lips. "And what do *you* think's going on in there?"

She shrugged. "Like I said, too soon to be sure yet."

Stella smiled. "Okay, back covered. Now tell me what you really think."

Kate smirked. "Fraud or embezzlement, maybe. Shoddy paperwork was the first thing she mentioned."

"Yeah, but she also mentioned that she'd already investigated the high mortality rate," Jimmy added. "So that indicates it was the first thing to deal with when she got there."

"Yes, but she ruled that out," Kate said.

"*Her* investigation ruled it out," Jimmy said. "But maybe she didn't go deep enough. I mean, she's not the police, is she?"

"Very true, Jimmy. Okay, I see your point. Don't let other people do a poor job of our work for us." Kate settled her feet back on the floor and reached for her notebook. "So we need to start looking at the deaths in the home as well as speaking to all these employees and ex-employees to see if we can ID our victim."

"Are we sure we need to start poking into this? These deaths?" Stella asked.

"Why? What're you thinking?"

"I'm having a Harold Shipman nightmare right now," Stella said.

"Christ, don't go there on me," Tom said. "I had a friend—we trained together—he worked in Tameside when they started looking into all that. He aged ten years in the first six months, and he's never gone to see a doctor since." He shuddered.

"Yeah, no one wants to come across something like that again, but if anything, that's more of a reason to make sure we look into this sort of thing. We can't—well, I can't—in good conscience ignore it now that it's come to my attention."

Stella sighed. "I know. I wasn't suggesting that we do. I was just meaning do you really think we've got enough justification to start poking around in this? It'll probably turn out to be nothing."

"All the better. But yes, I do. We've got dentures and clothes from multiple people from this place on our victim. All of them died there in the last three years. One on the night we know our victim died too. It's just too much of a coincidence, Stella. And before we all start worrying that there's something nefarious going on—"

"Ooh, big words," Tom crooned.

"Quiet in the cheap seats," Kate said and continued. "Even if there is more to the high mortality rate, it could be all sorts of reasons. We don't automatically have to suspect the worst possibility."

"Such as?" Stella asked.

Kate pursed her lips. "I'd be putting my money on negligence. Overworked staff, someone sleeping on the night shift." She tapped her lips with her forefinger. "I mean, if they're short-staffed like Diana Lodge indicated they were, then I'd suspect corners were being cut left, right, and centre. Staff is always the biggest cost. Minimise the staff, and you can keep them down."

"But patient care suffers as a result, and things get missed," Stella added, following Kate's line of thinking.

"Exactly. A patient doesn't get the best care, picks up an infection." She shrugged. "Nothing malicious, but definitely wrong. Negligence. I'd put money on it."

Jimmy held up a mug, the one that was never used for anything except their betting money. "Tenner, ladies and germs, gets you into the party."

Kate dipped into the pocket of her jeans and fished out a note.

"Ten pounds for the sarge on negligence. You, Tom?"

"Someone stealing the patients' drugs." Tom stuffed his own note in the pot. "They're all dying because they're not getting their blood pressure pills and laxatives," he added with a smirk.

"Nice," Jimmy said.

Kate and Stella groaned. "There's always someone who has to lower the tone." Stella slapped Tom across the back of the head while he kept on grinning. "Will you ever grow up?"

"Not if I can help it."

"I'm going with drugs as well," Jimmy said, adding his own cash to the mug. "But I reckon they're buying in cheap fakes to line someone's pockets."

"That's basically the same as mine, numb nuts," Tom protested.

"Hey, no it isn't. My idea was much more developed than yours. And made no mention of laxatives."

Kate sniggered. Sometimes it was like working with nursery-school kids. "All right, knock it off. You both reckon it's drug related." She shrugged. "Talk about one-track minds." She finished to a round of righteous anger. "What about you, Stella? Do you want a slice of the action?"

Stella bit her lip. "I'm going with natural causes."

Tom and Jimmy groaned and Stella held up her hands.

"I reckon an outbreak of a norovirus is killing them off 'cos the chef doesn't wash his hands after he goes to the loo."

Tom cackled. "And you accused me of lowering the tone."

Stella tucked her tenner in the mug. "I didn't mention any nasty bodily functions, and used the correct medical name. No tone lowering going on there, Detective Constable Brothers."

"Yeah, yeah, yeah. You keep telling yourself that, sarge," Tom said with a final snicker.

"Timmons isn't going to like it," Stella said.

"Who would?" Tom asked.

"True. Right, we've got a lot of work to do, kiddies." Stella rubbed her hands together. "So we'd best be at it. Kate, do you want to take Collier with you and go see Doc Anderson? Get her to pull the post-mortems on the residents of the nursing home and see what she can find."

"No problem."

"Tom, Jimmy, we'll start working our way around the employees with the picture while we wait and see if the databases come up with a match."

"On it, sarge." Tom tapped Jimmy on the shoulder as he passed him, heading for the door.

Collier was coming in as they left. He scowled at Tom as the two of them offered a paltry wave and let the door slam shut behind them.

Boys. "We thought you could come with me this afternoon," Kate said. "We thought seeing a different approach would be of benefit to you."

He sneered. "So he's given up, has he? Well, fine. I wasn't learning anything from him anyway."

Kate smiled. *Oh, this was going to be fun. Not.* "Come on, then. I'll fill you in while I drive." She followed him out of the room and looked back over her shoulder at Stella. "You owe me big for this one," she mouthed before carrying on behind him.

She quickly filled him in on the details as she drove the twenty-minute journey to King's Lynn's hospital. The car park was busy, and it took her several circuits of the tarmac expanse to find an empty spot.

Collier climbed out before she'd put on the handbrake and was back with a parking ticket for her windscreen by the time she'd turned off the engine and grabbed her jacket off the back seat.

"Thanks." She stuck it on the glass.

"No worries." He bounced on the balls of his feet a little as he waited for her.

He's like a kid who can't keep still. "This way." She led him up the small slope and along a path that cut between the two banks of trees that blocked the front of the hospital from the view of the road. Kate wasn't sure if they were there to save the eyes of the patients from having to look out on to the housing estate of identical houses, in identical rows, down identical streets, or if they were there to save the residents from having to look upon the eyesore that was the Queen Elizabeth II Hospital. Either way, poor trees.

The main entrance was a bustling hub of activity. People sat in uncomfortable chairs waiting for appointments that should have happened two hours ago. Patients were wheeled on huge beds from ward to ward, moved like pieces on a chessboard at the whim of an overseeing hand. The small essentials shop had a queue out of the door as the volunteer shop assistant tried to keep up with the demand for newspapers, fizzy drinks, biscuits, and tissues. The aroma from the coffee shop made Kate's mouth water and she steered them in that direction.

"One grande cappuccino please," she said when she got to the counter. "You?" she asked Collier.

"Oh, same please." He smiled at the barista.

"Actually, make that three, please." She handed her the cash. "Doc Anderson might be more amenable to what I'm going to be asking of her if I turn up with a little gift to grease the wheels."

"Bribing a government official?" Collier said. "Whatever next, sergeant?"

Kate chuckled. "Whatever the case demands, my friend. Whatever the case demands." She accepted her cup and took a grateful sip, careful to avoid burning her mouth. "Oh, that's good. You okay with the spare?"

He nodded and picked up the other two cups.

"So, Collier? What's your first name?" Kate led him down the long corridors as they wound in a predictable yet maze-like pattern through the hospital until they reached the morgue. She tapped on the door before pushing it open and held the door open for them both.

"Gareth."

"You okay if I use that, or do you prefer Collier?"

"No, I prefer Gareth."

"Good." She smiled. "So do I."

He blushed a little and stepped through the door.

"Anybody home?" Kate called into the room.

"Through here."

Kate followed the voice and found Ruth Anderson at a large desk covered in stacks of medical files and a computer. She had a pencil stuck through her ponytail, and her normally pristine white lab coat was covered in an array of stains that Kate didn't want to think about.

"We come bearing gifts, doc." Kate pointed as Gareth put the cup down on the desk before the harried-looking woman.

"Oh, bless you." She picked it up, took a big swallow, and closed her eyes as she clearly enjoyed the caffeine hit. "Hm. Heaven." She took another big swallow and waved them into seats. "My predecessor told me to beware detectives bringing gifts. But I think I'll risk it. What can I do for you today?"

Kate took a page from her pocket and handed it over. "These are names of all the people who have died at Brancombe House Nursing Home in the past three years."

Ruth's eyes widened as she flipped the pages over. "This is only three years?"

"Yes."

"Wow. Busy place."

"So we understand. We were wondering if it was perhaps a little too busy."

"Ah. I see." Ruth placed the page on her desk. "I'll pull the files and take a look. Am I looking for anything specifically?" she asked, not taking her eyes off the page.

"Don't know."

"Does this have anything to do with our unidentified skeleton?"

"Yes. The dentures and clothes he was wearing all came from this nursing home. I'm certain he did too, but there's no missing persons record. Nothing that matches the description of our victim, and nothing made by anyone associated with this place."

"Curious."

"Exactly."

"And nobody recognises the picture?"

"We only got the reconstruction this morning. Stella and the boys are out asking about it now. Have you submitted your report about the bones yet?"

"Not yet. I've been a little busy."

"Ah, good, good."

Ruth offered a conspiratorial smile. "Would you like me to refrain from sending it a little longer?"

Kate grinned. "I wouldn't want you to get into any trouble, Ruth."

"I won't. To be honest, I wanted to get a second opinion on the blood staining and a few other things I found on the bones before I submit it."

"You do?"

Ruth nodded. "Yes. It just doesn't sit right."

"None of this case does, Ruth. There's something going on. I can feel it."

"In your gut?" Gareth asked with a slight sneer to his voice.

"Yeah. It might sound old school or whatever, but I have a feeling. A lot of detectives get them from time to time, when they just know there's more going on than the sum of the parts they've got in front of them."

"So, what do you do about it?" he asked.

"We keep digging. Eventually we find the missing pieces."

Ruth lifted the page. "I'll see if I can find you anything in this lot while I wait for my expert colleague to come and see the remains."

"How long will that take?"

"He can't get here until Tuesday, so you have five days, Kate."

"That's more than I thought I'd get. Thanks." She turned to Gareth. "See? I told you it pays to bring a woman gifts."

"In the police force, we call it bribing an official," he jibed back.

Kate smiled. "I knew there had to be a sense of humour in there somewhere, Gareth." She held out a hand for him to shake. "Welcome to the team."

Kate fished her car keys and phone out of her pocket. She tossed the keys to Gareth. "I just need to make a quick phone call. You go ahead and I'll meet you back at the car."

"You sure? I don't mind hanging around."

"Nah, shouldn't take me long, but it's not a work call."

"Got ya. Tell Gina I said hi."

Kate turned to look at him. "Actually, I wasn't calling Gina right now." She softened her tone with a smile. "But I'll tell her next time I do speak to her."

He blushed again and walked away with his head down, muttering to himself.

Two steps forward and all that. Kate clicked through a couple of screens on her phone and then connected to the number she wanted. "Hi, this is Detective Sergeant Kate Brannon, can you put me through to Jodi Mann, please?"

"Of course. One moment please," the syrupy voice said before the tinny sound of a poorly-produced piano playing the "Moonlight Sonata" filled Kate's ears.

The static over the line made some of the notes hard to hear, but she knew the piece well enough to fill them in. It was a beautiful piece of music that always reminded her of her grandmother. It was one she'd played over and over when Kate was growing up. She'd told her once that it had been Kate's mother's favourite. Kate could understand why. It was a haunting melody, and Kate found it rather bittersweet that it seemed she and her dead mother had such a thing in common.

"Hello. Is that you, Kate?"

"Hi, Jodi, thanks for taking my call."

"Not a problem. What can I do for you today?"

"Do you have a space to see a new patient?"

"We can always find someone to see—"

"No, I think it needs to be you, Jodi."

There was a moment's silence on the line.

"Perhaps you better fill me in then."

"This woman was the victim of a knife attack six weeks ago."

"Was she badly hurt?"

"No. The cuts were meant to cause pain, not seriously wound. They've healed now, but..." Kate knew she wouldn't need to say any more. Jodi would understand what she meant.

"Ah."

"Yes."

"Give me her number, I'll get in touch and see if she wants to work with me."

Kate gave her the number. "Her name's Gina. Gina Temple."

"And why now? What's her impetus to work through her issues?"

"A new relationship."

Jodi was quiet for a moment. "I see." She cleared her throat. "Right, leave it with me, and I'll call her this afternoon. You could give her a heads-up that I'll be in touch."

"I'll let her know. And, Jodi?"

"Yes?"

"Thank you. I know you're always swamped, but she needs your help."

"And you need her, don't you, Kate?"

Jodi always did know how to filter things down. "Yes, I do."

Jodi was quiet again. "I'm happy for you."

"Thank you."

Kate hung up and quickly typed a message to Gina before heading to the car.

Gareth was waiting outside the vehicle with a grin on his face.

"What?"

He pointed to a parking attendant walking away from them. "She was going to give you a ticket."

"Why? I've paid for parking today. Well, you have."

"She said that's the first time you've paid for your parking in all the time you've been coming here."

"Did you tell her we were on police business?"

"Yeah. But I think she kinda enjoys the game. She's trying to catch you out now. She was smiling when she gave me this for you." He held out a parking ticket plastic envelope with a piece of paper inside it. Kate opened it gingerly and felt her cheeks warm. "What is it?" he asked.

"Erm, her number."

Gareth burst out laughing.

CHAPTER 12

The room smelt of stale urine and bleach. It was small; the bed in the centre took up most of the space. There was a scuffed wardrobe set in the bottom corner, next to the window, and the dresser next to it had a TV on it. The man feeding soup to the woman on the bed seemed far more interested in the TV than he was in making sure the soup went in her mouth and not down her chin.

Kate swallowed and tried to ignore the soggy strip of pasta clinging to the poor woman's chin. The indignity that came with old age and failing health. It made her feel sick. She was grateful she hadn't had to witness any of her loved ones decline like this. Even her gran in her battle with cancer had been strong up to the end. *Probably why she popped off in the end. Couldn't face the prospect of someone else wiping her arse for her.*

"Mr Warburton, could you take a look at this picture and tell me if you recognise this man?" Kate held out the page.

He turned his head towards the page but his eyes didn't leave the screen.

"No, don't know 'im."

Gareth picked up the TV control and clicked off the screen.

"Hey, what're you doing? Who do you think you are, pal?"

"The police," Gareth said. "Now, take a look at the picture and tell me if you recognise him." He wiggled the remote. "Then I'll put Jeremy Kyle back on for you."

Mr Warburton glared at him then looked at the picture. He squinted, then reached into his pocket and pulled out a pair of glasses, perched them on the end of his nose, and took the paper from Kate's hand. He examined the image carefully while he scratched his jaw and rubbed his hand over his mouth.

"He looks familiar." He handed the page back to Kate. "But I couldn't tell you where from." He shrugged. "He looks like every old bloke you ever see, really."

Kate understood. There was very little that stood out about the man they were trying to identify. Perhaps in life it had been different. *Perhaps there had been something about him that had made him stand out. But in death, he was the epitome of the grey man.*

"Thanks for your time," she said and pulled open the door.

She turned in time to see Gareth plucking a tissue from the box beside the woman's bed and wiping the dribbled soup from her chin. He tossed the wad into the bin and handed the remote to Mr Warburton.

"Maybe you should try keeping the TV off while you work."

"Why? She can't talk to me." He clicked the button. "Off her tits on painkillers. I'd go out of my box if I had to sit here in silence all day like these poor sods."

Kate shook her head in sadness at his attitude and a little in shock at the act of kindness from Gareth Collier. Perhaps the issues simply were a clash of personality with him and Tom Brothers. It was difficult to imagine anyone finding it difficult to work with Tom, but sometimes people just rubbed each other the wrong way. She had to admit she'd had her misgivings about working with the green detective, but he was making a pretty good show of himself so far.

"So who do we have next?" she asked.

"Jason Maxwell, thirty-two, lives in Docking."

"Hm. Like me. Whereabouts?"

"Number 2, Prince William Terrace."

"Oh, one of the new builds at the other end of the village."

Gareth frowned. "The ones they knocked down the old pub to put up?"

"Apparently." Kate smiled. "They were already in the works when I bought my place. I've heard stories about the old pub though. Did you ever go there?"

"Once. It was a party. Friend of a friend, you know."

"Is it true that there was a hole in the floor that the staff refused to repair so they could shout down when they needed more drinks upstairs?"

Gareth laughed. "There was a hole in the floor. Staff didn't use it, though. It had rotted through. It was so uneven, and water was dripping from a pipe somewhere. The only thing they did with that hole was put a bucket underneath it. It was a bloody death trap. It needed tearing down, that's for damn sure."

"Sounds like it." Kate wondered how much was exaggeration. Every story she heard about the Prince William Pub seemed more outlandish and farfetched than the last one.

"Sister Lodge said he'd be in room twelve." He pointed to the door at the end of the corridor. "Should be that one, I think."

Kate knocked and opened the door when a gentle voice called "Enter".

"Good afternoon, I'm Detective Sergeant Kate Brannon, and this is Detective Constable Gareth Collier." She held out her hand.

"Jason Maxwell." His grip was firm, his hand cool, and the corded muscles in his forearm bunched visibly with each movement. "How can I help you today, Detectives?"

"I understand you've worked here for a number of years?"

"Yes. Fifteen years now." He picked up a napkin and wiped the man's chin he had been feeding. "Excuse me, Reg, I need to speak with these people."

The old man didn't respond. He didn't look up even, just continued to sit in his chair and stare blankly into space.

Jason Maxwell indicated the doorway. "Should we talk outside?" He walked away, ducked his head to walk through the door and waited for them in the hallway.

Gareth held out the picture, looking up at the man. "Do you recognise this man?"

Kate watched him carefully, as she had everyone they'd shown the picture too.

"No. I don't think I do."

The same response as everyone else. There was just one difference with Jason Maxwell. There was a spark of recognition in his eye. Just for the briefest second. Then he fixed his features in a mirror of confused concentration. A little squint to his eyes. A little frown to his brow. A little purse to the lips. But it was there. She'd seen it. He knew their victim.

"Are you sure?" Kate asked.

Mr Maxwell frowned and stared again at the picture. This time his features were schooled. There was no flicker to indicate he knew the man in the picture. "Pretty sure. Where might I know him from?"

"Here," Kate said, watching every shift of his body language, every twitch of his hulking muscles. "We believe he was a resident here a few years ago."

"Really? What makes you think that?"

"We can't go into the details of an ongoing investigation, Mr Maxwell. I'm sure you can appreciate that."

"Of course."

"How long did you say you've worked here for?" Gareth asked.

"Fifteen years. I started as a cleaner. Didn't have much contact with the residents then. I've only been a care worker for the past two years. So maybe I did see him here, but not enough to really get to know him. Do you know what I mean? He looks familiar, but nothing more than that. I'm sorry."

There was a muscle at the corner of his right eye that twitched as he spoke. A tiny, tiny movement that Kate almost missed. One you wouldn't have seen if you hadn't been looking for something, anything, as a reaction. But it was there.

"Thank you for your time." Kate said. "We'll let you get back to your work." She produced a card. "If you do think of anything else, where you might know him from, or who he is, please call me."

"Of course."

Gareth and Kate walked down the hallway and started down the stairs. Kate pulled her phone from her pocket and dialled Stella's number.

"Hello there," Stella said.

"Anything?" Kate asked.

"Nada. Got a few people who think he looks familiar, but nothing more concrete than that."

"Same here."

"Anyone left on your list?"

"No. You?"

"Nope. We were just going to head back to the station."

"Right. I'm going to have another chat with Sister Lodge." She dropped her voice to a whisper to make sure she couldn't be heard. "Find out all you can about Jason Maxwell when you get back."

"Maxwell. The cleaner that turned into a care worker?"

"Yes."

"Why?"

"He recognised our vic and lied to me."

"Said he didn't know him?"

"Yup."

"How do you know he was lying?"

"Experience, a twitching eye muscle, and he was too nice to the old bloke in there."

Stella laughed down the line. "Aren't they supposed to be nice to the old folks?"

"Yeah," Kate conceded. "But how many of them have you actually seen do that?"

Stella was quiet a moment. "Fair point, well made. I'll see what I can find. Speak to you soon."

"Why wouldn't he tell us if he knew him?" Gareth asked.

"Well, if he has nothing to hide, I can't really think of a reason." She led Gareth to the back of the building and Sister Lodge's office. "Can you?"

"But what's he hiding?"

"That's what we're going to find out, Gareth." She tapped on the door.

"Come in."

Sister Diana Lodge sat behind her desk, the same as she had the last time Kate was in the room with her. She wore a dark blue uniform tunic, just like last time, and her dark hair was pulled back into a tight ponytail at the back of her head. Just like last time. This time, however, her smile seemed genuine and there was a twinkle in her eye as she waved Kate and Gareth into the chairs in front of her desk.

"I've been doing some research, Detective."

"You have?" Kate replied cautiously. The tone in the nurse's voice putting her on edge.

"Oh yes." She turned her computer screen towards them. "Quite the reputation you've built yourself already, Detective Sergeant Brannon."

On the screen was a picture of Kate from the night she'd saved Gina from Ally's attack. She was leading Gina out of her house while clearly shouting orders to her colleagues.

"Feisty."

Kate's cheeks warmed as she sat back in the chair. "Just doing my job." She swallowed and cleared her throat. "Sister, tell me about Jason Maxwell."

She frowned at the sudden change of topic. "What would you like to know?"

"Everything you can tell me."

She leaned forward and rested her elbows on the desk. "Why?" she asked quietly.

Kate raised an eyebrow at her. "I don't need to give you a reason, Sister. I'm here on an official police investigation. That should be reason enough for you to answer my questions." Kate leant forward, rested her elbows on her knees, and clasped her hands together. "Unless you're keeping something from me?"

Diana Lodge licked her lips and clasped her fingers together. Her eyes darted about the room suspiciously. Almost as though she expected that someone was listening to their conversation. "Perhaps we should go and get some coffee." She touched the lanyard around her neck, for a moment fumbling with the keys hanging from it, then climbed to her feet and led them out of the room. "Coffee would be lovely. What a fabulous suggestion, Detective," she said with an exaggerated wink.

Kate and Gareth stared at each other before shrugging and deciding to play along. Weird just got weirder.

Once the three of them had climbed into Kate's car, Sister Lodge spoke again. "Just head out to the lay-by outside of Brandale Staithe. No one will see us there."

Kate turned on the engine. "This better be good, Sister."

"It'll be worth your time," she said from the back seat.

Kate drove out of the car park and turned right on to the beach road, then right again towards Brandale Staithe. They were at the lay-by in less than five minutes. Kate pulled up next to the old black-and-yellow AA box. It hadn't worked in years, but it was something of a local landmark. She turned off the engine and twisted in her seat so she could see into the back more easily. "Okay, what are we doing here and what does this have to do with you telling me about Jason Maxwell?"

"Jason? Well, very little to do with him actually. Well, not that I know of, and I can't imagine any way he could be involved in this, but there's something very fishy going on at the nursing home."

"We could've told you that," Gareth said condescendingly.

"Right, but do you have any idea what?" Sister Lodge replied with equal condescension.

He glared at her but said nothing.

"As I thought." She fiddled with the key lanyard around her neck and pulled something off one of the rings. "This is all the records of the home. Everything since the records were computerised in 2004."

"Everything?" Kate asked.

"Yes. Accounts, invoices, patient records, drug charts, employee records, agency staff, disciplinary records. Everything." She handed the flash drive to Kate.

"And what am I looking for on here?"

"Do you know how many residents we have at Brancombe House Nursing Home?"

"Forty-two, no, forty-three."

"Correct. Do you know how many residents Brancombe House Nursing Home is receiving government funding for?"

Kate raised an eyebrow. "I'm guessing it isn't forty-three."

"The government is paying funding for forty-four residents to Brancombe House."

"So you have a spare," Kate said.

"What's the name of the spare resident?" Gareth asked.

"No name. Only a number. 3840."

"Any idea what that means?" Kate asked.

"None. But it's been on the system since December fifth 2013."

Kate smiled. "Now we're getting somewhere. So you've got a case of embezzlement on your hands."

"Yes, but I can't trace where the payment is being made to."

"I don't understand, Sister, you just said that the nursing home was receiving the funding from the government for the extra person."

She nodded. "Call me Diana. I've always hated being called Sister."

"Okay, but I'm still confused."

"Right, sorry. So the paperwork was all completed for our mystery person more than six years ago, and until the night of the fifth of December 2013, the payment came into the bank account of the nursing home. After that, it was redirected. It's now paid from the government directly in to a different bank account."

"But you have no idea whose account?"

"No."

"And no idea how to trace the payment?"

"Well, I tried calling the NHS accounts department this morning, but without a name or a reference to try and trace the payment, they didn't seem to be having much luck isolating the payment."

"And the number 3840 wasn't the reference number?"

"No."

"How much is the payment for?"

"Four hundred a week."

"And all the details of it are on here?" She held up the flash drive.

"Yes," Diana said.

"Okay. We'll get into this. We have a specialist who just loves to analyse data and can work miracles with it. Now tell me about Jason Maxwell."

Diana frowned. "What about him?"

Kate sighed. "I think he recognised the man in this picture, but he lied to me about it. Could he be the one responsible for this little embezzlement?"

Diana's frown deepened. "I don't see how. He worked as a cleaner and now he's a care worker. He doesn't have access to the finances or the bank accounts. Never has from what I can tell. And seeing him input the data for his patients, well, the man doesn't have what you'd call groundbreaking IT skills, if you know what I mean?" She mimed a person picking at a keyboard using both index fingers and nothing else.

"So why would he lie?"

"I don't know, Detective. Jason has been a godsend to us here at Brancombe House. He works double shifts whenever we're short-staffed. He's wonderful with the patients, and he genuinely does seem to care about them. He spends time with them. Talking to them, reading to them. I even found him putting nail polish on one of the old dears last week." She sighed. "I wish I had a whole staff full of Jasons, if I'm honest."

"Does he live alone? Married? Kids?"

"No. He never mentions anyone. Personally, I think he's gay."

"But no boyfriend?"

"No, like I said. He never mentions anyone. He comes in, does his work, and then goes home again."

"Any friends on the staff?"

Diana thought for a moment, her brow creased in concentration. "Not that I know of. He's a quiet sort of guy."

Another car pulled up in the lay-by and a woman with a dog climbed out. She crossed the road and headed up towards Barrow Common.

Kate frowned and made a note to make sure she took Merlin for a good walk later. "How did he come to start working here?"

"He told me once that he came to work here for his work experience from secondary school. He liked it so much that he never wanted to work anywhere else."

"And how did he make the jump from cleaner to carer?"

"Necessity."

"His or yours?"

"Ours, no doubt."

"Before your time?" Kate asked.

"Exactly."

"Can you think of a reason why he'd lie about knowing this man?"

"No." Diana crossed her arms over her chest. "I'm sorry, Detective, but I can't. What makes you so sure he is?"

Kate frowned. Could she have been mistaken? Could it just have been a nervous twitch? People get nervous all the time when they're asked questions by the police. It wasn't an unreasonable reaction. Was she mistaken? Was it really recognition she saw?

"I don't know." She indicated the flash drive. "We'll look into this and find out what's going on with your spare claimant. I might need some extra information from you, though."

"Anything."

"And I'll definitely need to know who was doing the books back then, and since."

"Okay. It's a woman by the name of Alison Temple who does the accounts now. She lives in South Creake. Works from home doing the accounts and payroll for small businesses in the area."

"And how long has she been doing the books?"

"About five months. I asked her to take on the work shortly after I started. It's taken us a while to get on top of things, but it was Alison who found the discrepancy and the 3840 number."

"And who did the books before?"

"A number of people, to be honest. I'll get you a list of the names and e-mail it over to you."

A campervan pulled into the lay-by and a couple climbed out, surveying their surroundings. No doubt deciding whether or not to call the spot home for the night, despite the no-overnighting sign on the AA box door.

"Okay. I can start with Alison. There's something else I'd like you to do, though."

"What's that?"

"Do you have photographs at the nursing home?"

"Hm, I see. I don't recall seeing any, but I'll speak to some of the staff. Eva maybe, or Anna. If anyone would have any or know of any tucked away somewhere it would be those two."

"Please, I need you to be discreet. I'd much prefer no one else on the staff knew about this, especially anyone who was there in 2013."

Diana frowned. "But—"

"This is an ongoing investigation and you've just given me a mountain load more work to do on this case."

Diana nodded and sighed. "Very well. I'll be discreet."

"Thank you. Now, who has access to all the computers?"

"Pretty much everyone on the staff. They all use them for something. Updating patient records, medication charts, notes."

"Even the carers?"

"Yes, they have to log when residents have a bath or shower, fluid input and output in some cases, and if residents are fed with an NG tube they document the nourishment given and when."

"So everyone has access to the computers."

"Yes. But different staff require different levels, and no one but me has administrator-level access."

Kate shook her head. "Someone who is any good with computers doesn't necessarily need you to grant them admin rights on a system like you have. They just need access. They can take care of the rest."

"You make it sound like I have a hacker on my staff."

"Maybe, maybe not. But you do have someone who is very good with computers. There's no other way they could pull this off and continue to hide."

"I understand."

"Why didn't you bring this to the police sooner?"

"Alison only told me last night that she'd found the number and finally got confirmation from the accounts department what was being paid, supposedly, to Brancombe House. She'd been trying to get to the bottom of some tax snafu. Like most things with the tax office, it took a while to get answers. And like I said, I called the accounts department myself just this morning to try and get more information, but they weren't much help."

"Okay, so last question."

"Yes?"

"Why the hell did we have to come out here for you to tell us this?" She twirled her finger around to indicate their surroundings.

Diana laughed. "Made it more exciting, didn't it?"

Kate raised her eyebrow and waited.

Diana sighed in frustration. "Fine. I'm not sure who I can trust either. Not when it comes to that information." She shrugged. "Whoever it is, is good enough to hide what they've been doing for a long time and I have no idea who it is. For all I know they could be listening to every conversation I have there. I'm afraid that if they know that I'm on to them, then they'll just disappear, or the trail will at least, and then we'll never catch them."

Kate had to admit, that despite the woman's obvious paranoia, it was a fair point, but it only brought up more questions. If their body and the embezzlement were connected, then wasn't it already too late? Wouldn't they already be on the run since the skeleton had been found? Why stick around to be caught?

"Sorry, I've thought of something else," Kate said.

"Please," Diana responded.

"Has anyone resigned in the last couple of days?"

Diana shook her head. "Trust me, you'd have heard me complain from here to Timbuktu if they had. I'm short-staffed as it is. Chronically. I'm already struggling to cover all the shifts I need on a day-to-day basis, what with people off sick, holidays, and the usual hangover sick days. Weekends are the worst, of course. If I lose another member of staff, I'll really be up the creek without a paddle."

"What about sick? Has anyone called in sick today?"

"Oh, yeah. Maja Hanin. She calls in sick regularly though, so I don't read too much into it. She's a cleaner, so it doesn't affect the patients too much, and she has asthma, so not the best career choice for her. She has an asthma attack at least once every couple of weeks."

"And she had one today?"

"No. She had one at work yesterday. Not too bad, but she'll need a couple of days to recover from it. She was on the evening shift."

"You saw her have this attack?"

"Yes. If any of the staff on site take ill, I try to see them. It gives me a better idea of how long I'll need to find cover for them."

"And you can check if they're faking or not," Gareth added.

"I'd never be so cynical, Detective," Diana said with a grin and a wink.

"Anyone else?" Kate asked.

"Hm, Tim Warburton left a short while ago. Said his wife's had a bad fall and he was at the hospital with her last night. Said he was going to try and make it through the shift but he was flagging. Asked for a day's holiday and apologised for the short notice." She twisted her mouth into a grimace.

Kate didn't believe for a moment that Mr Warburton's wife had fallen. *Well, not unless she'd been pushed...with a fist.* "I think we need to chat with him. Don't you, Detective Constable Collier?"

"I do, sarge."

Diana pointed to the flash drive. "His address is on there."

Kate tapped her temple. "His address is in here too. You gave it to us in the employee files yesterday."

"Oh, yes. Of course." She shook her head. "Sorry."

"No need to apologise. We appreciate your help, Diana." Kate shifted until she was sitting correctly in her seat again and reached for the key in the ignition.

"There is one other person who called in sick."

Kate turned back and waited for Diana to continue.

"David Bale."

"Is he someone who calls in sick a lot?" Kate asked.

"No. I've never known it to happen before."

"How long has he worked at Brancombe House?"

"Well, he started part-time while he was at college. Just weekends and so on about five years ago. When I looked at the records though, it appeared that he didn't take his wages. He had them put towards the care of a resident."

That got Kate's attention. "Which resident?"

"Edward Bale."

"Father?"

Diana shook her head. "His grandfather."

"And he's worked here ever since?"

"Yes."

"Thank you," she said to Diana, and glanced at Collier. She hoped he got the message that this guy just went to the top of their suspect list. Suspect in what crime exactly though, she still wasn't sure. The only thing she was sure about was that this case was one great big ball of string all tangled up and knotted together. She couldn't wait until they would finally be able to figure out all the pieces.

CHAPTER 13

Gina squeezed the trigger and fired a pungent plume of atomised liquid at the green-and-black patch of mould clinging to the grout between the tiles. Then another, and another, until the wall was covered and the bubbles of limescale remover began to do their work. There was something supremely satisfying in blasting the clinging spores to hell. Twenty minutes and she'd just rinse them away. If only every nasty, clinging thing was as easy to get rid of.

She left the light on behind her to keep the extractor fan filtering the air in the small en suite. Every room in the hostel had an en suite, but not all of them had windows. This one didn't, and she didn't like the smell of the noxious fumes from the spray. They gave her a headache.

Her phone rang while she stared at the bubbles and rubbed her temples. She answered it and held it to her ear without looking at the caller information. "Hello?"

"Hi, is this Gina Temple?"

"Who's this?"

"Sorry, my name's Jodi Mann. I'm a counsellor for the Victim Support team. I was given this number by Detective Sergeant Kate Brannon. Do I have the correct number?"

Gina's heart pounded and her palms were slick. "Yes. I'm Gina."

"Good. Glad I didn't call the wrong person." She chuckled. "Kate said you needed to talk to someone."

"She...did she..."

"She didn't tell me what about. I prefer to meet with people and find out their stories from them. Not from others. All she told me was that you were left with some scars."

"Yes," Gina whispered. A small track of bubbles slid down the tile, racing toward the grout-filled depression. It clung to the coarse filler like a climber clinging to a wall without a safety rope. Any moment its grip would fail and it would tumble and fall to the ground. Gina looked at her own feet, and for a split second she couldn't see the ground. There was nothing beneath her but empty air, and the sensation of falling was unmistakable. She groped around for something to hold on to. All she could find was the smooth porcelain of the sink. She clung tight until her knuckles turned as white as the pot.

"Well, okay. Would you like to meet up so that we can discuss what you need and whether or not you think I'm the person to help you?"

Jodi's voice sounded distant and distorted. Like Gina was listening to it through water. She took a deep breath. *Get a grip. How do you expect Sammy to talk about her issues if you won't even try?* She coughed to clear her throat. "Yes, I think that would be a good idea."

"Excellent. How about tomorrow? Say eleven o'clock?"

"Less time for me to chicken out?"

Jodi laughed. "Something like that." She paused. "Do you want to chicken out, Gina?"

"What I want is to not need to talk to you. Not that that matters, or even makes much sense. But that's what I want. I want to not need to do this."

"I understand that completely. Time travel isn't something I can help with, I'm afraid. But believe me, there was a time when I felt exactly the same as you do right now. When I just wanted the rest of the world to fuck off and leave me alone to wallow in my own self-pity. But there was someone out there who wouldn't let me. She showed me that it can get better. That *I* could get better if I wanted it enough."

"She sounds pretty awesome."

"She is."

Gina could hear the smile in her voice. "Are you still together?"

"Sadly, we never were together in the way you mean."

"I'm sorry."

"Please don't be. It wasn't meant to be. So tomorrow?"

"Where do I need to go?"

Jodi quickly gave her the address at King's Lynn's hospital. "I know it's easy to say, but try not to worry about tomorrow. I promise, I don't bite, and eventually it will help."

"I guess I'll have to take your word for that."

Jodi laughed. "Only until tomorrow."

Gina frowned. "I don't understand."

"You'll see tomorrow. Bye, Gina."

Gina hung up and sat heavily on the bed. She glanced down at her chest. Even through the thick fleece jumper and coat she wore, she still felt like she could see the scars. She could still feel them as they were cut into her skin. That cold tickle that turned to fire down each nerve ending. Searing them into her soul as they branded her flesh, and the memories came flooding back. She lay down on the bed and curled into a ball as tight as she could.

Memories of Ally standing in the middle of her sitting room after shoving her on the sofa. Demanding to know where Matt was. Her inability to convince the woman only made Ally angrier. And bolder.

Gina couldn't forget the smell. The pungent aroma of her own fear mingled with sea salt, diesel, and dead fish that had permeated Ally's clothes a long time ago.

Ally had laughed at her. Tried to goad her into letting Matt's location slip. And only Gina's sense of self-preservation managed to muzzle her pride as it squawked loudly.

But that hadn't been nearly enough to stop Ally Robbins. Nor had it stopped Gina from realising that it was Ally who had killed Connie, and telling her so.

Ally had laughed, but there had been something in her eyes, a flicker, a shadow, a ripple in the dead pools that glinted out at her. Fear. "You shouldn't be going around slandering people like that, Gina. It could get you into all sorts of trouble," she'd said, then pulled a gutting knife from her belt.

Gina had frozen.

"Come on, Gina. Where is he?"

Gina had shook her head. Her eyes fixed on the blade. The blade that was going to change her life. She'd thought death was the worst thing Ally could do to her then. Clearly Ally had a much better imagination than she did as she made promises and tried to cajole the information she wanted from Gina. Promises to leave her alone with nothing more than a little piss in her pants before Sammy got home. Or to start practising her knife skills. She'd promised crying, and blood, and then talking. Ally had put the tip of the blade to the corner of Gina's mouth and scraped the cold steel along her cheek, hard enough to feel, but not hard enough to draw blood. And made her final promise if Gina remained silent.

Ally had wrapped her fingers in Gina's hair and twisted her head to look her straight in the eye. "We wait a few hours for the tide. And then I'll take you out on the boat." She'd smiled and Gina watched spittle collect at the corner of her mouth. "Ask me what comes next, Gina," she'd said quietly.

Gina couldn't work up enough saliva to make her voice work.

"Ask me!"

"What comes next?" Gina had whispered, her voice shaking, crawling past her lips with barely enough force to be audible.

"Bait." Ally had whispered the word into her ear. Slow and low, dragging it out so it sounded like "Bay" and "T".

Even now, all she could see was the bait station that was on Ally's fishing boat. The steel table covered in chopped fish, guts, and dried blood. The wicked grinder bolted into place and designed to chop up frozen fish leftovers to use as bait. The noise was horrendous, and the bite of the grinder unforgiving. Bones, sinew, muscle, it all broke apart beneath the power of it. And that was all she could see. That and the dead eyes of the fish at one corner. Mouth hanging open, slimy, and its black, dead eyes covered in a film of mucus.

Tears ran down Gina's cheeks as she hugged her knees to her chest. Even then it hadn't been over. She wished it had been. That Kate and the police had come barging in to rescue her then, but they hadn't. Ally had yet more questions to ask. More games to play.

"Try not to worry, she says." Gina snorted. "Yeah, like that's not going to happen." She swiped at the tear on her cheek and grabbed a pillow to stuff under her head. The whirring of the extractor fan reminded her of what she'd been doing. "Fuck it. Who gives a shit?"

She curled her arm around the pillow and let the tears come.

CHAPTER 14

Kate didn't turn off the engine as Diana Lodge climbed out of the car and waved goodbye from the door. She dropped her phone into the cradle and waited for it to connect to the car's on-board system. "Call Stella," she instructed when it beeped at her.

"Genie of the Lamp, how can I direct your wishes today?" Stella's voice sounded like the secretary from every bad office movie ever made: dripping with condescending sweetness with an acidic underbite.

Kate burst out laughing. "What bet did you lose now?"

"You don't want to know."

She crossed the junction and took the back road from Brancaster to Docking. Keeping off the coast road was always quicker. Far less scenic, but quicker. Besides, there was bugger all to see on the scenic road today. The tide was out, the cloud was down, and the sun was already gone. Not worth the extra twenty-minute drive.

"Oh, I really do, Stella. Come on, spit it out."

Stella remained silent.

"You know the boys will tell me later with their spin on it. You may as well get it out of the way."

"The colour of Tom's underwear."

Kate tried to imagine what possible conversation or scenario had led to that bet. "You're right, I don't want to know. We've got work to do, Lady of the Lamp."

"It's Genie, you heathen."

"I prefer Lady. More classy, Stella. Fits you better."

"Gee, thanks. Now what do want?"

"We've got three no-shows from Brancombe House today, and a shit load of data that seems to lead us to an embezzlement case."

"How does it link to our body and all those autopsies we've got Ruth Anderson looking into?"

"At this moment in time, Stella, I haven't got a fucking clue. It's a rat's nest of shit. That's all I know."

"And what do you need from me?"

"The addresses of our absent employees and a run-down on them all."

"Okay," she said. The rustling of paper, indicating she was reaching for her pad. "Hit me."

"You shouldn't make an offer like that with the way your luck's going at the moment."

Stella sighed, but said nothing.

Kate laughed and pulled up outside the convenience shop. She pulled a fiver from her wallet and handed it to Gareth, pointing at the takeaway coffee sign, and added what she hoped was a pleading look to her face.

Gareth took the note, rolled his eyes, and closed the door behind him.

"Okay, okay. Enough fun. Tim Warburton. Left early this morning—asked for a day's holiday after spending the night at the hospital with his wife after she had a fall."

"Isn't he the domestic disturbance dude that's never had a charge?"

"That's the one."

"Bastard."

Kate didn't disagree.

"Okay. So what do you want on him?"

"Education background, family links, financials. Everything we can get our mitts on. Same for all of these please."

"Got it. Next name?"

"Maja Hanin. H-A-N-I-N."

"Foreign national?"

"Eastern European. Polish, Czech maybe. Something like that anyway. Diana Lodge said she had an asthma attack on site yesterday, so she thinks it's legit, but—"

"You can't be too careful. You said three?"

"Yes. David Bale. The grandson of Edward Bale."

"As in underpants Edward Bale?" Stella asked, referring to the scrap of underwear that had been found on the remains in the bunker.

"One and the same."

"Ooh. Now isn't that interesting?"

"It gets more so. He's worked there for five years. He started as a weekend worker while he was at college and paid his wages towards his grandfather's care."

"Any idea why?"

"Not yet. Send me whatever you find out and I'll fill you in on the embezzlement when we get there. This guy lives in Lynn so we'll drop the flash drive off to Grimshaw to get working on."

"Sounds like a plan. Don't spill your coffee while you're driving."

"I would never defile my pride and joy like that." She chuckled and pressed the button to hang up as Gareth came out of the shop, paper cups in hand. She reached over to take them as he climbed in. "Thanks."

"No worries."

She took a sip, careful to avoid burning her tongue with the hot liquid before stowing it in the holder and pulling away from the kerb.

"Do you think she's being straight with us?" Gareth asked as she approached the tight bend through the village of Flitcham.

"Who? Diana Lodge?"

He nodded.

Kate shrugged. "As far as I can see, she personally has much more to gain from being cooperative with us than not. She wasn't there when our vic went missing, nor when the funds were redirected from Brancombe House." She slowed for the junction at Hillington and indicated right towards King's Lynn, before surging across the road to avoid getting stuck behind a car towing a caravan. *Bloody menace on the roads.* "So I don't see any reason for her to lie to us."

"People lie to us just because we're us, sarge."

"Hm. True, I suppose. Sad, isn't?"

"Yeah."

They travelled the rest of the way in silence.

Kate stopped in the car park at the police station and handed Gareth the flash drive. "Will you run that in to Grimshaw and get him to start analysing the data on it? Tell him we need it as soon as possible. If not sooner." She winked.

"Got it, sarge." He took off walking as quickly as he could without looking like one of those Olympic walkers with the hip swing and runner's arms.

She picked up her phone and opened her message program. She clicked on Gina's name and started to type.

Thinking of you. Hope you're okay. Dinner tonight? xx

Kate hit send, put the phone back in its cradle and turned the car around. She wanted to be ready when Collier got back.

Your place? Merlin must've forgotten what you look like ;-) xx

Works for me. You know where the spare is if I'm running late. xx

Gareth was jogging back across the car park. She playfully gunned the engine and grinned at him.

He shook his head. "Sarge, I say this with the utmost respect, but you're a maniac behind the wheel."

"Maniac?"

He nodded.

"Oh, kiddo, you ain't seen nothing yet. I've been on my best behaviour!"

He gulped loudly and pulled his phone out of his pocket.

"What're you doing now?"

"I've got 3G, I was going to improve my life insurance."

"Funny, Collier. Funny." She threw the stick into gear and tore out of the car park, enjoying tossing Gareth around the car a little bit with a little wild steering. *Teach him to take the piss out of my mad skills.*

The closest address was for Maja Hanin, who lived in a flat just out of the town centre. The house was a converted old terrace, in the middle of the row, and was more than a little run down. The property to the left was boarded up with brown steel plates. No doubt to keep out vagrants and kids alike. The stippled render on the outside of the building was chipped and in desperate need of a coat of paint. The only properties on the street that looked well cared for were the off-licence and the kebab shop. It said all Kate needed to know about the area.

She climbed the deep concrete steps to the doorway. There were still some nice period features visible. The black-and-white mosaic tiled floor in the porch spoke of the former glory years of the house—when it was probably the family home to a wealthy, middle-class family. Maybe they'd had a servant or two downstairs to see to the family's needs. But that was clearly a very, very long time ago.

She buzzed the intercom and waited.

"Yes?" The voice was thin, reedy. Maybe wheezy was a better description.

"Maja Hanin?"

"Who is this?"

"Detective Sergeant Kate Brannon and my partner Detective Constable Gareth Collier. May we come in?"

"Top floor. On the left."

The door buzzed and the security latch released to let them in. Post was piled up on a small shelf next to the door, and the doors on either side of the hallway they entered were numbered. While it wasn't the tidiest place she'd ever seen, for a communal space in a block of flats, Kate was pleasantly surprised. There was no stale odour, no cobwebs, and it looked like the floor had been introduced to a mop fairly recently. The carpet on the stairs was worn in the middle of each step, but it looked as though it was hoovered regularly. The windows were clean, the sills dusted, and there was neither graffiti nor mould covering the walls. She glanced at Collier to see if he had spotted the details. He gave no indication he had. She sighed and started up the stairs.

Collier was in front of her, setting a fast pace, but she wasn't going to let the little punk try and show her up. She ran five miles every morning. More on nice days. She jogged up, enjoying the hint of competition that she knew would form between them.

Maja Hanin stood in the open doorway at the top of the stairs. She looked pale and tired, with a blanket wrapped around her shoulders.

"Maja, thank you for seeing us while you're ill. We'll try not to take up too much of your time," Kate said.

Maja nodded and led them into the room.

Collier had to cock his head to the side to prevent him from hitting it.

Maja had no such problems. She was a tiny woman. Kate wasn't sure if she'd reach five foot, but if she did, it wouldn't be by much. She was thin too. So thin that the bones in her wrist were overly prominent when she shook Kate's hand and offered them coffee.

"No, thank you. We'll try to be as quick as we can." She held out the reconstructed face. "Do you recognise this man?"

Maja took the page and studied it. She held one hand over the lower half of the face and squinted like she was trying to shift it slightly out of focus. Then she held it further away, before looking closer again.

At least she's giving it proper thought.

"I think I know him. Maybe. But I'm not sure where from."

"Do you know his name?"

Maja shook her head. "No. I don't think so. I'm not sure. It might be a face I know. The eyes look like...like someone I remember. But I'm not sure about the rest of the face."

"Could it have looked different? Maybe a beard? You said the eyes looked familiar."

"Yes, the eyes. Only the eyes. But I can't think what would make the face right." She shrugged. "I'm sorry."

"That's okay. Maybe it'll come to you later." Kate handed her a card. "If it does you can call me."

Maja took the card.

"How long have you worked at Brancombe House?"

"Only four years."

Only? "Do you like it there?"

Maja shrugged. "It's okay. The chemicals are hard for me. Cleaning chemicals. But it is all I can do."

Kate doubted that, but the background details that Stella had e-mailed her on Maja probably didn't give her an outstanding CV. High school education, no job history before Brancombe House. She looked so fragile, so childlike, that Kate felt sorry for her. Working a job that was probably killing her to live in a tiny flat, and eke out whatever meagre existence she had. "Are you okay, Maja? Do you live here with someone?"

Maja shook her head. "I live alone."

"Do you need anything? You're clearly not well. Do you have your medication?"

She smiled wearily. "Yes, thank you. I have everything I need. I just need to rest, to regain my strength. That is all."

Kate smiled sadly. "Then we'll leave you to it." Maja started to get to her feet, but Kate held out a hand. "We can find the door. You rest."

"Thank you." Maja closed her eyes.

Kate ushered Gareth out of the room and back to the stairs.

"That's it?" Gareth asked as they walked down the wide stairs.

"Yup."

"You felt sorry for her."

"Didn't you?"

"Why should I?" Gareth asked with a frown.

Kate sighed. "Never mind. She's not the person we're looking for."

Their next stop was Tim Warburton's semi-detached house, which sat in a plush suburb of King's Lynn. Wide, tree-lined streets were filled with parked cars, well-manicured lawns, and garden gnomes.

Kate shuddered. *The very picture of making it in the world.*

The Warburtons' gnomes were sitting around a fish pond that looked to be filled with koi carp. The TV blared from inside, the lights shining out of the window as they approached the door. This guy was a list of contradictions. The house, the fish, the gnomes, none of it fit with the football-hooligan image he presented. The shaved head, the missing teeth, the tattoos. They all jibed with the wife-beater his record indicated he was, but the picture she saw here...well, it didn't. But, domestic abuse can happen anywhere. It was far more insidious than people wanted to believe, so why not the middle of suburbia?

Gareth pressed the doorbell and they both looked at each other as "Jingle Bells" rang out. A festive door chime?

"Coming." Mr Warburton's voice echoed down the hallway and reached them easily from somewhere in the back of the house. A moment later he appeared sashaying down the hallway. *Is that... dancing?*

He pulled open the door, a broad grin on his face.

"Hello again, Mr Warburton," Kate said.

His smile faltered. "You again. What do you want now?"

"Tim? Tim, who is it?" A woman's voice called from the back of the house.

He appeared to hold his breath for a moment, then waved them inside.

"It's the police, darlin'."

A woman appeared in the back of the hallway. In her wheelchair. Her hair was perfectly coiffed, her make-up flawless, and did a marvellous job of hiding the black eyes Kate was sure would accompany the cut across the bridge of her nose.

"Look, I told them at the hospital. It was an accident." She approached them. "I wanted to take a bath. That's all. Tim was due home, but I was impatient. I thought if I could get the water run and get myself in before he got home, it would save him a job. He works full-time, you know? As well as caring for me."

Kate glanced at Tim Warburton. He was watching his wife as she defended him. Not in a way that made Kate worry for her. Like she had to say what she was telling them. More like in admiration. That she would so easily admit to the weakness that led her to her predicament to save his reputation.

"I have MS. It's well documented. I have accidents all the time as my condition changes and worsens. What I can do today, well, tomorrow I might not be able to." She threaded her fingers through her husband's. "It's the nature of the bloody beast. So I won't be pressing charges against my husband, thank you very much. There are no charges to answer. He helped me. He got me up, got me dressed, then took me to hospital to have my nose reset because I hit it on the sink. Before he got home."

"Mrs Warburton, thank you, but that's not why we're here." *Well, it isn't now. No wonder he zones out at work when he can. Caring's his life, 24/7.*

"Then why are you here?"

"We just needed to ask your husband a couple more questions about the remains that were discovered yesterday."

"What remains?" She turned to her husband. "Tim, what's this all about?"

"I didn't get chance to tell you last night. What with the fall and everything. I was going to tell you. It just didn't seem all that important today."

"Well, tell me now."

"I will, darlin'. Just as soon as the detectives ask what they need to." He looked back at Kate and Gareth. "Fire away, then."

"Does the number 3840 mean anything to you?" Kate asked.

Mr Warburton frowned. "Don't think so. What is it?"

"I'm afraid I can't go into that." She pulled out the facial reconstruction again. And held it so they could both see. "And you still don't recognise this man?"

He rolled his eyes. "No. Like I said this morning, he looks like every other old bloke out there."

"Do you recognise him, Mrs Warburton?" Kate asked still holding out the picture.

She shook her head. "I'm afraid not. Who is he?"

"That's what we're trying to find out." She smiled and backed towards the door. *Never judge a book by its hooligan-coloured cover, Kate.* "Thank you for your time, Mr and Mrs Warburton. We'll leave you to your evening."

She closed the door behind them and heard the latch fall into place. Then she heard raised voices as Tim Warburton started explaining why he hadn't mentioned something as...exciting...as a police investigation going on at Brancombe House.

"Strike two, sarge," Gareth said as they climbed into her car and set off for David Bale's home.

"Yup. Good job I'm not playing on any team, hey?"

He snickered but kept quiet.

"Have you got the directions for this next one? I don't recognise the address."

"Hang on, I'll get Google Maps up." He quickly opened the app and plugged in the address details. "Left out of here, then right at the end of the road."

Kate followed his smooth instructions for ten minutes and pulled up outside a property that looked empty. She couldn't see any curtains or blinds at the windows, and mail looked to have piled up behind the door.

"You sure this is the right place?"

Gareth looked up at the number on the door, then at his phone again. "Yeah. It's the address listed on his employee records. It's also his grandad's old house."

She tapped on the front door and peered through the window while she waited. "Doesn't look like he's been here for a while."

"What was that?" Gareth whispered. His body coiled, ready to spring into action as a cat wandered out of the bushes and hissed at them.

"Just an old tomcat, Gazza," Kate cooed mockingly. "The little putty tat, didn't scare you, now, did he?" She bent forward and held her hand out in a beckoning gesture and tried to get the cat to come towards her while trying to impersonate Tweetie Pie.

"I hate cats," Gareth muttered.

"That says a lot about a person." She looked up and a glint of metal caught her eye.

"Yeah, that they've got taste."

"Sh. What's that?" She pointed behind him, to the tall wooden gate that would lead around the back of the house.

"Erm, a gate, sarge," Gareth mocked.

She gritted her teeth. "I meant that brand new padlock that's attached to the lock on said gate, Detective."

"Oh. That."

"Yes. That." She walked over to the gate and pulled herself up enough to see over it. There was a bike parked under a makeshift lean-to. The lock on it was clean and new, there was a helmet strapped around the handlebars, and a pannier on the left of the back wheel. Someone was in there. Someone who appeared to be hiding. But she had no warrant.

"If anyone asks, the gate was open. Now give me a boost," she whispered to Gareth and raised her left leg. "I'm just going to take a little look around. No big deal."

"But, sarge—"

"Sh! We don't want to draw attention to ourselves. Just give me a boost."

She heard him sigh then felt his hands cupping her knee and pushing her higher up the gate. She managed to get her arms locked and then lifted her right leg so that her knee was supporting her weight. "Bloody hell, that hurts." She lifted her leg from Gareth's grip and swung it over the gate. It was awkward, she could admit it. But she was over the gate. She had to admit, she felt pretty smug. She used the cross-beams on the back to climb down and moved back to give Gareth room to get himself over.

The gate swung open.

Gareth held the open padlock in one hand and a lock pick in the other. "It's like magic, sarge. It was already open."

Kate's cheeks burned. *Bollocks.* She brushed her hair out of her eyes and straightened her shoulders while Gareth fought not to laugh.

"Why didn't you say something?"

"I tried to, sarge. You told me to shut up and not draw attention to us."

Bloody bollocks. "Right well, next time, try a bit harder."

"Sarge," he agreed and pressed his lips together, presumably to contain the rest of his mirth.

Bastard bloody bollocks. "Where'd you learn a trick like that, anyway?"

"My dad taught me when I was a kid."

"Your dad?"

He nodded. "He thought it might come in handy in the future."

"Why?"

"He said you just never know what you'll need until you need it." He pointed to the back of the garden. "Do you want to lead, or shall I?"

Clearly the conversation wasn't going to go any further. Her admiration for the young detective rose a notch at his skills—and her curiosity rose even more at the father who might think his son would need those skills.

She turned her back on him and started towards the back of the house, keeping as close to the wall as she could. If David Bale was in there, he clearly didn't want people to know it. Why else would he leave the mail piled up at the front door and leave the front of the house looking uninhabited?

She saw light spilling out of the window at the back, presumably the kitchen window. She gestured to Gareth, and he nodded, then walked back around to the front of the house. If he was going to run when she knocked, she wanted Gareth watching the front door.

She rounded the corner of the building and froze. She could make out a figure pacing in front of the window and gesticulation wildly with his hands. She held her breath and watched a moment. He was a big guy. Tall, powerfully built, with big hands that continued to wave in the air. The phrase "brick shithouse" sprang to mind. "You don't look very sick to me, pal."

She tapped on the door and smiled as David Bale dropped the phone and ran for the closed kitchen door. She pushed on the handle, amazed that it opened with no trouble, and chased him through the house. Well, she gave chase. But Gareth already had him on the ground by the time she ran out the front door.

"What're you running for, David? I only wanted to ask you a couple of questions," Kate asked as she regained her breath. "Get him inside so we can have a word."

Gareth nodded and hauled him to his feet.

The kitchen had a much warmer feel to it than she'd expected, given how uninhabited the front of the house looked.

"I haven't done anything wrong," David protested as Gareth pushed him into a chair.

"Then why did you run?" Kate asked.

"You scared the shit out of me. Knocking on my back door like that."

"Well, why didn't you answer at the front then?"

"I didn't hear anything at the front door."

"I knocked."

"Yeah? Well, not loud enough for me to hear you," David said. "Why are you sneaking around the back of my house, anyway? And how did you get in? I've got a padlock on the gate?"

Gareth held up the lock. "You must've forgotten to lock it." He put the lock on the table.

David grunted a disbelieving laugh. "Yeah, right."

"Your boss told us you called in sick today, David. You don't look very sick to me." Kate sat opposite him.

He stared at her.

"So why did you skip work today?"

"I had stuff to sort out."

"What stuff?"

"Personal stuff."

Kate nodded. Softly, softly. "Why don't you use the front room?"

"How do you know I don't?"

"I've seen it. The dust in there's higher than the dust on my telly, and there are no curtains or blinds or anything up at those windows. That room's south facing. The sun would be in your eyes all day if you didn't have anything up in there, but it would make it a lovely warm room. So why don't you use it?"

David glared at her. "It was where my grandad slept before he went into Brancombe House. It's got too many memories in it."

Ah. "Okay, I can buy that. So why weren't you at work today?"

"I told you, I had personal business to deal with."

"Yeah, I know, you told me that. But that's not really an answer to my question, is it?"

"I don't have to answer your questions. I've done nothing wrong."

She nodded. "Technically, no you don't have to answer, but think about it this way for a minute. I'm investigating how an old man, from the nursing home you work at, ended up dead, in a bunker, on a beach." She paused. "Then you call in fake-sick the day after the body is discovered. Discovered wearing some of your grandad's clothes, by the way. And now you won't answer even a basic question like why are you calling in fake-sick?" She paused again and watched his face redden a little. "Do you see how that looks, David?"

"Wearing Grandad's clothes?"

"That's the part of that speech you focus on?" Kate clicked her fingers. "David, wake up and smell the suspicion here."

His gaze snapped into focus and settled on her face.

"What personal business?"

"I found out my girlfriend was pregnant."

"Should I say congratulations or was this not happy news?" Kate asked.

"It's incredible news. Or it was." He leaned forward, rested his elbows on the table, and buried his face in his hands. *Is he crying?*

"What do you mean, was?"

"It was a friend of hers who told me. She wasn't going to. She was going to just break up with me and she wasn't even sure it was mine. She was going to have an abortion today. That's what I needed to sort out. I needed to talk to her. To find out what's going on. I mean, that's my kid too. I know it's her body. I get that. But I should get a say in my baby's life, right?" He cried openly now. "That's who I was on the phone to when you knocked on the back. Jessie, my girlfriend, well, ex now, I suppose. She said her new bloke was on his way here to kick my head in. Then I'd get the message to leave her alone. That's why I ran when you startled me. I thought it was him."

Jesus, was no one going to be what she expected them to be today? She pulled the picture from her pocket. "Do you know this man, David? He might have been a friend of your grandad's."

David shook his head. "By the time Grandad got to Brancombe he was past having friends." He wiped his face with his sleeve and picked up the page. He scrutinised it closely, tipping his head from one side to the next as he did. "I'm sorry. If Grandad did know him, I didn't meet him."

"It would have been from the nursing home," Kate said. "Do you recognise him from there?"

He frowned but looked again. "I don't think so. You've got to understand, when I was working there when Grandad was sick, I was mostly looking after him and a couple of the fellers on his floor. John Wood, Harold Fine, and Grandad. I didn't really see anyone else. Grandad was really bad, he needed a lot of care. His lungs filled up with fluid and mucus, and his throat didn't close properly. He couldn't swallow, so we had to suck the spit out of his mouth to stop him from choking to death on it." He shook his head. "Can you imagine that? Drowning on your own spit." He wiped his eyes again. "I spent every minute I could with him. I didn't pay attention to anyone else. Even though I know I should have done." He shrugged. "I loved my Grandad." He handed the page back to her. "So, I'm sorry, but no. I don't recognise this guy. I wish I could help you, but I can't."

Kate nodded. "Thanks for your time, David. And I hope you get everything sorted out with your ex."

He nodded and pointed to the padlock. "Would you mind putting that back on when you leave? I'd really like my bike to be there in the morning when I have to go to work."

"Sure." Gareth picked it up. "And sorry we gave you a scare, man."

He shrugged. "Just doing your job, right?"

"Erm, yeah. Right." Gareth led them out.

"Don't say it." Kate opened her car door.

"Strike three."

"Enjoy your walk home, Gareth," she said and pushed the button to lock the doors before he got in. She smirked and turned the engine on.

He banged on the window. "Aw, come on, sarge!"

She shifted into gear and pulled away a few yards, then opened the door. "Get in. I'm having dinner with Gina tonight."

CHAPTER 15

"Best behaviour, Sammy," Gina said as she parked up around the back of Kate's house.

"I'm always good, Mum," Sammy replied with a cheeky grin.

"Do I look like I was born yesterday? Don't answer that."

Sammy released her seatbelt and climbed out of the car. "Can I play with Merlin?"

"Ask Kate."

Sammy raced down the small back garden and knocked on the patio door.

A dog started barking instantly.

Gina closed the gate behind her and smiled at the sight of Sammy rolling around on the ground with a blur of grey-and-white fur.

Kate stood in the doorway, gazing at her. "Hi," she said softly.

"Hi." Gina felt shy. Shy like she hadn't felt around Kate before.

"Don't look so scared. I ordered pizza."

Kate had long ago warned her that she couldn't cook. Coffee, cereal, and toast were the limit of her culinary expertise.

"I'm not scared. I know how to use an oven." Gina relaxed a little under the self-deprecating humour.

"Sammy, do you want to carry on playing with Merlin inside? All the heat's escaping while you roll around on the ground." Kate winked at Gina.

"Sorry," Sammy said as she scrambled to her feet and scooted past Kate's legs. Merlin was right behind her, and the game did indeed continue: Sammy wrestling with the dog and holding out a rope toy to play tug of war with.

"Tea?" Kate asked.

"Erm, sure."

"I have wine, but I thought if you were driving—"

"Wine's good."

Kate looked at her.

No, that's more like scrutinising.

"Just the one."

"What's happened?" Kate asked quietly as she led Gina into the kitchen.

Gina shook her head. "Nothing."

Kate cocked her eyebrow.

"Really. Nothing's happened yet."

"But?" Kate poured two glasses of red and held one out for her.

Gina bit her lip and took the glass of wine. She took a big gulp before she wrinkled her nose and spoke. "I'm meeting Jodi tomorrow."

Kate's eyes widened. "That's fast."

Gina shrugged. "She had a space."

Kate pointed to the dining room table and pulled out a chair.

Gina sat down and waited until Kate was sitting next to her. The open-plan kitchen-dining room was large enough to accommodate a table big enough for six and still allow plenty of space to move around in. The kitchen was well-proportioned, white, and seldom used. By Kate, anyway. Gina found herself making use of it more and more. She felt more at home in Kate's house than she did in her own.

"Nervous?" Kate asked.

"No," Gina said. "Terrified."

Kate laughed. "Jodi's great, Gina. She can really help you."

"I'll have to take your word for that."

Kate shook her head. "Just give her a chance. You'll see."

"I'm going. The appointment's made."

Kate reached across the table and took her hand. "Want a ride?"

"I'm perfectly capable of getting myself there."

"I know you are. That's not why I'm offering."

"No, you want to make sure I turn up."

Kate pulled her hand back and wrapped it around her glass.

"I'm sorry." Gina shook her head. "I'm sorry. I know you're just trying to help." She took hold of Kate's hand again, threading their fingers together. "My mouth runs away with me when I'm scared."

Kate squeezed her fingers gently. "Okay. So you tell me what you want."

"A ride would be very much appreciated."

Kate smiled and tossed her long auburn hair over her shoulder. "No problem. What time's the appointment?"

"Eleven."

"I'll pick you up at ten."

"Do you know where we have to go?"

Kate nodded as the front door bell rang out, setting Merlin off barking again. "I'm coming. Sammy, keep hold of Merlin please."

"Okay." Sammy wrapped her fingers around Merlin's collar and stroked her while Kate paid for their pizza and deposited the boxes on the table.

"Hands, Sammy," Gina told her daughter and hid a smile as Sammy looked down at her filthy appendages before trundling to the sink to wash them.

"One margarita pizza." Kate opened the box in front of Sammy then plonked a bottle of sauce next to it. "And madam's ketchup." She also put a glass of water on the other side of the box. "And please don't feed Merlin all the crusts. She'll get fat."

Sammy grinned unrepentantly. "But she likes 'em."

"And you like crisps. Does your mum let you have all the crisps you want?"

"No, but she should."

Kate laughed. "I'll be counting. Any more than two, and we'll have to talk about your crisp consumption."

Sammy looked aghast and Gina chuckled. "Talk about hitting a kid where it hurts, sergeant."

"Tough times call for tough measures." Kate held up the wine again. "The spare room's always made up. If you'd rather not drive home..." She waved the bottle slightly.

140

Gina pushed the glass closer to Kate and glanced at Sammy. "You better make it a big glass, then."

Kate frowned and looked towards Sammy. "Oh right. Yeah. On account of having to sleep with the freight train." Kate poured, and poured generously. "I have painkillers for the morning too."

"Bless you," Gina offered as she picked up the glass and offered a silent toast. "So, tell me what's going on at work."

Kate groaned. "Do I have to?"

"Yes. You're taking my mind off things."

Kate glanced at Sammy. "You sure?"

"Keep it PG rated and we're fine. Right, kiddo?"

"Yeppers," Sammy said around a mouthful of pizza. "I don't mind all that blood and stuff, but mum gets pukey."

"Pukey? Is that a word?" Kate asked.

"Totes."

Gina frowned.

"As in, totally," Kate said.

"How is it you understand what she says more than I do? You're older than me."

"I work with the youth element. We have to go on courses to be down with the kids."

Gina giggled. "Right. Another wonderful use of taxpayers' money."

"Precisely."

"Yeah, yeah. Start with the blood and guts," Sammy demanded.

"I'm actually working on a case right now that doesn't have any blood or guts."

"Boring."

"It's all about the bones."

Sammy's eyes widened. "Cool."

"Yep."

"Where did you find 'em?"

"On the beach. Well, sort of. There's this bunker—"

"The one near the golf club?" Sammy asked.

"Yes."

"That's so cool. I went down there—"

"Samantha Temple, when were you running around the bunker at Brancaster beach?" Gina plastered on her stern face and watched Sammy over the rim of her glass.

"Erm..." Sammy gulped. "Dad took me there ages and ages ago. When I was just a little kid."

Gina sighed. Matt the Prat strikes again. She shook her head. "Fine. But do not think for one second you'll be going down there again. Got it?"

"Yes, Mum."

"Good." She turned back to Kate. "Sorry. You were saying?"

Kate cleared her throat. "Yes, right. Well, it was sealed off after the flood, but the guys at the National Trust had decided they were going to open it up properly for the kids to go in and learn and stuff."

"But they found a skelington instead."

"Skeleton. Yes."

"Who is it?"

"We don't know. We're trying to find out. Actually, you might be able to help me with that, Gina."

"I don't understand."

"We have a picture of what he would have looked like. We think we know where he came from, but we can't identify him. No one seems to recognise him. That or someone's lying to me."

"Okay, and where do I fit into this?"

"You've lived around here all your life. If I show you the picture, would you see if you recognise him?"

"It's not a creepy picture, is it?"

Kate frowned. "Define creepy."

"Something that would give me nightmares."

Kate screwed up her face then laughed. "No. This just looks like a computer drawn face. Nothing creepy about it."

"Okay."

Sammy dropped her pizza slice back into the box and scooted closer to Gina. "Can I look too? I might recognise him too."

"I doubt that, and no."

Sammy crossed her arms and pouted. "But Kate said it's not creepy, so why can't I look too?"

"Because I said so." *We're still dealing with the aftermath of the last dead face you saw, kiddo. I'm not adding another one to the list of issues you've got to deal with. Likewise, if you're not thinking about it, I'm not bringing it up right now either.*

"Sorry, Sammy. Your mum says no, so you'll have to go back over there and see if you can sneak that third pizza crust to Merlin while I'm not looking."

Sammy shuffled back to her seat and grudgingly reached for the third crust while Kate handed Gina a folded page. Merlin put a paw on Sammy's knee when she held the crust below the table.

Kate offered her a wink and an eye roll in Gina's direction. Gina pretended not to see, content to let them bond over a little mum teasing. Part of her didn't want to unfold the paper. She had visions of seeing Connie's face and throwing up everywhere. The other part of her knew she was being stupid and delaying the inevitable was only drawing more attention to the fact that she was struggling with this simple task. *What if I do recognise him? Another person I know, dead. And if I don't, I'm putting myself through this for nothing. Not even going to be able to help Kate.*

"It's a picture of an old man. Somewhere between sixty and eighty. He looks like every picture of a grandad I remember seeing in books when I was a kid. There is nothing scary or worrying about this image in any way, Gina. I swear. But you don't have to look at it. I'm sorry I asked." She spoke quietly enough that Sammy couldn't have heard as she played with Merlin and stuffed more pizza in her mouth. Then she reached over to take the page away.

"I'm sorry—"

"Don't be. I'm sorry for asking."

Gina pulled the page away from Kate's hand. "No, I'm being an idiot." She unfolded it and stared at the picture. Kate was right, there was nothing odd about the picture. He just looked like an old man. A little thin, balding head, a scruff of a beard, weathered cheeks, and wrinkles around his eyes told a story of a life well lived. But a life no one could relate to him. The artist had managed to inject some sort of thought behind his eyes. A look that said more than the empty sockets of his skull could have ever conveyed to them. He looked sad. Lonely. And Gina wished she could ease that by giving him his name. But she couldn't remember it. "I know him, or knew him rather. But I can't remember his name."

Kate stared. "That's okay. Where do you remember him from? I can go and ask them."

"I think he worked at the golf course."

"The golf course? The one on Brancaster beach?"

Gina nodded. "Years and years ago."

"How do you know?"

"I worked for a catering agency when I first left school. They'd call in agency staff for the clubhouse when they had big events on. I worked two or three of them. Silver service. It was good money. A few royals in attendance."

"Really?"

"Yes. Prince Michael of Kent was there on one occasion."

"And you're sure this man worked there?"

"Yes. He worked on the actual golf course, though, so I didn't really have much to do with him. I'd see him sometimes when we were messing about up in the dunes. He was always trying to run the kids off if they were sneaking across the links. Some of the boys used to try and nick the golf balls."

"You were playing around there with your friends?"

"Yes. When I was sixteen, seventeen. When I was seeing Matt."

"Ah."

Gina smiled as she heard the penny drop. "Indeed." Sammy was conceived amongst those dunes.

"Right. Well that gives me a place to start tomorrow. I'll take Gareth along and see if we can finally get a name for Mr Bones."

"Gareth? Who's Gareth?"

"Oh, yeah. That's another thing that's happened today. I'm not working with Jimmy at the moment."

"How come? Is he off sick or something?"

"I wish. Gareth Collier was partnered with Tom, but let's just say there's been some friction and we've had to come up with another solution." Kate took another sip of her wine.

"I see. Did you not consider throwing them a ruler?"

Kate laughed and put her hand to her mouth too late to stop the fine spray of red wine that escaped.

"Ew," Sammy shouted, pointing and laughing. "Say it, don't spray it!"

"Thanks for the advice, kid." Kate grabbed a fist full of paper towels and mopped up the mess around her laughing guests.

"Sorry," Gina offered.

"No problem. I don't know why Stella and I didn't think of that. But we decided to split them up, and now I'm working with Gareth and Jimmy's buddied up with Tom."

"And how is Gareth doing?"

"I have to admit, given what Tom has reported about him, I didn't hold out too much hope, but I've been very pleasantly surprised so far." She threw away the napkins and poured more wine in their glasses. "He's been receptive to my feedback, asked useful, intelligent questions, and shown signs of a sense of humour."

"So, you'll make a copper out of him yet."

"The signs are good."

"But he didn't get on with Tom."

"Oil and water get on better. And Jimmy doesn't think much of him either. I'll have to ask him about that."

"Well, if he's doing his job and listening to you, what more can you ask of him?"

"Not much at this stage really. But it would be nice to figure out what the problem is." She shrugged. "You know me and puzzles."

Gina was beginning to.

"Ooh, one more question. Does the name Alison Temple mean anything to you?"

Gina froze. She hadn't heard that name in a long time. Most people around knew the history between her and her parents. They'd long since gotten over bringing it up and watching her react to the latest news from Howard and Alison Temple. Ten years. It had been ten long years since Gina had told her parents that she was pregnant, and refused to abide by her father's wishes and get rid of the baby. Get rid of Sammy. Gina looked at Sammy. She was a pain in the arse most days, and more trouble the rest of the time, but Gina wouldn't be without her. She was her life.

"That's our surname," Sammy supplied.

"I know, kiddo. That's why I wondered. Gina are you okay?"

Gina nodded slowly.

"You sure? You've gone grey. Sammy, get a glass of water for your mum, please."

Sammy pushed her chair noisily away from the table and ran to the kitchen sink.

"I'm sorry. You don't have to say anything. I get it."

"My mum."

Kate nodded. "I get it. I'm sorry I asked."

"Do you know her, Mum?" Sammy asked as she carefully put the half-full glass of water in front of her.

"From a long time ago, baby. Before you were born."

Sammy's eyes widened. "Wow. That must've been ages, then."

Gina snorted. "Something like that." There was nothing like kids to bring you back down to earth with a bump. And Sammy excelled at it. She caught Kate's eye and mouthed the word "later" before taking a sip of water. "Thank you, Sammy."

"Welcome." Sammy climbed back on her chair and started in on the last slice of pizza. "Can I watch some cartoons after tea?"

"Depends," Kate replied.

"On what?"

"Do you have any homework to do?"

Sammy folded the pizza slice in half. "Nope. I'm all catched up."

"Caught up," Kate corrected.

"I'm all caught up." Sammy rolled her eyes.

"Okay. But only for an hour. Then you're getting in the bath before bed. Kate, do you have something I can stick on madam there for her to sleep in?" Gina asked.

"I think I can come up with something suitable. I've got a straitjacket in the loft, I think."

"We're staying here tonight?" Sammy asked with a delighted squeal.

"God, only if you never make that noise again," Gina responded.

"Cool."

"I'm glad you approve."

"Mum?"

"Yes, Sammy?"

"What's a straitjacket?"

Gina looked at Kate and waved her hand in invitation. "The floor's all yours, big mouth."

Kate gulped.

Gina pulled her legs up under herself and settled back on to the comfy sofa.

"Coffee?" Kate held out a bottle of Bailey's Irish Cream.

"Well, it'd be rude not to, I suppose."

Kate disappeared back into the kitchen and Gina clicked off the cartoon show that Sammy had been watching earlier. Giant green turtles were just not her thing.

When Kate handed her the drink and sat down next to her, she smiled and took a warming sip.

"Oh, that's good."

"Glad madam approves." She took her own sip and let out a satisfied "Ah" as she leaned back and got herself comfortable. "Sorry about earlier."

"What?"

"Alison Temple."

"Oh, right."

Kate's eyebrows climbed towards her hairline. "I remember you said they lived close by and refused to see you, but I didn't think you meant practically the next village."

Gina frowned. "I'm sorry, I thought I'd said where they were." She shrugged. "It wouldn't make a difference, anyway. They could be in the next village or the next continent. They don't want anything to do with me, and that's just fine by me."

"Really?"

Gina nodded as she stared into her mug. "There are more important things in life than trying to please people who can never be pleased and judge based on one mistake."

"Were you never close to your parents?"

"No." She rested the mug in the arm of the sofa and rested her head back.

"I can't imagine having parents around and not being in touch with them."

Gina bristled at the judgement she heard in Kate's words. "It was their choice, Kate. Not mine."

"Wait, I'm sorry. I didn't mean that to sound funny or anything. I was merely trying to imagine how what they did couldn't hurt you. And I can't imagine that scenario. No matter what, they're your parents, right?" She wrapped her fingers around Gina's hand. "I'm sorry if that sounded like anything else."

"They turned their backs on me. I was just a kid, I was scared, and he gave me a choice. Their way or get out and do it alone."

"What was their way?"

"An abortion."

"And you didn't want that?"

She shook her head. "It's the right thing for some people. Maybe everyone in the right circumstances, but it wasn't what I wanted. I wanted my baby. I wanted Sammy." She smiled as she spoke her name. "I knew I'd regret it if I agreed to what my father wanted."

"What about your mum? What did she want you to do?"

Gina shrugged. "I have no idea. She only ever went along with what dad wanted." She took another sip of her drink. "It was like she had no opinions of her own. She was just an extension of him. I always hated that. It was like I could never get away from him. Even when he wasn't in the house."

"What did they both do while you were growing up?"

"Dad was a farmer. He worked for the farm on the Holkham Estate."

"And your mum?"

"She did the books for the pub in the village. Then she started picking up a few other businesses' accounting work too. The village shop before it closed, the art studio, a couple of the campsites. That sort of thing. Why do you need to see her? Can you tell me?"

Kate shook her head. "I'm sorry, I really shouldn't say anything, Gina."

"Is she in trouble?"

"What makes you ask that?"

"You're a cop, Kate. You came across her name during an investigation."

"Fair point." She sighed heavily, clearly weighing her options before she continued. "Between us?"

Gina nodded. "Of course.

"I don't think she is, no. She's been doing the books at the nursing home for a few months. I just need to talk to her about some of the accounts from before she started there."

"Oh." Gina wasn't sure how to ask what she wanted to know. She wasn't even sure she really wanted to know, but she slowly found the words. "I always wondered if Dad was...well, he was always this larger-than-life personality, you know. Controlling, I suppose. But I always wondered if there was, I don't know, more to it. I guess."

"You want to know if he's abusive towards her?"

She nodded. "It doesn't make sense to me that she was so far up his arse. I mean, she's a clever woman. She had to have her own opinions on stuff, you know? So why did she always parrot his?"

"Do you want me to give you my opinion after I speak to her?"

"Would you?"

Kate frowned. "On one condition."

"What?"

"It's Kate's opinion. Not Detective Sergeant Brannon's."

"I understand." She finished the last mouthful of her coffee and put the mug on the coffee table. "Thank you." She let Kate ease her into an embrace, and rested her head on Kate's shoulder. "It wasn't always so bad."

"It rarely is, darling."

"Know-it-all." She pushed Kate in the ribs, then settled against her comfortably again. "She was a fabulous cook."

"Yeah? Is that where you learnt how to cook?"

"Must be. But, God, Mum's Sunday roast was a thing of legend. Yorkshire puddings as big as your head. I used to think that the only reason I had friends at school was because they wanted an invite to Sunday tea."

"You'll have to make me a roast then. I used to love Gran's roast dinner."

"You're on."

Kate ran her fingers gently through Gina's hair. Her eyelids grew heavy, her heartbeat slowed, and her limbs felt heavy as slumber called.

CHAPTER 16

There was one thing Kate hated about the beach. Sand. And there was nowhere she hated it more than in her shoes. Today was no exception. The short walk from the beach car park to the clubhouse entrance had plagued her with her nemesis.

Gareth pushed the buzzer while she hopped on one leg and tried to get the bloody stuff to shift to at least a comfortable temporary location within her shoe. But it was more stubborn than she had time for.

The door swung open while Gareth was laughing at her, and they were greeted by a short, wizened woman, with a slightly humped back, a crooked smile, and a windswept hairdo that reminded Kate of Doc Brown in *Back to the Future*. It wasn't a good look.

"Good morning. We'd like to see Mr Spink, please."

"And who might you be?" she asked.

"I'm Detective Sergeant Kate Brannon, and this is Detective Constable Gareth Collier."

"I'll see if he's available." She opened the door wide enough to admit them into the hallway. "I won't be long." She disappeared down the corridor, leaving them standing in the dark wood-panelled hall.

"Well this is..." Gareth paused as he searched for the right word to describe the decor.

"Testosterone-fuelled decor at its finest?" Kate sniggered.

Gareth chuckled. "Something like that."

"Not your style, Gazza?"

He scowled playfully at her. "No. I'm a metrosexual kinda guy." He held his hands out. "Can't you tell?"

Kate looked him up and down. He was certainly a modern bloke. His suit was sharp, well-fitted, and not cheap. That was for sure. It showed off his broad shoulders and trim waist, and hinted at the muscular physique she knew was underneath. His hair, as always, was gelled back neatly, parted to the left, but made no attempt to hide the pronounced widow's peak in the centre. If anything, he styled his hair to show it off. It seemed to enhance the symmetry of his face, the deep set of his blue eyes, the straight nose, and the wide, full lips. His strong, square, clean-shaven jaw completed the picture of a very good looking guy. And one who knew how to make the best of what he had.

"Is that what they're calling those *mani*cures you get these days?"

He dropped his arms to his side. "Very funny."

"I thought so." She winked. Just to be sure he knew she was messing with him. She didn't fancy dealing with one of the tantrums she'd seen him throw at Tom's offhand comments.

"Mr Spink says he has a few minutes for you," the woman said from behind them.

"Thank you." Kate followed her down the hall and up a flight of stairs. "Is he not in his office?"

"No, he's upstairs overseeing the remodelling of the restaurant."

"Ah."

The upstairs was as different as you could get to the man-cave downstairs. Light filled the room from the huge expanse of windows all around them. The pale grey-green walls seemed to soak it up and reflect it back with a pearlescent sheen. There were men on scaffolds all around them, fixing pictures to walls, touching up gloss on the coving, and fitting ceiling lights.

Mr Spink was at the far end of the room, amongst dozens of wicker chairs stacked in the corner, seemingly counting them as he spoke into his phone. He waved them over when he saw them and ended his conversation as they got to him. "Detective Sergeant Brannon, how lovely to see you again. Everything okay, I trust?

"Yes. I wondered if you could take a look at a picture for me and let me know if you recognize this person?"

He reached into his breast pocket and pulled out a pair of spectacles. "Of course."

Kate handed him the picture.

He frowned at it, then squinted his eyes. He cocked his head to one side. "Do you have a pencil?"

"A pencil? No. Why?"

"Well, I just wanted to see something." He looked around the room and wandered off a moment before coming back holding a decorator's pencil. He leaned over one of the stacked tables and shaded a full beard on to the picture, filled in heavier eyebrows, and drew a pair of glasses on to the face. "Yes, thought so." He took off down across the room and down the stairs.

"Mr Spink, wait." Kate followed him back down the stairs and into his office, where he was booting up his computer. "Who is it?"

"One moment, Detective."

Gareth came in behind her, and they both stared at Mr Spink as he stared at his computer screen.

"There." He turned the monitor towards them. "Alan Parr." He pointed to the picture on the screen. "He was the head groundskeeper here at one time."

Kate felt like shouting "hallelujah" and waving her hands in the air like they'd just scored the World Cup-winning goal, but it wasn't the time or the place. But finally, finally, they were starting to get somewhere. A name. They had his name.

"When was that?" Gareth took his notepad from his pocket and began making notes.

"Retired in 2002. We had a party here for him. He was a lovely chap. Hard-working, salt-of-the-earth type. Do anything for a friend. If ever we were in a pickle, Alan's the one I wanted to help. And my word, did he know how to keep a lawn. Grass hasn't been the same since he retired." He held his hands out. "Don't tell Malcolm I said that."

Kate smiled. "No problem." She winked. "If I can get a printout of that record."

"Certainly." Mr Spink clicked the mouse and sent the document to the printer. "It'll just take a moment."

"Thanks. Does Alan have any family?"

Mr Spink rubbed his chin. "If memory serves, he was a lifelong bachelor. No kids, parents long deceased. I couldn't tell you if he had any brothers or sisters, though."

"Do you know where he was living?"

"I believe he lived in Ringstead when he worked here. Couldn't tell you if he still has the house there or not. We didn't keep in touch. You know how these things go. We all promise to keep in touch, we all mean it at the time, but then things change."

"It happens, Mr Spink."

He nodded sadly. "Unfortunately. When he moved into the nursing home I went to see him a bit more at first. It was just down the road. I'd pop in on my way home, have a cuppa with him." He smiled at whatever memory he was recalling. "Then he seemed to stop recognising me. He'd stare at me with this blank look and ask who I was sometimes. Other times I'd be talking to him and he'd zone out. When he came back, he'd ask the same question I'd just answered." He wiped at his eye, subtly removing the tear that threatened to spill. "I let my own ego get in the way, I suppose. I went to take him a Christmas card back at the beginning of December in 2013. A few days before the flood, in actual fact. When I walked in he didn't recognise me at all." He shook his head. "I couldn't bring myself to go back again."

Kate watched him as she absorbed the first concrete corroboration that their victim had lived in the nursing home. Someone who not only thought he'd lived there, but had visited him there. Edgar Spink had sat in there with Alan Parr on numerous occasions. Finally it felt as though details of the case were shifting into place. "Do you know if anyone else on your staff kept in touch with him?"

"I'm afraid I couldn't tell you, but you're more than welcome to ask."

"Thank you."

"May I ask why you're looking for Alan?"

"I'm sorry, I can't go into that right now. Ongoing investigation."

"Was it..." he glanced out of the window toward the bunker on the beach. The tear in his eye finally fell as the realisation struck. "Was it Alan we found down there?"

"I'm afraid I can't comment on that at this time."

He met her eyes, understanding all she couldn't say. "When you can comment, Detective, we'd like very much to pay our respects to Alan here at the golf club. He was a friend. Despite how it must seem."

"We're all guilty of letting life get in the way of spending time with those we care about sometimes, Mr Spink. Especially if it's painful for us," Kate said softly. "It's things like this that help us to re-evaluate those choices and prevent us repeating the mistake."

"Very wise for one so young."

Kate waved her hand. "I'm not so young. And especially in this job. You age quickly. It's a bit like dog years. By the time we get to thirty in the police force, we're actually a hundred and two." She picked up the pages from the printer and held them up. "Thank you for this, and your time, Mr Spink. I'll talk to Malcolm again, if you don't mind. I'm assuming they worked quite closely together before Mr Parr retired."

"Yes, they did. Malcolm was practically Alan's apprentice." He glanced at the clock. "They'll be coming in for morning break in a couple of minutes. Can I get you a coffee while you wait?"

"Thanks, that'd be great."

Mr Spink left the room, and Kate turned to Gareth. "Bingo."

"Finally, sarge. We're getting somewhere."

Kate nodded. "Once we've spoken to Malcolm, we'll get this info back to the office. I need to run an errand for a couple of hours, and this afternoon we need to go and talk to Alison Temple. But while I'm out, I want you to find everything you can get me on Alan Parr. I want a next of kin if you can find one, Gareth."

"I'll do my best, sarge."

"I know you will." She handed him the pages. "I trust you."

Gareth's face lit up and she wondered if anyone had ever said that to him before.

"I won't let you down. Whatever there is to find about Mr Parr, I'll find it."

CHAPTER 17

Gina fiddled with the seatbelt as her hands shook.

"Do you want me to come in with you?" Kate asked.

She shook her head. "No, thanks. I think I need to do this part on my own."

"Okay." Kate leaned across the console and kissed her gently on the mouth. "It'll be okay, Gina. It really will."

Gina exhaled shakily. "I hope so."

"When you meet Jodi...don't be too shocked. Okay?"

"What do you mean?"

"She knows what you're going through," Kate said and ran her hand down Gina's cheek.

Gina flinched. Kate's meaning seemed clear to her. Jodi bore some sort of scar herself, maybe something she couldn't hide as easily as Gina could.

"Just give her a chance to help you and she will."

"How can you be so sure?" Everyone's scars were different. Everyone wore them differently, reacted to them differently. How could Kate be so sure that this woman was the one to help her?

"Meet her. You'll know what I mean then." She reached down and unclipped Gina's seatbelt. "Go on, or you'll be late." Kate pointed to the single-storey building they sat outside. "Just buzz the intercom and the reception staff will let you in."

"The doors don't open automatically?"

"It's a psych unit, Gina. They have safety protocols in place to keep the patients who need to stay in, well, in. One of those involves a lot of card-entry doors, and another is a front door that is only opened with a security badge or a buzz from the front desk."

"I don't want to go in there." The nondescript building suddenly felt more like a prison or a fortress.

"Don't worry. They don't keep people in who don't need to be there. More often than not, they have to let people out who they shouldn't rather than the other way round." Kate chuckled mirthlessly.

"You sound like you've had a lot of experience with places like this."

"Unfortunately. Every police officer does. A lot of crimes are committed by those who need help. Mental health help, and they can't get it, or don't take their meds because they don't trust the people trying to help them. Or the really sad cases where you're trying to talk someone down off the edge."

"The edge of what?"

"Life, usually."

"You mean suicide?"

Kate nodded. "Sometimes."

"How do you deal with stuff like that?"

Kate gazed at her. "I have to. To make sure I'm there when I can really make a difference, I have to deal with it." She squeezed Gina's hand. "When I can stop a really bad person from hurting someone who doesn't deserve it. Or so that I can catch the bastards and make sure they're punished for what they've done. So that I can at least give the victims and their families that comfort."

"Hero complex, huh?" Gina asked with a smile.

"You already knew that, gorgeous. Now get, before Jodi comes out here to see what's keeping us so long."

Gina opened the door and walked the twenty steps to the intercom before she had the chance to think about what she was doing or where she was going again. All she could think about was Kate, and how she'd been there for her to stop the scars Gina bore on her body becoming scars that her daughter would bear mentally for the rest of her life.

She didn't remember buzzing in, or waiting in the reception area for Jodi. She was too busy trying to control her breathing. To stop her fingers from becoming the claw-like talons that were a classic symptom of her panic attacks. Slowly she became aware of a soft voice telling her to breathe, a hand rubbing her back as she sat with her head between her knees. *Jesus, not again.*

"I'm sorry," she managed between the panting intake of breath. Gina tried to force her lungs to expel the air she was pulling in far too quickly, but they wouldn't listen. Black spots swarmed before her eyes, and she knew that the easiest thing would be to allow her body to shut down. To pass out and let everything reset to zero. To give in and let the fear win. But what was the point in that? What did that gain her? What was she here for if not to get over her bloody fears?

She tried to remember the things Kate had told her to help her ground herself. Five things I can see. Five.

"Lights," she whispered.

"I'm sorry, what?" the voice beside her asked.

But Gina ignored it. She couldn't see a voice.

"White tiles." She blinked, still drawing in breath too rapidly. "Magazines."

"Oh, I see. Good work. Two more."

"Chairs."

"Good. Last one."

"Shoes."

"Excellent, your breath's slowing a little. Four things you can hear."

"Buzzing."

The fluorescent lights overhead hummed like an angry bee about her head.

"Annoying, isn't it?"

Gina nodded. Her neck was stiff. "Telephone." The shrill tone was monotonous and seemed to never end.

"Yep. Two more."

"My heartbeat."

"Glad it's still there."

"Your voice."

"Will always be annoying. Now three things you can feel."

"Denim," she said touching her stiff fingers to her jeans and running them along the seam of her right leg.

"Good, what else?"

"Wool." She touched the deep green polo neck jumper she wore, and noted that her hands weren't as stiff. Her legs didn't feel so full of pins and needles either.

"Good."

"And your hand on my back."

"Excellent. How about two things you can smell?"

"Antiseptic."

The woman laughed. "Well, we are in a hospital."

"And your perfume."

"Angel. Do you like it?"

Gina nodded and sat up in her chair. She stretched her legs out in front of herself and closed her eyes as she rested her head against the wall behind her.

"Finish strong, Gina. Something you can taste?"

Gina smiled and flexed her fingers. "Victory."

"Oh, I do love a fighter." She squeezed Gina's arm. "Well done. I thought for a minute there I was going to be picking you up off the floor."

Gina snorted. "You almost were."

"Welcome to the Reman Unit."

Gina opened her eyes and looked into the face of the woman who had been talking to her. Her breath caught as she stared.

"Don't start panicking again, Gina." The woman smiled to diffuse the comment, but she was clearly steeling herself for an adverse reaction.

"Jodi?" Gina asked in a quiet voice.

The woman nodded. "I know it's a shock, but as you can see," she pointed to her own face, "I do know what you're dealing with."

Jodi's face was terribly disfigured. The right side of her face was a patchwork of skin that all looked to be different colours. All pale, but some paler than the rest. Her nose was more of a beak. Hooked but tiny, almost lost in the centre of her face, like it had been burned away and all that was left was what had been bone. Her right eyelid never closed. It never blinked. It wasn't there, and inside the socket was an eyeball that looked flat, lifeless. The hair over what was left of her right ear was missing mostly. A huge patch with just the odd tuft of blond hair here and there.

"What happened?" Gina asked without thinking. "I'm sorry, I shouldn't have asked."

"Why not? I'm going to be asking you the same question later. Turnabout's fair play, right?"

Gina sat quietly. Not sure what to say.

"Acid attack. An ex didn't want me to be with someone else, so decided to mutilate me with battery acid."

"Jesus."

Jodi shook her head. "No, sadly, he wasn't there that day."

"I'm sorry."

"Don't be. It wasn't your fault, and you haven't done anything wrong."

"Does it hurt?"

"Should we go to a more private room? Are you up to walking yet?"

Gina nodded and followed Jodi down a short corridor to an empty room with a small coffee table in the centre and two chairs.

"And yes. It still hurts. Inside and out, unfortunately." She smiled sadly and indicated for Gina to sit down. "The scars on my face don't hurt so much as the damage I sustained to my trachea. I get a lot of infections as a result, and I feel like I always have a cough. It gets irritating. My eye is always dry. The socket I mean. Because my tear duct was burnt out, I have to use drops to try and lubricate the socket. Or wear an eye patch. I haven't decided yet which I'm going to settle on. That's why I've only got a temporary eye." She tapped the false eye.

Gina shuddered and crossed her legs.

"Sorry, did that gross you out?"

"Yeah."

"Sorry. I forget about that sometimes."

"Is he in prison?"

"Who?"

"Your ex."

"She was."

"Was?"

Jodi nodded. "She was released five years ago after serving four years."

"Four years? But she tried to kill you."

Jodi shook her head. "She was ill. The judge passed a sentence of indeterminate length and she wouldn't be released until she no longer posed a danger to society. After four years she was released when her doctors assessed her to meet that criteria."

"Bloody hell."

"Yeah. It wasn't the best news I ever got. I couldn't be at the sentencing. I was in hospital having another operation."

"Another one?"

"Yes. So far I've had almost two hundred surgeries."

Gina stared at Jodi then glanced down at her own covered chest. She felt pathetic. This woman had gone through hell and on the other side she was helping other people with their own demons. She was so strong. Strong enough to give her strength to others. Gina couldn't imagine what it must be like to be that strong, that compassionate. It was as compelling as it was intimidating, and Gina was torn between basking in the warmth of her gaze and running from the overwhelming intensity of the woman. *What right do I have to sit in the same room as her?*

"I'm sorry, I have to go."

Jodi frowned. "Why?"

Gina shook her head. "I just do."

"I've seen that look before, Gina. It's the one that says my own scars are nothing by comparison, so why am I here? It's the look that tells me you're questioning your own worthiness to feel the way you feel." She reached forward and took Gina's hand. "You have every right to feel exactly how you feel. You have every right to feel violated. To feel angry. To feel hurt. Every single right." She squeezed. "My history doesn't lessen yours. It's simply mine. There is no right or wrong, no table of comparison. There's no judgement on what scars someone has to bear to justify this feeling or that one. It simply is. You feel what you feel, I feel what I feel. We deal with those feelings together. And the rest of the world," she said with a small conspiratorial smile, "well, they can just go and fuck themselves." She let go of Gina's hand and sat back in her chair. "If you want to leave, I won't stop you. But I can guarantee that you'll end up regretting it. And I think you know that. Don't you?"

Gina felt herself nodding, but it was like she had no control over her body.

"You don't have to talk to me, but if you want to stay, if you want to work through whatever it is you feel, then this is the only way I know how to do it. It was the only way that worked for me. And believe me, I tried a lot of different shit. Drink, drugs, suicide. None of it got me anywhere. Well, they did, but nowhere that I wanted to be."

"I have a daughter."

"All the more reason to avoid those coping methods then," Jodi said. "It can't hurt to give this a go. If it doesn't work, what have you lost? A few hours of your time. Okay, you can't get them back, but it won't cost you anything, and you can always say stop." She leaned forward and rested her elbows on her knees. "You're the one in control here. No one else, Gina. You." She caught Gina's gaze and held it. "Do you understand?"

Gina nodded.

"Good." She clasped her fingers between her knees. "So, where do you want to start?"

"Aren't you meant to tell me where to start?"

"Am I? I thought this was actually supposed to be all about you. Not me." She laughed gently. "But I usually find the beginning a good place to start. Why don't you tell me what happened?"

"Kate didn't tell you?"

Jodi shook her head. "I prefer to hear what you have to say. Someone else will always put their slant on an event. Makes it their story, then. You know?"

"Yeah. Might have made this easier, though."

"Easy doesn't always get the job done."

Gina took a deep breath and searched for the right words. She'd repeated them so many times to the police that she found they came quite easily. "I was attacked by Ally Robbins. She forced me into my own house with her. I went to make sure she stayed away from Sammy, my daughter."

"And what did she do?" Jodi asked her after a few moments silence.

"She wanted information. About Sammy's dad. He was working for her, smuggling drugs out of the harbour at Brandale Stiathe. But she couldn't get hold of him. He'd been arrested and was basically ratting her out to the police. Selling out her whole operation to try and reduce his sentence. She didn't know that. She just couldn't find him, so she came after me."

"Are you and Matt still together?"

"God, no. I haven't been with Matt in a decade. Matt was a mistake."

"One that left you with a daughter?"

"Yes. Sammy's the only reason I have—had—anything to do with Matt at all."

"So she wanted information about Matt?"

"Yes. She tried to get it out of me with a gutting knife."

"As in a fish-gutting knife?"

Gina nodded. "She tied me up. With my hands over my head tied to the banister railing. I was in the hallway. Right in front of the front door. I have to pass by that spot every single time I go in or out of my house. Every time I go upstairs to the toilet, I have to walk past that spot." Gina stared out, not seeing, not blinking. Her vision turned inwards, her eyes seeing Ally's face as she twisted the knife in the air in front of her. "She threatened to take me on to her boat and feed me into the bait station." She shuddered. "I can still see that grinder in my mind. It's effectively a massive blender. So big and powerful that it grinds bone and muscle and sinew to a pulp. She was going to turn me into bait."

Jodi waited before saying, "But she didn't."

"No, she didn't."

"So what did she do?"

Gina wrapped her arms around her body, trying to find a little warmth. "She cut my top off me and started to use her knife." She ran a finger across her own belly. "She sliced me here first." Then she traced a line across the top of her breast. "Then here." The other breast. "Here. And here." She finished with the second cut down her belly. "Then she got bored and decided she wanted to play noughts and crosses on my back. Then it was solitaire, so she started to carve out the game board on me." She hadn't realised she was crying until she felt the tears drip on to her hand.

"Then what happened?"

"Kate. Kate happened." Gina smiled through her tears. "She saved me."

"How?"

"She hit Ally with a rounders bat after she crept in through the back while her colleague distracted Ally at the front door."

Jodi smiled. "That sounds like the Kate Brannon I know."

"How do you know her?"

"She was the detective on my case. So this happened six weeks ago?"

"Yes."

"So it hasn't gone to court yet."

"No. We're still waiting for a date."

"In the meantime, she's in prison, and you feel what?"

Gina shrugged. She didn't want to voice her fears. To Jodi or anyone else. She just wanted to forget it ever happened and carry on.

"Come on, Gina. Tell me how you feel about what happened."

"I don't know what you want me to say."

"I don't want you to say anything. I want you be honest with yourself. Forget that I'm here. Pretend that you're in the room on your own."

"I can't do that."

"Close your eyes."

Gina frowned but did as Jodi asked.

"Good. Now, imagine you're here on your own. Just talking to yourself. What do you want, Gina?"

"I want for it to have never happened. I want to see myself when I look in the mirror, not this stranger that looks back at me. I want to be me again. I want to see me again. Not this patchwork quilt that she made me. I want to look at myself and believe that someone else could find me attractive again, because I certainly don't." She slumped in her chair. "I want to not be so vain that a few scars matter so much. I want to be strong enough that I can walk into somewhere new and not have a panic attack. I want to be able to say yeah, that happened, but I'm still here. I want to be what my daughter needs to get her through her own ordeal."

She let the silence stretch taut between them. She pictured it forming like a spiderweb across the room. Silken and shimmering in the light, but cold. So cold. She could see her breath beading on the strands, thickening them and adding moisture in the frozen air. The spiderweb turned instead to a giant snowflake. A fragile, brittle shield that would shatter and melt at the first touch.

"Instead of what?" Jodi asked quietly.

"I'm sorry?"

"You want to be what your daughter needs. You say that as though you aren't that at the moment."

"No, I don't think I am."

"Then what are you?"

"Someone she feels she needs to protect."

"Why do you say that?"

"Because she hid the fact that she was being bullied from me because I was dealing, or rather not dealing, with my own issues instead of helping her through hers."

"You think you're a bad mum?"

The statement held no judgement in it, yet Gina couldn't help but bristle. "I would do anything for my daughter. She's my whole world."

Jodi held up her hands to placate Gina. "I'm not suggesting you're a bad mum. Not for a moment. Quite the opposite. I think a mother who worries that she's doing what's best for her child is the epitome of a good mother. We're only human, Gina. We all make mistakes sometimes. If we don't question what we're doing and why sometimes, how can we be sure we are doing the right thing. I merely ask if you think you're a good or bad mum. Because I think motherhood is a huge part of your identity. And if you see yourself as failing in that part of your life, I think it will have major implications on other aspects too. Do you understand what I mean?"

Gina stared at her, not quite ready to let go of the anger. The anger felt good. It felt warm. It thawed out the cold fear and dread that seemed to settle in her soul.

"Honestly. I'm sorry I offended you."

Gina closed her eyes and let out a deep breath. "No, I'm sorry for flying off the handle. That was uncalled for." She smiled. "Did I also mention that I'm angry all the time?"

Jodi chuckled. "I'd be more worried if you weren't angry. It's a natural and understandable reaction to what's happened to you."

"Were you angry?"

"Some days I still am."

Gina was surprised and it must have shown on her face.

"Like I said, we're all human." She shrugged. "I spent a long time being angry, and some days it's hard to shake. In many ways, I found the anger helped me. At first, anyway. It let me function and make it through the pain. It gave me the drive I needed to get through another day filled with painful surgeries or the trial. But then it got to the point where it was holding me back. While you are angry, rightfully so, it doesn't seem to be the prevailing emotion you're suffering, Gina."

Jodi was right and Gina knew it. It wasn't anger that made her want to stay in bed and let the rest of the world pass her by. It wasn't anger that made her cry in the middle of the night. It wasn't anger that made her freeze when Kate touched her.

"So what is it?"

"I'm scared," Gina whispered and let the tears fall. She cried for the pain she could still feel from each of her healed wounds. Imaginary pain that never seemed to go. Pain that ate at each nerve like a flame devouring it. She cried for the vision of herself that she would never see again. She cried for the mother she could never be again. The more carefree Gina who had never seen anything to make her question everything and everyone around her. She wept for the loss of innocence—both hers and Sammy's.

Jodi held her, whispering soft noises meant to soothe her.

They didn't. They reminded her of the way she held Sammy when she cried, and she wept harder.

"Let it out, Gina. Let it all go then we can get to work on getting you back to normal."

Gina wished it were that simple, but she knew she'd be doing a lot more crying before she was normal again. If she ever got there at all.

Gina didn't remember finishing the session with Jodi or walking out of the hospital. She didn't remember getting back into Kate's car or taking hold of her hand. But she must have done. After all, they were sat quietly together, side by side, holding hands, watching a small bird hop across the grass picking up leaf litter and hunting for worms. She tried to remember what kind of bird it was, with its small, dark brown body and yellow beak. Starling? Wren? Did it matter?

She felt heavy. Numb. As though her limbs belonged to someone else. The only thing she could feel was Kate's thumb, stroking the skin at the back of her hand softly. Backwards and forwards in a steady circle. One inch in one direction, then the same back. It was hypnotic. Grounding. Something nice to focus on in a world that was ugly and hurt.

"You okay?" Kate's voice was barely above a whisper as she continued to stare out of the window.

Gina shook her head and swallowed.

Kate squeezed her hand gently then continued to rub with her thumb. "What do you need me to do? How can I help you?"

The bird dipped its head quickly and snapped up a tiny worm, gobbling it back in one before it carried on scratching at the ground with its claws. It lifted leaves with its beak and continued its hunt for the next morsel.

"Just be you," Gina said quietly.

A second bird joined the first, scraping at the ground, worrying the decaying debris, and the territorial hunter. The first bird squawked loudly and flapped its wings to scare away the interloper, but it seemed not to care. It merely turned its head from side to side and scuffed the ground.

"Is that enough?" Kate's voice was thick with emotion. She was clearly holding back tears, and Gina was grateful for it. She wasn't sure she could handle Kate's emotion on top of her own right now. As selfish as that sounded—as it felt—she knew she was at her limit for the moment, and any more could send her into meltdown. Kate's tender show of support was what she needed. No overly emotional displays, no overt PDAs; just holding her hand and showing her that she would be there. Always.

"It will be."

CHAPTER 18

Kate stared out of the windscreen. The field ahead sat fallow; the few geese still around feasted on the grubs and worms hiding amongst the rotting wheat stalks. The wind rustled slightly, making the hedges rattle their bare twigs, and the December sun sat low on the horizon, weak and watery, but just enough to make her squint.

"You okay, sarge?" Gareth asked.

Kate glanced at him then looked down the road to check the junction. "Yeah, why?"

"You've been checking this empty junction for three minutes now."

"Fuck off." She looked at him and clocked the raised eyebrow. "Really?"

"Really."

"Bollocks. Sorry, Gareth. Million miles away." She pulled out into the junction and headed for South Creake.

"I figured that out. Want to talk about it?"

Kate shook her head. She knew Gina wouldn't want her discussing things between them with someone else, especially not someone she worked with. "I'm just thinking about this case. Something about Mr Parr and this fraud stuff seems off."

"How do you mean?"

"Well, think about it. If we go and see Mrs Temple and she tells us that this Alan Parr is the mysterious 3840 that the government is paying a subsidy on, then not only is someone at the nursing home lying about not recognising him, but they also know what happened to him."

"Or they killed him," Gareth said.

"Or they killed him," Kate conceded.

"Which gives them a very good motive to lie to us about not recognising him."

"It does."

Gareth grinned. "It also explains why they put his body in the bunker."

"That's the part I can't get my head around."

"What do you mean? It's simple. The bunker kept the body hidden and the guilty party can go on claiming the benefits and reap the rewards. It was a good plan."

"Hm. Except for the obvious flaws in it."

"What obvious flaws?"

"Well, there are two flaws with that plan."

"Two?"

"Make that three."

"Three?"

"Yes. One, how did they get the body there?"

"Car?"

"The road flooded right after Malcolm Slater checked the bunker was empty. So no car could get down there."

"Carried it?"

Kate shook her head. "No way. That's a half-mile walk, maybe a bit more. No way could someone have carried him all that way to the bunker in the wind and rain that was coming off the sea that night. We were looking at ninety-miles-an-hour winds at some point. Have you ever carried a person?"

He shook his head.

"Well trust me, trying to carry a hundred and eighty pounds of dead dude into that wind is not going to happen."

"Dragged him through the water, then."

Kate tittered. "Clutching at straws now, Gareth."

"Fine, I don't know."

"Me neither. Then we have issue number two."

"Which is?"

"How did this person know the bunker would flood and get blocked off?"

"Locals maybe would know that."

Kate shook her head. "And the third one. How would they know, even if it did flood and get sealed, that it would be left sealed?"

Gareth frowned. "Ah, I get you. Otherwise the body would be found, identified, and they wouldn't be able to claim the money anyway."

"Exactly."

"Then how did it happen?"

Kate shook her head. "I haven't the foggiest right now." She indicated right and pulled up outside a small cottage.

A creek ran through all the gardens of the row of cottages, and they all had small bridges from the road to their front doors. The one they approached was a very pretty cottage, with climbing roses going up trellises outside the front and in an arch over the yellow front door.

"Quaint," Gareth said.

"Yeah." Kate knocked and waited for an answer. Gina's question played on her mind as much as the questions she needed to ask about the case. Were Alan Parr and the mysterious 3840 one and the same? If so, either someone was running a big gamble on Alan Parr's body never turning up, or there was a lot more going on in Brancombe House than Diana Lodge knew about.

"Hello." A woman in her mid to late forties opened the door, wiping her hands with a dish towel. Her dark hair was shot through at the temples with grey and tied back in a ponytail. Her eyebrows arched elegantly over azure blue eyes that looked just like Gina's. Even if she hadn't been expecting to see Gina's mother today, Kate would have picked this woman out in a room full of people. Their build and height were the same. The way she stood, with her shoulders slightly drooped forward, was the same.

"Mrs Temple?" Kate asked politely.

"Who's asking?"

"I'm Detective Sergeant Kate Brannon, and this is Detective Constable Collier."

"Of course. Diana said you needed to speak with me. Yes, I'm Alison Temple. Come in." She ushered them through the door. "Can I get you a drink? Tea? Coffee?"

"Coffee would be good, thanks," Gareth said.

"Only if you're making one. Don't go to any trouble on our account," Kate added.

"It's no trouble. It's nice to have bit of company, truth be told." Mrs Temple fussed with the kettle, mugs, and the milk before setting cups in front of them at a pine, country-style kitchen table. "I don't get many visitors, and I live alone. It's nice to be able to fuss once in a while."

"Oh, I thought you were married."

"I was." She glanced out of the window. "Still am I suppose. Separated." She sighed. "Three years now. But it's not common knowledge."

"That's unusual for a small village," Kate said with a smile.

Mrs Temple smiled cautiously. "We can keep a secret or two. When we have to. Speaking of secrets, you want me to tell you more about 3840."

"Please." Kate moved with the change of subject.

"Where would you like to start?"

"How long have you been working on the accounts for Bramcombe House Nursing Home?"

"About four, maybe five months. Diana Lodge is an old friend of mine. She asked me to take a look and see if I could help her sort out the mess that the previous accountant had made of them."

"Do you know who the previous accountant was?"

"I believe it was Viv."

"Viv?"

"Peterson. She worked for the big accounting firm in Fakenham, but did the nursing home books for a bit of extra cash in what little spare time a full-time worker and mother of four children has. Off the books too, from what I can tell. That should give you an idea of what we were looking at. Records were sloppy, to say the least. Downright fraudulent would be another. The VAT and PAYE payments were screwed up so royally that I've had to negotiate repayment plans with HMRC to prevent them from going after the nursing home for the outstanding amounts. It'll be years before they're up to date again, but at least they're getting there now. The only thing that seemed to be correct were the wages paid to the staff. One assumes that was to ensure Viv was paid correctly. I've passed on her details to HMRC and I'm sure they'll be pursuing her. It may yet cross your desk, Detective." She shrugged. "But that's a decision for better people than me to make."

"So, how did you find the anomaly in all that mess?"

"With great difficulty, I can assure you. That's why it took so long."

"So it was Viv who buried it—"

Mrs Temple shook her head. "No, she wasn't doing the books in 2013. I'm afraid I don't know who that was, but it wasn't her. She just didn't help me locate the issue."

"Can you explain what the exact issue is? I'm afraid accounts are not my strong suit." Kate smiled self-deprecatingly.

"You're not alone there, Detective. After all, if everyone were good with this sort of thing, I'd be out of a job." She crossed her arms. "I take it you're aware that the NHS subsidises the care of each person who needs residential or nursing care up to a certain amount each week?"

"Yes. Unless they have their own means, right? Then they have to pay for themselves."

"Yes. If a patient has no means, then the government pays the whole amount of their care, but they are put in whichever place will provide the care they need for the cheapest price. The nursing homes then have to go through a process to claim the payments or subsidies for each resident."

"I'm with you so far."

"Good. So once a resident is set up, it just ticks along, like a direct debit. Automatically deposited into the account of the nursing home until the nursing home files an update to the NHS database to change those details. Either to claim an increase for increased care needs or to notify of death. Sometimes a change of account details if a nursing home is taken over, etcetera. Still with me?"

"Yes."

"Now, all of the residents that Bramcombe House Nursing Home claims for are done by surname. Except for this one claim—3840. But the payment for 3840 isn't even going into Brancombe's bank account. It's going to a different account number all together."

"So if it isn't going into your account, how did you find out about it?"

"Oh, right. Well, while I was sorting out the tax issues, we came across a discrepancy. The NHS claimed to be sending 400 pounds a week more to us for resident care than our income showed we were receiving. Yesterday I finally received a breakdown of the accounts payable from the NHS accounting department and found the 3840 record. I managed to trace that back then to the eighth of December 2013. That's when this payment was started. Before that, it was all names, surnames."

"Do you have a record of all the payments that were being made prior to that date?"

"Yes, it's all in the data I gave to Diana. Didn't she give it to you?"

"She did. It just takes a while for us to go through so much information."

"Did you happen to notice if there were any names from before that went missing from the claim after the eighth?" Gareth asked.

"Unfortunately, there were several changes around that time and the records don't appear to have been made at the correct times," Mrs Temple replied.

"How do you mean?" Kate frowned.

"I believe someone wasn't declaring the dead as dead until they had another person to take their place in the home. Dates don't match up exactly as they should. So on the eighth of December there were a number of changes made. Annie Balding, Edward Bale, and Alan Parr all disappeared off the records."

Bingo. "So Alan Parr was a resident at Brancombe House Nursing Home?"

"Well, yes. He had to be for them to have completed the forms correctly. He or a next of kin would have had to sign them when he was first admitted to the facility."

"There's no other way around it? He had to have been there at that point?"

"Well, yes."

"But no one recognises him," Gareth interjected.

Mrs Temple shook her head. "I'm sorry, I'm afraid I can't help you there. All I know is that according to the NHS's records, he was a patient registered in the care of Brancombe House Nursing Home until the sixth of December 2013. You'll need to get the records of claimant 3840 to find out what's going on from there."

"No problem," Kate assured her. *I hope.* "We will need you to make an official statement about all the data you've passed on at some point. Would you be able to come to the station?"

"Of course. Now?"

Kate shook her head. "It might be better if you give us a chance to go over the data first." She smiled. "Hopefully we'll have better questions to ask about it all then."

"Just let me know when you need me to come in."

"Thanks. Would tomorrow afternoon work for you?"

"Yes, that would be fine."

"Thanks." Kate took a card from her pocket. "In the meantime, if you think of anything else you think we need to know, give me a call."

"Of course."

"We'll let you get back to your day, Mrs Temple."

"Alison. Mrs Temple was the wife of my bastard of a husband." She smiled brightly. "Fortunately, I don't have to play at being her any more. Now everyone just calls me Alison."

Looks like we have a pretty good idea about the answer to your question Gina. "Very well, Alison." She walked to the front door. "We'll see you at the station tomorrow."

"Tomorrow, sergeant." Alison nodded and closed the door behind them.

"Someone's got some balls then, sarge."

"Big brass ones by the look of it."

"You don't think it's a coincidence?"

"What? That our victim disappears at the same time as 3840 turns up, and no one recognises our victim?" Kate shook her head as she climbed into the car. "Nah." She started the engine. "There are coincidences and then there are criminals. They start with the same letter of the alphabet, Gareth, but they aren't the same thing."

He snickered.

"One is a random thing, my friend. While the other is just a coincidence," she said with a wink.

"Careful, sarge. Your cynical side is showing."

"Stick with this job long enough and yours will too."

"Humph. Guess we'll have to see about that."

She glanced at him from the corner of her eyes. "Tell me something, Gareth. Why you became a cop."

"Well, it was that or go into the army."

"Piss off."

"No, I'm serious. In my family, it's tradition. You either go into the police or the army. I didn't fancy crawling around in the mud so I thought the police was my best option."

"So why did you follow the tradition then? Why not follow your heart?"

"I guess, I've done both really. I always, and I really do mean always, knew that I'd end up following my dad."

"Don't tell me your dad's Commissioner Collier."

"Okay, then I won't tell you."

Bollocks. She slowed as she approached the speed change into Burnham Market. "Is that your plan? To follow him all the way to the top?"

He shrugged. "Well, yeah. He's always on at us about how the next generation has to do better than the previous one. So, yeah, I guess to make sure I don't let him down, I have to be a better police officer than he is."

Kate whistled. "Good luck with that, then."

"Yeah. I know I've got a lot to learn about being a good police officer, but it's about people too, right? About getting on to get up."

Kate chuckled, thinking about his oil-and-water relationship with Tom Brothers.

"What?"

"You're right that a lot of it is who you know, not what, and all that crap, and if that's the way you want to go, then I think you've got some work to do there too."

"How do you mean?"

She glanced at him. He looked totally confused.

"Well, you don't exactly get along with everyone." She shrugged. "I mean, take you and Tom, for example. You have different opinions, which is fine, but you two can't get along for more than a minute. If you're looking to make friends to help you move through the ranks, you're going to have to learn to politick. To get on, or appear to get on, with everyone. You'll need to learn to keep your opinions to yourself and swallow ones that you disagree with. If you don't, you won't get anywhere."

"He thinks I'm gay. That's why he doesn't like me."

She thought back to the conversations she'd had with Tom. She didn't think he was in any way homophobic. Certainly she hadn't seen any indication of it. But she was aware that men often saw lesbians and gay men differently. Lesbians were often a source of fascination to them, while gay men were a threat to their masculinity. Or some such bollocks. "Why?"

"Why what?"

"Why does he think you're gay?"

"Because I don't have a girlfriend and I take care of myself."

"Not exactly an exhaustive criteria."

"No."

"Are you?"

"What?"

"Gay. It's okay if you are. You can talk to me about it."

"I don't need to talk about it. I'm not gay."

Kate held up one hand in surrender. "Okay." She dropped it back to the wheel. "As long as you know you can talk to me about anything. Whenever. No judgement."

He turned to face her, eyes blazing. "I'm not fucking gay. All right. I can have any woman I want, whenever I fucking want. All I've got to do is ask them. I mean, look at me." He indicated his hands up and down. "There'd have to be something wrong with a woman not to want this."

Kate raised her eyebrow. "No offence intended, right?"

He frowned.

"See that's what I mean about needing to learn to politick, Gareth. You just said there was something wrong with any woman who doesn't want to sleep with you."

His frown deepened.

"You've just insulted every lesbian, every married and faithful woman, women who are older than you and not into younger men for whatever reason, hell, you even insulted nuns. Just because they won't find you attractive. Not very smart. I'm your superior officer, an older woman, compared to you anyway, and a lesbian. Do you think I'd feel very favourably right now to helping you further your career?"

He swallowed but continued to stare belligerently at her. "No."

"Do you see my point now?"

He nodded. "Yeah. I see a lot of things now." He forced a smile. "Thanks, sarge."

Kate frowned but decided to leave him alone to stew in his own bitterness for a while. Either he'd take her words to heart and learn from them, or he'd carry on being his mercurial self, getting nowhere fast and blaming everyone else for his misfortune. Either way, she didn't care. She had bigger things to worry about right now than Gareth Collier's ego.

CHAPTER 19

Kate tapped her pen against her notepad and stared at the wall. The picture of Alan's facial reconstruction was taped next to the picture of his skeleton, with notes of what they knew written all around the board. Date of birth: third of August 1940. Head groundsman at West Norfolk Royal Golf Course until retirement.

The details of the scraps of clothes and dentures were underneath his picture, including the names those items bore and their dates of death. Annie Balding, 5.12.13. Edward Bale, 10.10.13. Dorothy Kinder, 23.06.14. Rose Harvey, 19.02.14. John Wood, 3.04.14. At the centre of the board Brancombe House was circled. The number 3840 sat in its own bubble, a line connecting the two, and a big question mark underneath it.

"Do we have Alan Parr's address? Where he lived before he went into the nursing home?" Kate asked into the quiet room. She wasn't asking anyone in particular, just hoping that one of her colleagues had managed to trace the information.

"Yup." Tom said. "Docking lad. Not far from your house actually. 2 North Farm Cottages."

She frowned. "That's literally across the road from me."

"Like I said, not far. It was sold in 2010 to the current owners, a Mr and Mrs Pastor. The proceeds of the sale funded his time in Brancombe House until June 2013."

"How do you know that?"

"Based on what he sold it for and the cost of the fees, that's how long it would have lasted before it was all gone. Bloody criminal if you ask me. A man works all his life, pays his bloody taxes, and takes nothing back. Works hard to buy himself a home, make himself comfortable, and the bloody government takes every penny of it from him when he needs looking after."

"Well," Gareth started, "some people would say that the reason we work hard and build a nest egg is to give ourselves the funds to look after ourselves when we need the help."

Kate couldn't make up her mind if Gareth was taking the opposite position to Tom just to wind him up or if he truly believed what he was saying.

"Just because we're a welfare state doesn't mean we have to depend on the government for everything. If we can afford to pay to help ourselves, why shouldn't we? After all, if those who can afford to pay do, then there's more left in the coffers so that those who can't afford to pay aren't left to rot." He shrugged. "Isn't that the core value of the welfare state? To provide help for those who can't help themselves?"

Tom glared at him. "Don't tell me it doesn't grate on you that your taxes, the money you pay to the government from your own wage, goes to pay dole money for the very criminals we are looking to take off the streets in the vast majority of cases we work on?" He folded his arms across his chest. "You can't tell me that doesn't piss you off."

"That isn't what I said." He folded his own arms and mirrored Tom's pose. "It doesn't actually matter how I feel about it. It's the society we live in, and it is all perfectly legal. The government we voted into power made it so."

"Fine, then, pedant. It should be bloody criminal," Tom growled. "Better?"

Gareth smiled sweetly, but wisely held his tongue.

Definitely trying to wind him up. Why?

"Okay, so moving on from the highwaymen that are in government," Stella said, "where are we up to with the rest of this investigation?"

Kate sighed. "We've got a case of embezzlement that I swear is based on our victim's death, but I can't for the life of me figure out how someone could've killed him and dumped the body in the bunker on that night."

"So you think someone murdered him to claim the money from the government?" Stella clarified.

"It's the only thing that kind of makes sense given the facts we have."

Stella nodded and scribbled in the bible. "What about Dr Anderson? Have we heard anything from her?"

"Not yet," Gareth said.

"And have we heard from Grimshaw about the data from Sister Lodge?"

"Nope," Kate supplied.

"Right." Stella picked up the phone and punched numbers. "Len, it's Stella. I'm good thanks, you? Glad to hear it. Listen, how's your man getting on with that flash drive from the nursing home?" She paused to listen. "He is? That's great. We'll get a projector set up for him. When shall we expect him?" She frowned. "That long. How come?" She glanced at Kate. "No problem, Len. Kate needs to go and see Dr Anderson anyway. She and Collier will gladly give him a lift over here on the way back."

Kate nodded, hoisted herself out of her chair and grabbed her coat.

"Say an hour or so. That should give them time to get there and talk to Dr Anderson. Right, thanks, Len."

"Tell me he wasn't going to get the bus," Kate said, imagining how much equipment the young tech would likely be humping around.

"It was either that or wait for one of Len's field techs to get back, and he didn't know how long that would be. They're processing a scene at the moment."

Kate shook her head. "Right, we'll be off then. Play nice while I'm gone, kiddies." She waved her fingers behind her as she and Gareth skulked out of the door.

"You see?" she heard Tom saying as the door swung shut behind them. "You see what I have to put up with from him?"

The bang of the door cut off the rest of what she was sure would be a tirade of vitriol against Gareth Collier.

She waited until they were both in the car, belted in, and she was pulling on to the A149 towards King's Lynn before asking, "Do you enjoy winding him up or is there another reason for it?"

Gareth bristled and turned to look out of the window.

Kate waited.

"He thinks he's the dog's bollocks and it annoys me. He talks a load of shit most of the time, and cocky arses like that, well, they just need taking down a peg or two sometimes."

Wow. Talk about pot calling the kettle black. Kate snorted a quick laugh. "You do realise that he says exactly the same thing about you, don't you?"

"I'm not cocky, and I don't talk a load of shit."

"Ah, my friend," she said, "we all talk a load of shit sometimes." She slowed down at the roundabout, indicated left, and then crossed the junction. "Can I make a suggestion?"

She phrased it as a question, but as his senior officer they both knew it wasn't really a suggestion. It was a polite order.

"What?"

"Next time you want to take him down a peg or two, as you put it, I want you to smile at him, and say you think he's wrong, but agree to disagree with him."

He scowled at her.

"He is an experienced officer who has a lot he can teach you. If you're willing to learn. I don't care if you're best mates or you hate each other. It shouldn't affect us one way or the other. But you've made it a problem, you've let it affect you. That's why I'm sitting in the car with you today rather than Tom. I want to work with professionals. Professionals don't let a personality clash affect how they perform in their jobs." She turned on her windscreen wipers as the rain started to fall, distorting her view of the road. "Do I make myself clear?"

"Crystal, Sergeant."

Kate nodded but had nothing more to add so she concentrated on the road and left Gareth to stew. The bare branches on the trees shook and clattered in the wind, and the rain fell heavier. Spray from the cars in front of her and on the opposite side of the road added to the water accumulating on her windscreen. She turned the wipers up to full speed and slowed a little further.

"Sarge?"

"Yeah?"

"I'm sorry."

She smiled inwardly. *Points to the kid.* "Not me you need to apologise to, Gareth."

He sighed heavily. "I know. I'm just not sure I can bring myself to apologise to him."

"Then I'm disappointed."

"Why?"

"I thought you were a professional, Gareth. I was wrong. I'm disappointed in myself for getting that wrong."

"You're disappointed in yourself. Why?"

"Think about it, Gareth. Maybe then you'll figure out why it's so important to make an effort with Tom."

He sat in silence until they reached the outskirts of King's Lynn. "Can I ask you something, sarge?"

"What?" Kate replied tersely.

"Why do they all call Len Wilder 'sarge'? He's a civ. They all are over in CSI."

"Because he earned it."

Gareth frowned at her, his confusion clear.

"Len was a police sergeant running the crime scene techs back in 2009 when they changed SOCO to a civilian division."

"Because it's cheaper."

"In theory."

"It is. My dad said it was. Also, it means you've a dedicated force dealing with only that shit and they can keep up with scientific developments better than your average copper. I mean let's face it, if Tom was a CSI we'd never close a case."

"Gareth," Kate growled the warning.

"Sorry, but you've got to admit, it is more efficient this way."

"Yeah. Until we're stuck waiting on lab results, and forensics and can't do a damn thing because we're at the back of the queue."

He sat quietly while she navigated the roundabout. "So he was a cop?"

Kate nodded. "But he loved working in the crime lab so he'd stayed with it. Retired from the police force at fifty, having put in his twenty-five years."

"So he took the civilian equivalent post?"

"Yup. And he's never looked back from what I gather. His old friends still call him 'sarge', and it stuck."

She pulled into the car park, and again Gareth was out of the car before she'd put the handbrake on and turned off the ignition. He fed the parking ticket to her as she opened her door and slithered out of the small space. The car to her right was much too close to the line.

Ruth Anderson was sitting in her office, staring at an array of files cluttering the huge desk in front of her.

Kate tapped on the already-open door and leaned against the door jamb. "Hi."

"Hi, Kate. Gareth," Ruth said. She scratched her head and stuck the pencil in her hand into her ponytail. There were three others already sticking out of it at odd angles.

"How's it going?"

"Well, there are certainly a lot of reports to go over, but I'm afraid I don't have anything for you."

Kate frowned. "What?"

Ruth shrugged. "I've gone over a hundred and fifty reports so far, and I can't find anything that would support the theory that these deaths were anything but natural causes."

"But there are so many of them."

"Yes, but like we said, unfortunately, old, sick people die. It's a fact of life. These reports all fit with what would be expected as the natural progressions of the diseases they were suffering from."

"Such as?"

Ruth lifted the file in front of her. "This man had lung cancer. He'd been prescribed massive doses of morphine and he died in his sleep. Heart failure due to oxygen deprivation. The tumours were probably so advanced that he couldn't get enough oxygen into his body."

"Probably? Didn't the autopsy show if they were or not?"

"There was no autopsy, Kate. There was no need for one. He was dying of cancer. He was riddled with it. All his earlier tests showed that. A dying man died. There's nothing suspicious in that."

"Were autopsies performed on any of these people?"

Ruth shook her head. "An autopsy is only carried out if there is need of one. If the death was suspicious, untimely, or there are signs of violence or unnatural causes. In every one of these cases there was no reason to carry out an autopsy."

"So we can't be sure that there was nothing to find, because no one even looked."

"There was no reason to look."

"For fuck's sake." Kate banged her fist on the wooden desk. "We're talking about people here. People with lives, and families who loved them. Why didn't anyone look?"

Ruth shrugged. "It's easy to miss things in isolation. You know that. When you see things all together, with the benefit of hindsight, it's easy to see the missteps taken. But in the moment, with nothing else to guide your judgement, we tend to go with the axiom of whatever seems the most likely as being the right answer. Sick people die all the time, Kate. Old people die. There was no reason to think it was anything else. No reason to look any further."

"What about now? Is there reason enough to look now?"

"I can't."

"Why not?"

"Because almost every one of them was cremated. Most people are these days. Cemeteries are crowded, space is expensive, so cremations are the funeral method of choice. I can't examine ashes."

"So there's nothing?"

"Yes."

Kate scrubbed her hands over her face and ran her fingers through her hair. "Okay, thanks for looking." She pushed off the door jamb.

"Not so fast."

Kate turned back to Ruth.

"I've put an alert out to all GPs who attend Brancombe House. The next resident to pass away will come to me for examination before being released to a funeral parlour."

"So you'll do an autopsy then?"

Ruth shook her head. "No, I said examination. I won't perform an autopsy unless my examination reveals cause to."

"But what can you find in an examination?"

"I'll run blood tests and a toxicology screen. I'll also do a thorough examination of the body. If there is any evidence that the person didn't die of natural causes, I'll find it."

Kate pursed her lips. "Not that I want another person to die, but that may be the only way to put all our minds at rest."

"Unfortunately, I think you're right. That's why I put out the alert."

"Thank you."

"No need to thank me. I need to know as much as you do." She closed the file on her desk. "I'll let you know if and when I know anything more."

"Right." She closed the door behind them and walked slowly back towards the car.

"That wasn't what we were hoping for," Gareth said.

"No. But not really a huge surprise either. I mean if, and I do mean if, there is someone popping off old folks, then whoever it is has been getting away with it for quite a while. At least three years. To do that, they've got to be pretty good. So this was never going to be easy."

"I guess."

"Let's see what Grimshaw has to say. See if we can resolve this case his way instead of Dr Anderson's."

CHAPTER 20

"Will, can you check the stopcocks up at the top loos, please? We really need to shut the water off now. It was freezing last night, and I don't want to risk a burst pipe on top of everything else," Gina said into the small handheld radio.

"I'm already up here, Gina."

She pushed the button and lifted the handset again. "You're a star, Will. Don't know what I'd do without you."

"Don't worry, G. You'll never have to find out."

Gina put the handset back in the charging unit and turned to the spreadsheet she was trying to fill in. But she couldn't concentrate.

She hated payroll at the best of times, but she managed to take comfort in the fact that this would be the last cycle paying Sarah, Emma, and Rick. For the rest of the winter it would just be her and Will, and that would make her life so much simpler. But right now life didn't seem very simple at all.

All she could think about was her earlier meeting with Jodi. It was funny but she didn't see Jodi's face as a patchwork of scars now. She couldn't describe how she did see her. But it wasn't covered in scars. Yet for herself it was as though all she could see were scars. Even where there weren't any.

Her phone pinged, distracting her from her maudlin thoughts. She reached for it, half expecting it to be from Kate, but she didn't recognise the number. She opened up the app and clicked on the message.

Drinks tonight, gorgeous? xx

She frowned, and double checked the number against Kate's, then against any of the others in her phone, just in case. It didn't match any.

Who is this?

She put the phone down and grabbed the tax book full of national insurance contribution codes. Connie had called it a bible of sorts. She called it penance.

You know who it is. See you tonight xx

A picture came through at the same time as the message. A picture of a well-muscled male chest, stomach with cut abs, and an erect penis.

"Ew." She deleted the conversation, deciding that there was no point in getting drawn into a long text conversation to point out that whoever that picture belonged to was sexting the wrong number.

A sharp tap on the door drew her attention, and Sarah poked her head around. "Got a minute?"

Gina indicated the chair opposite her desk.

"I was, well, I was wondering if we could make a deal." Sarah looked more than a little sheepish.

"What kind of deal?"

"Well, this new job doesn't offer any accommodation with it." She paused, seemingly giving Gina a chance to jump in and save her from whatever she wanted to ask.

"And?"

"And the rents around here are humungous, and I really don't want to go back to my mum's."

"I repeat myself, and?"

"Well, can I stay here?"

Gina shook her head. "You resigned, Sarah. You're leaving as of tomorrow. Your decision. I can't let you stay here if you're not working here. You know as well as I do the insurance company won't go for that."

"They wouldn't have to know if I was registered as a guest."

"If you can't afford the rent around here, you can't afford to stay here permanently as a guest."

"That's where I was hoping we could make a deal."

Gina shook her head. "You've got to be kidding. You tried to blackmail me into making promises I didn't know if I'd be able to keep, increasing your wage, and now you want a favour from me after dropping me and Will in the shit?" She pointed at the door. "Get out."

Sarah scowled at her. "No need to be nasty about it, Gina."

"I'll show you bloody nasty. You're no longer required here at Brandale. Pack your crap and get out. Now."

Sarah paled. "You can't do that. I'm owed—"

"You'll get everything you're owed, Sarah Willis. Now get the fuck out of my office and off my campsite!"

Sarah offered her a fake smile. "It isn't yours, Gina. You'll only ever be a hired hand here."

"Which is a damn sight more than you are. Now get out before I call the police and tell them we have a trespasser."

Sarah slammed the door behind her. Then the gate.

Shit. Gina knew she was right. While she was running this place and making decisions as though it were hers, she was only another member of staff. And she had no more job security than they did. If they got a letter from HMRC they could be closed down, or an heir could be found who could come in and take over, or sell out from under them. Should she do what Sarah and the others were doing? Was that actually the wisest move? Close up the campsite and move on with her life. Let everyone fend for themselves. Including herself.

How would she support Sammy? Pay her rent? Put food on the table? How would she manage without this place? Without Brandale, she simply couldn't. She didn't have the luxury that Sarah and her pals did. She had responsibilities and no one else to turn to if she didn't meet them.

Her phone pinged again. She stared, not wanting to look at another penis, but Kate's number flashed on the screen. She smiled as she looked at the message.

Thinking about you. Wish I was there to give you a big hug right now xx

Me too xx

CHAPTER 21

Simon Grimshaw looked like he'd just rolled out of bed, grabbed his dirty clothes off the floor, and shoved a ratty beanie on his head to hide the fact that he hadn't brushed his hair. Ever. Kate almost didn't want him in her car. No, scratch that, she didn't want him in her car. Ever. Not without putting down plastic sheets to catch anything that was going to drop off and become a science experiment. She expected him to be very young underneath the unkempt beard and hair hanging in his eyes from under the rim of his hat. He wasn't. Well, he was compared to Len, but he probably had ten years on her. The moniker "Young Grimshaw" was obviously Len taking the piss again.

She watched him connect cables to his laptop with ease, seemingly oblivious to, or definitely uncaring of, the stares he garnered from Kate and the rest of the team. Stella's lip was slightly curled, her nose wrinkled, and Kate saw her reach for the bottle of alcohol gel that she kept on her desk for sanitation purposes. She stifled the snigger with a cough.

"Okay, so I've gone through all the data on the hard drive you brought me. I ran a few bots over it too, to make sure I hadn't missed anything—"

"Bots?" Stella asked.

"Yeah, these cool little programmes that automatically check for stuff. They're a lot more efficient than I am, and they don't miss anything. So we checked it all, and I found some weird stuff and some cool stuff."

"Cool," Tom said with a grin.

Gareth's jaw clenched. He didn't say anything though. *Good boy.*

"Yeah, it is. Your informant was right about the 3840 number. The money from the government is being sent to an overseas account, the National Bank of Poland in Warsaw."

"And the payments have been going there since the eighth of December 2013?" Stella asked.

"No. The payments started going there at the end of January 2014, but they were back dated to the eighth of December."

"How?"

"Well, I can explain it if you want, but it's all pretty boring and complicated at the same time. The basics of it are that the NHS's system back then was pretty easy to do almost anything you wanted with it. All you needed was the account password for the nursing home and the approved paperwork for the resident. Once you had that in the system, whoever accessed the account could change whatever details they wanted. It's not that easy now, by the way. There are multiple layers of access needed for this sort of thing now."

"Okay, let's start simple. Is 3840 our Alan Parr?" Kate asked.

"Yes. Your fraudster's told you that quite clearly," he said tapping the number.

"I'm sorry?" Stella asked.

"The number itself, 3840." Grimshaw looked at them all incredulously. "His date of birth, 3.8.40. You didn't see it?"

Kate banged her forehead down in the desk with a groan. "No. We didn't see it."

Grimshaw looked smug. Really fucking smug. "Well, I managed to access the records of the NHS's accounts—"

"Legally?" Stella asked.

Grimshaw coughed. "And when I accessed them, it was there in black and white who the reference code referred to. All his details were on there. According to his medical records he's showing as still living at Brancombe House Nursing Home."

"Right. And the bank account in Poland, do we have the name of who that belongs to?"

"No. I haven't been able to access those records. I have put in a request to get the data, but it will take a little while. Official channels take time, as we know."

"Do you have a rough idea?"

"Could be a few hours, could be a few days," he said with a shrug.

"Poland, though?" Kate asked.

"Yes. Definitely."

"And it stays in that account?"

He shrugged again. "Until I get the data from that account, I can't tell you."

"Okay." She turned back to her notes. "Who on the staff is from Poland?"

"We've got three blokes and eight women," Jimmy said.

Tom whistled. "Out of how many full-time staff members?"

"Twenty-five," Kate said.

"So we have eleven suspects to question and see if we can beat you to the information, right, Mr Grimshaw?" Stella said.

He sneered. "Good luck."

His haughty attitude told them all exactly how likely he thought that was. Given that they hadn't even spotted the reference number was the victim's date of birth, she had to concede that he had a point.

"Actually, we don't," Gareth said.

"We don't?" Tom queried.

Gareth shook his head. "Three of the women didn't work there until April 2014 or later, so they couldn't be our embezzler-slash-possible murderer."

"Good point. Anyone else we can rule out?" Stella walked over to the board and grabbed a marker pen.

"The sarge and I've already interviewed Maja Hanin."

"Okay." She turned to Kate. "You're confident she's clean?"

"She's five foot, and if she weighed eight stone I'd be amazed. There's no way she could carry out something as physical as this body dump would have to be."

"If it was a body dump," Stella said.

"True. But if it wasn't, then that means Alan disappeared and no one reported him missing, but our thief has enough knowledge of what happened to him to steal his subsidies." She shook her head. "It seems like too big a risk for it to be a separate crime."

"Desperate people do desperate things, Kate."

"True. But given her educational background and everything we saw at her flat, I'm pretty confident that she wouldn't have the skills to pull it off."

"Okay. Collier, read me off the names we need to interview."

"Stefan Podolski, Michal Boruc, Jacub Pazdan, Eva Kutenova."

"Jimmy, is she the one we met when we first went there?" Kate asked.

"I think so. Name sounds about right. Why?"

"I thought she was Czech or something," Kate said.

"Or something," Gareth said. "Polish. Says so in her employment records, sarge."

"I believe you. Carry on."

"Ola Dykiel, Anna Kolak, and Krystyna Cedinska."

Stella wrote the names as Gareth called them out. "Right, I want a full work-up of each of them. Don't leave anything out."

"That's going to start clocking up the phone bill, sarge," Tom said.

"Doesn't matter. We've a case to solve. Any luck finding a next of kin for Mr Parr yet?"

"Nothing. Looks like he didn't have a soul in the world looking out for him," Gareth said, loud enough for everyone to hear. "Now that, that's bloody criminal," he muttered under his breath.

Kate heard him, but she didn't think anyone else had. Certainly no one took any notice if they did. *That could be me. Forty years from now, that could be me.* She shuddered. *No it won't, I've got Gina and Sammy to care about now. I don't have to end up like this. Alone and forgotten.*

"Want me to run you back to King's Lynn, Mr Grimshaw?" Gareth offered.

"Thanks, that'd be great."

"That okay, sarge?"

"Works for me." She fished in her pocket and pulled out a twenty-pound note. "Get some coffees on the way back. The crap they've got in the cupboard downstairs is giving me a headache."

"Too much caffeine in it?"

She shook her head. "Not enough. I can't drink enough to get my fix without my eyeballs floating in my head and needing to pee all day."

"TMI, sarge." Gareth tapped his pants pockets checking for his keys, stuffed the note into his jacket pocket, and winked at Kate as he left.

Two hours later, they were comfortable with the information they had on each of their suspects, suitably caffeinated, and ready to talk to them all.

"So how do you want to do this, Stella? Get them all in here or go and see them?"

"I'm inclined to think getting them all in here would be more likely to rattle a cage or two."

"Agreed, but if we don't get our guy in the first couple, we'll have tipped our hand and they might run."

"Good point. Sounds like you have something in mind."

"Interviews at the nursing home, but get them all together and hold them in a waiting room until we get to them. Tom and one of the plastic policemen can watch them while we question the rest."

Stella nodded. "Yep. Works for me. Everyone else okay with that?"

Everyone agreed and quickly grabbed their coats as Stella called the home and set things up with Diana Lodge.

CHAPTER 22

Tom stood by the door. Arms crossed over his chest, his bald head gleaming under the fluorescent lights of the staff break room, and his eyes doing that creepy non-blinking thing that was such an effective interrogation tool for him. It creeped Kate out, and she hadn't done anything wrong. She could only imagine what it must feel like to someone with a guilty conscience.

She shuffled through the photographs that Sister Lodge had managed to find. Not looking at the pictures. She was looking at the people in the room. Some looked relaxed. Leaning back in their chairs, leafing through magazines, chatting to one another. Others looked worried. Sweat beaded on foreheads, trickled down necks, and grew in large stains under armpits. The odour in the room was stagnating quickly towards unpleasant. There were too many nervous people in the room. They only needed one, after all.

"Mr Podolski, would you come with me please," Stella said, and led the overweight, sweating man into a different room.

Jimmy closed the door behind them.

"Mr Boruc, would you come with me," Kate looked him directly in the eyes. They were bloodshot and half-lidded. Not overly surprising as the poor chap had been on the night shift last night and obviously hadn't had much sleep.

He was thin, maybe wiry was a better description, and not much taller than her own five-foot-eight. He yawned as he followed her up the stairs to a small sitting room on the second floor. Diana Lodge had done a good job on clearing spaces for them to set this up. Clearly she was as eager to have this over with as they were.

One of the portable recorders that Stella had organised sat on the small table. "I need to record this interview, Mr Boruc. Is that okay with you?"

He nodded and Kate pressed record. She quickly introduced herself, Gareth, and Michal Boruc, dated the recording, and stated their location. "May I call you Michal?" she asked as he sat in the chair furthest away from the door. Gareth sat next to Kate, between Michal and any means of escape from the room.

"That is fine," he said, his accent thick and heavy.

"Thank you." Kate quickly introduced herself before continuing, "I believe Sister Lodge told you we needed to speak to you about the man who has been missing from the home for some time—"

"I already told your baldie friend in there, I don't know the guy. I don't recognise him. If he ever lived here, I didn't have nothing to do with him."

Kate nodded. "I understand. We just have to be absolutely sure." She shuffled through the pictures until she found the one of Michal taken at Christmas 2012. She pointed to the picture. He smiled out from the page, a paper crown on his head and a broken cracker in his hand. "Is this you?"

He squinted at the image. "Yes. This is one of the Christmas parties we have here."

"Do you know when this picture was taken?"

"I would think, from haircut, maybe 2011." He shrugged. "Maybe 2012."

"It was 2012. It says so on the back of the picture."

"And?"

"Do you know who this man is?" She pointed to the bearded man with glasses sitting at the table next to him.

Michal squinted and frowned. "I don't remember him."

"You don't?"

"No."

She put another picture on the coffee table before him. "Does this help?" She showed him a picture of Michal with his arm around the shoulders of the same man as they sat at the table. They were both smiling into the camera. Both held drinks in their hands and were clearly toasting something.

Michal still frowned. "I'm sorry. No."

"This is Alan Parr. Does the name mean anything to you?" She watched closely for any flicker of recognition. For the slightest spark.

"I'm sorry, no."

She saw none. She put the picture down on the table. "Alan Parr was found murdered." She was increasingly certain that the old man had been killed and wanted to see his reaction to the news. She was hoping for some sort of give away. A twitch. A spasm. Maybe even a slight grin. All she saw on Michal's face was shock. This was not the guy. But she had to continue with the interview. They had so little evidence that witness testimony was going to be defining in this case. "If you remember anything, anything at all, about him or about things happening here at that time, it's important that you tell us. His family deserves that much. Don't they?"

Their research had shown that Michal was a devoted family man. Every month he sent the lion's share of his wage back to his family in Poland. She'd known this one would be a long shot. Why would he send so much of his own funds if he was sending £1,600 a month to them anyway? Playing to his family loyalties was their best chance at getting him to open up, but also to maybe getting him to make a mistake if they were wrong. If he knew Alan had no family, would he slip up and point that out to her?

"Yes, they do. But I'm sorry. I don't remember him." He picked up the picture of the two of them making a toast. "There are forty-three residents in here at all times. Forty-three. Do you know how many residents I have cared for here since 2013?"

Kate shook her head.

"Me neither. I couldn't even begin to work it out. But I can tell you, it's a lot of people."

"I'm sure it is, Michal."

"I work nights. I work six nights a week. By the time I come on shift, most of the patients, they are in bed already. They are old and want to sleep, so they go to bed early. And most of them don't get up until the morning shift starts. If this man followed that same pattern, I may have only met him this one time." He held the picture out to her. "I may have changed his pad if he messed himself. I don't know. But I don't remember this man. I'm sorry, but I can't help you, or his family."

His words made sense. It was perfectly logical. They came across witnesses every day who they could prove had contact with such and such person, but they had absolutely no recollection of it. The more she thought about it, the easier it was to believe that someone like Michal wouldn't be able to remember Alan.

"Okay, thank you for your time and I'm sorry we disturbed your rest."

He inclined his head and scuttled out of the door.

"You sure it wasn't him?" Gareth asked.

"As sure as I can be." She turned her neck, trying to get it to crack. "I couldn't see any spark of recognition and he didn't correct my errors in regards to Alan's family." She shrugged. "Without evidence, at the moment that's about as sure as we can get."

"Who do you want next?"

Kate thought about who seemed relaxed and who was sweating in the room. Eeny-meany-miny-moe. "Let's go with Anna. She seemed pretty relaxed."

Gareth frowned and then smiled. "I get you. Let the ones who are nervous about something sweat it out longer. It'll play on their nerves even more while we tick off the ones who don't seem to have anything to hide."

"Smart cookie, Gareth. Now, chop-chop."

Neither Anna nor Krystyna had anything they could add. They didn't remember him, had no knowledge of anything about him, and seemed to have nothing else to hide. Given the records they'd found on them both, just what Kate expected.

Ola on the other hand wasn't nearly so forthcoming. Every question was answered with no comment. Clearly someone had been watching too many police dramas.

Ola was a young woman, only twenty-three years old, but she had a look on her face that said she'd lived a hard life. The lines etched around her mouth and on her forehead were deep, like they'd been cut in stone, and her eyes were just as grey and hard as granite.

"You know, Ola, if you keep telling me no comment to even the most basic questions, I'm going to think you have something to hide. And then I'm going to have to go looking for whatever that is. Do you know why?"

"No comment."

"Probably a good job. I don't think I'd like it if you tell me I'm a nosey bitch. But that's probably what you think, right?"

"No comment."

"Right. So why do I feel the need to go looking if I think you've got something to hide?"

"No—"

"That was a rhetorical question. I was going to give you the answer. And the answer's simple, Ola." She waited a beat. "It's my job. Some people have the great pleasure of wiping shitty arses for a living. I get to figure out what people are hiding. And you know what, Ola?"

"No comment."

"I'm good at it." She opened an A4 wallet and pulled out a page. She glanced at it then placed it on the coffee table.

A trickle of sweat rolled down Ola's neck and disappeared beneath her tunic.

"I don't think you do remember my friend. Unfortunately." She tapped the picture of Alan Parr. "But I do know that you're hiding something."

"No comment."

"And I think it's this." Kate tapped the picture she'd put down. It was a photocopy of Ola's passport that was held on file by the nursing home from when she started working for them. "Am I right?"

"No comment."

Kate sighed. "Okay, looks like we'll be doing this the hard way. You know, I'd never seen a passport from Poland before today. Now I've seen seven of them. Well, six actually. Because this one," she said and tapped the picture again, "well, this one's a fake."

Ola's eyes widened and her face paled. "No comment."

Kate waved off the response. "I know it is, because you see here?" She pointed to the code at the bottom of the page. "That's a number assigned to another person."

Ola crossed her arms across her chest, but the move only served to highlight her shaking hands rather than hide them. "No comment."

"That's fine. You don't need to comment to me. Immigration services will be taking over with this. I just have one more question for you?"

Ola didn't say a word, but her eyes locked on to Kate's. She was clearly waiting to hear what else she'd have to say "no comment" to.

"Did Alan find out you were here on a fake passport so you killed him to keep your secret?"

"Killed him? I didn't kill anyone. I haven't done anything wrong."

"Well, except the whole false passport thing. Right?"

Ola squirmed in her chair.

"Is your name really Ola?"

"I thought you said you were done with your questions."

Kate smiled. "I lied. Just like you. So is it?"

Ola smiled back. "No comment."

"Beautiful. Detective Constable Collier, are our friends from immigration here yet?"

"I believe they are, sarge."

"Excellent. Please take Ola here to meet them."

Gareth stepped forward. "With pleasure." He ushered Ola out of the room.

One left. That was all. Just Eva Kutenova. The woman who sat in the room sweating, fidgeting, and constantly glancing out of the window. All signs of someone looking for a way to escape. Signs of someone who was in trouble, and knew it. She decided not to take her upstairs to the small, comfortable room. She decided to go in with Tom.

She glanced at the PCSO when she walked into the break room and indicated for him to step out. Tom didn't move. He just kept staring at Eva. Kate suppressed a shudder and sat on the chair adjacent to Eva's.

"Good to see you again, Eva." She smiled what she hoped was a sweet, innocent, disarming smile. Kate placed the portable recorder on the table. "I need to record this interview."

Eva nodded. Her brow creased and her cheeks paled as she swallowed hard. Kate wrinkled her nose. She could smell the fear that clung to the woman like the cheap eau de toilette her gran used to wear. It was thick and cloying, filling her nostrils and penetrating her brain. It was almost enough to give her a headache.

Kate pressed record. "Detective Sergeant Brannon in the room with Detective Constable Thomas Brothers and Eva Kutenova. We are at Brancombe House Nursing Home—"

"Why am I still here? I have much to do, I must be getting back to work."

"I have some questions for you and I need you to answer them. Honestly."

"I have always been honest with you." Her voice was quieter and she seemed unable to meet Kate's gaze.

Honest? Yeah, as the man said, my arse. "Then we shouldn't have any issues here. Do you recognise this man?" Kate held up the original facial reconstruction of Alan Parr.

Eva shook her head, but her eyes betrayed her. "I don't know him."

Kate took the image with the added beard and glasses. "What about now? Do you recognise him now?"

She shook her head again, but still her eyes betrayed her. The sweat that had beaded on her brow trickled down beside her ear before continuing down her neck.

Kate placed a picture of Eva with Alan on the table but didn't say anything.

Eva swallowed hard, her fingers twisting at the button on her cardigan.

Kate put a second picture next to the first. Clearly they were taken at a different time as they were wearing different clothes and Eva's hair was longer. The third picture was taken at the Christmas party in early December 2013. Eva was handing a knife and fork to Alan.

"I thought you said you'd only worked here a week when the storm hit. That's why you remembered it so clearly."

"I did."

"And in that week you managed to get photographed with this man on three separate occasions. But you don't recognise him."

"It was first week. There was much to learn. Much to remember. I don't remember him."

Kate leaned closer to her. "You're lying," she said quietly. "Don't you think so, Detective Constable Brothers?"

"Definitely," Tom said, no doubt the first word he'd spoken since walking into the room.

"Makes you wonder, doesn't it, why someone would lie about knowing an old man?"

"It does, sarge."

"I mean, we only asked if anyone recognised him. Knew his name. That's all."

"That's all we did, sarge."

"So why would anyone lie about not knowing him?"

"Got something to hide, sarge."

"You think?"

"Not a doubt in my mind."

"So, what do you think Eva here's hiding?"

"Well, we've got a dead victim, missing three years and not reported missing, and a woman who lies to us about knowing who he is." He paused and sniffed loudly. "Only says one thing to me, sarge."

"And that is?"

"She's our killer."

"What? No! I didn't do that. I couldn't. I liked Alan!" Eva said and then slapped her hand across her mouth as she realised what she'd just done.

Bingo.

Panic filled Eva's eyes and spilled out as she sobbed. Guilt and snot flowed freely as she started talking. "I didn't hurt him. I swear. I never knew what happened to him. I just know that one night he was gone and didn't come back. And no one missed him. No one seemed to even notice that he was gone. I didn't hurt him. I thought he'd just wandered off somewhere."

"And you thought that doing nothing about an elderly man wandering off somewhere was a good idea?" Kate said incredulously.

"I had no idea how long he was gone when I first noticed that he wasn't around. In all the commotion with the floods and Annie passing, it was a few days before I noticed that he was gone. But already no one had mentioned him. I couldn't find some of his things, but things always went missing in the laundry. So I didn't really worry. I thought sister would have been dealing with it, and that it was not talked about because someone was probably in trouble for letting him wander off."

Kate plucked a tissue from the box on a small table beside the chair. "Say I did believe you, that you didn't hurt Alan. Why didn't you go to the sister and ask her about it?"

"I did."

Kate looked at her sceptically.

"No, really, I did. As soon as I realised he was missing. It was maybe the Wednesday or the Thursday after."

Five or six full days, and no one else rang the alarm? What the hell kind of state was this place in? "Was the home evacuated? In the flood?" Maybe in a confusion like that she could understand how someone could be lost.

Eva shook her head.

"Then why was he never reported missing? Why did no one else ever notice that he was gone?"

"I can't answer for anyone else. We had lots of agency staff here at that time. More even than we have now. I only know that I tried."

"Then what went wrong? Because we've no record of Alan Parr being reported missing, and you lied to us and said you didn't recognise him."

"I pick wrong time to talk to sister."

"I don't understand, Eva."

"Sister was drunk. Very drunk. When I ask what she had done about it the next day, she looked at me blank then said it was all taken care of. That everything was fine." She blew her nose loudly. "It wasn't until a few weeks later that I realised that meant she didn't even know what I was talking about. She was so drunk that she didn't even remember." She wiped her eyes. "No one seemed to remember."

"See, that's what I don't understand. This is a modern nursing home. A modern facility. How could a resident just go missing and no one notices?"

She shrugged. "I was very new then, but most staff were agency staff. Very few working full-time. Some of the people who work here full-time now got jobs here after they started with the agency."

"And the agency staff were different all the time?"

"Some. But those who were the same weren't here all the time. They didn't comment if a patient was missing. They assumed they had died since they last worked at a place. One girl told me that happened all the time and it was too sad to try and remember all the people who were gone, so she just worked with the patient in front of her and then never thought about them again."

Kate's phone pinged. "Excuse me." She flipped through the e-mail from Grimshaw. Apparently the Polish bank wanted a case of international fraud sorting out as soon as possible. She nodded to Tom as she looked up from the device. He'd follow her lead. He was always good like that. "Okay, so I can see that with the transitory staff, but that doesn't account for the full-time staff or the records? Or his stuff?"

"When I noticed that he was gone, so were his belongings." She clicked her fingers. "Just like that, gone. So was his patient folder from the rack where we keep all the notes."

"Are those the only records?"

Eva shook her head. "They were the paper ones we had access to. So we could write in things that happened, medication records, fluid balance sheets, bathing schedules. That sort of thing. The rest of the records are kept on the computer." Eva's lip quivered.

The net was closing in on Eva. Kate could feel it, smell it closing as Eva talked herself tighter and tighter into it.

"And what about the computer records, Eva? Because they're gone now."

Eva stared at her lap and started to twist the button on her cardigan again.

"You wouldn't happen to know anything about that, would you?"

"Me? How would I know anything about that?"

"I was hoping you'd ask that. Weren't you, Detective Brothers?"

"Definitely, sarge."

Kate laced her fingers together, inverted her hands, and cracked her knuckles loudly. "So, Eva Kutenova, thirty-two years old. Worked in the UK since 2013 after gaining a master's degree in computer science at the University of Warsaw. Married Peter Kutenova in 2010 and had a little girl in 2011. Shortly after which your husband was killed in a car accident, leaving you alone to provide for your daughter."

Eva stared at her wide eyed.

"How am I doing so far?" Kate asked.

Eva just continued to stare but her face paled even further and her fingers wrung the hell out of her cardigan.

"Good, good. So after you were widowed, I'm guessing you needed to find work and fast. I'm also guessing that your options were limited in Poland so you came to the UK to try and find a job in the IT sector. Correct?"

"Yes."

"But they wouldn't recognise your credentials?"

"Yes."

"Bummer. So you end up working here."

"Yes." Eva wiped at her eyes again.

"So what happened next, Eva? How did you get from new worker to stealing the money that was supposed to pay for Alan Parr's care? The missing person that only you seemed to be aware was missing."

Eva covered her mouth like she was going to be sick.

Kate moved back a little but didn't relent on her questions. "Did the sister give you computer jobs when she found out about your skillset? Ease her workload and make extra time for drinking?"

Her cheeks puffed out, and Kate grabbed the waste paper bin. Thankful that it was a solid metal one with a bag in. Not like those useless wicker ones. She held it in front of Eva.

"You do realise that the innocent don't throw up when they're caught, don't you?"

Eva's dark eyes swam with tears.

"They haven't had to swallow the bile of their own lies." She held the basket under Eva's face. "We traced the account." She waved her phone at Eva. "We know that the account in Poland is held in your name. And we know that the payments were started at the end of January 2014. We also know that the payments were backdated to the eighth of December 2013. I can prove all of that. I can also prove that you were here throughout that period. And I can prove you knew the victim."

Eva finally gave up the battle and threw up.

The smell made Kate's own stomach churn.

"Eva Kutenova, you are under arrest on suspicion of fraudulently receiving monies from a government agency. You do not have to say anything unless you wish to do so, but you may harm your defence if you do not mention, when questioned, something you later rely on in court. Anything you say can be used as evidence. Do you understand your rights as I have explained them to you?"

Eva nodded. "Yes." She let her head fall to her chest. "I know it was wrong. I just needed the money. No one else even noticed he was gone. I didn't hurt him. I liked Alan. But he was an old man, and he wouldn't have survived long out there. The government didn't miss him. The staff didn't miss him. He had no family, but he was a kind man. He would help anyone in trouble if he could. That is the kind of man he was. Was the kind of man he was." She heaved again. "He would have wanted me to take the money if he'd known how much I needed it."

"Tell me everything, Eva. From the beginning. What happened that night?"

"I wasn't here the night he went missing."

"So how do you know when he went missing?"

She shook her head. "I was never certain until you told me. I only knew when I had last seen Alan, and that was the Friday afternoon before the flood. When I came back to work after the weekend, he was gone. I didn't realise though until halfway through the week that I hadn't seen him. I went to his room, but there was someone else in there."

Kate nodded and let her continue in her own time.

"His things, his belongings were all gone, and the folder with his notes in too. At first I wondered if he had died too. But no one had mentioned him passing. Not like Annie's death. Everyone was talking about that."

"Why?" Kate leaned back in her chair making it feel more like a conversation than an interrogation. She'd found in the past that once they started talking, it was easier to keep them going if there was less pressure. It seemed counterintuitive at first, but it really did work.

"It was so sad. She was a lovely lady, but so poorly. It was the first time I had seen death to be a blessing. I was still so angry at my husband's death then that I couldn't think of it as the release that so many of the people here see it as." Eva twisted the button on her cardigan again. Round and round, through the button hole, then back out again.

"I see."

"When I realised that he wasn't dead but that no one seemed to be missing him, I tried to talk to Sister Ama. But she was drunk and didn't remember what she was supposed to do. By this time I realised that, if he hadn't already been found by someone, it was likely too late to help him."

"When was this?"

"Just before Christmas." She frowned and stopped twisting the button for a moment. "Yes, maybe a day, two at the most, before."

"Christmas 2013?" Kate asked to clarify.

"Yes."

Kate scribbled a note on her pad. "Thank you. Please carry on."

"Just before Christmas, Sister Ama started getting me to take care of her paperwork on the computer. She would dictate letters and medical notes, but a lot of the data-entry-level stuff, she just left me to take care of while she drank herself into a stupor."

"You didn't think to tell anyone about this?"

"Who was I supposed to tell? I was new to the country, my colleagues changed from day to day, only the night staff seemed to be full-time at that point, and my boss was an alcoholic. Who was I supposed to turn to?" She pushed the button out of the buttonhole again. The thread was starting to fray.

"You could have come to the police."

Eva barked a laugh. "Right. And you would have taken me seriously? Excuse me, officer, but I think there is an old man missing from home but no one else remembers him. Can you go take a look, thank you." She laughed again. "You would have laughed at my face."

Kate wanted to tell her she was mistaken, but sadly she didn't think she was. She recalled a moment from her previous case where the victim had gone to the local police for help. They'd effectively laughed at her and their dismissal had cost Connie Wells her life. Did she have complete faith that Eva Kutenova would have been treated with any greater respect? Erm, no. "I'm sorry you felt you couldn't come to us for help. Please carry on."

Eva closed her eyes and reached for another tissue. "My daughter's hair was like yours. Red and long, and beautiful." She wept into the tissue. "She was sick. I needed more money than I can earn here to pay for her care. Sister Ama had me updating the accounts payable and I saw opportunity. Alan wasn't here, but the home had been receiving his money from the government all that time. Why shouldn't my daughter have it instead?"

"When was this?"

"End of January 2014. I entered all data in the new year. Sister Ama said it was to make sure that there was enough money coming in to cover wages over the holiday period while we had to wait for new residents."

"Sister Ama sounds like a peach. I don't suppose you know where I can find her, do you? I'll need to speak to her about her numerous crimes too."

"Good luck." She smoothed the tissue open on her lap and tried in vain to straighten the soft paper.

"What do you mean?"

"She's dead. Liver disease."

Bollocks. Diana Lodge had said her predecessor had passed away from illness. Kate hadn't realised it would be the same woman. "I see. So you decided you needed Alan's money more than she did?"

She shrugged. "Yes."

"And what did you do?"

"I changed the details on our computer system and deleted any record of Alan Parr, then I changed the reference name on the payment and changed the account it was paid into. It was quite simple in the end, and I could do it all by computer. All I needed was Sister Ama's password."

"How did you know his body wouldn't be found?"

Eva shrugged. "I didn't."

"You didn't, but you still went ahead and took the money?"

"I didn't have a choice." She scrunched the tissue in her hand.

"Yes, you did, Eva. No one forced you to steal the money. No one forced you to stay quiet about Alan's disappearance. No one forced you to lie to us about who he was. You've made choices all along. Bad ones. So why should I believe that you didn't know where Alan's body was? You've lied to me from the start."

"I didn't know. I swear."

Kate shook her head. She had to push. She had to be sure. "You've given me no reason to believe you. Why shouldn't I be charging you with murder?"

"No, no. I didn't." She reached for Kate's hand and tugged it towards her, begging, pleading with her eyes that Kate believe her. "I didn't hurt him. I have lived the past three years waiting for today. Waiting for him to come back." She let go of Kate's hand and pulled another tissue from the box. She wiped her eyes and her nose. "A part of me wished that he would just walk back in the door and that he was okay, but most of me knew he would not. That this would only happen when his body was found." She tossed the tissue on the table. "The more time that passed, the more I could sleep. I had prayed to God over and over to help me. To help my little girl. And then this happened. He answered my prayers. He showed me how I could help my daughter."

"God helped you?"

"Yes. He answered my prayers."

"Just a little FYI, Eva. God, doesn't answer prayers by making people perform criminal acts. That's the bloke downstairs."

"It was not a criminal act. I only took what I needed. I was going to stop when I didn't need the money any more. It wasn't for me. It wasn't."

"You were going to stop?"

Eva nodded.

"For the recording please."

"Yes."

"And how did you plan to do that?"

"I planned to stop the payment or reroute it back to the nursing home if he was found or when I didn't need the money any more. It was just while she needed the care."

"And she still needs it now?"

Eva looked down but didn't answer.

"I'll take that as a no. So why haven't you stopped the payment like you planned?"

"Sister Lodge is here now. I can't get access to the computer any more. I don't have her passwords. The system has changed, there are many passwords that you need now to do things like this. And a little machine for a card. I couldn't stop the payments."

"So your daughter's only just recovered?"

"No." She squeezed her eyes closed. "She passed away."

Ouch. She couldn't help but feel a pang of sympathy for the woman. Eva had lost everyone, and now she was going to lose her freedom too. "I'm very sorry for your loss, Eva."

Eva nodded and wiped at the fresh tears down her cheeks.

"You said only the night staff were full-time back then. In 2013. Who was on the night staff then?"

Eva shrugged. "Michal. He's always worked nights. I think Anna worked nights then. Maybe one or two of the nurses. I'm not sure. The rotas should be on the computer in Sister Lodge's office. In the back-up drives. They go back five years."

"Thank you. We'll take a look for that." She leaned forward and rested one hand on the arm of Eva's chair. "Given what you've told me, there's still compelling motive for you to have killed Alan."

Eva's eyes widened and her hand shook as she lifted it to her mouth. "I didn't. I swear." She reached out towards Kate but stopped before she touched her. "You have to believe me. I couldn't do something like that."

"Do you have an alibi for the night in question? The night of the flood."

"Well, I was at a flood party in Hunstanton. I met up with a lot of Polish people who live and work there."

"You told me before that you got the bus to King's Lynn to go home."

"I did. Then my friend, Maja, she lives in King's Lynn too, she picked me up to go to the party."

Kate handed her a pen and piece of paper. "I'm going to need the names and contact details of all the people you can remember being there that night."

Eva wrote quickly and gave the names of five other people who were there that night.

"Thank you. Eva, are you absolutely certain that you can't think of anything else that could help us find out what happened to Alan?"

She frowned clearly deep in thought. "No. I'm sorry."

Kate nodded. "Okay. I'm going to have to take you to the station now."

"I understand. I wish I could tell Alan how sorry I am. He didn't deserve this."

"No one does," Kate whispered as she led Eva out to her car. She caught a flicker of the curtains from the corner of her eye but by the time she looked up she couldn't see anyone behind the glass.

CHAPTER 23

"Sammy, get a move on or we're going to be late," Gina called up the stairs before she hurried out of the hallway. She couldn't stop the shudder that ran up her spine. "That's getting old now." She opened the fridge door, grabbed the milk bottle, and deposited it on the table as Sammy ran in.

"Sorry, Mum. I was brushing my teeth."

"Hm. Did you wash your face while you were at it?"

"You said I was running late so I didn't have time."

Gina pointed at the door. "Get upstairs and wash your face, you little madam. If you're quick about it your cornflakes won't be all soggy by the time you get back."

"Aw, Mum."

"Don't give me that. Now, go."

Sammy reluctantly scooted down from her seat and trundled out the door.

"Hurry up or they'll be soggy." The heavy footsteps on the stairs quickened. "Bloody kid'll be the death of me one of these days."

A soft beep from across the room alerted her to her phone. It was still plugged in. She retrieved it and sat back down, enjoying her cup of tea as she opened the app.

How are you doing this morning? xx

Kate. Gina couldn't keep the smile from her face as she replied.

I'm good. How're you?

Really? You're okay after yesterday?

Gina frowned. She didn't really want to think about yesterday or her meeting with Jodi. She especially didn't want to think about how she felt about it all. Nor how she hated living in her own house now.

Yeah, I'm fine.

"Mum, can I have a drink please?"

"Yes, water or milk?"

"Milk, please." Gina poured a large glass while she was still waiting for Kate to respond. It didn't normally take so long unless she was already at work. She passed the glass to Sammy and bent over her to kiss the top of her head.

"Love you, munchkin."

Sammy grinned. "Love you too, Mum."

"Are you still happy about the school thing? Ready for another day of protection punishment?"

The name had been Sammy's idea. Gina hated it, but it kept it a little bit fun for Sammy, and she was happy to go with whatever made it easier for Sammy.

"Yeppers. It really wasn't so bad yesterday. Mrs Eastern's actually kinda fun. Not like Mrs Partridge. She just made me sit and talk to her all through dinner time."

"How could she? Sit still and talk? You? Never."

Sammy giggled. "I did, though." She stopped giggling and frowned. "It was hard to start saying the fings."

"Things."

"Right. But when I started, it got easier. It was like when you take the plug out of the bath and the water starts to run away. At first it's a bit hard to pull the plug out, 'cos of all the water just pushing it down and keeping it stuck in place. You know?"

Gina nodded but didn't speak. She didn't want to stop Sammy.

"But when it comes out it all starts to run really fast. It was a bit like that. With my words."

"Do you want to tell me what you told Mrs Partridge?"

Sammy shrugged. "I don't fink—"

"Think."

"Right. I don't think I can remember everything I said. It was a lot."

"That's okay. You can just tell me the parts you remember."

"I told her about how I thought I'd shot Connie's face off. And how I thought I was a bad person and should go to jail but that it wasn't really me what did it. She said she knew it wasn't me, but she didn't know that I'd been there. That I saw what happened to Connie. Well, sorta saw." She pulled a face and put her spoon back in her bowl. Appetite clearly lost. "I asked her if she thought I was a bad person 'cos I saw that. And she said no, but she could understand why it upset me. She said it would've upset her too. And she's like a gazillion years old. So that made me feel a bit better."

"Why?"

Sammy shrugged. "Didn't wanna be a baby. But if Mrs Partridge would be upset seeing someone's face blew off, then I'm not being a baby." She looked at Gina as though the logic was completely reasonable and she couldn't understand why everyone else just didn't get it.

In a Sammy way, Gina did get it. And she wished again that she could go back in time and stop Matt from taking Sammy that night. She'd do anything for Sammy to have been safe in their house that morning. Then none of it would have happened.

"I asked her if it really was my fault that everyone's going to jail and all the kids won't have dads any more. Like me."

Gina bit her lip. "What did she say?"

"She said no. That it was Ally's fault, and my dad's fault a bit, but it was just as much the other kids' dads' fault as his. They didn't have to do the bad stuff, and if they hadn't, they wouldn't be going to jail. It's kinda simples really."

Gina smiled. "I guess it is. Did that make you feel better?"

Sammy nodded and reached for her glass. "Yeppers. Even if I did have to sit still for hours and hours and hours."

"Sammy, dinner time is only an hour long."

"And?"

Gina chuckled and her phone pinged. She ignored it. Sammy was talking and she needed to focus on her. "What else did you talk to Mrs Partridge about?"

"Hm. Well, we talked about the scary dreams."

"You did?"

Sammy nodded.

"Do you remember them?"

Sammy nodded and put her empty glass down. "But I don't like to. I wish I could forget them."

"Are they all the same or are they different?"

"They all start the same, but sometimes they end different."

"What happens in them?"

"They all start with me on the marshes, just like it was the day Connie died. In the dark, then watching it get lighter, with all the water all around. Then I hear the bird scarers and the shooting, and I try to get that rabbit for Dad, and then it changes. Sometimes I just wake up then. I can go back to sleep after those ones. They're not so scary. It's the other ones that I don't like."

"What happens in the other ones?"

Sammy tucked her hands under her thighs and rocked from side to side like she was trying to bury them further and further away.

"It's okay. You can tell me. Sometimes telling people helps to make the dreams less scary."

"That's what Mrs Partridge said."

"Did she?"

"Yes."

"Do you believe her?"

Sammy shrugged. "It didn't stop me being scared last night when the bad one came. I still woke up and cried."

"That's okay. It takes time for the scariest ones to go away. For them to get less scary. It happens over time and the more you talk about them, kiddo."

"Kate calls me that too."

"I know."

"I like Kate."

"Me too." She ran a hand down Sammy's cheek. "Tell me about the dream last night."

Sammy gazed into her eyes. It wasn't the gaze of a nine-year-old. It was the gaze of a child who had seen too much. The gaze of a lost childhood, lost innocence, but most of all a child who'd lost belief in the wonder of the world. She'd seen the black horror of what human beings could do to each other. She'd survived it, come out the other side. But it had left its brand upon her.

"It started just like the other ones. On the marshes, but when I go and look at what Merlin's upset about, I don't see Connie." Tears welled in Sammy's eyes, but they didn't fall.

"What do you see, baby?"

"Sometimes I see you there instead of her." The tears trickled down Sammy's cheeks. "And sometimes I see me."

Gina tugged Sammy on to her lap and wrapped her arms about her skinny frame. "Who did you see last night?"

"Me." Sammy sobbed. "I saw me dead with my face blew off."

Gina didn't want to imagine the horror of waking up after having seen your own body like that. She didn't want it to be true that Sammy did. But she couldn't change that. She couldn't take those images away from her daughter's mind. It was just one more way in which she felt helpless. Powerless to do even the smallest of things to help her little girl.

She held her as she wept, content to sit with Sammy in her arms for as long as Sammy wanted to stay.

Eventually it was a knock at the door that drew them apart. Both with their faces tear-stained, their hair a mess, but both feeling a little lighter than they had in quite a while.

"Feel a bit better?" Gina asked.

Sammy nodded.

"Good, go wash your face again and get your coat. You're late for school." There was a second knock at the door. Louder this time. "Coming," Gina shouted and tapped Sammy's bum to get her moving.

She hurried to the front door and pulled it open to a huge bouquet of flowers. Roses. Beautiful yellow roses. And lots of them.

"Georgina Temple?" The voice behind the bouquet asked.

"Yes, that's me."

A clipboard appeared from underneath the display. "Sign on the line, please."

Gina did and handed the board back as she reached for the flowers.

"There's a card in there too."

"Thanks," she said as she closed the door and went back to the kitchen. She placed the flowers on the table and searched amongst the fragrant heads for the card. Counting as she did so. Fifty. Fifty yellow roses. Why fifty? Wasn't it supposed to be a dozen red roses for a lover? What was the significance of fifty yellow ones? She remembered reading somewhere that the amount as well as the colour of the roses given always signified something. She wondered if Kate was into all that kind of traditional thing. Must be to send this.

The message was short and sweet.

Missed you last night. How about tonight we make it special? The Victoria, 8pm? xx

"Oh, Kate, what am I going to do with you?" she said to the empty room. She picked up her phone and checked the last message Kate had sent.

Okay. Sorry.

Damn it. The best and worse things about text messages. You can't hear the tone of voice on the other end. You couldn't tell if someone really was fine, or just pretending. You had to trust them or your gut. Clearly Kate trusted her gut a lot more than Gina's response right now. It was instincts like that that made her so good at her job.

Sorry, I'm just a little stressed right now. Sammy had a meltdown this morning and I don't really want to leave her with a babysitter so while I'd love to see you tonight, can we do a night in rather than out? Your place would be perfect. You're there so little anyway, it's practically a night out anyway. xx

She hoped the conciliatory tone she was feeling right now made it across the text. *Damn, I forgot to thank her for the flowers.* She shook her head and grabbed her coat and ushered Sammy out of the door. *I'll do that tonight.*

CHAPTER 24

Kate stared at her phone and frowned as she tried to make sense of Gina's text message. She tried to recall if they'd arranged to go out, but couldn't for the life of her remember if they had. Was this some sort of seven-week anniversary thing they were supposed to be doing? Was this something she should just know? Shit. What if she was making a huge fuck-up because she couldn't remember the stupid dating rules? She didn't want to fuck things up with Gina.

She read the message again. No. There were no further clues in the text as to what she was missing, but she didn't want to go out anyway. Gina wanted to stay in. At her place again. She liked that. That Gina felt comfortable there. Sammy clearly did, which was cool, and it made it easier with Merlin. Who Sammy also loved. So, no drama. Just play it cool and agree.

Night in at mine sounds great. Want me to pick up food? You know I have nothing in. Lol. Is Sammy okay? Need me to do anything for her? xx

She read the message back three times before she was sure she couldn't be making anything any worse, then hit send, and beeped her horn. She was quickly discovering that waiting for Gareth was just as bad, if not worse, than waiting around for Jimmy had been. At least Jimmy usually brought food with him. Hot toast, bacon butty, coffee on a good day. Gareth just stood at the mirror, checking his hair was gelled to within an inch of its life. God forbid that one strand tried to move of its own accord. It'd probably be plucked and tossed into the wind. She snickered to herself. *Now, now, Kate. Play nice with the little children. One day he'll probably end up being your boss if he can figure out how to play nice with the other kids.*

"Sorry, sarge," Gareth said as he got into the car. "Had some stuff to do this morning that put me behind schedule."

"Nothing serious, I hope."

"Nah." He smiled a little Mona Lisa smile and buckled his seat belt as she pulled out on to the road. "Where to this morning?"

"Brancombe House. We need to have a talk with Sister Lodge to check out some of those details Eva Kutenova gave us yesterday. See if they pan out."

"Do you think this will cause problems for the home?"

"Undoubtedly."

"Will it have to close?"

She shook her head. "Not on the back of one relatively small case of fraud that didn't harm any of the residents." She indicated and pulled out of the junction. "I don't think so. There will need to be an investigation on how it could have happened in the first place, but given the fact that Eva couldn't get into the system again to stop the payments, I'd say Diana Lodge has already taken significant steps ensuring that it can't happen again. Wouldn't you?"

"Yeah. I just don't like that place."

"The nursing home?"

"Yeah."

"Why not?"

"It's just, I don't know. Sad, I suppose. I mean, we've been there loads of times now. Stuff about Alan Parr's been in the newspaper, on the news, online, but have you seen a relative visit any of them?"

"Nope."

"Exactly. And they've got family. I checked on them all. I mean, yeah, there's one or two who don't have kids, or they live abroad and stuff, but most of them have family living within a twenty-minute drive. And not a one of them's been to check up on them. It's like they've already buried them, dumping them in there."

"It won't be like that for all of them."

"No?"

"No, I think that for some of them it may hurt too much to see their loved ones like that. To walk into the room with your mum or dad, and have them not recognise you. Can you imagine how much that must hurt? To watch them wasting away and know there's nothing you can do to help them?" Kate tapped the steering wheel. "That's got to be one of the most powerless feelings in the world. And the people in the home aren't aware of what they're missing because they have no memory of it. How can you miss what you don't know?"

"So you'd agree with it?"

"With what?"

"Euthanasia. Assisted suicide. Whatever you want to call it. You agree with it?"

"Where did that come from?"

"It's been playing on my mind a lot since this case started. Seeing all of those people like that, just wasting away. It's cruel, sarge, and it got me thinking. I mean, oh, I don't know, I guess I was just curious about your opinion on it. As a theoretical thing."

Kate shook her head. "Whether I agree with the idea of assisted suicide in theory or not, I uphold the law. It is against our law. So no, I don't agree with it. As for euthanasia, that's a different thing to assisted suicide."

"How so?"

"Euthanasia is the caregiver making the decision for someone who doesn't have the capacity to make it themselves and actively participating in the act. Administering the drugs or whatever. Assisted suicide is helping someone who has the mental capacity to make the decision, but lacks in some way the physical capability to obtain the means to perform the act. They could depress a plunger on a syringe, for example, but couldn't get the drugs needed. Maybe they could take the pills, but they couldn't open a container. Those are the distinctions."

"So you've been looking into it too?"

"Not recently." She swerved around a parked car and tried to stop herself remembering all the websites she'd visited when her gran had finally told her what was ahead of them both. Kate had cried when she'd told her that she didn't want to die in a home pissing on herself and relying on other people to clean her up. She didn't want that to be her end. Kate hadn't realised it then, but she knew now that her gran was feeling her out. Seeing what her reaction would be had she asked Kate to do the unthinkable. To help her end her own life.

In the end she'd never asked. Kate was sure she'd seen the answer she needed that day and took matters into her own hands when she was ready. But Kate had wondered ever since she'd been old enough to really understand what she was being asked that day. Could she have helped her gran if she'd asked? Could she have popped the pills and put them in her hand, knowing she wanted to die? Would Kate have been willing to risk everything to prevent someone she loved suffering any longer?

She didn't know then, and she didn't know now. She truly hoped she'd never have to find out.

She cleared her throat and continued. "If we were to legalise either act, the question would become where do we draw that line? Who is eligible to be put down? Anyone who can't walk? Who loses the use of a limb through injury or stroke? For one person, that wouldn't matter. They'd still live a life they were happy with. To someone else, the idea of living in a wheelchair or with an amputated limb is devastating. They simply couldn't cope no matter how much you helped them. So who decides who qualifies for the law to apply to them?"

Gareth merely frowned as she glanced at him and continued driving.

But she wasn't done. "If the patient doesn't have the capacity to make the decision, then who does?. Say they were in a car accident and have a traumatic brain injury or a stroke. Or maybe they no longer have communication skills but they're completely aware of what's going on, and can enjoy that for what it is. Seeing their loved ones interacting with them in whatever capacity they can. For some, that would be enough to make life worth carrying on with. For others, it would be hell. But if they can't communicate that, who makes that decision? Who decides which of those people want to live and which of them want to die? It's too big, too vague a question, Gareth."

"Isn't that where the experts come in? The doctors and lawyers who know enough about the medicine to be able to make those decisions."

She shook her head. "I don't think it's a question that can be answered for each person as a rule or a law. Or at least I don't think it should be. I think every person has to make their own decision on what they can or can't live with, and let their families and loved ones know their personal decision. Because it is a personal decision that will differ from one person to the next."

"And if the families disagree with their decision?"

"Many will, I'm sure. Some people will think those who don't want to live because they're stuck in a wheelchair are selfish for wanting to end their lives. Others will think they're selfish for wanting to continue life in a wheelchair." She shrugged. "But it has to be up to them. Then if they're prepared to honour the patient's decision in the event that such a tragedy occurs, or if they can't live with that act on their conscience."

"And you think something like that could be legislated?" Gareth said sceptically.

"Probably not. At least not well enough to be certain that coercion couldn't be brought to bear. Think about it. You'd have to have sworn testimony from the patient that they wanted to die in the event of x or y circumstances. Then you'd have to have a doctor, if not a bank of independent doctors, confirm that x or y criteria were met, and then the family member would have to perform the act of euthanasia." She shook her head. "Can you imagine what that would do to the family member? Can you imagine what they'd have to live with from that point on? The stress, the guilt." She shuddered. "The money saved on the NHS in caring for the elderly or disabled that are now dead would instead be spent on counselling all the living family members who couldn't handle what they did."

"So it's not really something you've ever thought about, hey, sarge?" Gareth tried to lighten the tone in the car.

She sniggered. "You asked, Gareth. If you don't want to know…" She decided to leave the rest unsaid as she parked up and got out of the car.

Anna answered the door when she rang the bell.

"Hello, again. Is Sister Lodge in her office?"

"Detective. I believe so. Want me to go and check for you?"

"No, that's fine. I'm sure you're busy. We'll just head on back, if that's all right?"

"Sure, sure. You know where you're going now."

"Thanks." She brushed past her as she closed the door behind them and went back to whatever task she'd been doing before they arrived. Since it was early, she assumed breakfast feeding, maybe helping people get dressed still.

Diana Lodge sat at her computer staring at the screen.

"That looks engrossing," Kate said as she tapped on the open door.

"Ah, Detective. I wish it were as interesting as I'm trying to pretend it is. But it's like watching paint dry. I hate spreadsheets."

Kate pursed her lips, and waited.

"Please sit down, both of you. How can I help you today?"

"We've come by to let you know the outcome of yesterday's little enquiry session."

"Ah, right."

"I'm sure you know some, if not all, of it, but we have to do this as part of our debrief as you're the one now in charge of the business at the heart of the matter."

"Of course. Thank you for filling me in."

"There are some details we can't share until after the trial, but others that you'll need to know in order to guard against them in the future, if you haven't already."

"I appreciate it. Before you start can I get you something to drink? Tea? Coffee?"

"Coffee would be great, thanks."

"Same, please," Gareth said.

"I'll be right back." Diana stood and squeezed her body around the large desk.

"Do you think she knew?"

"Knew what?"

"That it was Eva?"

Kate frowned, but thought about it seriously. If she did, why hadn't she said so, or at least pointed them in Eva's direction when she came to them with the funky number and missing money? Would she cover for her? Did she know of Eva's circumstances and sympathise? If that was the case, then why bring them the information at all? Why not just let the investigation peter out as it seemed to be doing?

If Diana Lodge hadn't given them the data, they wouldn't have found out that 3840 was Alan Parr, and they wouldn't have been able to trace the money to Eva's bank account. It didn't make sense that she knew who the culprit was, or that she had any kind of sympathy for them if she did. "No, I don't. But I'll ask her."

"Ask her what?" Diana asked as she came back in with three mugs balanced on a tea tray.

"If you suspected that Eva was behind the mystery of 3840?"

"Good heavens, no." She handed them each a cup and sat back down in her chair. "I always thought she was a lovely woman. Very sad." She took a sip. "She has a haunted look, that one."

"Did you know about her daughter? When she died I mean?"

Her eyes widened in surprise as she shook her head. "Her daughter died? I didn't even know she had one." She put her mug on the desktop. "Eva was always very distant from me. Kept very much to herself, and played her cards very, very close to her chest. I can see why now. I mean, if anyone knew anything about her past and started asking questions, where would they end up?"

"I see."

"It made her very difficult to know. But she was a hard worker, and I never saw any reason not to trust her. She came to work, did her job, well, I might add, and went home. What she did after that was no business of mine, and frankly, I was glad that I didn't have to worry about dramas with her. No boyfriend dramas, or drunken-night-out dramas. She was easy to manage." She took another drink. "Watch the quiet ones. Isn't that what they say, Detective?"

"I believe they do."

"But you're here to debrief me on what I need to know. So fire away."

Kate was quick but thorough as she went over the details she could divulge.

When she'd finished, Diana looked stunned. "That poor girl."

"Excuse me?" Gareth said.

"She lost everyone she loved, and now she's going to prison for trying to help them."

"With respect, Sister, she broke the law."

"I know. But sometimes we do the wrong things for the right reasons. You learn that as you get older."

"The law is still the law." His jaw was clenched tight. The muscles on either side of his neck were corded and strained, but he kept his voice quiet.

Dangerously quiet. He reminded Kate of a coiled snake. Power that was twisted and harnessed, and ready to pounce. Ready to spring into action at a millisecond's notice and strike down his enemy. For a second Kate was acutely aware of how glad she was not to be facing that venomous glare.

"Yes, I know. And she'll pay the price for breaking it. You've already put the wheels in motion to see to that, haven't you?"

"Yes."

"Well, then. A little sympathy from me will do the law no harm. Will it?"

Kate smiled and offered Diana her hand. "Thank you for your time, and your help, Diana."

"No problem, Detective. Anything I can do for you in the future, my door is always open."

"I appreciate that." She led Gareth out of the door.

"You're right, sarge. She didn't know or she would've let her get away with it."

Kate wasn't so sure Diana would've let her get away with stealing more money. She might, however, have stopped further payments and let her off with what she'd already managed to take. That she could see. Sort of. "Maybe, but maybe she has a point."

"What? Don't tell me you'd let her steal from the government too."

"Not what I said. Don't be so blinkered, Gareth. If you want to be a good detective, sometimes you need to be able to look at things from the other side of the coin. You need to be able to put yourself in someone else's shoes and think the way they do. Then you can catch the criminals because you see what they see."

"Like what?"

"Like a woman who has nothing, but sees an opportunity to help her daughter that won't hurt anyone else. To us, she broke the law. To many people out there, yeah, it's illegal, but who did it hurt? No one. So where's the harm?"

"That's not right."

"The world isn't just about black and white, Gareth. It isn't all right and wrong, good and bad. There are shades in between that most of the rest of the world fall into. Think of Robin Hood. He was a thief, yes?"

"Yes."

"Yet he's revered as a folklore hero, and the prince and the sheriff are the bad guys. Why?"

"Because Disney made Robin Hood funny."

She tutted. "Fine, forget it."

"No, no. I'm sorry, sarge, you were trying to make a point."

"Robin Hood is a hero because he helped the little guy at the expense of the big bad, government agency."

"So?"

"Well, people still have that mentality. Who does it hurt if the government loses out a bit so the little guy gets a handout?"

"But it hurts everyone in the long run. Those small losses mount up, and the NHS has to make cuts. Cuts to drug availability, staff. Waiting times are affected, patient care is affected—"

Kate laughed. "And how many of Joe Public out there actually think like that, Gareth? How many of them think past the end of their noses?"

He stared at her.

"We see every day the great unwashed, the masses. We pick them up, lock them up, and half the time we throw away the key. Do you think any of them think about how a scheme like this would affect their health care? Their benefits, maybe. But not health care."

"Careful, sarge. Your bias is showing."

"I'm trying to teach you something here, Gareth. I'm trying to teach you how the other half think. The other half that you have to deal with every day. I'm trying to teach you how to be the cop you want your dad to see." She ran her fingers through her hair. "But you can't even see that, can you?"

"I see more than you think, sarge."

"Really? Then start showing me. Start acting like the professional you're supposed to be, Detective Constable Collier." She got into the car and slammed the door.

The office was empty when Kate got back but there was a note from Stella on her desk.

Interview room 2. Alison Temple. Video suite when you get in. S.

"Come on, Gareth. Let's go and see what Stella's got to say to Alison Temple." She held the door open as he skulked past her. "And for God's sake, stop sulking. I've known teenagers with fewer mood swings than you."

He mumbled something but she couldn't make it out. Probably a good job, she decided. She was pretty sure she could take an educated guess at the names he was calling her.

The video suite was an elaborately-named broom cupboard. Or at least it had been in its previous incarnation. It housed racks of monitors and video-recording equipment, two chairs, and a small desk just about big enough for a couple of notepads, a clipboard, and a cup of coffee. Tom was sitting in one chair watching the monitor in front of him, where Stella and Jimmy sat opposite Alison Temple. The view was a little grainy, black and white, but perfectly clear as to what was going on.

"Hey. How much have we missed?" Kate asked Tom.

"Hey. We're nearly done really. She's pretty articulate, and answered every question as straightforward as you'd expect. Doesn't seem to be hiding anything."

"Anything new?"

He shook his head. "Nah. A bit more in-depth. Nearly put me to sleep a couple of times. This accounting shit's not exactly edge-of-your-seat stuff, is it?"

Kate smiled. "Not really. Did she confirm if Eva's sequence of events was possible?"

"She did. She said that back then the NHS system was pretty open and this wasn't the first case of fraud like this that had happened. And may not be the last to be discovered either. It's why a lot of the new measures were put in place. Including those PIN-number generator machine thingies that work off an account card. Like the ones you get to do your online banking."

"Just like Eva said."

"Yup."

Stella reached over and shook Mrs Temple's hand, turned off the tape recorder in the room, and led them towards the door. Kate led Gareth out of the video suite.

They were only a few doors down from the interview room, and Mrs Temple saw her as she stepped out of the room. "Detective Sergeant Brannon, might I have a word with you, please?"

Kate was surprised but curious too. "Sure."

"In private, if you don't mind. It has nothing to do with the case."

Kate frowned. "Well, I'm not sure what else I can help you with, Mrs Temple—"

"Alison, please. Like I said yesterday, I hate being called Mrs Temple. And it's to do with Gina."

Kate swallowed and met Stella's gaze over Alison Temple's shoulder.

Stella nodded, and led Jimmy and Gareth back to the office.

"Downstairs?" Kate pointed to the landing.

"I was thinking maybe we could grab a coffee."

Kate raised her eyebrows, but followed Alison out of the police station and across the street. The coffee shop was a few minutes' walk away, and Kate chafed at her arms. She wished she'd thought to run back in for her coat as the December wind cut through the fleece jumper she wore like it was nothing.

Alison was quick to the counter and ordered coffees to be brought to them at a table by the window.

The shop was almost empty. Kate was glad of that as she wasn't entirely sure where this conversation was going to lead them. "Mrs Tem...sorry, Alison. What is it I can help you with?"

Alison slung her coat over the back of her chair and sat down, pointing to the space opposite her.

Kate sighed and sat down.

"I did a little research last night. Spoke to a few people. Broached a few topics that my friends and I usually avoid, Detective."

"Such as?"

"Gina."

"Why do you avoid talking to your friends about your daughter?"

Alison smiled sadly. "Because it hurts too much."

Kate held her tongue. She didn't want to get into an argument with her girlfriend's mother in the middle of the town.

"Let me see, I think I can probably guess what you know about me. Or rather what Gina's told you about me. Tell me if I'm right. I was a mother who lived in her father's shadow, and when she got pregnant my husband ordered her to get an abortion. She no doubt told you that I agreed with him, and when she refused, we kicked her out of the house and haven't spoken to her since."

The waitress put their cups on the table and walked away.

"Does that about cover it?" she asked and reached for her mug.

"Yes."

Alison nodded. "Well, it's all true."

Kate took a small sip of her drink. "So what are we doing here?"

"My friends told me that you're seeing Gina. Romantically. Is that true?"

Kate nodded warily.

"They also told me she was attacked a few weeks ago."

"Six weeks ago."

Alison swallowed and seemed to find it difficult to speak. "Is she okay?" Her voice was hoarse, full, like it held too much emotion.

"Physically, her wounds have healed."

Alison's eyes opened wide. "But?"

"It will take her some time to really be okay again. Things like that take their toll on a person."

Alison nodded knowingly. "Yes, they do, Detective."

"Mrs Temp...sorry. I don't mean to be rude, but I do have a lot of work to do, so please, why are we here?"

Alison lifted her mug to her lips, then put it back on the table without taking a drink. She cleared her throat. "I married Howard when I was sixteen. I know now that it was to get away from an abusive father, and I ran straight in to the arms of a husband who proved to be worse." She snatched the napkin from beside her cup and twisted it into a long straw. "Gina was born when I was eighteen, and Howard was so disappointed that she wasn't a boy. I don't think he ever forgave me for it." She tore the corner off the napkin and dropped it to the tabletop. "He was angry before. Whatever went wrong for him was always someone else's fault, but after she was born, he just got worse and worse. It was easier, and safer, to just agree with him. About everything. If he insisted the sky was green, I'd have agreed just to get through a day without pain."

"He beat you?" Kate asked quietly.

She nodded. "Sometimes." She swallowed. "More as the years went on. After Gina left." She smiled ruefully. "It seems it was my fault she got pregnant too."

"I'm sorry."

She waved her hand. "It's in the past now. I've finally got rid of the old bastard."

"How?"

"He lost his job on the farm at Holkham. Hit his boss, and he pressed charges. He went to prison for a few months. When he came out, I'd changed the locks and told him I didn't want to see him again."

"And he just went?"

She shook her head. "He kicked in the door, and it took three policemen to pull him out of the house. He broke my arm, my nose, three ribs, and I lost most of my teeth, Detective. He's back in prison."

"Christ. Are you okay now?"

She smiled ruefully. "Probably as okay as Gina is."

"Ah." Kate let the information sink in and remembered how Alison had said her split from Howard was a bit of a village secret. "How the hell did you keep that quiet?"

"Howard had a friend. Inspector Savage."

"And?"

"He told him that he'd keep it quiet if Howard agreed to plead guilty and never come back when he got out. That he'd move on."

"And Mr Temple agreed to this?"

"Yes."

"When's he due to be released?"

"Next year."

"Will he stick to it?"

She took a sip of her drink. "I hope so."

"I'm very sorry for your trouble, Alison. But I still don't understand what it has to do with me."

"I want to see...well, I wondered if...I thought maybe you could tell me if..."

"You want to see Gina." It wasn't a question. She didn't need to ask it. She could see the hopeful look on Alison's face. "Then you're talking to the wrong person."

"I've hurt my daughter terribly. I was weak. I should have stood up to Howard when she needed me to. Not years later. I know all that. What I want is a chance to explain it all to her. To give her a chance to understand what happened. To beg her to forgive me, if she can."

"And I say again, Alison, you're talking to the wrong person."

"Will she speak to me? Will she give me a chance to explain?"

Kate leaned her elbows on the small table and took her own napkin. She pulled a pen from her pocket, and scribbled the address and phone number of the campsite on it. She didn't want to give Gina's personal information away. She wasn't entirely sure she'd want Alison to have it. But the campsite information was available anywhere. She could have got it from any one of her friends with a simple question.

"I don't know if she'll want to talk to you, or if she can forgive you for all the hurt, Alison. I know it's affected her very deeply for a long time, and in ways you can't even begin to imagine. But the one thing I do know is that if you don't try, you'll never know." She held the napkin out to her. "I never knew my own mother. I lost her when I was a baby. But I would given anything to have a chance to get to know her."

Alison reached out. "Thank you."

"Don't thank me," Kate said and finished her drink. "If you hurt her again, just know that you'll have me to answer to. She's my priority. Gina and Sammy. Not you. Are we clear on that?"

"Perfectly."

"Good." Kate stood up.

"Detective?"

"Yes?"

"Will you tell her? About this?" She held up the napkin.

"I tell her everything."

Alison nodded.

"So I'd suggest you not wait too long before you use that."

CHAPTER 25

Kate stood in the open doorway as Sammy charged down the path and Merlin jumped up to greet her. Sammy giggled and rolled around on the wet paving stones as she wrestled with the squirming mass of dappled grey-and-white fur.

"Sammy, get off the wet ground! That's your last dry coat!"

"Sorry, Mum." She wriggled to her feet.

"Best get inside quick," Kate said. "Hang your coat over the radiator."

"'Kay," Sammy called from inside the house.

Kate continued to watch Gina close the gate behind her. She held out her hands to take some of the bags that Gina carried, and leaned in to kiss her. "Hey, gorgeous."

Gina smiled. "Thank you," she whispered and leaned in to kiss her again, slowly letting her tongue sample Kate's mouth.

"Hm. I'll have to call you gorgeous all the time if that's what it gets me."

"You can call me gorgeous all you like, but that kiss was for the flowers," she said, and brushed past Kate into the warm house.

Sammy and Merlin were playing tug-of-war with a rope toy.

"Ew. Don't put that in your mouth, Sammy. Use your hands like a human being."

Sammy rolled her eyes, but did replace her teeth with her much more boring hands.

"Erm, Gina?"

Gina turned back to Kate and smiled.

"Not to risk the loss of any future kisses like that, but, well, what flowers?"

Gina laughed. "It's okay, I know they were from you. You don't have to pretend." She plopped the bags down on the kitchen counter and started to unpack them, tapping Kate's stomach as she passed her.

Kate frowned and bit her lip. "I wish I was pretending, Gina, but I'm really not. I'm sorry. I don't know what flowers we're talking about."

"Oh my God." Gina stood with her hands in one of the bags and looked at Kate over her shoulder. "You really didn't send them?"

Kate shook her head.

"The roses."

"Roses?"

Gina nodded. "Yellow roses."

"Okay. At least they weren't red ones," Kate said with a gentle smile, but a worried look on her face.

"Fifty of them."

"Fifty?"

Gina nodded again. *Who else would send me fifty yellow roses if it wasn't Kate?*

"Gina, is there something we need to talk about?"

Kate's voice drew her out of her thoughts. "What?"

"Is there something you need to tell me? About who else is sending you flowers?" There was a slight edge of anger to Kate's voice.

"What are you talking about?" She planted her hands on her hips and noted that the noise from Sammy and Merlin had suddenly stopped. "Sammy, go and play with Merlin upstairs a minute. Kate and I need to talk about boring grown-up stuff."

Sammy scampered up the stairs while telling Merlin that that meant Mummy and Kate were going to have an argument. *Bloody kid.*

"Now would you like to explain what you mean by that, Kate Brannon?"

Kate took a deliberate breath and exhaled through her nose. "I'm sorry if I've got the wrong end of the stick here, but when I said longer than a weekend, I also meant just the two of us. I'm not interested in open relationships of poly-whatevers. If you want to see other people, then you need to see them and not me."

"You're joking?"

"No. I'm sorry, Gina. But I—"

"I'm not seeing anyone else." Gina threw her hands in the air. "Jesus, I can't even see you properly till I get my fucking head sorted.

I'm not interested in anyone else." She ran her hands over her face, then clasped her fingers under her chin. "I thought you sent the flowers because you're my girlfriend. You. No one else."

Kate looked unsure of herself. "You sure?"

Gina rolled her eyes. "Positive, you big dope." She pulled Kate into a hug. "Isn't it me who's supposed to be worried that you'll run off with someone else?"

"No. You've got nothing to worry about. No one else...wait. So who are the flowers from?" She frowned.

"Now you get it." Gina sighed. "If they're really not from you, then I've got no idea."

"Fifty?"

Gina nodded.

"Roses?"

"Yellow ones."

Kate whistled. "That's some serious cash, Gina. You sure no one's been, I don't know..."

"Sniffing around?"

Kate shrugged. "For want of a better phrase."

"No one. I'm the village pariah."

"Was there a message with them?"

"Yeah. It said 'Missed you last night. How about tonight we make it special? The Victoria, 8 p.m.?' With two kisses at the end."

"Okay, that explains the text you sent me. About staying in instead of going out."

"Yes. You were confused?"

"Just a bit. I wasn't sure if I'd missed some sort of weird seven-week anniversary or something." She laughed gently.

"Why didn't you ask me?"

"Didn't want to show my ignorance of the dating rules."

Gina chuckled. "Idiot."

"Yeah." Gina felt Kate's lips against her forehead. "But I'm your idiot."

"Lucky me."

"Nah. I'm the lucky one." Kate covered her mouth with a tender kiss and threaded her fingers into Gina's hair.

Tenderness quickly gave way to passion and Gina found herself pressed against the kitchen counter.

"How long will tea be? I'm starving."

Sammy's voice was like a bucket of cold water as they jumped apart. Both breathing heavily, both heavy-lidded with lust. *Bloody kid.* "About half an hour," Gina said and reached over to put the oven on to warm.

"I'm dying," Sammy whined.

"You'll live."

"Can I watch cartoons?"

"Yeah," Kate said. "You know how to work the remote, kiddo." She reached into the bags and started to help Gina unpack. "We'll talk about it more later."

Gina nodded and unwrapped a frozen lasagne, before sticking it in the oven. Gina was distracted and let Sammy and Kate carry the conversation throughout dinner. Who the hell would send her fifty yellow roses? Why yellow? It had to have some significance. She reached for her phone and quickly opened her web browser. Her search was fast and the results came up just as fast. *Shit.* She gulped down a glass of water. Kate looked at her with a frown. She shook her head. "Later."

Kate read Sammy a story while Gina paced back and forth in the living room. Before long Sammy was snoring like the freight train that Gina was used to, and Kate was back with her.

"What?"

Gina held out her phone to show Kate the page she'd found.

"The yellow rose given as a gift signifies friendship and new beginnings."

"Friendship's good."

"I haven't made any new friends. I told you, I'm the village pariah. They won't even talk to me, never mind shell out God knows how much on a bunch of flowers like this."

"So who do you think it's from? You're pacing, you look terrified. What do you think this is all about?"

"Could this be Ally sending some sort of sick message?"

Kate frowned. "She's in prison, Gina."

"So? I've seen enough documentaries on prisons to know they can get all sorts of stuff in there."

"And you think Ally Robbins has got a phone in there and sent you a couple of hundred pounds worth of flowers just to fuck with you?"

"Can you think of a better explanation?"

Kate sighed. "No." She ran a hand over her face and pulled Gina into her arms. "I'll call the prison tomorrow and speak to the warden. Get them to toss Ally's cell and make sure she doesn't have a phone stashed."

"Thank you."

Kate took another big sigh. "Okay, now for my surprise."

"Uh oh, that doesn't sound good."

"Well, I don't really know. That's kind of up to you."

"I don't think I like the sound of that."

"You have to promise to hear me out before you react. And then, whatever you want, that's fine. Okay?"

"I really don't like the sound of that."

"Please?"

Gina swallowed hard and bit her lip. "Fine."

"I saw your mum again today."

Gina stiffened. "Well, you said she was a part of the investigation you're doing so..." She shrugged.

"Yes. And she came in to give a statement, but then she asked to speak to me. We went for coffee."

Gina could feel her face shifting to a scowl. "You had coffee with my mother?"

"Yes."

"Why?"

"Because she said she needed to talk to me. And that it was about you."

"She doesn't know a damn thing about me."

"I know that, and so does she."

"So what did she want to talk about?"

"Seeing you."

"Fuck off." Gina pushed Kate's arms away from her and returned to pacing the room.

"You promised you'd let me explain."

Gina stopped and stared at her. "Fine. Explain."

"Your dad's in prison for beating her up. They're separated, and she'd like to speak to you. She wants to explain why things ended up the way they did all those years ago. I think she wants a chance to get to know you and Sammy, and to make up for those mistakes."

"And you told her I'd speak to her?" she asked incredulously.

"No. I told her she was speaking to the wrong person. I told her that she needed to talk to you if she wanted to ask forgiveness. So I gave her the phone number at the campsite."

"You did what? Why would you do that? Why would you give her my contact details without speaking to me first?"

"The details of the campsite are easy to get hold of. She could actually have got them without me giving them to her. But I did it for a reason. Well, a couple actually."

"They better be good ones, Brannon."

Kate smiled.

"What are you grinning at?"

"You've never called me Brannon like that before."

"And I won't again if you don't get on with this."

"Okay, firstly, I gave her those details so she wouldn't go fishing for your home stuff. I know she'd be able to get it by asking around. It's a small community. Giving her that info keeps yours and Sammy's personal stuff, well, personal, unless you decide otherwise. Not someone else."

Gina thought about it for a moment. "Okay, I'll agree that's a halfway decent reason."

"Thank you. Secondly, I told her that I'd tell you I gave her the information."

"So if she doesn't call, then we all know she isn't serious about it."

"Yes."

"I guess this is why you're the detective. Any more?"

"Yes, but this one's more a personal one for me than a good one to you."

"I don't...oh." Realisation hit Gina in her stomach. It felt heavy and dull, like an ache that would never go away. Just like she imagined it must feel for Kate. "Your own mum."

Kate nodded. "I know it's totally different. Totally. But I'd give anything to have a chance to talk to my mum. I know Alison hurt you. But I think she had her reasons, and I think half of those were to protect you. It might not be good enough, Gina. But I don't think it could hurt you more to know than it has harmed you guessing all these years." She swiped at a tear before it fell. "I'm sorry. I just wanted to give you a chance to know her, I guess."

Gina wrapped her arms around Kate's waist and leaned into her. "I get it."

"Does that mean I'm forgiven?" Kate's arms wrapped around her back.

"Probably."

"Phew." She pulled back a little and kissed Gina's lips gently. "I don't like it when you're angry at me." She kissed her again. "Even though you are really cute when you are."

"Not helping your cause any, Brannon." She puckered her lips as Kate chuckled and kissed her once more. Softly, gently exploring with her tongue. Her hands slid up and down Gina's spine, along the nape of her neck, and into the fine hairs at the base of her skull. *God, that felt so good.*

The shrill ring of Kate's phone tugged her out of the sweet sensation as she pulled away to answer it.

"Brannon." She gazed at Gina with hooded eyes and mouthed "sorry" as she listened. "You're joking?" She stood up straighter and Gina could see her switch from Kate, her girlfriend, to Kate, the cop, in a split second. "No, of course you wouldn't." She patted her pockets, and fished out her keys. "Okay, cheers. Bye." She ended the call and grimaced at Gina. "I'm so sorry."

"It's fine, Kate. I know you're on a big case."

"I wish I didn't have to go."

"Seriously, it's fine." She reached for Kate's hand and squeezed her fingers. "I'll go get Sammy—"

"No. Stay." She threaded her fingers with Gina's. "There's really no need to wake Sammy up just to drive back to your house and try and get her back to sleep. You know where everything is. Help yourself. I don't know how late I'll be, but I really like the thought of you being here when I come home."

Gina gazed at her. This was the Kate she was falling for. The sweet, wonderful Kate that spoke from the heart.

"Please." She reached for Gina's other hand, pulled their bodies together, and touched her forehead to Gina's.

"You just want me to let Merlin out for you."

Kate grinned. "That too."

Gina chuckled. "Fine. Now go to work."

Kate gave her a quick peck on the cheek, grabbed her coat, phone, keys, and rushed out of the door with a quick bye tossed in Merlin's direction.

"And for God's sake, be safe out there," Gina whispered to the closed door.

CHAPTER 26

"This better be good, Ruth."

"Why? Did I interrupt a hot date?" Ruth asked with a giggle.

Kate just stared at her.

"Oh shit, I did. How is Miss Temple?"

Kate glared, and Ruth laughed.

"Fine, I can take a hint. Seriously though, I thought you'd want to be here for this."

"You're right I do. What do you have?"

"Eighty-three-year-old male. Reginald Barton. Passed away this evening at Brancombe House Nursing home."

"I saw him." Kate spoke softly as she leaned over the body.

"When?"

"Couple of days ago. He was being fed but he looked to be completely away with the fairies."

Ruth nodded. "I'm not surprised. He was on big doses of lorazepam."

"For?"

"Seizures."

"And why was he having seizures? Do we know?"

Ruth smiled. "The royal we, Kate? Really?"

"Hey, a girl's got to do something to get you to open up. It's like pulling teeth."

"Fine. He was having seizures because he was in end-stage cancer. He has a tumour in his brain."

"Poor old sod."

"Indeed."

"So we're...sorry, you're looking at another dead dying man and nothing more, right?"

"You'd think so, wouldn't you?"

Kate looked up. "You're not?"

"I'm not." Ruth pointed to the nose and mouth area. "Do you see it?"

Kate looked closer and noticed a slight difference in the colour of the skin.

"Here, let me put the big light on it. You'll see it more clearly then." Ruth adjusted the moveable fluorescent lamp over the face of the cadaver and turned it on. "There."

"Oh my God."

"Finger marks."

"Bloody hell."

"Our poor Reg wasn't even allowed to go in his own time."

"Is there any way those marks could have been made by someone giving CPR or anything like that?" Kate asked. "Just so no one can claim that happened."

"No." She placed her hand over the marks without touching the skin. "See how the shape of my hand lines up approximately when it's flat like this?" She shifted her hands to place them as you would to administer CPR. "If someone was giving the kiss of life, then the marks would be here and here." She indicated then chin and nose. "Not here." She demonstrated her hand across the mouth again. "Whoever did this had to have large hands though. Definitely a man."

"Okay." She pulled her phone from her pocket and dialled Stella.

"Do you know what time it is?" Stella said hoarsely, her voice full of sleep.

"Too early for you to sound like you've been slumbering for a hundred years."

"Funny. Why are you bothering me?"

Kate sniggered. "Because I'm standing in the morgue."

"I thought you were seeing Gina tonight. I don't want to hear about your creepy fetishes."

"Ooh, look who's woken up her sense of humour. Do you want to know why I'm bothering you or not?"

"Please, continue."

"Remember I told you that Dr Anderson was going to examine any other residents who passed away from Brancombe House?"

"Yes." She heard the bed clothes rustle. "You've got one already?"

"Yup."

"Bloody hell. Tell me she found something or Timmons is going to shut this investigation down now we've got the embezzler."

"How does a faint hand print over the victim's nose and mouth work for you."

"Bloody hell."

"You said that already."

"All right then, smart arse, how does 'bollocks' work for you?"

"Much better, thanks."

"Right, I'll get the lads out of bed and get them to round up all the staff at Brancombe House and take them to Hunstanton."

"Just the guys who were on shift tonight. Ruth said the size of the hand print makes our suspect male."

"Is she willing to change the open verdict on Alan Parr given this finding?"

"Don't know. How about it, Ruth? Does this make you more inclined towards a suspicious death for Alan Parr?"

Ruth shook her head. "I have no soft tissue to examine. I can't possibly suggest that our skeleton was murdered based upon the evidence presented. It would never stand up in court even if I did. I'm sorry."

"But this one you're certain of?"

"Absolutely."

"So why didn't the GP who pronounced death spot it?"

"Well, under normal lighting conditions the marks would be pretty much invisible. The slight discolouration also becomes more pronounced over time as the blood in the body settles and lividity sets in. The bruising here becomes more visible. If you weren't looking for it, though, you could easily miss it. And when a dying man—"

"Dies, who's looking for anything more. Right?"

"Right."

"So, Stella, did you catch that?"

"Yes. I'll call the boys now and get them to round up the chaps on shift. Not too bright, whoever it was that did this. I mean, we were only there this afternoon. Why do this now? Why take the risk?"

"Don't know, Stella. I can't really figure out why you'd want to kill someone who was already dying anyway."

"Fair point. Meet you at Hunstanton police station?"

"Yup," Kate said and hung up.

"It's not a new idea, Kate. There have been a number of killers who have killed the sick and injured."

"What do you mean?"

"Angel-of-mercy killers."

"Like Harold Shipman?"

Ruth shook her head and looked disgusted. "No. Shipman killed for gain. Angel-of-mercy killers do it to spare the victim any further suffering."

Kate pointed to Reginald Barton. "Do you think his last moments were peaceful ones? While some bastard stopped him breathing and watched him die?"

"I didn't say I agreed with the idea, Kate. Just that they believe it."

"Sorry. You're right." She twisted her neck to crack the vertebrae with a satisfying crunch. "So our killer thinks he's doing the best thing for the patient. That he's saving them from pain."

"Maybe."

Kate felt it like a vibration in her chest as she realised who the killer was. "Compassionate?"

"Yes."

"Caring?"

"Definitely."

"And big, you said?"

"Yes."

Kate grabbed her phone again. "Stella, find out if Jason Maxwell was on shift on the fifth of December and tonight."

"I'll swing by the office on the way to Bramcombe House. You think it's him?"

"Dr Anderson just gave me a psychological profile of our killer."

"I did not!" Ruth shouted.

"Well, sort of," Kate explained.

Stella chuckled. "You can fill me in when you get there. I'll let Tom know who our target is, but we'll hold them all until we've spoken to them."

"Good plan. See you there." She hung up and turned back to Ruth. "Do you think you'd be able to get prints off the body?"

"You've been watching too many *CSI* episodes." Ruth laughed. "That stuff only works in Hollywood."

Kate stuck her tongue out. "Fine. Can you get me anything, forensically, that will link our killer to the crime?"

"I'll start the rest of the post-mortem now and see what I can find. I have to warn you though, whatever I'm likely to find will be fairly easy to explain away as your suspect not only worked where the victim lived, but was one of his carers. All he has to say is he did x, y, or z with Reginald as part of his job, and hair, fibres, even traces of DNA will be useless as evidence."

"Fair point. But maybe our suspect won't know that."

Ruth raised her eyebrow sceptically.

"A girl can hope, Ruth."

"Don't pin your case on hope."

"I'm not. I'm pinning it on a confession. I just need something to try and get that confession from him."

Ruth stared at Reginald. "Okay, I'll try to get a hand impression cast based on the shape of the bruising left."

Kate looked at her in awe. "You can do that?"

Ruth smiled. "Yes. But it won't hold up in court."

"Then—"

"But your suspect won't know that."

"Ruth, you're brilliant. That's just awesome. Awesome, I tell you. I owe you a drink."

Ruth sighed. "Well, if I must."

Both laughed as Kate walked to the door.

"Bring Gina with you and we'll make a night of it."

"I'll ask her," she said as she let the door close behind her. "I knew you were too nice to be true, Maxwell. No one who works with people is always nice to them." She hurried across the car park to her car and groaned. "People suck." She reached across the windshield and peeled the sticky yellow and black envelope off. "It's the middle of the night, for fuck's sake." She peered inside and pulled out the parking ticket. £60. Half price if she paid within fourteen days instead of the requisite twenty-eight. "Bollocks. I hate people."

CHAPTER 27

"Kate, how far away are you? We've got a problem," Stella said.

"Two minutes from the station." Kate pulled the car into a lay-by. "Why? What's the problem?"

"Jason Maxwell's running."

"Running?"

"Yes. He saw Tom and Jimmy at Brancombe House and scarpered. They lost track of him between the nursing home and the beach."

"Where between the nursing home and the beach?"

"I don't know, on the road."

"The Coastal Path, Stella. It's about twenty yards from the boundary of Brancombe House. Did they see which way he was heading at least?" Kate pulled the phone from her ear as a loud, scratchy sound filled the line while Stella covered the microphone and presumably asked them.

"Jimmy said he was on the right-hand side of the road."

"And how long ago?"

"About two, maybe three minutes ago."

"Okay, tell them to start running, and I'll try to get to Brandale Staithe before we lose him completely. If you drive along the road you might see him pop out of a garden along the way."

"Towards the campsite?"

"Yes. He might carry on along the Coastal Path if he's feeling lucky."

"I'll get the PCSO with me to carry on further."

"Good."

Kate disconnected the call, threw her car into gear, and gunned the engine as she pulled back on to the road headed east on the A149. Fortunately, the road was quiet. Given the time of night, that wasn't really a surprise, but she was always grateful when the traffic gods collided to make her life a little easier.

Stella's car was parked at the entrance to the harbour, the full beams lighting up the expanse of mud, bare masts, and grasses filtering in the wind. The right-hand side of the harbour was filled with little boats. Tenders, toppers, racing boats, all lined up one next to the other against a fence that separated the main harbour from the sailing club's parking area. That bit they closed off to Joe Public. The left-hand side was the salt marsh, with clay-filled creeks, sea birds, and the popping and fizzing of the water skulking back out to sea as the tide departed. At night it was a black and empty expanse as far as the eye could see.

"I saw him," Stella whispered as Kate got out of her car. Stella pointed towards the end of the harbour. "He slipped between those boats."

Kate nodded. What she wouldn't give right now for an armed unit... or even a rounders bat. But no. She had a Stella and her mobile. Great.

"Where are Jimmy and Tom?"

"Still running."

She glanced at her watch. "They need to up their game, Stella. This just isn't good enough."

"I'll be sure to tell them they need to improve their fitness to stop us from having to fight the bad guys just as soon as I see them." She slapped Kate's shoulder. "On second thought, why don't you do that?"

Kate ignored the sarcasm. "Come on then, let's try not to read guilt into this, and go and find out why our Mr Maxwell decided to do a runner." She pointed to the fence that the boats on dry land were parked up alongside. "I'll go down there, use the boats for cover."

"Need a distraction?"

"Well, since it worked so well last time we tried it, it'd be rude not to."

"Ready?"

Kate nodded and manoeuvred herself in a crouch to the edge of the fence. Stella stood up tall and stepped into the beam of light from her car.

"Jason Maxwell, I know you're down there. Come on out."

Kate crawled along the fence line as fast as she could. As her eyes adjusted to the darkness, she could make out more and more details of the harbour. The moonlight glistened off puddles allowing her to avoid splashing through them. The clink-clink of the steel cables along the masts disguised her footsteps, and the shadows softened and grew as she moved further away from Stella's car.

"There'll be an armed response unit here any minute, Jason. But if you give it up now, we can talk about it."

The straight lines of the highly polished hulls reflected the moonlight too. Until the last boat. The sleek lines of its hull were broken and the light was absorbed rather than reflected. The knobbly shape that broke the profile could only be one thing. A large hand.

"Whatever you did, we can sort it out, Jason. We know people run for all sorts of reasons. I mean, it doesn't have to mean you did anything that bad really."

Kate crawled closer. One of the fingers moved.

"I mean, you were probably just having a wank or something, and we surprised you, right?"

Kate was within touching distance of him now. She concentrated on keeping her breath quiet and hoped like hell he couldn't hear her heartbeat because that seemed to be all she could hear.

"I mean, it's a bit pervy, I'll grant you, but it's not criminal to have a wank at work, Jason. Not unless you were doing it over one of the old dears."

She inched closer still.

"You weren't doing that were you? Because that's just wrong, mate. On so many levels."

Kate stood up and reached out. "Jason Maxw—"

He roared and sprang from his hiding place. Powerful thighs propelled him towards Kate and knocked her flat on her back. The air was forced from her lungs as he lunged for her and managed to cover her body with his own. He wrapped his huge hands around her neck and squeezed.

Bollocks. Spots floated before her eyes as she tried to suck air into her lungs. But his grip was too tight. Her pulse throbbed in her temple under the unrelenting pressure from his massive hands. She clawed at his fingers and the soft skin of her own neck as she tried to pull them away from her throat. She didn't have long. Oxygen was being expended. Nothing new was coming in. If she didn't break his hold quickly, she was dead.

She kicked her knees beneath him and threw her fists at his bulk with no more effect than a kitten against a full grown lion. She had to do something, and she had to do it fast.

She stopped fighting for a second and gathered what was left of her energy. As she lessened her attack he leaned forward. His eyes bulged and the veins in his neck stood out. She could see his pulse in them. She could feel her own pulse beating in her neck, trying to push blood to her brain against the dam of his massive hands.

She reached up. This was her last chance. She didn't go for his neck; it was his eyes she wanted. She wrapped her fingers over the top of his head to give her the best possible purchase and pushed with her thumbs. Driving the nails into the soft meat of his eyes.

He screamed and let go of her neck to grab her wrists.

She twisted to get away from him but his weight on top of her was too much. He had her pinned. And now he had hold of her wrists too.

"Bitch," he spat out, and wrapped one hand around both of hers.

She still couldn't break free.

He wiped a trickle of blood from the corner of his right eye and looked at it before pulling back his fist. "That wasn't very nice."

He drove his fist toward her face. Time slowed as she watched his meaty hand descend. The second it touched her she knew she was going to be out cold and then he would kill her and get away.

Not today.

She twisted as far to the left as she could and used his own strength holding her arms as a lever to hurl herself up and away from the worst of the blow.

His ring caught her on the jaw before he landed with his fist buried in the mud where her head had been.

Then the weight was gone. She breathed as though it was the first one she'd ever taken. Deep and sweet. Then coughed so much that she parted with her dinner. She could feel hands helping her to her feet and rubbing her on the back. She could hear the mumble of words that went along with the hands, but couldn't make sense of them. She wondered briefly if her brain had died from lack of oxygen. Then comforted herself with the knowledge that she wouldn't have been able to have such a thought if she was brain-dead.

She looked up to find Tom and Jimmy wrapping handcuffs around Maxwell's wrists as he lay face down in the dirt. Tom was arresting him as she leaned back against the fence post.

"Next time," she said to Stella with a croaky voice, "you take down the criminal while I do the distracting."

"What makes you think I'd switch roles?" Stella pushed her hair back off her face and prodded her jaw. "You're bleeding."

Kate lifted her hand to her aching jaw and felt the warm trickle of blood. She wiggled her jaw, pleased when nothing new cracked or ached. *Well, no more than I'd expect it to given that punch.* "I'll live."

Stella put her hand to her chest. "My hero."

"Bitch. I just took a punch for you."

Stella raised her eyebrow.

"Okay, I just took a punch on behalf of justice and freedom and democracy and all that good shit. I should get time off from sarcasm."

Stella nodded sagely. "Fair point. I'll take a break from taking the piss when you go and get some stitches in that cut."

Kate blanched. "Stitches? Really?"

"Yup."

"Bollocks."

"Don't worry, we'll save the interviews for the morning. Bloody PACE. I've said it before and I'll say it again. If they're awake enough to commit the crime, they're awake enough to be interviewed about it. Namby-pamby coddling."

"Closes the defence loophole, though, Stella."

She sighed. "I know. Anyway, Collier can drive you to the hospital and you can get that taken care of."

"He's not driving my car."

Stella shrugged. "Okay, then we can leave it here at the harbour."

The last car she'd left in the harbour while she went to hospital had drowned. Literally. When she came back it was blaring its alarm and wiping the windscreen while the engine was off. "Bollocks." That was not a risk she was going to take again.

"Don't you have any other profanities in your vocabulary?"

"Bloody bollocks?" Kate offered.

Stella stood up and held out her hand to help Kate to her feet. "Note to self, get Kate a thesaurus for Christmas."

"You're going too fast," Kate complained, holding a wad of gauze to her jaw.

"I'm doing thirty on a sixty road, sarge. I'd be getting grief off the tractor drivers if it wasn't so late."

"Funny." She wriggled in her seat. She was starting to ache, and her throat was killing her. "Everyone's a comedian."

"I promise I won't hurt your precious car. I know it's more than my life's worth."

"See? There you go again with the funny."

"Want me to just shut up?"

"Whatever gave you that impression?"

Gareth didn't respond.

Kate sighed. "Sorry. I'm a bitch of a patient."

"Really? I hadn't noticed."

She snorted but managed to refrain from saying anything. She owed him a freebie.

"Will it scar?"

She pulled down the visor and held the wadding away as she looked in the mirror. "Probably."

"They do plastic surgery for facial scars."

Kate shrugged. "Maybe, but I won't have it."

"Why not? You're a good looking woman, why let a scar ruin your face?"

"There're more important things than a little scar. More important things to me. If someone can't see past a small scar like this might end up being, then I've no interest in looking past any of theirs. Wherever they may hide them."

"I don't understand."

"No." She pressed the wadding back in place. "And that's the real shame of it, Gareth."

They travelled the rest of the way in silence. He dropped her outside the entrance to the accident and emergency room, promising to be quick and put a parking ticket on her car so she didn't get another fine.

She booked in and was waiting for the triage nurse to see her when he came back. He held out a coffee cup. "I stopped at the coffee shop. Cappuccino, right?"

"Thanks." She took the drink and took a small sip.

"Sorry."

"What for?"

"Pissing you off in the car."

"You didn't. It's not your fault if you have a different opinion in something. A wrong opinion, definitely. But it's not your fault." She winked and took another sip. "You're young. You'll learn."

"Ha ha. Now who's being funny."

"Aw, Gareth. Haven't you learnt that yet? I'm always funny." She twisted slightly in her chair and grimaced.

"What's hurting most?"

"You mean besides my pride?"

"Yup," he said with a smile. "Besides that."

"Well, it's a toss-up between my back, my shoulders, my neck, my arms, my wrists, my backside, and my head."

"That all?"

"Yup. Legs and feet are good to go."

"Excellent. How can I help?"

Kate closed her eyes and rested her head against the wall. "Distract me from this bloody uncomfortable chair."

"How?"

"I don't know, juggle, sing me a song, tell me about the life and times of young Gareth." She shrugged.

"Well, I guess there is something interesting I can tell you."

"What's that?"

"I'm seeing someone."

"Well, well, well, Mr Collier. Do tell."

"She's a little bit older than me, but not much. Couple of years, that's all. Gorgeous."

"Of course."

He smiled. "Of course." He stopped.

"And?"

"And what?"

"Well, what's she like? What's she called? Where did you meet her? How long's this been going on? You know, just those tiny little details."

He chuckled. "Never stop with the questions, hey, sarge?"

"I'm a detective. It's what I do. So?"

"Well, it's still really early days. We met a little while ago, but I suppose you could say she needed a little convincing to take a chance on me."

"Ah, stubborn. A challenge."

"Oh, yes. She's definitely a challenge. But it'll be all the more worth it in the end." He stared at his hands as he steepled his fingers then slid them together.

There was an odd little smile on his face that she couldn't quite understand. It wasn't the goofy smile of the newly in love, it was more a secret smile. Of someone trying to hide what they truly felt. It made her a little uneasy, but he did look happy. No, not happy, more pleased with himself. Perhaps it was conquering a challenge that made him happy more than anything else. *Well, whoever she is, she's a grown woman. She can deal with Gareth herself, no doubt.*

"Well, good luck with it, Gareth. I'm glad you've met someone. It looks like she makes you...happy."

Gareth's smile widened but he still didn't look up. "Oh, she does, sarge. She's just got so much going for her. She's perfect."

"Detective Sergeant Brannon?" A nurse leaned out of an open door and smiled. "Let's take a look at that wound for you."

CHAPTER 28

Kate opened her front door and quietly locked it behind her. Merlin greeted her in the hallway, tail wagging, and rubbing herself up against Kate's legs.

"Hiya, girl," she said and crouched down to fuss around her ears and neck. Merlin swiped her tongue up Kate's cheek. She quickly turned her face away to protect her stitches. "Good girl, that's enough now." She stood up, shucked her coat from her shoulders, and hung it on the peg. She could see the lights from the TV coming from the living room, and smiled to herself. Gina must have fallen asleep on the sofa.

She rolled her shoulders, trying to ease some of the ache from them, and crossed the dining room to the lounge. Gina lay with her head on the arm of the sofa. The soft throw covered her legs, and there was a large Merlin-shaped depression at the back of her knees. The TV was muted, but the lights of the late-night infomercials flickered across her face. She looked beautiful. And so at peace. Kate didn't want to wake her, but Merlin's attempt to regain her place at the back of Gina's knees managed to do the trick anyway.

Gina opened her eyes and smiled sleepily when she saw Kate. "What time is it?"

"Almost four."

"You okay?"

Kate bobbed her shoulders. "Mostly."

Gina rubbed her eyes and squinted at Kate. "Oh my God, what happened?"

"Suspect resisted arrest."

Gina sat up and reached out to touch the wound across Kate's jaw. "How bad is it?"

"Not bad at all, really. Couple of stitches. Few days and I'll be good as new."

Gina stroked gently underneath the cut. "Why is it always you that ends up at the action end of these things?"

"The boys are wusses?" she said with a grin.

Gina chuckled. "I don't think so, Sergeant." She gave her a little peck in the lips. "I think you're a control freak who needs to be the hero."

Kate pulled back, and gave Gina her best innocent look. "Me? No. You've got me all wrong. I'm not like that at all."

"Of course not," Gina said, clearly not fooled for a second. She touched Kate's jaw again, focused on the cut. "Will it scar?"

Kate froze. "Probably. Just a little one." She saw tears build in Gina's eyes. "Does that matter?"

Gina's gaze shifted to Kate's. "Does it matter to you?"

Kate frowned, wondering exactly what she wanted to know. There seemed to be so much more behind the question than the question itself portrayed. "It doesn't bother me in the slightest." She shrugged. "It's just a little reminder to move a bit faster next time. I don't need another to match it." She winked.

"It doesn't change how you feel about yourself? About how you look?"

Ah. "No. I'm the same person I was when I left the house this evening as I am now. The fact that I've got a couple of stitches and a scar to show my evening's work doesn't change that. It doesn't lessen me, in any way. What I learnt tonight, and what I achieved make me a better, stronger person, Gina. Not less of one."

"That doesn't answer my question."

"Yes, it does. How I feel about myself, and how I feel about you, aren't tied up in superficialities. A scar, a mole, a freckle, grey hairs, wrinkles, age spots, skin tags, none of that stuff matters. Because all of it changes over time. Looks fade, Gina. They change. It's the person inside that matters. And the person inside me hasn't changed in any negative way because of this little cut." She put her hand on Gina's belly. "Just like those scars don't change the way I feel about you." She leaned in and kissed her softly. "Or how much I want you." Gina's lips were soft under hers. Her breath was warm, and the tiny moan she gave as Kate slipped her tongue over her bottom lip sent shivers down her spine. "It's the woman inside that I fell for, Gina." She touched her chest, right over her heart. "She's the one I fell in love with."

"You...you...but..." Gina's eyes were wide open and her breath came in short, ragged pants. "But we haven't even..." She flicked her hand between the two of them. "You know? How can you know that?"

Kate laughed. "I don't need to sleep with you to know how I feel about you. I know it's going to be amazing." She placed a hand on each of Gina's cheeks. "When you're ready." She kissed her again. She tried to convey everything she felt for Gina in that kiss. She tried to show her every measure of love and passion she was able to in every caress of her lips. With every breath she made a promise that she would treasure every second they had together.

"I don't know how long—"

Kate put her finger to Gina's lips. "Doesn't matter." She chuckled at Gina's sceptical look. "Think of it like an old-fashioned courtship. Those folks had the patience of saints."

"Yeah, and how many shotgun weddings?"

Kate laughed, relieved that the tension was broken. "True. But this won't be one of those relationships." She took hold of Gina's hand. "We've got all the time in the world, Gina, because I'm not going anywhere." She kissed her knuckles. "As Richard Marx once said, 'I will be right here waiting for you.'"

Gina groaned.

"Too corny?" Kate asked, wrinkling her nose.

"Just a bit." Gina leaned in and rubbed the tip of her nose to Kate's. "It's a good job I already love you, or that could've hurt your chances, Brannon."

Kate grinned and wrapped her arms around Gina's shoulders. "I'll work on my material." *She loves me. She said it, and she can't take it back now.* She tightened her arms and ignored how much her back ached. And her shoulders. And her head. And her arse.

CHAPTER 29

Stella's and Tom's cars were both parked on the gravel car park. They were just waiting for Kate, who felt nauseated. Why would someone do that? How could someone do that? Kill people who were dying already. What was the point? What did it gain them?

She knew who her chief suspect was. She'd seen it in his eyes when he'd had his hands wrapped around her throat. He was too comfortable with what he was doing. It hadn't been the first time he'd held someone down and snuffed the life from them.

"You okay?" Stella asked when Kate approached her down the corridor to the interview room.

"Yeah, I'm fine. Just a couple of stitches, and a few aches and pains. Nothing a good night's sleep and a few paracetamol couldn't take care of."

"Good, because our three amigos are a little belligerent. Did Dr Anderson give you anything we can use in the interview?"

Kate quickly told her of the hand cast Ruth was making up for them to try and rattle their suspect.

"Perfect," Stella said.

"I thought so too. Who do you want to start with?"

"You said the hand impression was big?"

"Yup."

"And we know we've already got him for assaulting you, so let's start with the littler ones and work our way up."

"Where are they all at the moment?"

"In cells."

"I want to put Maxwell in an interview room with Tom doing his creepy eye thing while we interview the other two."

"I like it." Stella quickly instructed the others what to do, and had Stefan brought into the second interview room. "I spoke with Stefan yesterday. Do you want to take it this time? A different approach might get us what we need if he's our guy."

Kate shrugged. "I don't mind. But we both know it's not him."

"I know. But we do this by the book. We've got bugger-all evidence on Maxwell for anything but assaulting a police officer. Without a confession, we're looking at circumstantial evidence only. And I'm not having this guy get off because we didn't pursue all lines of enquiry to their full potential. We need his confession to tie this up, and I'm not convinced he's going to give us one."

"Of course." Kate looked at Gareth and indicated with her head towards the door.

He followed her and sat next to her inside the small interview room. The window was high on the far wall, with steel struts between each of the four-inch squares of safety glass. The table was bare except for a small plastic water cup. Stefan Podolski scowled at them while he twirled the cup on its side, flicking the last drops of water out on to the table before smearing them under its centrifugal force.

"What you want with me now?" he demanded.

Still, his English is a lot better than my Polish.

Gareth started the tape and introduced them all. "Before the tape started, you asked us a question. Would you please repeat it for the tape?"

"Why am I here? I have done nothing wrong."

"I'm sorry for the inconvenience, Stefan. Do you mind if I call you Stefan?"

He shook his head.

"For the purpose of the tape Stefan shook his head. So, Stefan, the reason that you're here with us today is because of the resident who died at Brancombe House last night."

"What about him? Reg was sick. Very sick. Sick people die." He shrugged. "It is a shame, yes, but he is no longer in pain at least."

"Yes. Sick people do die, Stefan. But they don't normally die by being suffocated."

"Suffocated? I don't understand. He died of his illness." Stefan stopped. "Didn't he?"

Kate shook her head. "No, he did not." She laid out three pictures that showed the bruising on Reg's face. "From these marks we know, absolutely, that Reg was murdered." She let the word sink in and watched Stefan's reaction.

He was too stunned to do anything but blink and stare at the pictures.

"So where were you when Reg died?"

"Me? I was working. Putting Harold to bed when Anna shouted that Reg was dead."

"Shouted?"

"Yes. It was the first time she's found one of them dead. She panicked and shouted."

"I bet that disrupted everybody."

"You think so, wouldn't you? But no. Most residents they not really there any more. Medications, dementia, deafness. They no know what she shout for the most part."

"Can Harold vouch for you?"

Stefan appeared to think about it. "I think so. He pretty sharp, is Harold. Just a bit deaf, bad on legs. You ask him. I with him from about ten minute into my shift until Anna found Reg."

"What were you doing that took so long?"

"Giving him a bath. He has once a week. But he in a wheelchair so it's not very straightforward procedure. It take a while."

Kate glanced up at the camera and knew Stella would understand that she needed that information checked. "Explain it to me."

He crossed his arms over his chest. "You want me tell you exactly how I give an old man a bath?"

"Yes."

He rolled his eyes. "I run hot water in bath tub, and throw in a thermometer. It must not be too hot or we will be accused of abusing the residents. Then I collect towels while water is running."

"And what was Harold doing while the water was running?"

"He taking a shit. Great big, stinky shit." He grinned. "Need me to describe smell in more detail?"

Kate wanted to roll her own eyes but managed to pluck a smile from somewhere instead. She only hoped it didn't look as sarcastic as it felt. "I get the idea."

"When he finished shitting, I help to take off rest of his clothes and wrap sling around him. Harold is big guy and he no can walk. We have to use sling and hoist to move him from wheelchair to toilet, toilet to bath chair, to bed. Whatever. He no like hoist. And he especially no like it when we have to move the hoist while he's hanging in the air." He shook his head. "Is very undignified. To hang in mid-air with everything on show. So we have to be fast for him. Is only fair." He shrugged like he was doing the man a great favour. "When I fix bath chair to winch I can then lower him down into the water. Need me to describe how I wash feet and arse for him?"

"I get the picture, Stefan. I'm sorry, but we have to do this. It's for the safety of your patients, you know?"

Stefan stared at her.

"If one of those people was your father or grandfather, wouldn't you want to be sure they were somewhere safe?"

He stared some more then sighed heavily and nodded. "It took an hour and a half before Harold was dry, in wheelchair, and back in his bedroom. I was about to get him cup of tea and biscuit when I hear Anna shout. I was with Harold whole night." He leaned forward and rested his elbows on the table. "They are safe with me. I do my best. I try to give respect. You know?" He twitched one shoulder in a half shrug. "I no always get it right, I'm no always in good mood. But I never hurt them. Never."

There was a tap on the door before it opened and Stella pushed her head around. "Harold confirms."

"Thanks." Kate turned back to Stefan. "I'm sorry for the inconvenience, Stefan. And thank you for answering all my questions. You're free to go."

"I am?"

"Yes."

"Fine." He looked at his watch. "How am I get back to work now?"

"We'll sort you a lift as soon as you're booked out."

"Interview terminated at 9.32 a.m.," Gareth said, and stopped the tape. He was labelling it up as Kate led Stefan out of the room.

Stella was waiting for her. "I'll run the same with Michal now."

Kate nodded. "How's Tom doing in there?"

Stella waved her towards a bank of monitors and pointed to one of the small screens.

"As he usually does. But look."

Kate watched Jason Maxwell. He seemed totally calm, serene, almost. Unfazed by Tom's stare as he leaned his chair back on its rear legs, folded his arms behind his head, and looked to be asleep. His balance was perfect. Not a shudder or a shift to betray any unease.

"I'm looking forward to this one," Kate said under her breath and tapped the screen, wishing the motion would've knocked him on his back.

"Are we ready for Michal?"

"Show me what you've got, Stella."

"I was going to let Jimmy have a crack at him. You think he's ready?"

Kate bobbed her head as she thought about it. "Yeah. I think he can handle it. You'll be right there if need be, so yeah, let him have a crack."

"That reminds me, we need to have a chat about Collier before long."

"Okay. We can do that once we wrap up this case."

Jimmy's interview went smoothly for the most part. His questions were a little rough in places, perhaps not as open-ended as they could have been in others. Overall though, not bad. But it was quickly evident that he also wasn't the man they were looking for. His hands shook, and they were far too small. Smaller than Kate's own, with short, stubby fingers. There was no way he could have left the impression on Reg's face that she'd seen. That had left their impression on her own neck.

Time and again she was drawn back to the monitor where she could watch Jason Maxwell sleep in his chair.

She loved bringing down the cocky ones. The ones who thought they were so much better than they were. The ones who thought they could do anything and they'd get away with it.

CHAPTER 30

She was convinced that Jason Maxwell was their killer. She was just as convinced that getting him to admit it was going to be painful. Like a root canal without anaesthetic.

"We didn't even show him the picture of Alan, did we?" She asked the question more for herself than anyone else.

"No, sarge," Gareth answered anyway.

"Go and grab the pictures, and any photos of him with Alan from the ones Diana Lodge supplied. Let's do this from the beginning and see how much we can rattle your cage, bud."

Stella picked up the headphones and held them ready to slip over her ears. "Are you taking Collier in with you?"

Kate shook her head. "Tom's been in there all this time."

"Doesn't seem to have had much effect on him."

"No, but I want to keep personnel changes as options for later, just in case."

Stella nodded and slipped the headphones over her head. "Good luck."

Kate closed her eyes, swallowed, and ignored what Stella had said. Luck was what you needed if you were crap at your job. Luck was what you needed when you were grasping around in the dark. She wasn't. She knew.

Gareth handed her a document wallet full of pictures and notes. She slipped it under her arm and pushed open the door.

Maxwell opened one eye, smiled, and lowered his chair to the floor. "Good morning, Detective. Are you coming to speak to me at last? Your ape over there doesn't seem to have a tongue in his head."

Kate sat down and reached across to start the tape recording. "This is Detective Sergeant Kate Brannon interviewing Jason Maxwell. Also in the room is Detective Constable Thomas Brothers. It is ten-fifteen on the morning of the thirteenth of December. Can I get you anything? Coffee, tea, water?"

"Thank you, but no. I'm fine," Maxwell said.

"Very well. Let's get down to business then. Before I ask you any questions, though, I must advise you of your rights. At this moment in time, you are under arrest for assaulting a police officer and resisting arrest. You were advised of this by Detective Constable Thomas Brothers at Brandale Staithe Harbour and then brought here for further questioning to help us with our enquiries."

"I understand."

"As such, and in regards to these separate questions, you do not have to say anything unless you wish to do so, but you may harm your defence if you do not mention, when questioned, something you later rely on in court. Anything you say can be used as evidence. Do you understand your rights as I have explained them to you?"

"Absolutely."

"Good. Do you recognise this man?" Kate placed the picture of Alan on the table. The one without the beard. "For the tape I am showing Mr Maxwell exhibit BB047A."

Maxwell picked up the page and studied it carefully. "No, I don't think so." He put it back on the scarred wood.

"Do you mind if I call you Jason? It feels so cumbersome to say Mr Maxwell all the time, doesn't it?"

"Erm, yeah. Okay."

"Thanks, Jason. So what about this one?" She placed the altered image in front of him. "I'm showing Jason exhibit BB047B."

He lifted it and squinted at the photo. "Hm. This man seems familiar, but I'm afraid I couldn't tell you any more."

She put the first picture back in the document wallet and sat a 4x6-inch photo next to it. "I am now showing Jason exhibit BH0238. Is this you?" She pointed to the photo.

"Yes, that's me."

"And who is that in the photograph with you?"

"I believe that's a resident. I can't think of his name. Perhaps he was a respite patient."

"Respite patient?"

"Yes. We sometimes have people come in for a short time. A few days, a week or two, when their families need a rest. If they're being cared for by elderly spouses and the like, it can be necessary for their good health to get respite on occasion."

"I see." Kate paused. "What if I told you this gentleman had no family?"

"Hm. Then I'm afraid I don't know."

Kate placed four more pictures of Alan and Maxwell together on the table, each one clearly taken at different times based on clothing and haircuts.

"I am showing Jason exhibits BH0349, BH0279, BH1003, and BH0847. Can you please identify the people in these pictures?"

He scowled.

Kate felt like pumping her fist in the air. The first reaction.

"They all show me and this same man."

"But you don't know who he is?"

"I'm sorry, no, I don't."

"Okay, we'll come back to this in a little while." She gathered up the photos and slipped them back into the document wallet. Next she let the picture of the skeleton slide out and sit on the table in front of him.

He pushed his chair away from the table as though it were on fire. "Get that away from me. That's disgusting."

One-nil.

"I'm sorry about that, Jason. That just slipped out of the folder. Please accept my apology." She noisily slid it back into the folder. "Can I get you anything, Jason? You look a little pale there. Some water, perhaps?"

He nodded, still staring at her. His eyes were wide and his eyebrows drawn up. Not in a frown, more like a shocked expression. He'd prepared himself for the images of Alan in life. Even the pictures of the facial reconstruction were expected. He hadn't expected to see the bones.

Jimmy stepped in with a plastic cup.

"Detective Constable Powers has entered the room with some water for Mr Maxwell."

Maxwell chugged it down in one and Jimmy took the empty cup away. Now they had his DNA too. She knew Jimmy would be bagging the cup and sending it over to Ruth to be processed.

She wanted to smile that he'd let his guard down so easily, but she bit it back and continued with her next question. She placed a picture of Reginald Barton on the table. "Do you know this man?"

Maxwell nodded.

"For the tape please, Jason."

"Yes."

"Thank you. I'm showing Mr Maxwell exhibit BH2310. A photograph of Mr Reginald Barton. Jason, could you please explain how you know Mr Barton."

"He was a resident at Brancombe House for the past few years."

"And you were his care worker?"

"We all worked with everybody. No one specifically looked after any one resident."

"I understand, but Diana Lodge told us that you were his key worker."

"Yes, I was."

"And what does that entail?"

"Making sure that Reg had everything he needed, that he wasn't running out of socks and whatnot. Getting in touch with his family if he did need anything. Making sure he got his baths every week, scheduling his chiropody appointments." He shrugged. "Just stuff like that."

"And how many residents are you the key worker for?"

"Ten."

"That seems a lot."

"I've been there a long time. It's not difficult work." He clenched and unclenched his fists against his thighs. The tendons and muscles in his forearms flexed with each movement. "It's stuff I'd do anyway, really."

"So as his key worker you'd have to be privy to exactly what Reg's medical prognosis was."

"Yes. He had a brain tumour that was causing severe seizures."

"Did you administer any of his medication?"

"No, I'm a carer, not a nurse. Only the nursing staff can do that sort of stuff. We do the things that are considered beneath the trained medical staff."

Kate cocked her head to the side as she caught the note of bitterness in his voice. *A chink in the armour?* "Did that make you feel like a second-class citizen?"

"What?"

"That there were people working there doing things that you weren't allowed to. That they considered themselves too good to do what you had to do, day after day. I bet that pissed you off."

He clenched his fists tight and kept them balled on his knees. "No, that's their job. Most of them do it pretty well. They do their job and I do mine. I'm not trained to do their job and they can't do mine. Not the way I do."

She watched him as he realised what he'd said. "Meaning?"

His Adam's apple bobbed as he swallowed hard, thinking about his response. "The nurses don't care about the patients. They've got too many to look after at any one time. They don't even know their patients' names unless they're in their rooms where their names are on the door." He tapped his chest. "Not me. I'm not like that. I know my patients. I know what they need, what they want. I care for them." He shook his head. "I care about them. And because I care about them, I can do things for them that no one else will."

Kate pulled the photo of Reg on the morgue table from the folder and put it in front of Maxwell. The picture showed a close up of Reg's mouth with the bruising revealed under the harsh light. She pointed to the bruises. "Is this something you did that no one else would?"

He stared at her, refusing to look at the picture.

"I'm showing Mr Maxwell BH2311. Is this what you did?"

Kate waited.

Maxwell said nothing.

"Very well." She left the picture on the table. "So tell me about the seizures Reg was suffering from."

Maxwell squinted at her quick change of subject. "The seizures?"

"Yes. What did they do to him? How often did he have them? That sort of thing. You were his key worker, weren't you? You know this stuff? Or should I ask one of the nurses to check his notes and tell me the answers?"

"Pfft. The seizures started off irregular. Maybe one a month. But during a seizure, blood flow got restricted and parts of his brain would get damaged. The more damage there was, the more seizures he had, so the more damage was created. It was a vicious circle. One that the medication didn't work for, and one he was never going to get better from."

Kate nodded sadly, and echoed Eva's earlier statement. "Death was a release for him."

Maxwell's eyes lit up and she saw a glimmer of excitement in them. He thought she understood his perspective. He thought she agreed with it.

His shoulders relaxed and his fists unclenched. He wiped a hand across his face, swiping away his anxiety with the sweat he removed. "Exactly. Every day was worse than the one before. A week ago, he could speak. He could communicate enough to tell us what he wanted. But then he had another seizure on Monday." Maxwell bent his head and clasped his hands on the table. He looked deflated. As though he really missed the relationship he'd had with Reg.

Kate suddenly realised that Maxwell didn't see Reg as a victim or a patient. He saw him as a friend.

"It wiped out what was left of his communication skills. He was just turning into a vegetable where he sat."

"It must have been terrible to see your friend like that."

He nodded. "It was. Reg was such a strong man. A good man. To see him sitting there day after day dribbling and pissing all over himself. What kind of life is that for a man? For anyone?"

"None at all," Kate agreed.

"He didn't deserve that."

"No."

He looked at the picture of Reg. Not the one showing the bruises. The one showing him alive and smiling. "This is the Reg I'll always remember. Not seeing him after he started dying, one piece at a time. Not the way he looked after he died."

Bingo. "I thought it was Anna who found him when he died. I didn't realise you were with her." She shuffled through her pages, pretending to locate a report she knew by heart while she watched him. "Yes, that's what I thought. Anna found him and it was called in by the nurse on duty. They were with him until the GP came and declared Reg dead. When did you see him?"

"I didn't."

"But you said you didn't want to remember him the way he looked after he died. What did you mean, Jason?"

"I...I..." he stammered, his gaze darting about the room, and his breathing quickened for a beat or two. "I meant the picture you showed me." His breathing slowed a little and a smug, relieved smile twitched at the corner of his lips.

Yes, it was plausible. But it's not fucking true. "Hm." She shifted tracks again. "Do you know that we're going to be able to prove who made this mark on Reg's face?"

"Excuse me?"

"Yes. The coroner and crime scene people are using the bruise to make a cast of the hand that made this bruise. We'll be able to match it to a person when it's finished."

He paled and a bead of sweat formed on his upper lip.

She smiled and shook her head in awe. "Science is truly amazing, don't you think?"

He didn't respond with words but his jaw clenched.

Is that grinding teeth I can hear? "Now we know we aren't going to be able to get a print or anything conclusive like that. But that's actually okay. It doesn't really matter at this point. Should I tell you why?"

He folded his hands across his chest. His tunic bunched under his armpits and pulled tight across huge pectoral muscles.

"It's actually quite simple. See, what this cast will show is the exact size of the hand that killed Reginald Barton."

His chest rose and fell as his breathing sped up.

"Reginald Barton never left Brancombe House."

Maxwell's right eye twitched. A tiny, tiny little movement.

"So his killer had to be there. In Brancombe House, and his hand had to be that size." She tapped the photo again. "And that took a big hand, Jason." She splayed her fingers out. "I've met the other men who work at Brancombe House. The ones who were on shift last night." She closed her hand and held her finger and thumb about an inch apart. "And they've all got tiny hands." She pointed to his where he had them tucked under his armpits still. "Except you."

His lip curled into a sneer but he still said nothing. He just stared at her. The look in his eye had gone from feeling understood to one of anger. He felt she'd let him down by not being able to understand what he'd done for Reg. She could see it. She needed to keep him off balance. She needed to keep him thinking on his feet until he slipped up again.

"Was Alan Parr ill?"

"What?"

"Like Reg, was Alan ill?"

"No." He paused. "I don't know. How would I know that?"

"You said no, first. You did know him."

"No, I didn't."

"Yes, you did. We've got photographs to prove it."

He waved a hand in her direction. "I mean I don't remember him."

"That's not what you said. You said you didn't know him. That's different."

"I meant, I don't remember him."

"Then why didn't you say that?"

"Because you're trying to confuse me." He put both hands flat on the table and leaned forward, his chest almost parallel with the surface. "You're trying to get me to say things that aren't true."

Kate shook her head. "No, Jason, far from it. The only thing I'm trying to do is get you to tell the truth."

"You don't want the truth."

"I can assure you, that's all I want."

"No, you couldn't deal with it."

"Try me."

He opened his mouth, but stopped the words from tumbling from his tongue. He sneered at her again and shook his head as he sat back in his chair and crossed his arms over his chest again.

Damn it, that was close. She could feel it. "Pathetic." She sighed. "For the purposes of the tape Mr Maxwell is shaking his head." She needed another line of attack and his ego was ripe for a little prodding. "Why didn't you become a nurse?"

"Excuse me?"

"You said you care about your patients, more so than the nursing staff. Surely if you were a nurse you'd be able to help your patients more than you can as a care worker."

"I can do everything my patients need me to do for them just as I am, thanks."

"But carers are the bottom of the food chain in the medical profession. So why wouldn't you want to better yourself and thereby do better for the patients you profess to care so much about? Did you ever apply to go to nursing school or medical school?"

"No. Like I said, I don't see the need."

"Yes, I heard. You can do everything they need of you as you are."

"That's right." He smiled smugly.

"Do you know what that says to me?"

He didn't respond.

"You didn't have the stones to try." She crossed her own arms, mirroring his pose, and leaned back in her chair. "Don't you think, Detective Constable Brothers?"

She heard Tom chuckle behind her. "Definitely, sarge."

"You don't know anything," Maxwell hissed through gritted teeth.

"Maybe," Kate conceded. "But I *think* I know an awful lot, Jason. And in this job, thinking I know something is the first step to me being able to prove the truth of it. That's the position I put myself in by becoming a detective rather than remaining a uniformed officer." She leaned on the desk again. "That's what I mean about getting yourself off the bottom rung of the ladder, Jason. As you climb, you start to see things a bit differently. Other options open up to you. Other possibilities. New abilities." She shrugged. "But you don't know any of that, because you're happy wiping shitty arses and thinking you're the only person in the world who can do it."

Tom sneered behind them both and Maxwell's glare shifted to him.

"What is it that makes your arse-wiping technique so much better than anyone else's?" She waited until he was looking at her again. "Do you use balm on the tissue?"

He didn't respond but the vein at his temple thumped and a bead of sweat ran down his reddening cheeks.

"No balm then. Do you use a wet cloth to ease the chafing?"

His jaw clenched tighter. Tom must have been able to hear the grinding.

"Come on, Jason. Enquiring minds want to know. What's your secret?"

"You want to know what my secret is?" he asked, his voice little more than a whisper through his teeth.

"Oh, yeah," Kate whispered back. "I'm waiting with bated breath."

Maxwell sneered. "You wouldn't understand. You couldn't. You don't have the capacity to perceive my secrets, my truths."

"Try me."

"You sit here in your little box and think you're all powerful. Don't you?"

She didn't respond. She could feel he was on the verge of letting go.

"You think you've got it all under control. You think you've got me under control. With your giant ape in the back of the room to protect you." He laughed and held his right hand up. He positioned his hand as though it were wrapped around her neck and flexed his fingers and thumb.

She could almost feel those fingers around her neck. Feel the squeeze. But she refused to react.

He sneered again. "You haven't got a fucking clue what control is. What power is." Spittle gathered at the corner of his mouth and his cheeks reddened. "True power."

"Then why don't you enlighten me, Jason."

"Because you don't deserve the truth."

"No? But Reg deserved to die?

"Reg didn't deserve to live! Not like that. He wanted to die, you stupid bitch. He wanted it over with."

"How do you know that? You're the one who told me he couldn't speak any more. Sat there dribbling and pissing all over himself, I believe was the phrase you used."

"I know, because I always know."

"You always know?"

"Oh, yeah. I always know." He curled his hands into fists. "I know when they're ready to go. I know how they want to go. I can see it in their eyes. Begging me to set them free. They beg everyone, but there's only me who can see it. There's only me who's got the bottle to do what needs to be done. Only me who cares enough. You talk about not having the stones to go to nursing school. Bollocks. No nursing school can teach me what I already know. What I can already see every time they look at me. I've got more than enough balls to do what they need from me."

"You kill them." It wasn't a question. It didn't need to be.

"No, Detective." He shook his head. "No, I don't kill them. I set them free!"

"Free from what exactly?"

"From the pain. The misery. The loneliness. I set them free from this pathetic excuse of a life that they're forced to endure because we have the medical skill to keep them alive, but not the decency to know when to stop. When we shouldn't use our wonderful advances. So I give them what they crave." He tapped the picture of Reg's bruises. "Even while he kicked and tried to breathe again, I could see his eyes thanking me. He didn't want to live like that."

"But he fought you."

"They all do. I think it's their way of saying goodbye to life. They all fight a little. A little kick or a cry. But none of them wanted to live the way they were. None of them."

"None of them?"

"That's right. Annie, Reg, and the rest of them. They were so grateful to be free of the pain." He shrugged. "What I did for them was the right thing to do."

"The right thing?" *Life is precious. Life is all we have. How could someone think that snuffing that out was the right thing to do?* But he was convinced. She could see the certainty in his eyes as he looked at her. He was convinced that he was the answer to these people's prayers.

"Definitely the right thing to do." He snorted a derisive laugh. "We put down dogs, Detective. When they're old, in pain, incontinent. We say that there's no quality of life for them, and we just give them an injection. Then we feel all self-righteous about ourselves, that we did what's best for them, and that it had nothing to do with the fact that they'd become inconvenient to us. We don't put down our elderly and infirm. No. We stick them in homes where we can forget about them and the inconvenience of an elderly, incontinent mother or father. We dump them in places like Brancombe House to rot. Why do human beings qualify for less humanity than a bloody dog? Why are we made to suffer pain and anguish and humiliation in ways that we don't even subject an animal too?" His eyes blazed with passion and fury as he spoke. "That's not right, Detective. That's cruel. And you sit there in judgement of me. All I did was give them relief from the shithole their loved ones had dumped them in." He banged his hands on the table. "I gave them wings, Detective, and let them fly. I unshackled them from the chains of drugs and pain that held them captive. I set them free!"

She nodded, preparing herself for the answer to her next question. "Tell me what happened on the night of the fifth of December 2013."

He leaned back and folded his beefy arms over his chest. "Annie. That's what happened."

"Tell me about Annie."

"It started before her, really."

"You've killed before Annie?"

He shook his head. "No. I watched Edward die. I cared for him up to the end. I saw the misery of his final days." He chafed his biceps as though a shiver had run through him. "I decided then that I wouldn't let anyone else suffer like he had."

"Instead, you killed them first."

"Annie had lung cancer. Every breath was a struggle for her. Every single breath. Have you ever watched someone die of cancer, Detective?"

Kate thought of her gran. How she'd gone so fast in the end that she hadn't had time to watch her suffer the way Maxwell was describing. But she'd seen the pill bottles. The amount of painkillers she'd been taking just to make it through the day was incredible. Would she have been able to stand it? How awful would it have been to watch her gran, the woman who had raised her, the only family she'd ever known, fade to nothing before her eyes? "Yes," she whispered. "I've seen what it does."

"Then you know. You know the pain when they cry out even through the morphine-induced dreams. You know how they're here but not really here at all. It's like their minds are already gone, but their bodies haven't caught up with them yet." He cast his eyes down to the table glancing at the pictures. "That's not living, Detective. It's barely even existing. And the families. Well, it's like some kind of weird limbo for them. They're waiting for the phone call that tells them they can set the wheels in motion to get on with the funeral. To get on with packing up whatever's left of mum's life. To getting on with their own."

"Very thoughtful of you." Kate couldn't bite back the sarcasm, but he appeared not to even have heard her.

"Annie was so tiny, so frail. She could barely even kick the covers when she said her goodbye. Her cry was so quiet I didn't think anyone would have heard it. But even if they did, no one comes running in a place like Brancombe House. I should have accounted for Alan, though. I knew he was sweet on her, but I didn't realise he came visiting at night."

"So you killed him too?"

Maxwell shook his head. "I just pushed him against the wall. I told him I was helping her, that he should just go back to bed. If he had, he'd have forgotten what he saw by the next day. Dementia's like that. But he didn't go back to bed. He tried to stop me. Was going for help, he said." He leaned back on his chair legs. "You're three years late."

"So you slammed him up against the wall?"

"Pushed. I just pushed him a bit."

"Did he hit his head?"

"Well, yeah, I guess. I mean it was bleeding a bit. I had to clean it up when I couldn't find him."

"You couldn't find him?"

"That's right. He walked, well, shuffled away really. Wearing a stupid frilly dressing gown with big stupid flowers on it."

"So you pushed him against the wall, hard enough to make his head bleed so profusely that you had to clean blood off the carpet, while you killed Annie Balding. How did you kill her?"

"I held a pillow over her face."

"What kind of pillow?"

He shrugged and frowned at her. "Just a pillow from her bed."

"A normal-sized one that you sleep on or a throw pillow of some sort?"

"Why does it matter?"

She shook her head. "I'm just trying to picture the scene with you, Jason." She clasped her hands on the table. "So that I can understand what happened."

"Just a normal head pillow. We don't have those fancy touches in Brancombe House. That just makes more work and gives us more to clean up."

"You said their eyes begged you to kill them while you were doing it."

"That's right. They craved the release I could give them."

"How could her eyes tell you she wanted to die if you couldn't see them? A normal-sized head pillow would have covered her whole face."

He blanched a moment. "I knew it was what she wanted. She needed to die."

"No, Jason. You needed to kill. Your justifications don't excuse that. Jason Maxwell, I'm arresting you for the murders of Reginald Barton, Annie Balding, and Alan Parr. You do not have to say anything, but your defence may be harmed if you do not mention something which you later rely on in court. Anything you do say will be used against you as evidence. Do you understand these rights as I have explained them to you?"

"I didn't kill Alan."

"You caused the injuries that resulted in his death. Murder, manslaughter, whatever. That's for the crown prosecution service to figure out, and you to defend." She sneered at him. "As if you could."

"I knew you wouldn't understand. None of you can understand what I did for those people. Do you blame a doctor when they do what I do?"

"Doctors save lives, Jason. They don't take them."

"Really? What about when they just let them go? I believe that's the phrase they use. Let nature take its course."

"Do you understand your rights?"

"Do you ask them to justify their actions when they withdraw care when there is no hope left?" He stood up and towered over her.

She leaned back in her chair but she refused to move. She refused to let him see fear. "I'm not one of your elderly patients, Jason. Do you understand your rights as I have read them to you?"

Tom stepped deeper into the room.

"You're pathetic. If Annie had been in hospital they would have stopped feeding her, stopped giving her water, and let nature take its course. She would have died slowly, with only pain medication to make her more comfortable. Doctors and nurses do this up and down the country every single day. Multiple times a day. I don't see you marching them all in here and charging those pussies with anything. They withdraw the care the patient's become reliant on and think they're being kind in not prolonging their suffering any more."

She'd seen that done when she'd visited her gran. They stopped treating the human being and just medicated for the pain. It had been horrible to watch, but some had gone quickly. They'd been ready to pass. She'd seen others linger for days and days, though. Waiting for something to let them fade away while their breathing became more laboured, more tortured. Skin clung to bones like a wet sheet, hanging and sagging in a sickening mockery of life. There had been no life there. Sure, the heart had beaten its rhythm and the lungs had filtered oxygen from the air, but there had to be more to life than that.

"You've seen what I mean, haven't you?"

She tried not to react, but she knew her eyes had given her away.

"And you think I deserve to be punished for sparing them from that end?" He leaned a little closer, and Tom edged nearer to them both. "They don't have the stones to do what a patient really needs at that point. To truly put them out of their misery rather than letting it drag on for days, sometimes a week, before they finally die." He beat a fist against his chest. "I did it quickly for them. When they were ready, I did it." He clicked his fingers. "Just like that." He sat back down, a smug smile on his face. "I'm the only one who truly has the balls to do that for them."

"I'll ask you one more time, do you understand your rights as I have explained them to you?"

"Yes," Maxwell said through gritted teeth.

"I'm sure there will be other charges to add once we've finished discussing your time at Brancombe House with you. Interview terminated at 2.02 p.m." She turned off the tape. "Get this animal out of my sight, Tom."

"With pleasure, sarge."

Stella walked in as Tom ushered Maxwell out of the room. "Well, that didn't go how I expected it to."

"No?"

Stella shook her head. "I didn't think he was going to confess."

"He wanted to confess. He's had to hide his good deeds for too long and it's grated on him." A chill ran through her body. She rubbed her hands up and down her arms. "He needed to confess. He thinks he's God."

"God has a following."

"I know. Maxwell bestowed himself with the power of life and death. In his eyes, at least. With all that should come recognition."

"The world is full of crazy fuckers."

Kate laughed. "That's the truest thing I've heard all day."

"Something's bothering you."

Kate shrugged.

"Come on, tell your Auntie Stella."

Kate snickered. "It bothers me that I can sort of see his point."

Stella frowned.

"I've seen people die horrible deaths. We've seen results of violent deaths, traumatic deaths. And while no death is a good death, the prolonged suffering of those dying from illnesses and old age seems far crueller than some of the traumatic deaths we've seen. And far more torturous than some of the violent deaths we've seen. Or at least that I have."

"Human beings are capable of such cruelty, Kate."

Kate nodded. "Yes, we are. But we're capable of acts of kindness and compassion too."

"You think what he did was kind? Compassionate?"

"No. What he did was to gratify himself. He's just twisted it all up in a righteous excuse. But that doesn't mean I can't see the merit in the argument. What's better? A prolonged torturous death or a fast torturous death? Dead's dead, right?"

Stella's eyes widened. "You're not gonna start popping off old folk, are you?"

"Nah. I haven't got the stones."

Stella chuckled. "I'm sure Gina's very pleased about that," she said with a wink.

Kate stared at her. "I can't believe you just went there." She slapped her hand to her forehead. "What am I saying. Of course I can. While we're on the subject of Gina, I have a little problem."

"Trouble in paradise?"

Kate screwed her face up and sniffed. "Yes, but not the kind you're alluding to."

"Come on then, out with it."

"Gina got a huge bouquet of flowers yesterday."

"And?"

"Fifty yellow roses."

"Fifty?"

"Yup."

"And I take it they weren't from you."

"Nope."

"And she's got no idea who they might be from?"

"Well, she has a theory, and I was kind of hoping you might help me rule it out."

"What's the theory?"

"She thinks it might be Ally messing with her."

"Christ." Stella ran a hand over her face. "And what do you think?"

Kate shrugged. "In the light of a lack of other ideas, this seems like a fairly good possibility."

Stella sucked in a huge breath and blew out slowly. "Right, I'll call the prison and get them to toss her cell. If they find something, great. If not, I'll get them to keep an eye on her."

"She's in prison already. What more do you want them to do to her?"

"Well, if this is potentially witness intimidation, then they can monitor her communications more closely. They could isolate her for a time." Stella shrugged. "You know the drill, Kate."

"And if it isn't her?"

"Maybe you just have some competition for your lady's affections. This could be nothing more than a secret admirer."

"Fifty yellow roses, Stella."

"Yeah," Stella said, trying to hide her grimace.

"Fifty."

"Okay. One hell of a secret admirer." She clapped Kate on the shoulder. "You'll have to up your game if it isn't Ally."

"Not helping, Stella."

"Sorry. But at least we've wrapped up this case now."

Kate raised her eyebrow at her.

"We've caught a killer we weren't sure we were looking for and stopped a case of embezzlement."

"Hm. But who wins the pot? No one got the right result."

"Fair point. Looks like it'll have to go towards the Christmas party fund."

"You sure?" Kate asked and put on her best smile.

"What's that creepy look for?"

Kate frowned. "I was hoping you'd take pity."

Stella laughed.

"Hey! You're the one who said I was going to have to up my game."

"I think it's going to take more than a measly forty quid, kiddo."

"Bitch."

"It's why you love me."

"Yeah, yeah. You just keep telling yourself that."

Epilogue

Gina picked up the vase full of flowers and carried them to the bin. She dumped the beautiful blooms in, then emptied the water down the sink. She felt bad for throwing them away, but she couldn't stand to look at them any longer either. The thought that it might be Ally's way of needling her again was too much for her to stand right now. Not when she was just starting to make progress.

She took a deep breath and picked up her phone. Now all she had to do was put the steps into action to move things forward with Kate. She dialled a number and waited.

"Hello?"

"Stella?"

"Yes. Who's this?"

"It's Gina."

"Gina?"

"Yes, Kate's Gina."

"Oh, right. Erm, Kate's not with me—"

"I wanted to talk to you."

"Oh. Okay."

Gina could hear her groping around for something to say and smiled. She quite liked the thought that she'd caught the cool, calm, and collected Stella on the hop. "I have a favour to ask you."

"Well, Kate's already asked, Gina. It's fine. I've been in touch with the prison and they're going to check it all out—"

"It's not about Ally."

"Oh. Then you've got me beat. What can I do for you?"

"It's Christmas in a couple of weeks and I want to get something special for Kate."

"Good, good. That's the time of year to do that sort of thing." Stella chuckled. "But what does that have to do with me?"

"Fancy a girly shopping trip?"

"A girly shopping trip?"

"Yes."

"What's different about a girly shopping trip to a normal shopping trip?"

"Well..." Gina scratched her chin and wondered if she'd have the guts to actually tell Stella before they got to the shop she wanted to visit.

"Is there coffee involved?"

"Probably."

"Cake?"

"More than likely."

"Norwich?"

"I was thinking King's Lynn."

"Hm."

"And Ann Summers."

Stella burst out laughing. "Now you're talking. I'll pick you up. When?"

"Some point this weekend. Would that work for you?"

"No problem." Stella was still chuckling. "I'll text you a time when I've had a look at my shifts."

"Okay. Thanks. And Stella?"

"Yeah?"

"Please don't tell Kate."

Stella groaned. "Spoil all my fun."

Gina snorted. "Yeah, like I believe that. See you at the weekend."

"Yeah, yeah."

Stella disconnected and Gina could still hear her chuckling in her ear.

She looked in the mirror over the fireplace. "I am a strong, independent woman. I am beautiful and I can do this." She smiled at her reflection. "I can do anything I damn well please."

About Andrea Bramhall

Andrea Bramhall wrote her first novel at the age of six and three-quarters. It was seven pages long and held together with a pink ribbon. Her Gran still has it in the attic. Since then she has progressed a little bit and now has a number of published works held together with glue, not ribbons, an Alice B. Lavender certificate, a Lambda Literary award, and a Golden Crown award cluttering up her book shelves.

She studied music and all things arty at Manchester Metropolitan University, graduating in 2002 with a BA in contemporary arts. She is certain it will prove useful someday...maybe.

When she isn't busy running a campsite in the Lake District, Bramhall can be found hunched over her laptop scribbling down the stories that won't let her sleep. She can also be found reading, walking the dogs up mountains while taking a few thousand photos, scuba diving while taking a few thousand photos, swimming, kayaking, playing the saxophone, or cycling.

CONNECT WITH ANDREA

Website: andreabramhall.wordpress.com
Facebook: www.facebook.com/AndreaBramhall

Other Books from Ylva Publishing

www.ylva-publishing.com

Collide-O-Scope

(Norfolk Coast Investigation Story – Book 1)

Andrea Bramhall

ISBN: 978-3-95533-573-1
Length: 370 pages (90,000 words)

One unidentified dead body. One tiny fishing village. Forty residents and everyone's a suspect. Where do you start? Newly promoted Detective Sergeant Kate Brannon and King's Lynn CID have to answer that question and more as they untangle the web of lies wrapped around the tiny village of Brandale Stiathe Harbour to capture the killer of Connie Wells.

Benched

(Love and Law Series – Book 2)

Blythe Rippon

ISBN: 978-3-95533-833-6
Length: 322 pages (87,000 words)

On the heels of their win for same-sex marriage equality, Supreme Court Justice Victoria Willoughby and LGBTQ rights lawyer Genevieve Fornier are thrust into the spotlight again. A photo of them almost kissing rocks their careers and new relationship, just as a same-sex parental law heads to court.

Requiem for Immortals

(The Law Game – Book 1)

Lee Winter

ISBN: 978-3-95533-710-0

Length: 363 pages (86,000 words)

Requiem is a brilliant cellist with a secret. The dispassionate assassin has made an art form out of killing Australia's underworld figures without a thought. One day she's hired to kill a sweet and unassuming innocent. Requiem can't work out why anyone would want her dead—and why she should even care.

Four Steps

Wendy Hudson

ISBN: 978-3-95533-690-5

Length: 343 pages (92,000 words)

Seclusion suits Alex Ryan. Haunted by a crime from her past, she struggles to find peace and calm.

Lori Hunter dreams of escaping the monotony of her life. When the suffocation sets in, she runs for the hills.

A chance encounter in the Scottish Highlands leads Alex and Lori into a whirlwind of heartache and a fight for survival, as they build a formidable bond that will be tested to its limits.

Coming from Ylva Publishing

www.ylva-publishing.com

Rock and a Hard Place

Andrea Bramhall

Expert mountain climber Jayden Harris has the world at feet until an avalanche at Everest base camp sweeps it all out from under her. She wants nothing more to do with the mountains, and turns her back on it all.

Rhian Phillips is a successful London marketing executive who has the chance of a lifetime fall in her lap. She's sent to produce a reality TV series on competitive climbers, while showcasing the stunning beauty of a Patagonian glacier and the Cerro Fitz Roy range.

An accident brings Jayden and Rhian together, and outside pressures keep them at each other's sides. When you're stuck between a rock and a hard place eventually something has to give. The one thing they never counted on was them both wanting to stay together.

A lesbian romance about pushing onwards and defying expectations.

Under Parr
© 2017 by Andrea Bramhall

ISBN: 978-3-95533-744-5

Also available as e-book.

Published by Ylva Publishing, legal entity of Ylva Verlag, e.Kfr.

Ylva Verlag, e.Kfr.
Owner: Astrid Ohletz
Am Kirschgarten 2
65830 Kriftel
Germany

www.ylva-publishing.com

First edition: 2017

Credits
Edited by Astrid Ohletz
Proofread by Zee Ahmad
Cover Photo by Andrea Bramhall
Vector Design by Freepik.com

Lightning Source UK Ltd.
Milton Keynes UK
UKHW03f2107240418
321596UK00001B/56/P

9 783955 337445